To Bronwyn, Raydon and Russell
and to the memory of Bob Disher 1921–2019

1

This close to Christmas, the mid-north sun had some heft to it, house bricks, roofing iron, asphalt and the red-dirt plains giving back all the heat of all the days. And this Thursday morning a grass fire to top it off.

Hirsch toed a thick worm of softened tar at the edge of the Barrier Highway, watching the mop-up. Country Fire Service trucks from Tiverton, Redruth and Mount Bryan in attendance. One of them at the seat of the fire behind an old farmhouse set back from the road, the second chasing spot fires, and the Tiverton unit patrolling the fence line. Not a blazing fire—a slow creep through sparse wheat stubble. And not a big one—only a corner of the farmhouse hedge and the road paddock. No wind today. Cloudless, as still as a painting.

A suspicious fire, though.

'Suspicious in what way?' Hirsch asked.

He'd parked his South Australia Police 4WD nose-up to the tailgate of Bob Muir's ute, nudging the words *Tiverton*

Electrics. If Hirsch had a friend, a male friend, in the district, it was Muir. A mild man, unhurried, but capable of a hard, exacting competency whenever he used his hands or his brain. He was what passed for the local fire chief.

'Not a firebug, if that's what you're thinking,' Muir said. 'I'll show you once they've given the okay.'

All Hirsch could see right now was a corrugated-iron roof with flakes of farmhouse-red paint still clinging, and a towering palm tree.

The Tiverton unit drew near, Kev Henry the publican at the wheel. Two men on the back, hosing fence posts: Wayne Flann and some guy Hirsch didn't recognise. A shearer? Windfarm worker? Didn't matter. Flann mattered, at least to some extent. He was mid-twenties, with sleepy eyes, loose limbs, almost good-looking. Always privately amused, as if he knew something the rest of the world didn't. Getting a kick out of this fire. Flicked his wrist when he spotted Hirsch, landing a loop of water on his uniform shoes.

'Knock it off, Wayne,' Muir said.

The truck trundled on and then a radio crackled. Bob Muir listened, said, 'Good oh,' and jerked his head. 'This way, Constable Hirschhausen.'

A long, rutted driveway took them down to a gap in the hedge and the house and sheds on the other side. The house had been unoccupied for years, the stone walls ceding to the dirt, the rocks and the dying grass. Ants teemed where once had been lawns and flowerbeds. A wheelless pram beside a crooked garden tap; a ladder busted down to three or four rungs leaning against the tank stand. Nothing seemed whole. Cracked windowpanes, grass in the rusted and drooping gutters. Only the palm tree showed any splendour, and its base was littered with dead fronds.

Hirsch parked behind Muir in the side yard and got out. Here the smoke was more acrid—burnt vegetation with an overlay of scorched rubber? The sunlight was queer, too, winking hazily where it came through the ragged fringe of palm fronds, casting blurred shadows on the dirt.

Looking up, Hirsch said, 'These old country places with their palm trees.'

Muir grunted. 'Over this way.'

He took Hirsch along the flank of the house and around the tank stand to the backyard. The cypress hedge sheltered the house and garden on three sides, Hirsch realised. To his eye, the fire had started in one corner, charring the patchy grass before scorching its way through the hedge, leaving a spidery tangle of blackened, leafless twigs in its hunt for better fuel on the other side—the wheat stubble.

'What do you make of that?' Muir said, pointing at the blackened dirt.

Hirsch looked down. Ash on his toecaps now, not only dust. He felt sweaty, greasy, a sensation of grit in his teeth. And still early in the day. 'Kids playing with matches?'

Muir might have been disappointed in him. 'Mate, the wire.'

Coiled in the ash at the base of the hedge was a length of insulated cable. Now Hirsch understood the taste of the smoke: molten plastic. But mostly his gaze was caught by a stripe of copper glowing bright.

'Ah.'

'Exactly,' Muir said, spreading his arms. 'I mean, why go to the bother of slicing off insulation with a knife when you can burn it off? Lovely hot summer's day, dead grass all around...'

Hirsch grinned. 'Maybe they felt better-hidden in here.'

Muir pointed to the dead ground between the house and the sheds. 'They would've been just as invisible from the road over there in the dirt.'

'Who called it in?'

'Your girlfriend, in fact.'

Hirsch visualised it. Wendy Street heading down to Redruth at seven-thirty to arrive at the high school by eight, same as usual. Saw the fire, called Bob, knew Bob would call him.

'Early start for your average copper thief,' Hirsch said. 'Maybe it's the country air.' Back in his CIB days in the city he could rely on the bad guys sleeping till noon. He glanced dubiously at the old house. 'They didn't strip it out of there, surely?'

'Nope. Not worth their while. What this is, is their base. Big metal skip full of copper in the barn.'

Hirsch gazed across a stretch of dead soil broken only by abandoned harrows, a rusty fuel drum and a silvery gum tree. A barn, an open shed collapsed at one end like a mouth in rictus. 'So they've been at it for a while.'

'Be my guess,' Muir said.

Hirsch recalled a department memo: two thousand reported thefts of semi-precious metal in South Australia this year, estimated value $2.5 million. Mostly copper, mostly from building sites; also powerlines, rail networks and storage depots. Electrical wiring, antenna cables, transformers, hot-water pipes. Police members advised to keep an eye open for unusual activity or reports that might indicate blah, blah, blah...

He ran a mental gaze over the district, the thousands of square kilometres he patrolled. A couple of new houses going up in Redruth, but that was his sergeant's headache, not Hirsch's. Some kitchen remodelling here and there. The long-abandoned railway service. Not much in that. Maybe the stuff was brought here from far and wide to be stripped, stored, shipped elsewhere. He didn't know where to start with it. Sometimes, it seemed to Hirsch—newcomer to the bush—that his job was as much probing the landscape as probing the circumstances of the crimes committed in it.

'Prints,' he muttered, thinking of the paperwork ahead, wondering about the likelihood of getting a forensic team here so close to Christmas.

Hirsch photographed the wire coil in the ashes, the charred grass around it and the skip piled with stolen copper, much of it dulled by oxygenation. Then he looped crime-scene tape across the entrance to the barn and called his sergeant, who was underwhelmed but promised to notify CIB in Port Pirie.

Finally, Hirsch reassessed the day ahead. On Thursdays he took a swing through the back country south and west of Tiverton, on Mondays he patrolled north and east. Hundreds of kilometres a week, checking in. An elderly grazier here, a widow with a schizophrenic son there. A police presence— meaning a cup of tea, a chat, a follow-up. I'm afraid your car was found down in Salisbury, burnt out. Your neighbour claims your dogs have been troubling his sheep. I'm required to ensure that your rifle and shotgun are properly secured. Any further sightings of that mysterious truck you saw last week?

Some of the people he called on were lonely, others vulnerable. Some got into trouble through a lack of foresight; a handful were actively dodgy. It was the variety, the different people and experiences, that Hirsch enjoyed about his Thursday and Monday patrols. He liked to start early, about 7 a.m., but today it was almost nine and he was still only a few kilometres south of Tiverton. He'd have to take a few shortcuts to make up the lost time. Phone some of the people on his rounds rather than dropping in.

'You off?' Muir said.

'Yep.'

His face a picture of innocence—so that Hirsch was instantly on guard—Muir said, 'All set for tomorrow night?'

In a moment of weakness that he'd been trying to spin as building good community relations, Hirsh had agreed to be Tiverton's Santa this year. He'd be distributing presents to the town and farm kids on the side street near Ed Tennant's shop, then announcing the winner of the town's best Christmas lights, while looking ridiculous in a smelly red suit.

'Fuck off, Bob.'

'That's the spirit,' Muir said, clapping him on the back.

*

Hirsch set out south along the Barrier Highway. Window down, Emmylou Harris in the CD slot, a hard country lament that suited his mood—the isolation, the bushwhackery he sometimes encountered. Down the shallow valley, low dry hills on either side, greyish brown with the darker speckles of shadows or trees clinging to the stony soil. Stone ruins close to the road, distant farmhouse rooftops, a line of windfarm turbines along a nearby ridge—the settler years, the struggling present and the future, all in one. Halfway up a sloping hillside a motionless dust cloud. A vehicle on a dirt road? A wind eddy? It all seemed unknowable, a world poised for action, but unable to proceed. Hirsch had been the Tiverton cop for one year now and was waiting for a mutual embrace, but the place kept him at arm's length. If life was the search for a true home—a welcoming place, a constant lover or a mind at peace—then he was still looking.

Kind of. There was Wendy in his life. In the eyes of the district they were 'going out', and that was just fine with Hirsch. And he was close to her clever, amusing daughter Katie, who'd saved his life last year. He had plenty to be thankful for.

Hirsch turned west onto Menin Road, the boundary between the Tiverton and Redruth police patrol areas. Place names mattered up here, where they didn't in the city, it seemed to him. Menin Road, Lone Pine Hill, Mischance Creek, Tar Barrel Corner, Mundjapi—all putting down layers of meaning and significance. Menin took him up into better wheat country. Better rainfall west of the Barrier Highway than east of it. 'Barrier': another signifier. Better crops and fencing, better roads, shorter distances between farms. But, all the same, Hirsch drove for a further twenty minutes and saw not a soul.

And then he saw Kip.

He was past the dog before he realised it and braked hard, sending road grit and choking dust over the poor mutt. He got out, crouched, offered his upturned palm. The kelpie halted, skin and bone, ribs and prick. Panting, deeply fatigued. A low growl in his throat—it seemed to break free before he bit it back as if ashamed.

'Kip,' Hirsch said. 'Kippy. Here, boy.'

The world stopped. Not a breath of wind and the day soundless but for galahs screeching in the gums beside a cracked-mud dam and the tick of the cooling motor. Kip gave a slow tail-wag.

'You're thirsty, right?' said Hirsch.

He always carried plenty of water. In the rear compartment of the Toyota, where he sometimes had to transport prisoners, was a locked metal compartment for spare hand-cuffs, flares, ropes, a torch, evidence-collecting bags and a couple of Tupperware containers. Hirsch tipped a shallow layer of water into one of those and set it down on the crown of the road, halfway between the driver's door and the dog.

Kip dropped to his belly, stretched and twitched his nose. Got to his feet, limped forward, dropped again. Then, by degrees, he was at the water, testing it. Started lapping all at once, drops flying about, before looking to Hirsch for more.

'Not yet, bud. Too much too soon, bad for you.'

Hirsch drew near, reached a hand to the bony skull,

stroked the dog between the eyes. Kip turned, licked his hand, and let himself be coaxed by the collar into the passenger seat, where he circled twice before curling head to tail as if he'd come home to his favourite blanket. Snout on paws, alert to Hirsch's every movement—but trustingly alert. Trusting Hirsch to know the way home.

'Poor old boy,' Hirsch said, giving the dog a last pat before turning the key. 'You've been in the wars, haven't you?'

Cuts, blood flecks, a torn ear, the sheen gone from his tawny pelt.

Hirsch glanced at his watch, did the maths again. He'd lose even more time returning Kip to his owners. He checked for mobile reception—zilch.

Half a kilometre along, steering with his right hand, one eye on the road, the other on his phone signal, he suddenly had two bars. Stopped, got out, consulted his notebook and made four calls to his non-urgent clients. Wouldn't matter if he didn't pay these people a visit this week.

First, Rex and Eleanor Dunner. She picked up. Sorry, but he had no leads on the graffiti artist who'd tagged their heritage-listed woolshed.

'That's very disappointing, Paul.'

Hirsch took that philosophically. He was always disappointing someone.

Next he told Drew Maguire it wasn't a police matter if the neighbour's sheep strayed onto the Maguire property through a hole in the fence.

'What if I flatten the bastard?'

'Then it becomes a police matter.'

Next, a call to the owner of a wallet that had been handed in. No cash or cards in it, but he'd drop it off next Thursday. Finally he checked on Jill Kramer, a single mother who'd been robbed and hospitalised by her ice-addict daughter.

'She's in rehab.'

'Doing okay?'

'Well as can be expected.'

That was a kind of mantra in the bush. Hirsch heard it once or twice a week. Acceptance. Not daring to hope for better times. 'Will she come home to you when she gets out?'

'She's got nowhere else to go.'

'Let me know when,' Hirsch said...And I'll check in more often than once a week.

He drove on, past a homestead with a windsock on a landing strip, down and around and in and out of old, eroded cuttings in the folds of the earth. Along a sunken road between quartz-reef hillslopes, and across the Booborowie valley, a patchwork of wheat stubble, crops awaiting the harvester and green-black lucerne, darker where massive, computer-controlled sprinklers crept over the ground.

Then up. Over Munduney Hill and onto a side road—and now Kip knew his home was drawing near. Climbed to his feet, stuck his snout into the airflow and barked.

'You bet,' Hirsch said.

He slowed for the cattle grid at the front gate—not that the Fullers ran stock anymore. Then onto a track that wound past star thistles and Salvation Jane to a transportable house on stumps. No weeds here. It was as if a switch had been flicked: vigorous couch-grass lawns, rosebushes and native shrubs. No sign of Graham Fuller's old Land Rover in the carport, but—perfect timing—Monica was there, unloading groceries from the open hatch of her Corolla. She turned with an expectant smile, a lonely country woman who didn't get many visitors, the smile growing curious when she saw she had the police on her doorstep.

Then she spotted Hirsch's passenger and simple joy lit her face. She let the shopping bags go, wiped her palms on her thighs and came at a little run to yank open the passenger door. 'You found him!'

Kip whimpered and slobbered, his tail whipping the seat.

'Where have you been, you monster? You poor thing, you're filthy.'

A glance at Hirsch as if uncertain of the proprieties. 'May I?'

Hirsch grinned. 'He's not under arrest, if that's what you mean.'

Monica Fuller laughed, helped the kelpie to the ground. 'Thank you so much. Where on earth did you find him?'

Hirsch explained, Monica cocking her head as if mentally tracing a route on a map. 'So he was more or less on his way home,' she said. 'God knows where he's been. Come and have a cup of tea. I'll text Graham, he'll be that thrilled.'

She chattered on, a simple release of tension. Within minutes she'd settled Kip on the veranda with a bone to chew, stowed tins and packets into pantry and refrigerator, and placed a mug of tea and a slice of Christmas cake at Hirsch's elbow. A tired kitchen, a hint of 1970s orange here and there, Formica and laminated chipboard. A house where there was a kitchen reno on the to-do list, but money was tight. Some meagre light came through a window above the sink, more from a screen door to the veranda. Hirsch could see staked tomato plants in the backyard, an old stone dunny and an implement shed. No implements these days, only rusty ploughshares and rotting hay and empty grain sacks.

Monica's phone pinged. She was round-faced, comfortable in herself, her wiry black hair laced with silvery filaments. About forty, a face in the crowd if you saw her on the street, but Hirsch sensed her shrewdness, her quality of watching and waiting. She read the message on her phone and grinned happily at him.

'Graham says he owes you a beer.' She frowned. 'Is that allowed?'

'I've been known to go off-duty.'

She grinned again. 'So I've heard. Mrs Street, Wendy, teaches my youngest.'

I'm the talk of the high school? wondered Hirsch. 'I'll take down the wanted posters when I get back to town.'

She laughed. 'Wanted posters.'

Graham Fuller had come into the police station on his way to work Monday morning with a dozen A4 printouts in his hand: a photo of Kip on his haunches, sizing up the photographer. *Have You Seen Kip? Reward Offered* in big black letters. Hirsch had pinned one to the wall next to the wire rack of police, district council and public health notices, and all week he'd seen Kip's face elsewhere in town: on power poles, fence posts, the shop window. Privately, he'd thought it was a lost cause. Kip had been bitten by a snake or shot by a neighbour or stolen. Or, worst case, he'd run away because he'd been beaten once too often.

Now Hirsch was wondering if perhaps the Fullers' dog had been stolen. He sipped his tea. 'I understand Kip has won some ribbons in his time.'

Monica shrugged, modest. 'Best sheepdog at the Redruth Show, four years running—back when we had sheep.'

It was a common story. The family farm no longer sustained a family. It was either sell out to a richer neighbour or a Chinese-owned agri-company, or shift career gears and stay in the district. Graham Fuller now serviced windfarm turbines; Monica worked two days a week at the Clare hospital. A lot of driving involved.

Hirsch said, 'All those prizes...How did the other dog owners take it? Anyone get their nose out of joint?'

Monica moistened her fingertip, dabbed at the crumbs on her plate, looked at him wryly. 'It was ages ago. And I mean... the Redruth Show? It's small-time.'

'People store grievances.'

Monica shook her head. 'Actually I'm wondering if it's related to the time our phone line was cut—though I don't see how.'

An evening last January. Monica and Graham had just gone to bed when they heard noises in the yard and a knock on the door. Kip barked and strained at his chain until it broke—Graham was just in time to see him charge into the darkness—as Monica tried to call the police and realised the phone was dead. Kip returned eventually. Meanwhile Graham found the phone line severed, a neat, clean snip through insulation and wiring, and some garden tools missing.

Copper, again. Not much copper, though, and it had simply been cut, not stolen. 'A long shot,' Hirsch said.

Monica waved a hand as if to deny the direction her mind had taken her. 'I know, I know; hard to imagine they saw the kennel and thought, ah, a dog, we'll come back and steal him at the end of the year.'

'Anyway, he's back, that's the main thing.'

Still, two incidents involving police within twelve months. That was well over par for this area. Hirsch stood, stretched his back, said he'd better be going. He could see, through the little archway that dated the house, a sitting room with a small, overdecorated pine Christmas tree, cards on a string looped beneath the mantel above a fake log gas fire, loops of red, green and silver tinsel. 'Season's greetings,' he said. 'Thanks for the cake.'

'You too. And thanks heaps for bringing Kip home,' Monica said.

She took him out onto the veranda, watched him bend to knuckle the kelpie's head. 'Those cuts—someone's taken a stick to him.'

Hirsch allowed that that was one possibility. 'Or he got into it with another dog.'

'No, that was a stick,' Monica Fuller said flatly.

She walked with Hirsch to his 4WD. 'I hate to add to your workload, Paul, but there was a bit of excitement in town just now, while I was doing the shopping.'

No one had notified Hirsch. Maybe he'd been out of range. 'Do I want to know?'

'Brenda Flann.'

'Yeah. I didn't want to know,' Hirsch said.

2

Every city suburb and bush town had its Flanns. They lived in run-down houses with car bodies and washing machines rusting in weedy, untamed yards. Rangy dogs and snot-nosed toddlers sitting in the dirt. No obvious means of support but no apparent shortage of cash either. Always a couple of family members rotating through jail or 'known to police'. Flashpoint tempers in the pub, the shop, the schoolyard, at the football. You didn't look sideways at a Flann.

Brenda Flann and her brood lived east of Tiverton, out in rain-shadow country, where the early settlers had been conned by one year of bumper rains then damned by decades of drought. Her husband, Stu, was serving five years for robbery and her sons were headed that way. Brenda herself wasn't light-fingered—or she hadn't been caught yet—but she was heavy-footed. She racked up fines and demerits the way some other women collected handbags.

And that morning—no more than an hour ago, according

to Monica Fuller—Brenda had tried to enter the main bar of the Tiverton pub without exiting her car first.

'There was this almighty bang and I ran out of the shop and there she was, wedged under the veranda.'

'Was she hurt?'

'Nine lives, that one,' Monica said. 'But she'd knocked over one of the support posts and part of the roof had come down on the car.'

'Already drunk,' Hirsch muttered.

'Well, is she ever really sober? Anyway, next minute her wheels are spinning and she's trying to reverse off the veranda. She didn't get very far, Ed and Martin managed to pull her out and confiscate her keys.'

Ed Tennant owned the shop; Martin Gwynne was the town stickybeak. Hirsch closed his eyes briefly, thinking of the paperwork. Citizen's arrest, if that's what it was. Police arrest. Damage report, witness statements...And he'd rather take a DNA swab from a hungry pit bull than try to breathalyse Brenda Flann.

'Where is she now?' he asked, thinking that if Ed and Martin had her locked in a room, he'd be facing another stretch of legal quicksand.

'They drove her home in her car.' As if reading his mind she added, 'But they have her keys and with any luck she's passed out on her bed.'

Hirsch shook his head, thinking of the other vehicles owned by the Flanns.

Monica was giving him a sly smile. 'Want a squiz?'

Enjoying herself, she took an iPhone from her jeans

pocket, tapped and swiped. Shading the screen from the sunlight, she showed Hirsch a series of photos: the tail end of a dusty 1980s Falcon wagon, a sagging section of curved corrugated-iron veranda roof, a snapped post, Ed and Martin holding Brenda by either arm.

'Like me to email these to you?'

Hirsch nodded, gave her his address. 'And perhaps keep them to yourself? No need for them to go viral,' he said lightly.

Monica gave a good-humoured shudder. 'Get on the wrong side of the Flanns?'

Hirsch felt depleted suddenly. 'She's a complete pain in the arse.'

Monica patted his arm. 'Good luck.'

By 1.30 p.m. the spine-jarring back roads were behind him and he was on the Barrier Highway again, slowing for the southern outskirts of Tiverton. A couple of crouching farm-houses, the disused railway station, the grain silos. When Hirsch was posted to Tiverton a year ago, the silos were glum, grey, weather-stained. Since then an artist had painted a huge flowering bottlebrush and a Sturt desert pea on one, merino ram heads on the other. There was something uplifting about them, he thought. The artistry, the incongruity, the sense of liberation from the buttoned-down lives all around. Others felt it too, a kind of pride and delight.

He drove on, passing little stone houses behind hedges, the Catholic church, a disused garage, the Uniting church, the institute with its stone Anzac standing guard, the pub—a couple of early drinkers contemplating the mangled veranda iron—and finally, on the northern edge of town, the shop and the primary school opposite the police station.

Police station. The front room of a tiny redbrick house, in fact, with a chest-high counter to separate Hirsch's desk, swivel chair, filing cabinets and computer from the great unwashed. Behind his office, a door that led to his cramped living quarters. Out front, a patchy bit of grass and a wire fence, a little blue-and-white *Police* sign beside the gate. A short, badly potholed driveway, his old Nissan in the carport at the side of the house. Owing to the yawing, pitching back roads and the weight of his equipment belt, Hirsch's back was a nagging mess, so he U-turned to park in the street rather than thud over his driveway potholes. A couple of the council's road-maintenance guys had promised him a shovelful of leftover asphalt one day, but nothing had eventuated so far.

He locked the police Toyota and stood for a moment, mentally sorting the rest of his afternoon. He was still to eat the sandwiches he'd packed this morning. Check the landline answering machine, read departmental emails, deal with Brenda Flann and the fallout from her little adventure. And take Katie Street home. Last day of the school year tomorrow, Christmas next week: Wendy's daughter would be bursting out of her skin.

In the end, Hirsch ate his lunch under the drowsy chop of the ceiling fan. Stale air, too warm. No messages, and only a couple of SA Police memos in his email, the words swimming before his eyes. What was an 'information cascade'?

More to the point, what was he expected to do about it? He got to 'service performance indicators' and logged out, having lost twenty minutes of his life.

An envelope addressed in his mother's large, rounded hand sat in his in-tray, rebuking him. As expected, it contained one sheet of cramped, minimally formatted type, the form letter his parents mailed to everyone at Christmas. Hirsch shifted in his chair: love, embarrassment, compassion, cynicism. Sometimes he thought he wasn't a very nice man; certainly not a very nice son.

He ran his gaze down the page. Trips his parents had made during the year. Who they'd seen. The garden. Bowls and golf. Who'd died, remarried, procreated, retired to the Gold Coast. The achievements of their only child, *now one year into his posting at Tiverton and loving life in the bush!!!* Always liberal with the exclamation marks, his mother.

And with the usual poignant tug, a blue biro message just for him: 'To our darling Paul, always in our thoughts, let your Christmas be happy and safe and may we see each other soon, your loving Ma and Pa.'

This year's card was a cartoon of two chimney-tops, a policeman nabbing a masked burglar emerging from one, Santa stepping from his sleigh into the other. Hirsch placed it with his other cards, all five of them: the general store, Martin and Joyce Gwynne, Katie Street and Wendy Street, the Muirs, Rosie—his only remaining friend at police HQ.

He returned to his rickety chair and contemplated infinity again. A cloudless, windless day with a high, hot sun. He had no wish to be out in it. But it was 2 p.m. now and Katie got out of school at three. He'd better get cracking on the Brenda Flann case.

Yet he continued to sit. Presently he heard a vehicle screech to a halt outside. A door slam, determined footsteps. Hirsch was attuned to the engine notes of his neighbours' cars, the general sounds of the Barrier Highway. This was someone in a hurry for police attention.

Martin Gwynne barged in, quivering with emotion. Sixty and retired, a neat package, a man of bubbling energy, he was always about the place somewhere. The street, the shop, council meetings, the tennis club, the Saturday football match.

And, more often than not, bearding Hirsch in the police station about something or other.

Hirsch swivelled in his chair. 'Afternoon, Martin. Heard about your bit of drama this morning.'

Gwynne sniffed. 'Yes, well, you weren't here so we had to act.'

I'm never here on a Thursday or a Monday morning, you know that, Martin. He didn't get up.

Gwynne slammed a set of keys onto the counter. 'Brenda's. And I hope she doesn't get them back in a hurry.'

Oh, right, thought Hirsch, hauling himself to his feet, crossing to the counter.

'The woman's a menace. She's going to kill someone, the way she's going.'

A house key, a key to a Ford, a short, silvery chain with a tiny pair of dice on the other end. 'Take me through it,' Hirsch said.

'Where to begin,' Gwynne said. He inflated slightly, stretching his faded pink Lacoste shirt. A little belly over a pair of ironed cargo pants. Deck shoes.

Hirsch put up an abrupt hand. 'Actually, Martin, first I need to know if you made an arrest. I mean, did you actually say those words to Brenda?'

Gwynne looked astounded, doubly irked. 'Arrest? That's your job.'

'Just sorting through the proprieties,' Hirsch said, relieved. In the end, he rattled off a series of questions, the only way to cut through Martin Gwynne's waffle. The sequence was simple: Martin had been chatting with Ed Tennant at the petrol bowser outside Tennant's shop. They saw Brenda's distinctive station wagon—rusty, dented blue body, sun-faded red bonnet—enter the town, stop briefly while Adam Flann, Brenda's youngest, got out, and continue towards the pub.

'She was swerving all over the road. Next minute she was up on the pub veranda.'

'Go back a bit. Where did she drop Adam?'

Martin frowned in irritation. 'I don't know. The Cobbs' place? He's mates with Daryl. What matters is...'

What mattered was, Martin and Ed had run to the pub to see if Brenda was all right. 'Or should I say, see if she'd hurt someone else. But when we got there, she tried to reverse off the veranda, so we pulled her out and I confiscated her keys.'

'Wise move.'

Martin stood a little straighter. 'In the end, Ed drove her

home in her car, and I followed and brought him back. We left her sleeping it off on her sofa.'

Where she's choking on her own vomit? wondered Hirsch—while also thinking it was a good thing Ed, not Martin, had driven Brenda. Martin would have lectured her the whole way, and she might now be going down for assault. 'So her car was driveable?'

'If you can call it that,' Gwynne said.

Hirsch added to his mental to-do list: photograph Brenda Flann's car, photograph the damage to the pub. His afternoon was stuffed. Maybe Katie could go home with a town friend when school broke up? Or watch TV at his place—he'd shown her where the back-door key was hidden. He'd text her as soon as Martin Gwynne was out of his hair.

Now Gwynne checked the time. 'I assume you will arrest the bloody woman?'

Hirsch grabbed Brenda Flann's keys. 'Thanks, Martin, I'll take a formal statement from you later. Great job, by the way.'

It was the right thing to say. In the hot, still air of the little waiting area, as the sluggish fan stirred the public notices and tipped over one of Hirsch's Christmas cards, Martin Gwynne beamed.

Milking the moment, he gave a tut-tut shake of his head. 'I hate to think what damage or injury might have occurred if I hadn't got to her in—'

'Actually, Martin, did you check Brenda for injuries?'

Gwynne blinked. 'What? No. She's fine. Snoring her head off when I left.'

Hirsch thought of Brenda Flann with more urgency now. Alone—husband in jail, Adam in town, Wayne on the fire truck...

'I'd better get going,' he said, grabbing his uniform hat, strapping on the service pistol and equipment belt that helped keep his chiropractor's kids in private schools.

Gwynne seemed reluctant to see him go. 'You still haven't collected the Santa suit, Paul.'

Martin, keeper of the town's Father Christmas costume, had been asking for days when Hirsch might be expected to come by and collect it. And stay for dinner. Another dinner in the Gwynnes' oppressive dining room, Martin's avid questions, his fierce gossip, the meek wife he called Mother.

'Thanks for reminding me, Martin. I'll come by tomorrow morning some time.'

'Or tonight, stay for dinner. You can tell me how it went with Brenda.'

'I'll be judging the Christmas lights tonight, sorry,' Hirsch said, gabbling a little. 'But maybe I could come for a meal once the seasonal madness is over?'

'Holding you to that, Paul.'

Hirsch locked up, pinned his mobile number to the front door and followed Martin Gwynne into the drenching sunlight. A gritty wind had been added to the mix, pushing paper scraps along the footpath, rattling the Fullers' missing-dog poster on a nearby power pole. Hirsch tore it down, screwed it into a ball and said, 'Thanks again, Martin.'

'You'll be checking the pub first, I expect, so you're in a better position to know what charges you'll lay on Brenda?'

Martin had no doubt been telling people their jobs all his life. His wife, his employees, repairmen, next-door neighbours, the district council. Public servants. Hirsch was beginning to understand why he, not Martin, was this year's Santa. It was the town avenging itself.

'Actually, Martin, the first thing I need to do is check if Brenda's okay,' he said. *In case she's got whiplash, concussion, internal bleeding, vomit in her dead lungs, okay?*

Gwynne wasn't quite sure it was okay, the disapproval clear in his eyes as they stood there next to the driver's door of Hirsch's police vehicle. But he didn't get to express it. Instead, within seconds, he was saving Hirsch's life.

3

Hirsch put it together later.

Brenda Flann woke to find herself at home, on her sofa, with a thirst on. In some lizard corner of her brain the notion stirred that she should have been at the pub—*had* been there, in fact, so why was she back home? Looked out the window: there was her car. Meanwhile, a stronger notion was taking hold, that she still had plenty of drinking to do, so she searched for her keys. Couldn't find them, but instinct took her to the kitchen drawer, repository of the world's lost and spare crap, and she tottered out to the car with her spare key aimed vaguely at the ignition. Blinked to see the front banged up, the bumper caved in and the off-red bonnet corrugated with dents. She couldn't recall any accident. One of the boys? What the hell, it was a shit car anyway.

She steered down the empty back roads to Tiverton and was about to turn onto the highway towards the pub, when a third instinct asserted itself—the need to right the wrongs done to her. For there, fifty metres away, was the police station and Martin Gwynne and that prick of a cop out the front, yacking away. Arseholes, both of them. The cop had busted her more times than she could count, and Martin Gwynne seemed to keep a permanent sneer on, just for her. There was a dim memory of something more, quite recently: Gwynne's hands on her? Brenda was fuzzy on the detail but she was certain the bastard had taken liberties of some kind. She planted her foot and yanked on the wheel as she shot onto the highway. Oops, too wide. She yanked again, over-corrected, and found herself fishtailing towards Hirsch and Gwynne, screaming obscenities at them.

Anyway, that was how Hirsch later reconstructed the workings of Brenda Flann's sozzled brain. Right now, Brenda was intent on his annihilation, her crazed face nose-up to the windscreen, the crumpled front end of the Falcon looming, motor howling, bald tyres smoking, radiator steaming.

Good sense evaporated in him. He gaped, motionless in a half-crouch, his heart knocking behind the paltry defence of his skinny ribs. He might have died.

Martin Gwynne reacted first and shot out his arm. He clamped his pale, spidery fingers on Hirsch's forearm and tugged hard, meeting no resistance from Hirsch. Their feet tangled; both men toppled into the gap between their cars as Brenda blew past, sideswiping the roo bar mounted on Hirsch's police 4WD. A percussive thump, the shriek of metal peeling open. The old Ford paused briefly, as if to shake off a hindrance, then ricocheted across the highway and through the primary school boundary fence, wires twanging.

Peace, when it gathered itself, saw Brenda's car stalled in

a cloud of steam and dust halfway between the footpath and the nearest classroom. Small heads filled the windows. Birds resettled on the powerline, muffled talkback radio buzzed in a nearby house, a breeze filled the lungs of a supermarket bag and set it dancing. Then mundane reality as a semi-trailer load of hay rolled through the town, the driver craning to get a good look.

Hirsch extracted his arms and legs from Martin, brushed himself down. Glanced at Martin and said, 'You okay?'

Gwynne used his please-take-note voice. 'I think we can safely say it's a good thing my reaction times are above average or you'd have been a goner.'

Hirsch breathed in and out. His thoughts leapfrogged to the ramifications: there was no way he could avoid a dinner invitation now.

'I'll just check on Brenda,' he said.

Hirsch was surprised, and also relieved, to find that Brenda had been wearing her seatbelt.

'Her injuries would have been a lot worse otherwise,' the ambulance driver said, thirty minutes later. Broken nose, gashed forehead, whiplash, possible cracked ribs. Still unconscious.

'And just as well you didn't try to shift her,' the other ambo said.

Hirsch said his thanks, waved them off, had a word with the primary school headmaster, retrieved Brenda's shoulder bag from the footwell of the Falcon and crossed to the police station, where Martin was hovering. Didn't the guy have anything at all to do?

As if replying to Hirsch's inner grumbling, Martin said, in his managerial voice, 'I think you'd better take my statement about both this and the pub incident while the details are still fresh.'

'Good thinking,' said Hirsch amiably.

He ushered Gwynne inside, ducked around the counter to his cramped bit of office space, tumbled Brenda's bag into the bottom drawer of his desk, hunted out the relevant paperwork.

Martin watched, frowning, a man who required order and rarely found it. 'Since we're both involved in the most recent Brenda incident, let's get that out of the way first.'

'Good thinking,' Hirsch said again.

Settling on a working ballpoint, Hirsch began to write, half-talking to himself: 'Date, time, location. Who, what, where, when and why...'

Martin Gwynne, reading upside down, said, 'It was more like two-twenty, not two-fifteen.'

'Well spotted.'

'Conditions calm,' Gwynne said, 'visibility clear despite a slight haze.'

'Right.'

Martin gave Hirsch time to catch up, then dictated a first-person account: sequence of events, locations, distances. Possible witnesses. Three cars parked in the vicinity—one next door to the police station, two outside the shop. Their numberplates.

Hirsch blinked. He looked up. Martin was reading from a small spiral notebook.

'You're a thorough man, Martin.'

Gwynne nodded: it was his due. 'Finally, owing to my quick reactions, a possible fatality or serious injury to Constable Hirschhausen was averted.'

Hirsch almost wrote it. 'They like witness statements to be, ah, neutral. Just the facts.' In the face of Martin's faintly affronted air he added, 'Unadorned language. How about you say this: "I pulled Constable Hirschhausen out of the path of Mrs Flann's car"?'

Gwynne considered the rewording and seemed to find it wanting. 'You know best, Paul. But the fact is clear, if I hadn't been there, you might have been killed.'

Bridling a little at Martin Gwynne's neediness, Hirsch nodded his head at the many fickle ways of chance. 'Damn right,' he said, still amiable. 'Makes my skin crawl to think of it.'

Gwynne, satisfied, went on with his narrative, which Hirsch copied word for word since Martin would read it back before signing.

Then, a shorter account of the pub incident. When it was done, Gwynne clapped his hands together. 'I think we could both do with a restorative cup of tea. Come around to my place for a quick cuppa, and you can collect the Santa suit while you're about it.'

Hirsch visualised it: the dire sitting room; Martin telling him what was wrong with the world; Mother hovering.

'Raincheck? I still need to gather other statements, write up reports, let Brenda's sons know what happened.'

A brief tightening of Gwynne's features, a glint of suppressed disappointment. 'Fair enough. Dinner?'

'The Christmas lights, remember?' Hirsch babbled, 'Maybe the weekend?'

'Sunday, six-thirty,' Martin Gwynne said, turning on his heel.

Hirsch took statements from an out-of-work shearer who'd reflexively spilled his beer when Brenda mounted the veranda next to him, the publican, and an elderly woman deadheading her roses on the other side of the road. Their accounts varied little, although the gardener believed that Mr Gwynne had been unnecessarily rough with Mrs Flann. Then Hirsch headed to the shop for a word with Ed Tennant.

Stepping from sunlight into dimness, he blinked to adjust. A woman from an outlying farm was browsing with a shopping basket in the crook of her arm. Gemma Pitcher, the young woman who occasionally worked the cash register and stacked the shelves, was flipping through a catalogue. Otherwise the shop was a silent place frozen in time. Along from the cash register was the post office counter, and beyond that a case of books that constituted the Tiverton branch of the Redruth Library Service, half an hour down the highway. On the far wall, rubber boots, work overalls, tools, trays of nuts and bolts, fuel cans, an aluminium ladder. And, massed in the centre, everyday household goods on rows of metal shelves: breakfast cereals, tinned peaches, laundry detergent, tampons, aspirin, shampoo.

Hirsch stalked through to the rear. He found Tennant in his office, a small space crammed with filing cabinets, desk, chair and a boxy old computer.

Ed, tidy, precise and middle-aged, said, 'Heard what nearly happened to you.'

Hirsch nodded. Any news at all soon flashed around this town. 'Live another day. Meanwhile, about this morning...'

'One thing I want to make clear: it wasn't my idea to take frigging Brenda back to her place. That was Martin's brainwave.'

'He can be forceful,' Hirsch allowed.

'I thought she should have been seen by a doctor, frankly. When we got her home, there was no one to keep an eye on her. God knows where the boys were.'

'Wayne was on the fire truck,' Hirsch said. 'Adam was visiting Daryl Cobb.'

Tennant shook his head: indifferent or philosophical, Hirsch couldn't tell.

'Quick question, Ed: did you and Martin arrest Brenda? Say those actual words?'

'God, no.'

'Hurt her in any way?'

Tennant gaped. 'I'm starting to wish I'd kept my nose out of it. Are you saying this is all going to come back and bite me?'

'Nothing to worry about, Ed. I doubt she remembers a thing.'

He shook Tennant's hand and went in search of Brenda Flann's sons.

4

Hirsch sought Wayne first, the responsible older one—
'responsible' having other nuances when applied to any
member of the Flann family.

On the little fire station forecourt, Hirsch found Bob
Muir hosing down the elderly CFS truck, a mess of road
dust, pollen and chaff swirling at his feet. Hirsch waited and
watched. Muir was methodical: top to bottom, front to back;
wheels last.

'Good as new,' Hirsch remarked, as Muir coiled the hose.

Muir patted the shiny flank. 'Held together with fencing
wire and sticky tape. What can I do you for?'

'Wayne here?'

Muir stowed the hose, taking his time. Contemplating
his cop friend as if weighing his loyalties. Wayne Flann
belonged to the district; he was a CFS member—but he was
also trouble. Hirsch was accustomed to seeing these mental
machinations in the locals. He let the process play out.

'Went home an hour ago,' Muir said finally.

Hirsch explained: Brenda, the pub, Gwynne and Tennant, Brenda's blazing return.

'What you might call a busy morning,' Muir said, unsurprised. He'd heard and seen a lot from Brenda over the years. 'She in hospital?'

'For a few days at least.'

Muir calmly shook water from his hands, wiped his palms on his thighs. He cocked his head at Hirsch. 'You know about her husband, right?'

'Currently incarcerated.'

'Half a dozen armed holdups over a two-year period,' Muir continued. 'We're not talking guns—Stu prefers screwdrivers and cricket bats. Service stations, the odd milk bar. Last time he stepped it up a bit—knocked off a bookie after the Clare races, got away with close to thirty grand.'

Hirsch nodded; there was a story coming on. A point to it, knowing Bob.

'On his way home, he feels a bit peckish. Pulls into a roadhouse, grabs a Coke and a packet of chips.'

Muir eyed Hirsch sleepily. The point was coming.

'There he is, swimming in cash, but does he pay for his little snack? Not our Stuart. Shoves everything under his jumper and walks out.' Muir paused. 'The whole thing caught on CCTV. Arrested a couple of hours later.'

'It's called an incapacity for consequential thinking,' Hirsch said.

'Oh, is that right?'

The men grinned at each other. Hirsch understood Stuart Flann's actions because he'd seen it a hundred times before. Bob Muir understood them because he was a smart man.

'Was he a drinker?'

'He was,' Muir said. 'Brenda not so much, not before she married him. He was a nasty drunk. Knocked her around.' He paused. 'I went to school with her. She was just one of the gang. Stu fucked her up.'

'The boys, too.'

'Count on it.'

Hirsch glanced at his watch. 'I need to let them know about Brenda.'

Muir pulled a leather flip case from his pocket. 'Landline number. Wayne should be home by now.'

He scrolled through his contents, touched the screen, listened to the dial tone and thrust the phone at Hirsch. 'Here you go.'

'Wayne?' Hirsch said. 'This is Paul Hirschhausen on Bob's phone, I'm calling about your mother.'

He explained. Not too badly hurt. Redruth hospital. The car? Still on the school oval. 'A write-off, I'd say,' Hirsch said.

Silence on the other end, then Wayne Flann said, 'Understood,' and ended the call.

'Profuse with his thanks,' Hirsch said, returning Muir's phone. 'A wailing and gnashing of teeth.'

Muir gave him a look: mates or not, don't overstep the mark.

A Land Rover rolled through the town, caked in back-country dust, plates obscured, only a half-moon of windscreen available to the driver. Hirsch geared up for the chase, then slumped. He was tired, overloaded, been running around all day. He'd notify Redruth to pull the vehicle over. Or not.

He checked his watch again. Twenty minutes before he was due to collect Katie Street from school, and Wayne Flann's last question echoed in his mind: the car?

He said, 'Bob, if you're free, maybe you could—'

'Help you tow Brenda's heap of junk somewhere.'

'Amazing how your mind works.'

'I could have been a professor.'

Yes, you could, Hirsch thought.

They used the Tiverton Electrics ute and a fire-service rope to drag the damaged Falcon back along its path of destruction and onto the highway. Then, hooking the rope to the front of the car, they towed it to the outer edge of town, where a cyclone fence housed a storage shed and the district's sole grader and road-maintenance truck. The area was a wasteland of hard baked red soil and dead grass; a couple of heat-stunned gum trees. Muir had the key. He has the keys to the town, Hirsch thought. Literally and figuratively.

'It can't sit here forever,' Muir warned, coiling the rope hand to elbow, hand to elbow.

But it probably will, thought Hirsch, gazing glumly at Brenda Flann's wrecked car.

Feeling sticky, grimy and fatigued, Hirsch walked through to the highway and on to the Cobb house, hoping he'd find Adam Flann there with Daryl, the boys glued to an Xbox or watching a DVD. Ten minutes until the school bell sounded.

The Cobbs lived in a small 1970s brick veneer ravaged by time and the inland sun, sitting low in the dust as if waiting for further blows. No front garden, no decoration, no Christmas wreath, just weariness and stored heat. Marie Cobb was rarely seen in the town. Unemployed, chronically shy, she suffered from bipolar disorder and her children were her carers. If families like the Flanns were not uncommon, nor were families like the Cobbs, Hirsch had discovered in his brief career.

He set himself to knock, wondering who would answer. Daryl Cobb, seventeen, a big, soft, sloppy boy with a touch of ADHD, easily led by someone like Adam Flann? Laura, his younger sister? No: Laura wouldn't be back from high school yet. She was the calm, practical, organised one. Did well at her studies and earned a few dollars after school grooming miniature ponies for a local breeder. That left Marie, who, in all probability, wouldn't answer the door.

Hirsch rapped his knuckles, waited in the heat. The house seemed to grow tense, barely breathing, and he could sense Marie Cobb alone in there, either manic and afraid or depressed and asleep.

Laura would be home on the bus soon, but where was Daryl? Hirsch shrugged; nothing more he could do. With any luck, Adam had scrounged a lift home with someone, and would hear about his mother from Wayne.

He walked back to the police station just as the final bell sounded in the school on the other side of the road. Fished out his car keys and got behind the wheel of his ancient Pulsar just as the kids poured from their classrooms.

Ignition: nothing.

Flat battery.

'Six fours,' he was saying a couple of minutes later, behind the wheel of the police Toyota.

'Twenty-four.'

'Four sixes.'

'Twenty-four.'

'The square root of the third integer taken as a percentage of the hypotenuse.'

'Three-and-a-half.'

'I didn't think you'd get that one, frankly,' Hirsch said. 'Very good.'

Katie Street touched her shoulder to Hirsch's briefly. She was a wisp in the passenger seat, skinny legs, short dark hair damp on her neck. Wearing the Tiverton Primary School uniform of tan shorts and dark blue polo shirt. Scuffed sneakers with yellow laces propped on the dash, a massive backpack in the footwell. A solemn, watchful kid when Hirsch had first met her, but different around him now. A practical kid. She'd had some trauma in her short life, but seemed okay. No nightmares, no tendency to take a memory out and agonise over it. He didn't think so, anyway.

But a withholding kid sometimes. Finally she said, 'Is Mrs Flann okay?'

'She's in hospital. She'll be okay.'

Another silence. 'Was she drunk?'

'Yes.'

Katie wasn't looking for a life-lesson, so Hirsch said

nothing. He'd let her ruminate and prod the matter into a shape she'd find satisfactory. He began to accelerate, heading out of the town, past the shop, the sign to the side-street grain dealer, past Martin Gwynne and his wife attacking their box hedge with electric clippers. Martin paused in the act, narrowed his eyes to see Hirsch sail by. Joyce Gwynne paid no attention. Hirsch saluted and then he was on the outskirts, passing the silos.

A kilometre further on—mirage shimmers on the unspooling highway, the afternoon sun high and hot—he saw two figures in the distance. They clarified: not mirages. Daryl Cobb and Adam Flann on the other side of the road, heading for the town.

Hirsch braked and pulled onto the gravel verge. All around were grain heads and wheat stubble behind drooping wire fences choked with parched roadside weeds. Farm tracks, a couple of exhausted gums, and one distant farmhouse roof behind a cypress hedge. Nothing else under the vast blue haze. What were the boys doing out here in the heat? No water, no hats, no shoes—just rubber thongs on their feet.

He wound down his window, propped his elbow on the sill. 'Want a lift?'

They gaped at him, burning up, exhausted. 'Come on,' urged Hirsch, 'hop in.'

Daryl Cobb stared down at the softened asphalt. A shapeless, indistinct boy, the down on his cheeks adding to his general blurriness.

Adam Flann was sharper: slight and calculating. 'We're good,' he said with sleepy insolence.

'Don't be idiotic, get in,' Hirsch said, intentionally harsh. 'I'll run you back to Daryl's, take all of two minutes.'

Adam glanced uneasily back the way they'd come, murmured to Daryl, and they crossed together and slid into the rear seats with barely a disturbance of the air. Hirsch said, 'Buckle up,' U-turned and headed back towards the town. 'You guys know Katie, right?'

Daryl grunted. Adam said, 'Her mum's your girlfriend.' A hint of smartarse in it.

Katie swivelled and leaned into the gap between the seats with friendly interest. 'Hello.'

No hello in return, but Hirsch sensed shoulder shrugs from each boy. He imagined their jumble of emotions: not cool to say hello to a kid; embarrassing to ride with a cop; now he's going to ask us what we were up to.

Hirsch said, 'What on earth were you two up to?'

'Just having a walk,' Adam said.

'Right.'

A minute later, Hirsch braked outside Daryl's house. He switched off, turned to the boys and said, 'Before you get out.'

'What?' said Flann, hostile now.

'Adam, your mum's in hospital.'

Explaining, he watched confusion, contempt and acceptance flicker on the kid's face. 'Wayne know?'

'Yes.' After a pause, Hirsch added, 'Look, if you'd like me to run you out to your place...?'

'Nup,' and it was final. Adam poked Daryl in the upper arm and yanked on the door handle.

'Suit yourself,' Hirsch said, but by then the doors had slammed and the boys were gone.

'Now,' said Katie in a sunny voice, 'where were we?'

Hirsch snorted. They had a mutual regard for each other.

Five kilometres south of Tiverton, Hirsch turned onto Bitter Wash Road, riding the now-familiar curves and undulations, passing an 1880s stone wall, property gates, grain stubble, skinny sheep in threadbare paddocks. The road climbed gradually, bisecting a range of low hills staked with wind-farm turbines and offering a brief glimpse of distant ashen ground, the morning's grass fire. Then onto a flat stretch, more grain heads and wheat stubble; finally a driveway and a small red-roofed house.

As arranged, a neighbour was there, her little Mazda parked in the partial shade of a massive oleander. Katie used to argue that she'd be fine alone until her mother got home. But she was linked to Hirsch, who probably had enemies, being a cop, and this was a back road. And violence, he'd learnt, was often random. So: an after-school minder. Giving him a peck on the cheek now, twinkling her fingers at him, she ran inside, backpack dragging and bouncing.

He turned to go. Then he realised: this was the last time. When school got out tomorrow she was going to a friend's house. After the summer break, she'd start high school, the same school Wendy taught at. She'd be travelling there and back with her mother.

Hirsch headed for the highway, feeling an odd sense of loss. He slowed for the intersection, turned north, accelerated. And then, owing to the altered perspective on the return leg, he saw a flash of sunlight on glass a short distance from where he'd picked up Daryl Cobb and Adam Flann. A vehicle, half concealed by roadside grasses, was parked along a rutted farm track a hundred metres in from the highway. *Ah hah.*

Hirsch stopped to check it out.

5

Hunched in an airless hollow, partly screened by grain crops and dry grass on either side: a Holden ute. At least thirty years old. Dents, rust in the tailgate and wheel arches, bald tyres, a chipped windscreen, a frayed tonneau cover. Pungent warmth rising from the engine compartment, a stink of unburnt petrol and hot oil. It hadn't been there long.

Hirsch opened the driver's door. The glove box was open—the boys, probably, rifling through for anything of value—and the key was in the ignition. Dust caked the dash, the instrument panel and the shelf behind the seats. Not road dust, dust-dust—suggesting disuse and long-term storage. He turned the key, watched the fuel gauge climb to the quarter mark—so that wasn't what had stranded Adam and Daryl out here. The edge of an ejected cassette poked from the tape player: The Seekers' greatest hits. Hirsch's mother, a sly stirrer, liked to bawl out 'Morningtown Ride' whenever her menfolk lapsed into their brooding silences at the dinner table. Hirsch wondered if Adam or Daryl had played the tape. Would they even know how to work the player?

Hirsch returned to his Toyota and entered the plate details into the MRT, an onboard computer in tablet form. Unregistered since 2016; last known owner Nancy Washburn, 11 Kitchener Street, Tiverton.

Hirsch shook his head; it made sense. Nan Washburn bred prize-winning miniature ponies on a five-hectare block at the edge of town; Daryl Cobb's sister earned pocket money helping her. If Daryl had also worked there, or visited, or gone there to fetch Laura because their mother had flipped out, he'd have known about the ute.

But would he have stolen it if not in the company of Adam Flann?

Back to the old ute. Hirsch tried the ignition key. The motor caught, shuddered on four of its six cylinders for half a minute, then belched and stalled in a cloud of toxins. Cracked head? Vapour lock?

He closed the door, walked around to the rear and unclipped the tonneau cover. More dust, rat droppings, straw, ropes, stirrups, a small cracked saddle, a plastic bucket, a five-litre fuel can, empty grain sacks. And under everything a coil of insulated copper tubing. Left over from some renovation project? Heating for the stable block?

Copper, anyway.

Locking the ute, pocketing the key, Hirsch drove back to the highway, paused for the Redruth High school bus and followed it into town.

*

Nan Washburn probably had the best of two worlds, rural and urban. Her lovely old stone house faced farmland and the distant ranges in one direction, the town in the other, and was close to everything. In thirty seconds she could be halfway across her property; three minutes to the shop, a friend's house, the community tennis courts.

Hirsch rolled up Kitchener Street and into her driveway, noting the looping strands of fairy lights draped over shrubs, garden trees, the veranda and around several wire shapes: reindeer pulling a sleigh, a Christmas tree, Santa with a sack. Just now—unlit, bleached by sunlight—the display was nothing much, a pale ghost of Christmas. But it was stunning at night, and Hirsch had pretty much decided that Nan would win this year's Best Christmas Lights award. He'd make one more tour of the town tonight, to make certain.

Following the driveway along the side of the house to the yard at the rear, he parked alongside a Volvo station wagon and got out. Engine heat wafted from the Volvo: she's just got home, he thought. He checked the grounds: concrete troughs, four huge concrete tanks, a windmill, an old corrugated-iron shed, quince and apricot trees, a stable, two holding pens and a paddock for an old Clydesdale and ten faintly ridiculous miniature ponies. Only the Clydesdale registered Hirsch's arrival, sticking its head over the top of a sturdy post-and-rail fence as if welcoming an old friend.

Hirsch returned the gaze balefully. Back when the town council had informed him the vote was more or less unanimous, he was this year's Santa and *expected to appear on a horse, kindly provided by Nan Washburn*, he'd said why couldn't he drive up in his police vehicle, lights and siren? That idea was shot down: it would terrify the little ones. Or how about he arrived on the back of a farm ute? No. Or simply strolled in from out of the darkness? No. Nan's horse it was. Call it building bridges. He was fairly new to the district and it had been a rocky start.

He passed a tangle of staked tomato plants and a line of roses as he made his way along a crazy path to the back veranda. There was no clear indication that he was approaching a rear entrance: no external laundry, kitchen or bathroom plumbing, just generous windows and a wide doorway under a deep veranda set with worn decorative tiles and hung with grapevines. He stepped onto the veranda; knocked on the flyscreen door. Beyond it, the main door was open, revealing a dark hallway, closed doors on either side. He could hear a radio, drawers slamming, general kitchen business.

He knocked again. The noises stopped and the house seemed to listen, making certain. A third knock and Nan Washburn appeared, a woman in her fifties with untamed wiry grey hair, wearing a denim apron over loose tan pants and a white T-shirt. Stripping off rubber gloves as she approached, she saw at last who her visitor was. 'Paul. You here to ride Radish again?'

The Clydesdale. Hirsch shuddered. 'Another matter.'

'Then come in, come in.'

Hirsch stepped into cooler air. Scented. Not furniture polish, not air freshener or perfume. Potpourri?

'I'm in the kitchen. Cuppa?'

Hirsch realised a cup of tea was exactly what he needed

and followed Nan's comfortable shape into a kitchen at the side of the house. It was a vast, well-lit room with French Provincial-style sinks, copper-bottomed pans hanging above an island bench, a farmhouse oven, a burnished steel fridge and a sizeable wooden table with cane-bottomed chairs.

'Sit.'

Hirsch sat. The window looked over more roses, a clothes-line and a side fence and farmland. Nan put the kettle on and rummaged for biscuits. Good, Hirsch was starving, too. Still bustling about, she turned off the radio, reached for cups and side plates, filling him in on her day. Had he stopped by earlier? She'd been out since breakfast, just got back. First her mother, in a nursing home over in Port Pirie, then visits to the bank and her accountant, had her hair done for tomorrow night, generally a day trying to fit everything in. It isn't nerves, Hirsch thought, she likes to talk. There was a husband, but he lived in a caravan out east and spent all of his days ranging the back country with a metal detector. A bit cracked in the head, apparently, but harmless.

Finally, tea made and biscuits delivered, Nan said, 'Now, what can I do for you?'

Hirsch took a sideways approach. 'Did you happen to look in the shed when you got back?'

'No. Why?'

'So you wouldn't have seen that your ute is missing?'

A look of pure astonishment. 'Missing?'

'Have you driven it today, by any chance? Did it break down on you?'

'It's undriveable. What are you getting at?'

'I found it abandoned just off the highway a little while ago. Not far, about a kilometre past the silos.'

'How did it get there?' As if aware that she'd asked a silly question, she added, 'I never drive it, it just sits in the shed.'

'So you haven't let anyone borrow it?'

'They'd be in for a shock. It conks out after a couple of minutes.'

'Where do you leave the key?'

She wriggled uncomfortably. 'In the ignition. No one was going to steal...Well, I guess someone has.'

Hirsch reached for a biscuit. His fingers melted the chocolate. 'How do you manage without a ute?'

'I don't really need one. Things like hay or oats I get delivered, and I can always load things in the back of the wagon. I use the wheelbarrow if I need to move hay from A to B.'

'Heavy lifting?'

'There's always someone I can call on,' she said, and Hirsch saw a glimmer of understanding reach her eyes. Looking away, she added, 'Laura Cobb helps me with the grooming and feeding and her brother lends a hand if we need extra muscle.'

A pause developed. Hirsch said, 'Is Daryl ever here with his friend, Adam?'

'Adam Flann? Once,' Washburn said, and she straightened her back and shut her mouth.

Hirsch said gently, 'And?'

'And let's just say Daryl hasn't made the wisest friendship choice.'

True, but as far as Hirsch could tell, there were no other

boys Daryl's age in the town. He told her about spotting the ute, half-concealed on a side track, and earlier spotting Daryl Cobb and Adam Flann nearby. 'Walking back to town along the side of the highway.'

Another silence. When it grew uncomfortable Nan said, 'People say you're fair.'

Hirsch said nothing.

'Please don't charge them with anything.'

He sat back. 'Of course, it's always possible they didn't take it.'

She shook her head. 'We both know it was them.'

'It's theft, Nan,' Hirsch said. 'And driving an unregistered, unroadworthy vehicle. And if Daryl was at the wheel it's driving without a licence.'

With some heat, Nan Washburn said, 'But no harm done, and it would have been Adam's idea, and think what a court appearance would do to Daryl, not to mention his poor mother or Laura.'

Hirsch folded his arms. 'What do you suggest?'

Nan gave him a half-humorous grin. 'A stern talking-to?' She warmed to the theme. 'Neither of those boys has had a proper father-figure in his life. They'd listen to you.'

Hirsch wasn't so sure. He said, 'First, was there anything of value in the ute?'

'Maybe they were just joyriding, not stealing.'

'Nan, listen to me. Was there cash in the glove box? Or tools, a mobile phone, prescription painkillers?'

'Nothing like that.'

'Any kind of firearm?'

49

'No.'

Good. If the boys had removed anything from the ute, they'd have hidden it in the grass, and Hirsh didn't fancy poking about. This weather brought out the snakes. 'Copper tubing?'

'Oh.' A look of mild amazement, a memory returning. 'Actually, yes, left over from when I had the laundry done.'

But would those boys know the copper was worth a few dollars? Had they even looked under the tonneau cover? Hirsch said, 'Will this affect your relationship with Daryl? And his sister?'

'Laura's lovely. She's not involved, and no way am I tarring her with anything. She thinks both boys are idiots, anyway. As for Daryl, the only useful mothering he gets is from his little sister. And me, to a lesser extent. I'll talk to him. It'll be okay.'

'Adam?'

'Adam I want nothing to do with. But I suppose the police can't take it up with one boy and not the other—how about you deal with him and I'll deal with Daryl?'

'No, I don't think so,' Hirsch said. 'We need something... stronger. More formal.'

Leaving Nan to retrieve the ute with the help of a neighbour, Hirsch drove back to the police station, parked, and made for Marie Cobb's house on foot. He phoned the Redruth hospital as he walked: Brenda Flann was awake and cranky. Cuts, bruises, reset nose, rib fractures. She'd be in for another three or four days.

He was stepping off the footpath onto the weedy dirt that was the Cobbs' front yard when Laura appeared from the rear of the house, wheeling a bike. She had changed out of her school uniform and into an old T-shirt and torn jeans. Pale skin, dark hair; chipped pink nail polish on the fingers curled around the handlebars. A pannier hung over the rear wheel, crammed with a small backpack and a variety of curry combs. On her way to Nan Washburn's, Hirsch thought.

'Laura.'

'Hello.'

She was shy, embarrassed, whenever she met him. It dated from an incident earlier in the year when she'd knocked on Hirsch's door to say that her mother was acting weird, ranting, hadn't slept for days, she and Daryl couldn't cope. After checking for himself, Hirsch had called an ambulance. Rehab, a different medication, and two weeks later Marie was back with her children.

Now Laura gave him a frightened look. 'Did Mum do something today?'

Hirsch smiled. 'Nothing like that. I need a quick word with Daryl and Adam. Are they here?'

Worry creased Laura's face, emphasising the curious half-centimetre-wide white flash across one eyebrow. An old injury? Finally, she said, 'They're in Daz's bedroom.' She stuck out her jaw. 'Whatever he's done, Adam would've put him up to it.'

'Just a few questions,' Hirsch said.

She was marking time, anxious to be off to her job,

anxious to protect her brother. Her face cleared. 'Is it about Mrs Flann?'

'That's one of the things,' Hirsch said.

Still not satisfied, she propped her bike against the side wall and said, 'Come around the back.'

They never use the front door, Hirsch thought, following her. Expecting more dirt and weeds, he found three raised garden beds. The staked tomatoes, broad beans and silver beet he could identify but there was a patch of leaf heads that defeated him. He crouched to read the small plastic tags stuck in the dirt: carrots, radishes.

Creaking upright, he asked, 'Who's the gardener?'

'Me. Nan showed me. Mrs Washburn.'

'Great,' said Hirsch inadequately.

She led him through a warped screen door and into the kitchen. It was as unlike Nan Washburn's as any kitchen could be: cramped; worn linoleum; elderly electric stove and refrigerator. Marie Cobb was sitting side-on to a round chrome and laminate table, one elbow propped beside an ashtray piled with butts, the other elbow flexing as she drew on a cigarette. Her hair was greasy, eyes vacant. She didn't look at Hirsch or her daughter but flopped her arm straight down, spilling ash onto the floor, then seemed to forget that she was smoking.

'It's one of her good days,' Laura said. 'Through here.'

Down a short, airless hallway to a door halfway along. Hanging at eye height was an earthenware sign in crooked, primary-school letters: *Daryls room*. And Daryl—or someone—had booted the bottom of the door at one point, the plywood outer shell jagged and splintery.

'See ya,' Laura said.

So Hirsch knocked, and walked into a dope haze. Adam recognised him first. Seated on the floor between a narrow single bed and a plywood wardrobe, his back to the bedside table, he edged an ashtray beneath the bed with his right hand. 'We meet again.'

Hirsch ignored him. 'Daryl? I need you to wake up.'

'He's out of it, man.'

'Anything stronger than pot? I'm not here about the pot, by the way.'

Adam smirked and Hirsch wondered if pot was a word kids still used. He took in the dirty clothes dumped on the floor and draped over a rickety chair, a pile of graphic novels under the window, and three posters: a Formula 1 car, one of the Transformer movies, the Adelaide Crows. Daryl himself was sprawled face up across the bed.

Adam grabbed one of his feet and yanked. 'Hey, bro. Visitor.'

When the boy was upright and more or less focused, Hirsch jumped straight in with a couple of lies. 'We have witnesses to you two boys driving off in Nan Washburn's ute, and I'm confident your prints will be a match to prints I took from the vehicle.'

Daryl crumpled, casting his friend a sulky look. 'Told you.'

'He's bluffing.'

'You told him what, Daryl?' Hirsch said.

Daryl was casting about for a palatable lie. 'Look, Adam just needed to get home. Because of his mother and that.'

'Yeah,' Adam Flann said. 'I mean, how was I going to get home? Mum totalled her car.'

'It's called theft,' Hirsch said. 'And I notice you're in no hurry to get home now. Or go and see your mother, for that matter. She's regained consciousness, incidentally.'

'Wayne's coming to get me. We're going to see her.'

'Why didn't you call him in the first place, instead of stealing a motor vehicle?'

'Couldn't get hold of him. Me phone died.'

'Perhaps you should settle on just one excuse.'

'Couldn't get hold of him.'

Which was probably true.

Tears in his eyes, his hands bunching the grimy bedcover, Daryl said, 'Are you arresting us?'

'First offence, I'm wondering if a judgment call is in order,' Hirsch said, stroking his jaw as if not fully convinced.

'What's that mean?'

'It means that while I do think it would be a shame if you guys found yourselves sentenced to some young offenders' program, a part of me is also thinking it'd be the best thing in the long run.'

'Please,' Daryl said wretchedly.

Hirsch checked Flann. Felt the full force of the boy's concentration.

'All right.' Hirsch addressed the air. 'Full admission of guilt, and a full apology.' He held up a forestalling hand: 'Not to me, not now, not here.'

The boys waited.

'Admit you stole the ute and apologise to Mrs Washburn,

in person, tomorrow morning at ten, the main meeting room of the Institute.'

'No problem,' Flann said.

He's thinking: *suckers*, thought Hirsch. 'By apology I don't mean some vague, mumbling, sorry I took your ute without permission, won't do it again kind of bullshit. I mean a carefully considered, heartfelt apology, with me as a witness. And if for one moment I doubt your sincerity, I'm charging both of you.'

Daryl was beside himself. 'Does my mum have to be there?'

Hirsch shook his head. 'No reason to stress her.'

A horn sounded in the street. Adam rose from the floor in one fluid movement, touched his knuckles to Daryl's. 'Good one, bro.'

'Good one.'

He turned with lazy charm to Hirsch. 'You have a good one, too, Constable Hirschhausen, sir.'

Hirsch gave him a look.

When Flann was gone, Hirsch turned to Daryl. 'When you're with Adam, think before you act, okay?'

Daryl stared at the floor.

Hirsch let himself out, returned to the police station. The Santa suit sat reprovingly on the doormat, stowed neatly inside a David Jones bag. Shit fuck bugger damn. The only cure was a shower and a beer before Wendy and Katie arrived for dinner.

6

They'd intended to dine at the Tiverton pub, where in winter the cook was apt to stand in the dining-room doorway and yell, 'Hands up who wants soup,' but Hirsch had scotched that idea.

'I'd spend half the evening fielding questions about Brenda, and the other half being stared at and talked about.'

Wendy Street had patted his arm. 'Poor darling.'

Now, small-boned, quick and watchful like her daughter, she was watching him prepare his famous taste-free spaghetti bolognese. The TV murmured in the corner, Katie watching *Home and Away*.

'Did Bob tell you I reported a fire?'

'He did,' Hirsch said, draining the pasta, telling her about the stolen copper.

'Huh,' she said. 'Sounds like a lot of work for not much reward. It also sounds like local knowledge.'

Hirsch considered that. She was right.

Bowls filled, more wine poured, they abandoned the

cheerless police station dining nook and ate in the backyard, once a concrete square, now transformed by Hirsch with a shade cloth, Ikea outdoor furniture and a few geraniums in terracotta pots. Twilight drew in. He lit tea candles; the evening wrapped them in balmy shadows. Wendy Street's half-smile as she toasted him was sleepy, heavy-lidded—desire that she cloaked with her daughter present.

'So,' she said later, when darkness had fully settled. 'One last review?'

Hirsch groaned, creaked upright, and pulled the two of them out of their chairs.

They strolled the town arm in arm, past others checking out the Christmas lights on foot; the occasional prowling car. About a third of the town's dwellings were decorated. Hirsch kept his voice low as he defended his judgments. Some displays were too busy, others dreary and clichéd. The Hannafords' swagman Santa was clever, ironic; the Bolgers' kangaroo Santa was just kitsch. Santa with one foot in a chimney was cheesy. A single, beautifully lit tree counted for more than a garden-wide mishmash of motifs. Martin Gwynne, by outlining his boxy carport with lights this year, had fatally skewed the elegance of his main display with its strings of lights draped around his shrubs and garden trees, its wire tableau of Jesus, Mary and Joseph in the manger.

That left Nan Washburn's effort; imaginative; not too cluttered. A story unfurled if read from left to right.

'Behold,' Hirsch said. 'This year's Best Christmas Lights.'

Wendy clamped herself hard against him. 'Agreed.'

Their arms around each other, they walked back in the oddly lit evening air. The low point was saying goodnight, see you tomorrow evening.

Friday, 5.30 a.m., Hirsch stabbing blindly at his iPhone to cancel the alarm.

He collapsed back onto the pillow. He rarely remembered his dreams. They meant nothing and he wasn't interested. But fugitive dream traces were in his head this morning, coils writhing and poised to strike. Snakes, only they were copper pipes and wires.

He liked to walk every morning, the dawn a time to cherish with only the birds busy, the air quite still and everything sharply etched. He generally made the most of it—by 9 a.m. the mid-north would be lying limp and stunned beneath a molten sun and the overnight reports of villainy, idiocy and shitty luck would have landed on his desk. But this morning he cut it short, got a quick breakfast inside him and shot down the highway to the abandoned farmhouse.

The barn was bare.

All Hirsch had were shreds of crime-scene tape, tyre tracks, indentations where the rubbish skip had compressed the dirt. The tracks meant little: Bob Muir's ute had come and gone; fire trucks, his own SA Police Toyota.

He checked the time, six-thirty, and called his boss.

Hilary Brandl's voice was strained and gasping. 'This had better be good, Constable Hirschhausen.'

'Morning jog, sarge?'

The new region sergeant was a fitness fanatic. She ran the

little hills of Redruth every morning, to the bemusement of the locals, who, if they weren't actually overweight, were generally unhurried.

'A morning jog that I fear has been interrupted,' Brandl said with good humour. 'What's up?'

As Hirsch explained, he visualised her lean face and the intensity of her concentration. When he'd finished she said, 'They were game. You'd think they'd stay well away after causing a fire big enough to get the fire crews out. Locals, do you think? Watching and waiting?'

'Hard to say, sarge. Five minutes of pub gossip would have been enough to keep them informed. It's possible they came back because the haul was worth a bit of money—they might have stolen the copper to order, been paid in advance, who knows. Prints and DNA might be on record; they wouldn't have wanted to leave it too long.'

Hirsch's sergeant snorted. 'I have to say, Paul, it's been an adjustment, being posted to this place. If this was the city I would've had CIB on the scene within the hour and you or one of the children guarding the copper until we could get it off for forensic testing.'

The 'children' were her two young Redruth constables, Jean Landy and Tim Medlin. 'It's an adjustment, all right,' Hirsch said.

'You've been here a year. You're used to it.'

Not quite.

'I'll knock on a few doors,' Hirsch said, 'see if anyone saw or heard anything last night.'

Doubtful. The nearest occupied dwelling was three

kilometres away on the other side of a hill. And last night was a full moon—a truck could have been and gone, no lights, in a couple of minutes.

The fruitless doorknock sucked up an hour, then it was time to oversee the Cobb–Flann apology.

Hirsch returned to the police station, changed into a crisp, clean uniform and grabbed a briefcase: a touch of authority. He pinned his mobile number below the supermarket Christmas wreath on his front door and cut diagonally across the highway to the Institute. The sun was hot on his back, the road tar was soft underfoot, and his mind was on the stolen copper.

The Institute, a fine stone building on a corner block where a side street met the highway, was separated from the primary school by a house that had once been the Methodist manse. A white stone soldier stood, head bowed, above a granite memorial. A World War II cannon on a patchy lawn protected against approaches from the side street. Lavender beds. Rose bushes. A slender column on either side of the main door.

Hirsch paused to tear down one of the Fullers' *Have you seen Kip?* posters and entered the foyer. A shock of transition from heat, dust and diesel fumes into a hushed, echoing space. Polished wooden floors, wooden half-panels on pastel blue walls, high pressed-tin ceilings. A gleaming staircase on one side of the foyer, a corridor leading to meeting rooms on the other. Passing a series of 1920s and '30s photographs—town councillors and prize-winning merino rams—he stopped at a door marked Conference 1.

He knocked. Went in.

The room was bare but for a massive mahogany table, several chairs, a sideboard under a curtained window and a photograph of the young Elizabeth II on the wall. Hirsch glanced at his watch: 9.35. That's what you get for efficiency, he thought. Twiddled his thumbs. Paced the room; left it to pace the corridors, then explored the ballroom with its gleaming floorboards, a stage at one end. The whole building seemed deserted.

He returned to the meeting room and straightened the Queen in her dusty gilt frame and idly opened sideboard drawers and doors. 'Huh,' he said.

Stacked at the bottom, their labels faded and chewed by silverfish, were three old film canisters. *A Night to Remember*, 1958, starring Kenneth More. *The Back of Beyond*, 1954, made by the Shell Film Unit. *The Shiralee*, 1957, starring Peter Finch. Hirsch shook each canister. The reels were missing. Lost? Archived somewhere? Was there an old-timer in the district whose job it had been to thread dreams through a projector on Saturday nights?

On a shelf above were two ancient-looking bound journals, musty and friable. Hirsch lifted one out and rested it on the table. The powdery binding leather coated his fingers. The title, handwritten on a label, read: *A History of Keirville Station in the Hundred of Whyte, the Colony of South Australia, by Mrs Elizabeth Keir, Volume the First, 1839–1869.*

Hirsch tingled. There was a Keir Road south-east of the town but no locals named Keir, to the best of his knowledge. No farming property named Keirville. Sold off and renamed?

Mrs Keir had used a medium nib and her penmanship was precise, if crowded. Hirsch had no difficulty skimming through the story of her husband, a Scottish carpenter called Douglas Keir. Quoting liberally from his daily journal entries, she related how he'd arrived in South Australia on board the *Palmyra* in 1839, worked in the colony for some years then, in 1851, trekked overland to the Ballarat gold-fields. By the time he returned two years later—*nuggets to the weight of twenty pound strapt around my waist, for there are persons hereabout that would take your life for an ounce of gold if you was not well upon your guard*—Hirsch was hooked.

Douglas Keir, restless now and unable to settle, but married to Elizabeth and with a young family to support, moved north to Redruth when news broke of a copper oxide find in the local stone. This time he set up as a builder, not a miner, grew rich, and eventually moved with his wife and children to a vast lease north of Redruth. Here the Natives (as related by Mrs Keir) gave 'a great deal of trouble', stealing sheep and bags of flour and spearing one of the shepherds. Douglas and his station hands took action:

Where life has been taken, those who do not know its value should be made to feel and see how Sacred we hold it. As a consequence, the men did not retreat until they had left many Blacks stretched on the grass. As has been proven from the start of time, a little cold lead soon forges an understanding between the Races.

Christ, a local massacre, thought Hirsch. He wondered if the story was passed down. There were no Aboriginal people in the Tiverton area. To his knowledge, only two families in Redruth. He had never thought to wonder about it.

He glanced at his watch again: 9.55. Bundling Mrs Keir's journals into his briefcase, brushing dust from his hands, sleeves and trousers, he stood, straight-backed, and waited.

Right on time, Nan Washburn tapped on the door, stuck her head around it, finally walked in. 'Paul.'

'Nan.'

She rubbed her hands together, a dry rasp. 'So far, so good. Daryl's walking from his house and I just saw Adam's brother drop him off.'

Hirsch pulled out a chair. 'I think you should be at the head of the table, one boy on either side.'

He'd given some thought to the dynamics. Sitting at the head of the table would grant her some authority. And the boys, if separated, would be denied the opportunity for warning kicks or insolent nudges under the table.

Just as she got comfortable the door swung wide and Adam Flann sauntered in. 'So—this where it's all at?'

He turned, beckoned, and Daryl entered, shoulders hunched, eyes darting.

'Good morning, Daryl,' Nan said. 'Good morning, Adam.'

Cobb, soft and gingery, bumfluff on his cheeks, shot her a look. 'Hello, Mrs Washburn.'

He glanced at Hirsch. Was he supposed to do the apology now? Hirsch shook his head minutely.

Adam Flann was looking at Nan. Not hostile, just detached. He said nothing.

'Sit,' Hirsch ordered. 'You there, you there.'

'What, here?' Adam said, slipping onto his chair in his graceful, effortless way, apparently enjoying himself. Nan exchanged a look with Hirsch, then turned to Daryl with a smile and a be-seated gesture of her hand.

Daryl flopped into the chair. He stared at the table. The window light revealed a faint layer of irresistible dust. Hirsch watched him lift a hand from his lap, reach out, swiftly finger-stripe the dust, snatch back his hand. Flann, looking on, shook his head.

Sensing the older boy's impatience, and thinking the kid had a point, Hirsch began. 'Daryl, Adam, I want to begin by thanking you both for coming, and we should all thank Mrs Washburn for her goodwill and generosity in this matter. As you know, we're here for you to acknowledge that you stole from Mrs Washburn and to apologise. It's not a court-ordered procedure, but it's still to be treated seriously. Daryl? We'll start with you.'

Cobb darted another desperate look at Washburn. 'Sorry, Nan, Mrs Washburn. It was stupid. I wasn't thinking. I'm really sorry.'

'Thank you, Daryl. What I would like now is for us to put it behind us and move on, what do you think?' She paused. 'How's your mum?'

Daryl Cobb wouldn't look at her, didn't know where to look. At last he whispered, 'She's okay at the moment.'

Hirsch turned to Flann. 'Adam?'

Flann said levelly, 'I'm sorry.'

A lengthening silence. Hirsch was about to break it when Nan Washburn said, 'Are you, Adam?'

Hirsch winced. He watched, waited.

Flann took a deep breath. 'I'm sorry I broke into your shed and drove off in your ute, but I had to get home, me mum had an accident and I couldn't get hold of Wayne, and you know how it is.'

Hirsch watched Nan. Judging by her expression, she was unmoved by the apology. She probably sensed what Hirsch did: that the boy took this lightly. Stealing her ute was no big deal, and anyway what sort of an idiot left their keys in the ignition? He'd go on loading his apology with extenuating circumstances until the cows came home.

She gave Hirsch a bleak look, turned back to the boys. 'Thank you, Daryl, thank you Adam.'

'That's okay,' said Cobb reflexively.

But Flann stood. 'That's it? We can go?'

No one wanted to prolong the session. 'You may go,' Hirsch said.

'Come on, Daz,' Flann said, jerking his chin at Cobb.

When they were gone, Washburn said, 'Well, that went as well as could be expected.'

'Can't win them all,' Hirsch said. 'Thank you for making the time.'

They wandered along the corridor, across the foyer, out into the sun. A hundred metres away, a dozen people were gathered outside the shop.

Spotting Hirsch, Martin Gwynne broke away, trim and

natty in chinos and a short-sleeved shirt, and approached at a run, carrying an iPhone.

Nan Washburn gave him a dazzling smile. 'Hello there, Martin. Lovely morning. Is something wrong?'

She can't stand him, Hirsch thought, amused.

Gwynne gave her a grimace intended to function as a smile and fixed sternly on Hirsch. 'There's a kiddy locked in a car.' He gestured at the sun. '*In this heat*, Paul.'

7

It seemed very likely that Martin was enjoying himself. The avid eyes, the smiling earnestness.

Hirsch snapped out of it. What mattered was a kid locked in superheated air. Today's forecast top was thirty-five degrees and it was high twenties already: the temperature would be close to fifty inside a car.

He forged along the footpath as Gwynne struggled to keep up. Then a soft thud and Gwynne wailing, 'Oh, no, oh no.'

Hirsch darted a look. The guy had dropped his phone. Idiot. Hirsch ran on, and after a beat, Gwynne was at his heels again, gasping: 'All good, no damage to the screen. Talk about lucky.'

Hirsch shook his head. 'Did you call an ambulance?'

Gwynne faltered, then was labouring close behind Hirsch again. 'Should I have?'

Doctor Pillai, thought Hirsch, Gwynne already gone from his mind. The doctor, based at a little medical centre in Redruth, held a clinic in Tiverton every Friday—and there was her dusty Forester, parked outside the ex-Bank of Adelaide building.

By now Hirsch was sprinting along the shopfront veranda. This close to Christmas, there were a dozen cars parked snout-up to Ed Tennant's little supermarket: farm utes, station wagons, sedans, all as dusty as Dr Pillai's Subaru. Everyone—Ed, his wife, their customers—clustered around a rusty pink Hyundai. Panting from the heat, the fast jog, Hirsch asked if anyone had thought to fetch the doctor.

'I sent Gemma over,' Tennant said.

Sliding through the mix of farmhands and townspeople, Hirsch peered into the rear seat of the little car. A toddler slumped in a baby seat. All of the windows were up. He tugged on a door handle.

'Already tried that,' someone said.

Scouting around for a rock, a metal bar, anything, Hirsch said, 'Whose car is it?'

No one answered.

Frustrated, Hirsch said, 'Ed, check the shop.'

'Already done. Everyone's accounted for.'

Hirsch glanced both ways along the street. The shut-up houses crouching for shade, Tiverton Hardware, closed for forty years, the old stone bank with a sign in the window, *Friday Clinic 8 a.m–6 p.m.* His gaze flicked over a house brick and swung back. An open-fronted wooden box beside the petrol bowser, the brick anchoring unclaimed copies of the *Advertiser* at the end of each day. Hirsch grabbed it and belted it against the Hyundai's side window. It bounced off the glass, jarred his wrist. Again, and the glass fractured. He stabbed the brick at the remnants, tossed it aside, reached in for the lock as hot air poured out. Now he was heaving the door open, one knee on the back seat, fumbling at the straps that secured the child. A girl, about three years old, flushed, clammy, unresponsive. Hirsch backed out with her in his arms and then a woman was clawing at him in a shrieking panic.

'*Give her back. What are you doing? She's mine, give her back!*'

Hirsch lifted the little girl aloft instinctively, twisting away from the woman, this way, that way. He stumbled against Gemma, who had trailed the woman from across the street.

'She was in seeing the doctor,' Gemma explained. Exhilarated, in her stolid way, to be caught up in the drama.

Still trying to dodge the mother, Hirsch escaped from the confines of the closely parked cars and trotted towards the clinic. Dr Pillai was emerging with her bag, a hand up telling him to stop. 'It's like an oven in there,' she called as she started across the street.

Hirsch flinched. The child's mother was clawing at his forearm. '*Give her back to me!*'

The ridiculous dance continued. Hirsch freed a hand and shoved the woman aside as her arms windmilled at him. '*Calm down.* The doctor needs to examine her.'

'*Give her to me!*' shrieked the woman.

She ducked under his arm. Slapped, punched and kicked as he tried to keep the little girl out of her mad reach. Then his shirt buttons were popping, his shirttails flapping, and, somehow, she had his service pistol in her hands.

Time seemed to stop.

The woman trembled. Blinked, stared aghast at the pistol.

Hirsch moved first. Turning in a circle, he proffered the child, seeking willing arms, but the onlookers were stunned, so he turned back to the woman. 'Let's all take a deep—'

The woman dropped the pistol. It smacked butt-first beside her sandalled feet and Hirsch flinched and ducked, expecting it to go off. Time stopped again. And then he scooped up the pistol with his free hand, holstered it, fastened the strap, watching warily as the woman shrank away and flailed her hands as if caught in a spider's web. 'I didn't mean...I don't...' she stammered.

By now Dr Pillai was there, trapping her wrists. '*Denise*.'

The woman said dazedly, 'I didn't mean...He was going to take my daughter away.'

'He's a policeman. He won't hurt her. You need to be calm. Do you think you can do that for me?'

The woman blinked. Pillai said, 'Just let me check on Anna for you, okay?'

No response, so the doctor turned to Hirsch. 'Let's get her into the shop, next to the refrigerated cabinets.' She glanced at Tennant. 'Some damp towels, please, Mr Tennant. Ice if you have it.'

Hirsch followed as they trooped inside, the child moulded hot and damp to his shoulder and uttering shallow, panting breaths. The woman named Denise kept close to him, calmer now.

He blinked as he moved from sunlight to dimness. It was always murky in Ed's shop, maybe to hide the cobwebs in the corners of the pressed-tin ceiling. Warped floorboards creaked as Hirsch hurried down an aisle between shelved groceries to the banks of refrigerated units along the back wall. Frozen food behind glass; butter, milk, cheese and processed meat on open shelves. The air was markedly cooler.

And then Dr Pillai was gently taking the child from his arms and stripping off her pants and top.

'Poor little thing, she's so hot.'

'Ed! Wet towels,' said Hirsch, an edge to his voice.

Tennant was standing with Martin Gwynne and a couple of others, and seemed torn between the little girl's plight and the desire to keep an eye out for light-fingered customers. It was Gwynne who replied. 'Should I...?'

'I'm on it,' Gemma said, trotting to a door in the corner.

Hirsch had been in town for a year now; he knew the door led to a storeroom, a tearoom and the staff toilet. Presently he heard the rush of tap water and Gemma was hurrying back with a pair of sodden, threadbare towels, intent and capable. She pushed past Gwynne, who gave her a sour look.

It occurred to Hirsch that Gemma Pitcher might do all right if she got out of Tiverton. She was a soft, slow-moving twenty-year-old, her usual outfit a vast T-shirt above sandals and knee-length black leggings. Limp brown hair to her shoulders, cropped raggedly above her eyes. A nostril stud, an eyebrow ring, a barcode tattooed on one fleshy calf. Nothing and no one to stimulate her—but now this little emergency. And she was equal to it, shoving one of the towels at Hirsch and folding the other into a square the size of a breadboard and placing it on the floor.

Pillai nodded her approval and settled the toddler's

tiny spine on the moist pad. She reached wordlessly for the second towel and began to dab the flushed face, neck and trunk and brush away the perspiration-damp hair. She looked up. 'Another towel, please.'

Gemma came back with a wet, grimy handtowel. 'Sorry.'

'So long as it does the trick,' Pillai said, draping it over the child's torso.

By now she was reviving. A cough. Dazed eyes opening, unfocused, then full of fear under the gaze of all those looming strangers. She whimpered, reached her arms to her mother. 'Mumma.'

The woman named Denise knelt, stroked her daughter, saying wretchedly, 'Sorry, bubba. So, so sorry.'

She turned to Hirsch. 'Really sorry.'

Hirsch was silent.

She said, 'Please, I was only gone five minutes. I needed a repeat prescription.'

With Hirsch still unforthcoming, she added, 'I've never left her like that before. I had no idea. I wasn't away that long.'

'It doesn't take much,' the doctor said.

Hirsch nodded his agreement. He didn't know what he was going to do about the incident. He needed to know the child would recover fully before he went into punitive-cop mode.

Gemma was hovering. 'Does she need a drink?'

Pillai looked up. 'Thank you, Gemma. Water, nothing else. Unrefrigerated if you have it. And a cup.'

Gemma returned with bottled spring water and a paper

cup. 'Easy does it,' Pillai said, dribbling water into the child's mouth. 'A bit at a time.'

Hirsch asked, 'She going to be okay?'

The doctor shrugged minutely, her slim brown fingers testing the child's forehead and cheeks. She smiled down, murmuring words of comfort. The flushed face looked back, still dazed, but then broke into a shy smile. Hirsch thought: shame certain people aren't present to see this.

Most of the locals welcomed a weekly clinic in the town and they seemed happy to be treated by a Sri Lankan doctor. But he'd heard pub talk disparaging Pillai's credentials and one day, seated in the clinic's waiting room, worried that his pollen allergies had tipped into asthma, he'd overheard an old woman hiss at Pillai, *'Don't you touch me.'*

The doctor seemed to come to a decision. 'I'd be a lot happier if we could monitor her in hospital for a few hours, possibly overnight.'

She took the mother's hands in hers. 'Okay, Denise? It's for the best. We don't want her to relapse. Her temperature's coming down and her vital signs are good, but we need to monitor her fluid intake and just keep a general eye on her.'

The woman looked stunned, afraid. 'Hospital?'

'The one in Redruth,' Pillai said.

'Ambulance?' asked Hirsch.

The doctor shook her head. 'Could take ages to get here. We'll take her ourselves. You drive, Paul, I'll sit in the back with Anna and Denise.'

*

Aircon cranked high, Hirsch sped south along the Barrier Highway, passing the disused grain silos at the end of the little town, their shadows like blockish brushstrokes across the highway, then down through a shallow valley, distant, dirty grey hills on either side. A corrugated-iron hayshed here, a scrap of red farmhouse roof there, closeted behind cypress trees. Otherwise the world was populated by wind turbines silhouetted against the sky, wheat stubble, a tiny dust eddy on a hillslope that might have been the wind, might have been a farmer checking sheep. For now, Hirsch was calling it home.

Lifting his forefinger to greet an oncoming car—a kind of rural benediction that he'd adopted—he waited for the road to clear and reached for his iPhone. Shielded it from view, set it to record, popped it into the cup holder between the seats.

'Denise, do you mind if I ask you a few questions? We might not get an opportunity later.'

A long silence from the back seat. Then Dr Pillai murmuring. Hirsch waited.

'She feels pretty bad about what happened, Paul.'

Hirsch nodded. 'I know. But it was witnessed, and there will be a hospital admission, meaning a bit of paperwork. Just general questions, form-filling questions.'

The woman answered this time, her voice a dry-mouthed croak. 'Okay.'

'What's your last name?'

'Rennie.'

'And your daughter's called Anna?'

'Yes.'

'Where do you live?'

Another long pause. 'Does that matter?'

'Paperwork, Denise. I need a street address.'

With an effort, the woman said, 'Hope Hill Road, number fifty-eight.'

He'd been along Hope Hill Road plenty of times, probably twice a month on one of his long-range patrols through the dry, outlying sheep-station country. Hope Hill wasn't a town, or even really a hill; it certainly didn't offer much hope.

'Are there others in the family?'

Another pause. This is a seriously private woman, he thought.

She said, 'Ne...Noel, my husband.'

Had she been about to say 'Neil'? 'And what do you do for a living?'

Marginal country, he was thinking. Surely they don't farm.

'*Noel* has stocks and shares,' Rennie said, stressing the name. 'I have an online business. Gift cards, things like that.'

The internet would be pretty patchy near Hope Hill. Basic ADSL? Satellite? 'Have you lived there for long?'

'No.'

She didn't elaborate. Hirsch said, 'And no other children?'

She seemed to find the question difficult. 'No.'

'Does Anna go to kindergarten?'

'No,' she said, her voice dropping to a hollow croak.

'Do you usually shop in Tiverton?'

Dr Pillai cut in, probably sensing that Rennie was

struggling. 'Denise usually shops in Redruth, isn't that right, Denise?' She leaned into the gap between the seats as if to create a huddle of kind souls. 'I first met Denise when she brought Anna in to see me. She gets ear infections, poor thing. How's she doing, Denise?'

'Good.'

Anna had been asleep, lulled by the movement of the Toyota. Using the mirror, Hirsch had seen the doctor touch the child's forehead from time to time. Then suddenly a little voice was piping, 'The wheels of the bus go round and round.'

'We're feeling a lot better, aren't we,' cooed Pillai.

Hirsch tuned them out. Twenty minutes later, Redruth appeared, streets named after Cornish towns. Old stone houses and an abandoned copper mine set in the folds of seven small hills. Down past the high school, the council chambers and a car repairer, through the square where a scene from *Breaker Morant* had been filmed, and out along the southern entrance to the town. Redruth and District Hospital, the sign said. Hirsch knew it didn't have the staff, equipment or expertise of a city hospital—was more of an aged-care facility than anything—but better the kid be monitored for a few hours than sent home with her mother just yet.

'Am I in trouble?' Denise Rennie said, in a low, wretched voice.

Hirsch chewed on that. Then Pillai was looming between the seats again. She touched his upper arm. 'Paul?'

Hirsch came to a decision. 'Not from me.'

After a moment, he clarified. 'Unless Anna's condition deteriorates. I'm sure you understand.'

'We do,' Pillai said.

Hirsch would keep quiet about it. Denise Rennie had learnt a hard lesson. She'd committed some kind of misdemeanour, though, and another cop might have taken action.

Pillai was saying, in a jolly tone, 'So no more leaving kids unattended in the car on a hot day, Denise.'

'I won't.'

And no more grabbing your friendly local policeman's service pistol, thought Hirsch.

Rather than wait around at the hospital, and conscious that Tuesday was the twenty-fifth, Hirsch went Christmas shopping. As if Christmas would bring much joy to him this year. Wendy and Katie were going to a family thing in the Barossa Valley and he was on duty. Either staring at a wall, just another Christmas orphan, or mopping up after drunks, pulling bodies out of car wrecks and breaking up family brawls.

The main Redruth shops were clustered around the square. Hirsch knew from reading a local-history booklet that a 1960s primary-school headmaster, dismayed that no one recognised the town's historical significance and tourist potential, started a movement to restore and preserve the copper mine and the Cornish miners' cottages and other colonial-era buildings. That had been okay with everyone. Less okay, as far as town-square business proprietors had been concerned, was the proposed removal of neon signs and banner advertising from shop facades. Right now the streetscape was more commercial present than colonial past.

First, Redruth Antiques and Gifts, where he bought a tall, slender, unadorned vase. 'You can't go wrong with a vase, right?' he asked the woman serving him.

She was young and tanned, and gave him a sceptical smile that filled him with doubt. 'Christmas present,' he explained, as if she might come clean about her misgivings.

'Wife? Girlfriend?'

'Girlfriend.'

'She likes long-stemmed flowers?'

Hirsch didn't know for sure. What he did know was that *he* liked the vase and hoped that would be enough. This was a nightmare and all he could do was come through it intact, and a minute later he was leaving the shop with the vase securely and beautifully wrapped.

Katie was next on his list. The latest Andy Griffiths title and four iPhone cases similar to her current case, which was chipped and inky. Also gift-wrapped in Christmas paper.

Then cards for friends and family which, if posted instantly, should arrive well after the big day, in keeping with every Hirsch Christmas. But he'd caught up. Items crossed off list. Back to police work.

He returned to the hospital carpark, stowed his shopping, and stepped into the blessed cool of the foyer just as his phone beeped for an incoming text. Dr Pillai: *Releasing the little one soon.*

Time to check on Brenda Flann.

Hirsch found her in a ward with three elderly patients who seemed to shrink from her purpling bruises, ballooning eyes and foul tongue. The sons were sitting on either side of her and all gave Hirsch scowls of such malevolence that he told Brenda he'd catch up with her another day and backed out.

Half an hour later he was making the return trip with his passengers. Exhaustion had set in; few words were spoken, the child slept. As they drew into Tiverton, he mentioned that he was putting on the Santa suit that evening and would Denise like to bring Anna along...?

All he got was a grunt.

8

Saturday, 5.30 a.m.

> Insomuch as the Natives are slippery to a degree almost
> inhuman, it behoves the police to be proportionally
> canny, lest they be outwitted.

Hirsch closed Mrs Keir's handwritten history and drained
the first coffee of the day, feeling unready for the dawn.
After playing Santa—what, a mere ten hours ago?—he was
bone-sore, bone-weary, completely addled.

He activated his phone and replayed Katie's video. The
ghostly dimness of evening in Kitchener Street, which ran
from the side wall of Ed Tennant's shop to Nan Washburn's
little horse stud. The darkness deepening as the last shreds
of sunlight winked out along the western hills, then unnatu-
ral light creeping in: mobile phone screens, sparklers, one
or two cigarettes flaring, and the fairy lights on a Christmas
tree in a builder's bucket in the middle of the street. Bright

voices on the soundtrack, the town and farm kids gathered with their parents and grandparents.

Finally, glee. Hirsch appearing, barely upright, on Radish the Clydesdale with a bulky sack of wrapped presents across his lap: one for every child in the district and a handful marked B and G just in case. Now he could be heard booming, 'Ho, ho, ho,' and trying to read Joyce Gwynne's handwriting. Tilting dangerously in the saddle as he dispensed his gifts, stretching muscles he didn't know he had. Radish letting go thunderous turds and the kids cracking up.

Sight and sound, but what Katie's video failed to record was Hirsch's tortured tailbone and spine, the stink of sweat and horse, Santa's whiskers feathery in his mouth.

Santa. It was 'Father Christmas' when Hirsch was a kid. He replayed the clip, began to smile, his muscle strains temporarily forgotten. The kids had been beside themselves with excitement. And they'd appreciated the joke, Santa on horseback. But distributing the presents had taken forever, so Katie had begun to use the pause button, filming freely again when it was time to award the prize for the best Christmas lights. Hirsch watched himself slip dangerously, grab Radish by the mane, haul himself upright, clearly trembling, before gingerly handing Nan Washburn her award, a framed certificate and a plum pudding wrapped in cellophane.

Thus ended Hirsch's fifteen minutes of glory.

Walking would ease his stiffness.

But there on his bedroom chair was the Santa suit. He couldn't return it unwashed—what would Martin say?

Reflecting on the legions of people who went through life anticipating what Martin would say, Hirsch hand-washed and rinsed the pants, jacket, cap and beard and pegged them out on his backyard clothesline.

Then he stuffed a large garbage bag into his pocket and set out. First to the oval—football in winter, cricket in summer—circling the low rail fence twice. Tall, smooth, silvery gum trees around the edge of the park, galahs screeching among the branches, constantly rising and settling. He walked the town's perimeter roads and occasionally up and back down one of the side streets. A distant kookaburra joined the bird chorus. Otherwise Hirsch heard only the scrape of his rubber soles and small creatures rustling, clinging to the last vestiges of night.

He passed a fence strung with Christmas lights, the colours washed out now, with the sun above the horizon. Hirsch was sick of looking at Christmas lights, sick of Christmas.

Six-thirty. The sun was above the droughty hills and slanting through the trees now, promising another cloudless, windless, stifling day. Time for his shower and shave, his second breakfast. But first he passed by the shop, quickly confirming that it had been a good idea to bring the garbage bag. Bending, pushing against his aches and pains, he scooped up plastic bottles, scraps of wrapping paper, dead sparklers, paper hats, cigarette butts. He moved further up Kitchener Street, hunting and pecking, and came upon a significant pool of blood.

*

Hirsch froze for a moment, then knelt. Touched his forefinger to it. Still sticky; spilt recently, then.

He gazed along the street. Kitchener was a short street, six homes on either side. He ran a mental checklist: who was capable of violence? Who was likely to be on the receiving end?

None of these people.

Movement alerted him, a shape behind a garden hedge, a disturbance of the sparse leaves. The house belonged to an elderly widower named Cromer. Calling, 'Mr Cromer?' Hirsch approached the driveway entrance.

A cry, just as he stepped onto the footpath. A queer, soft, alien cry, not of warning but of distress. And more blood. Spooked now, Hirsch entered the front yard. Blood new and glistening on the couch-grass lawn. A panicked sound, high-pitched, and Hirsch jumped in fright as one of Nan Washburn's miniature ponies retreated, trembling, into the corner between the hedge and the side fence.

He tried to make sense of what he was seeing. Not a person in distress. A little horse—covered in blood.

He took a breath and slowly approached, one hand reaching, his voice gentle. Who was he kidding? The pony lunged past, knocking him to the ground, smearing his baggy old morning-walk shorts. It was gone quickly, but one thing Hirsch was certain of: stab wounds. He knew what stab wounds looked like. And the poor creature had been stabbed several times.

He followed. The pony, weak and listing badly, headed back the way it had come, to the end of Kitchener Street and through Nan Washburn's front gate.

Where it stopped to sniff at and nudge one of its mates, a bloodied shape on the ground. Sensing Hirsch again, it stumbled along the side wall of the house, then, tottering, a great shudder in its hide, settled onto its knees, its hindquarters, and toppled over.

Hirsch felt sick. Pausing to check the animal at Washburn's front gate—lifeless eyes, intestines oozing across the dirt—he approached the fallen pony. It was still alive, snorting, eyes wild. Nothing he could do at this point, so he continued around to the pens, the small paddock and the stable block at the rear. Gates were open. More blood, gouts of it here and there. A further three bodies. Survivors, too: five traumatised miniatures and Radish at the far end of the paddock, the latter tossing his massive head; backing away as if doubting Hirsch had come in peace.

9

Hirsch knocked on the back door.

No answer, so he walked right around the house, knocking. Locked tight, no lights, no breakfast radio or TV leaking through a window. But Nan's Volvo was parked beside the back veranda. A victim? he thought. Or sound asleep. He needed to know.

He found the spare key in a magnetised tin stuck behind the hot-water tank and let himself in. Sounds—deep breaths in and out. Laboured? Injured? He couldn't tell.

He traced the sounds to a bedroom. Door ajar. He nudged it open.

Nan lay on her back, her legs entwined in a sheet. Intact, unharmed, deeply asleep. He crossed to wake her, explain why he was there, then reconsidered, picturing her shock and distress. He felt unequal to it. And he had a crime scene to preserve. He let himself out, locked up, replaced the key. A string of calls to make.

The Muirs were Nan's closest friends in the district. Apart

from the support, they'd know if she had family who should be notified. They'd know how he could contact her husband, the reclusive gold prospector.

Yvonne Muir answered, the voice conjuring the woman in Hirsch's mind's eye: slight and nervy in contrast to her stolid husband, a woman whose hands were constantly at her hair and clothing, rotating her wedding ring.

He sketched the situation and she gasped, appalled; said she'd come immediately.

'No,' Hirsch demurred. 'Wait for my word. I'd like to get a vet here before she wakes up.'

Yvonne was alarmed. 'Are you sure she's asleep? What if she's been hurt?'

Hirsch said he'd heard snoring.

'Well...I know she takes sleeping pills sometimes.'

'Meanwhile,' Hirsch said, 'perhaps Bob could give me a hand?'

'You just missed him,' Yvonne said. 'He's rewiring a house in Spalding today.'

So Hirsch would have to examine and preserve the crime scene alone. He wasn't confident that trained forensic officers would arrive before the end of the day, and half the town could be expected to traipse through Nan Washburn's yard by then.

'As soon as the vet gets here,' he said, 'I'll text you to come over.'

'Okay.'

Next, Hirsch called his boss. Jogging again.

'You're ruining another perfectly good run, Constable Hirschhausen.'

Then she listened, asking good questions—almost as if she could visualise the scene—and rattled off instructions: secure the area, take photographs of the dead and injured horses, preserve footprints and tyre prints. 'As best you can in the circumstances. I expect the horses have trampled over everything? Better establish a radius too—search for discarded clothing, knives, machetes. Doorknock. I'll try to get you a forensic team or at least a couple of CIB officers from Port Pirie.' She paused. 'Do you know who might be responsible?'

Hirsch did. He said, 'Early days, sarge.'

'All right.' The sergeant grunted. 'I sometimes jog with one of the vets. I'll give her a buzz.' She finished the call.

Hirsch began scanning the dirt for signs of vehicle and foot traffic. No good: the areas not churned up by panicked horses or hidden beneath carcasses were baked hard by the sun. Maybe forensic technicians could isolate partial tyre or shoe treads.

He took photos: the blood-smeared railings, the dead ponies with their slit throats, the survivors with their stabbed and slashed pelts.

There was no other evidence. No discarded blades or bloodied clothing along the fence lines or in the shrubbery. Head down, he worked a grid pattern, advancing deeper onto the grounds of the property. Stopped before he reached the horses huddled in the back corner: he was distressing them. The bloodied miniatures were surging around Radish's withers, eyeing Hirsch wildly, snorting, tossing their heads, one or two uttering little squeals of panic. He took more photos and backed away. Seven o'clock. The town was stirring, distant doors slamming, motors firing, breakfast table radios tuned to the ABC news.

Unwilling to leave the property unsecured while fetching crime-scene tape, he sealed off the driveway and entire backyard with a length of nylon cord from Nan's shed. He could feel a bite in the sun now. He was damp and sticky, and soon the air would stink, the sun super-heating the carcasses, the blood and shit.

At seven-thirty a forest-green Nissan twin-cab fitted with a camper shell rolled up Kitchener Street, *Redruth Veterinary Services* scrolled along the side panels. The driver parked short of the pony in the driveway entrance, got out, crouched as if to ascertain it was dead. She looked young, barely out of vet school, and Hirsch saw that she had the slight, hard grace of a runner.

He quickly texted Yvonne Muir—*Come now*—and ambled over, offering his hand to the vet, conscious of his shorts, T-shirt, battered Dunlop Volleys and overnight whiskers. They shook. He told her to call him Hirsch.

Her grip was dry, firm, brisk. 'Cathy Duigan,' she said, already looking past Hirsch at the pony he'd found on his walk. 'That one's still alive.'

'It was down the street, in someone's front garden,' Hirsch said. 'There are three more dead ones near the stable block, and a couple in the paddock with what look to me like stab wounds.'

'Where's Nan?'

'Still asleep. But one of her friends is on the way.'

'She'll be devastated.'

'You know her?'

'I do. You might call me the district horse vet.'

She looks about nineteen, Hirsch thought. 'Look, this is a cop question, okay? Do you think—'

'...that Nan was responsible? Absolutely not,' Duigan said, unlocking the camper shell; plastic crates, metal lockers and sets of drawers containing vials, syringes and bottles. She shouldered a bulky surgical case and pushed past Hirsch, ducked under the rope, squatted a moment at the wounded pony, and disappeared in the direction of the backyard. Hirsch stayed where he was. Yvonne Muir was hurrying up the street.

A minute later, hovering just outside the bedroom and hoping his presence would be reassuring, Hirsch watched Yvonne shake Nan Washburn's shoulder. The air was stale, overwarm; Nan propped on her elbows in a singlet top, slow to respond. Then slow to comprehend.

'Dead?' She sounded amazed more than anything. Then she scooted to the side of the bed.

Muir put an arm around her. Hirsch stepped into the room, began a clumsy explanation, tried to finish on a positive note. 'But Cathy Duigan's already here, looking after the others.'

'I should get dressed.' Nan cast about the room helplessly. 'She'll need help.'

Hirsch stepped out of the room. 'I'll put the kettle on.'

Into the kitchen, where he filled the kettle, spotting Nan's Best Christmas Lights certificate under a fridge magnet. With the water heating, he searched the overhead cupboards for mugs and tea, and then footsteps sounded in the hallway. Glancing at the open door, he saw both women pass by, Nan in shorts and a T-shirt, finger-combing her hair.

'Tea?' called Hirsch inadequately.

No answer. He abandoned the tea-making and followed the women onto the back veranda. Stopped abruptly, because they had stopped.

Nan, gasping, doubled over, groping with one blind hand for a veranda post.

'Oh, sweetheart, sit a moment,' Yvonne said, helping her into a deck chair.

Hirsch tried to see the yard through Nan's eyes. The lumpen shapes in the dirt; blood pooled here and there; blood smears on the white railings; the survivors with their flayed red hides. They were less wild-eyed now, though. The vet's a horse whisperer, he thought, watching Duigan among the jostling creatures.

'She needs my help,' Nan said, her strength returning. 'Is it okay if I...?'

'Go ahead,' Hirsch said.

But he kept Yvonne Muir with him. 'They know Nan, they don't know you or me.'

Muir was wound tight, started to argue, then nodded and sank into a deck chair.

Hirsch sat beside her. 'Thanks for coming.'

'You did the right thing, asking me.'

They watched as Nan entered the little paddock. 'Does she have children?'

'No. No brothers or sisters. Only me and Bob and a few other friends.'

'What can you tell me about the husband?'

'You think Craig did this? I very much doubt it,' Yvonne said.

Craig Washburn's story came out haltingly. He'd been the district council surveyor until he lost his job. 'He was getting quite eccentric and paranoid. He thought hidden forces were altering the landscape when he wasn't looking, that kind of thing. Some places he refused to survey. He said the mallee scrub out east was the only pure area left, and that's where he lives now, in a caravan Nan bought for him. He goes out prospecting with a metal detector, which somehow doesn't upset the landscape balance. We all keep an eye on him—take him food, check that he hasn't fallen down a mineshaft or died of snakebite. He's not completely bonkers, he takes his meds. But he is odd.'

'Odd as in paranoid, voices telling him to kill Nan's horses?'

Yvonne Muir slapped the back of Hirsch's hand. 'No. Do *not* go there. Craig's harmless, he doesn't need you hassling him.'

Hirsch raised his hands and Yvonne backtracked. 'If you *do* talk to him, go easy, okay?'

'Okay.'

Hirsch's default position, an amiable okay to everything.

*

A short time later, they joined Nan and the vet by the pony in the driveway. Squatting in the dirt, Duigan said, 'Sorry, Nan, but this one'll have to be put down.'

'I know,' Washburn said, tears flowing. Sitting cross-legged, she lifted the pony's long neck onto her lap. 'But it's hard, they're not just show ponies, they're pets. They're *family*.'

'Of course they are, dear,' Yvonne said, crouching with her.

The vet nodded, busy with a syringe. First a sedative, she explained, then an overdose of barbiturates.

Hirsch looked on, feeling helpless. Nan, stroking, crooning, watched askance as Duigan slid the needle into the pony's neck and depressed the plunger. A shudder in the hide, then, quite soon, the legs grew still, the eyes less frightened. Nan continued to stroke, blink away her tears.

'She'll go quickly now, Nan, no pain,' Duigan said, administering the kill shot.

But Hirsch was alarmed to see muscle tremors and leg movements. The pony took in a great breath.

'It hasn't worked,' he blurted.

Duigan said gently, 'What you're seeing is involuntary. All part of the process.'

Quite soon after that, Hirsch experienced a curious sensation of loss, as if he'd been linked to a life that had suddenly drained away. He peered at the pony: simply a carcass now, all tension gone. It might never have been alive.

A hundred metres away, Radish screamed and whinnied. Tossed his head and wheeled around and dashed from end to end, kicking up paddock dust and divots.

Nan looked over at him, wretched. '*He knows.*'

'Yes,' Duigan said, also upset, 'I think he does.'

Yvonne squeezed hard and Nan wept, and no one spoke for some time until Duigan, quietly packing her gear, said, 'That's it, Nan, she's at rest now, you can let her go.'

'I just want to be with her a while longer,' Washburn said.

Duigan touched the blood-smeared forearm, got to her feet and walked to her Nissan. Hirsch, trailing her, asked, 'What about the other horses?'

'Superficial injuries, thank God. But they're traumatised, so it'd be good if people could be kept away for the time being.'

Hirsch felt wrung out. How could he achieve that? CIB officers were on the way, and townspeople—ghouls and well-wishers—would soon hear what had happened. 'And the bodies? A mass grave?'

'Not here,' Duigan said firmly. She blew a strand of hair away from her bottom lip. 'The property's too small, and it's semi-urban.'

'Dump them in the bush?' Hirsch was improvising wildly.

The vet frowned at him, as if he were slow. 'I've just administered *poison*. If a fox or a dingo feeds on the carcass...' Then her face relaxed. She touched his forearm. 'I'll make a call. There are professional cremation services for the disposal of large animals.'

She cocked her head, itching to say something. Hirsch waited for it.

'As a policeman,' she said slowly, 'you'll have seen this kind of thing before...'

Out with it, Hirsch thought. 'Actually, no—but I've met

the odd axe murderer type who probably tortured cats as a kid...'

'I did a special subject in my honours year,' Duigan said. 'The psychological underpinnings of animal cruelty.' She paused. 'It was interesting.'

'Interesting,' echoed Hirsch, giving her a look. 'Does that mean you have a theory about this?'

Duigan countered with a question. 'Does it seem random to you?'

He'd decided against that notion in the first thirty seconds. 'As in a warped stranger happened to stumble on the place? No.'

'No,' Duigan agreed. 'This was personal.'

'And?'

'Whoever did this was targeting Mrs Washburn—in particular, her emotional attachment to her ponies.'

'Mm.' That seemed obvious to Hirsch. 'Why?'

Duigan shrugged her bony little shoulders. 'A grudge of some kind? Payback.'

'It's extreme, though. This is a seriously screwed-up person we're talking about.'

'Yes. Someone with a sadistic disorder of some kind, which he keeps hidden...under control...except that one day Nan offended him in some way.'

'He?'

The vet looked at Hirsch levelly. 'Don't you agree? And he'd be local. Maybe you already have your suspicions?'

Hirsch smiled, shook her hand goodbye. 'Thanks for everything you've done.'

'Tell Nan I'll call in again tomorrow.'

'Will do.'

Hirsch wandered back to the house, planning his day. Wait for other police to arrive, then knock on doors. The Cobb house first—because it was within walking distance—and then Adam Flann's. How likely was it, though, that a pair of vacant, unmotivated boys had risen before dawn with blood lust in their eyes? Unless they'd been up all night—drinking, maybe taking ice—and been hit by a sudden brainwave. Or they'd been smouldering with humiliation since the apology. Or both. Hirsch thought he should probably pounce now, before weapons and clothing could be hidden or destroyed, but found himself halting in the driveway. Nan Washburn, desolate, frail, diminished, was still cradling her pony. Yvonne was at her side.

He crouched with them. So much blood on Nan: her cheek, arms, hands, torso, probably her lap. And darkening the dirt all around. 'The vet will drop by again tomorrow,' he said. 'And she'll arrange for the, ah, disposal of the bodies.'

'Okay.'

'Do you mind if I ask a few questions?'

'Paul, *no*,' Muir said.

But Washburn was practical. She gently touched the other woman's arm and said, 'I'm fine now, Von, thank you.' Turning to Hirsch she said, 'Give me twenty minutes, okay? Both of you wait on the veranda while I reassure Radish and the others.'

They did as they were told, watching Nan tip a haybale

and a bag of oats into a bouncy green barrow and wheel it through the paddock gate and down to the far corner, slowing her pace as she neared the surviving horses, calling in a singsong voice. Radish reacted first, snorting, scraping at the dirt with his front hoof, but then, like an elegant machine set in motion, he walked to greet her, his big shoulders rolling. The ponies trotted behind.

Nan rested the barrow and went to each animal, stroking, patting, crooning. They responded with nudges and head tosses, before passing on either side of her, bound for the tucker. She hauled the hay onto the dirt, cutting the twine, separating the compressed stalks into clumps, breaking these apart with her shoe. Then she poured a long, thick runnel of oats along the ground and stood, watching, as her horses began to eat.

Hirsch looked on, and wondered if a man—or a kid—with a taste for mutilating animals might one day want to try it on humans.

The questioning took place at the kitchen table. 'You didn't hear anything?' Hirsch asked, gesturing at the world beyond the room, simultaneously glancing at Yvonne Muir, wondering how much she should be a part of this.

'I took a sleeping pill,' Nan said, regret on her face.

'Do you have any thoughts on who might have wanted to harm you?'

Nan blew on the surface of her tea. 'I know *you* have thoughts, Paul. You're thinking Daryl and/or Adam.'

'What do you think?'

'I think some people might say those boys had a motive, they felt humiliated because they had to give a formal apology, but...really? It's not as if I rubbed their faces in it. I didn't quibble, didn't insist on taking it further, didn't go complaining to their parents, nothing like that. And the apology was your idea.' She shook her head. 'When it boils down to it, they're basically good kids.'

In Hirsch's experience, a kid like Adam Flann might consider the apology an insult, and Nan Washburn a softer target for revenge than a policeman. 'You raise pedigrees, right? They're valuable? You win prizes with them, you sell to other breeders?'

She glanced at him shrewdly. 'Yes.'

'Is it a cut-throat business?'

Too late, he realised what he'd said. Nan gave him a crooked smile. 'I take it you mean figuratively? It's not. I suppose some of the other breeders might be envious, but I can't see any of them hurting any animal.'

'Perhaps you sold someone a dud pony and didn't offer a refund?'

'Nothing like that. I haven't bred a single dud, as you call it. If I had, I'd have given a refund, no questions asked.'

The iron roof flexed in the growing heat, a series of cracks and creaks above their heads. 'Your husband.'

Yvonne Muir bristled, but Nan Washburn said calmly, 'What about him?'

'You're separated. Perhaps he doesn't want that? Perhaps he thinks there's someone else in your life? I'm sorry, Nan, but I have to ask these questions.'

'Paul, stop it,' Muir said.

'It's all right, Von, he does have to ask these questions. And I can say categorically that there's no one else in my life, and it was Craig who left me, not the other way around. And not because we were fighting.' She paused. 'He has mental health issues. He needs to be alone. I see him once or twice a month and we get on fine.'

'*Non-violent* health issues,' Yvonne Muir said, with emphasis.

Nan touched Muir's forearm, but followed up. 'Yes, non-violent, he wouldn't hurt a soul. Nuts, but harmless. It started a few years ago, and at first I made allowances. But it became too much in the end, he wanted to be by himself. I worry, of course. We all try to keep an eye on him, take him food and clothing from time to time, a quick chat, that kind of thing, whatever he can bear. Sometimes he's lucid, other times...not, but in a gentle way. Muted.' Tears came to her eyes. 'One day a snake will get him, or he'll wander off and die of thirst.'

Hirsch drained his tea. 'Have you had any threats lately? Letters, emails, phone calls, social media posts?'

'No.'

'Rocks through your windows?'

'No.'

'Tyres slashed?'

'Nothing at all,' Washburn said irritably. 'I live a quiet life, okay? I don't make enemies. I don't yell at the neighbours for leaving their bins out or letting their dogs yap. I don't gossip. I don't make waves. Breeding miniature ponies isn't everyone's cup of tea, but it's a quiet business, I keep the place tidy, there are no bad smells, no mistreatment, no gates left open, no horses roaming the district. All this'—she gestured at the carnage on the other side of her wall—'seems personal in some way, but I have no idea how or why. You're looking for someone who's, I don't know, sick. And I've no idea who that is.'

Nor do I, thought Hirsch, but he had to start somewhere. He said goodbye and had barely reached Kitchener Street when the Port Pirie team arrived: one lone CIB detective, one lone forensic technician. They accepted Hirsch's report and photographs without comment.

'We'll take it from here,' said the detective, a bruiser named Comyn, looking intently at Hirsch with wide-set, doubting eyes.

He knows who I am, Hirsch thought. He's thinking whistle-blower, dog, maggot, rat. Thinks I caused the resignation of some good CIB men and the suicide of another.

Hirsch smiled sweetly and set off to do some police work of his own.

10

He raced home, showered, shaved, stuffed himself into his uniform and hung his towel on the backyard clothesline. The Santa suit was dry. Note to self: return to Martin Gwynne asap.

Settling his broad-brimmed uniform hat at a stern angle on his head, he left the police station. A huddle of townspeople across at the shop; one of them beckoned to Hirsch. He waved cheerily and set off in the opposite direction. They know about Nan's ponies, he thought. They want the official version. And reassurance.

Two minutes later he knocked on Marie Cobb's door. Waited. Walked around to the rear. Laura was there in shortie pyjamas, plugged into an iPod, watering the tomatoes. And Hirsch thought: Shit, what will the news do to her? Unless *she* mutilated the ponies? Hirsch rejected the notion as soon as it popped into his head. Me in cop mode, he thought: trust no one, suspect everyone.

Laura caught him in the corner of her eye and started

reflexively, placing her hand over her chest. Then, her expression resentful—masking apprehension, Hirsch thought—she released the hand-spray trigger, hooked the nozzle over the trellis and removed the headphones. The garden, still in shade, smelt coolly and cleanly of tomatoes and damp mulch.

'Morning, Laura.'

'Can't you leave us alone?'

This was a kid who got up early and filled her days, thought Hirsch. Shopping, cooking, gardening, schoolwork, housework, work-work. Watching over her mother and brother. The little household's youngest member, she shouldered most of the responsibility; had no other choice. But how was she going to cope by the time Year 12 came around? She might get some leeway if she broke a leg or caught glandular fever, but if her brother was in jail? If—when—her mother acted out? Shy, shamefaced, Laura had told Hirsch some of it: Marie staying in bed for weeks at a time; talking non-stop for days at a time; calling her kids out of class to say her sore throat was cancer; bundling them into the car at 2 a.m. because the secret police were coming.

Hirsch removed his hat and found that his mouth was dry. He swallowed, feeling clumsy. 'Laura, there's...I have to tell you something awful has happened to some of Mrs Washburn's ponies.'

Her hand bunched the neck of her pyjama top. Fear. 'What?'

He told her, and she was silent but tears ran down her cheeks. Then she gathered herself. 'I need to go around there,' she said. Paused minutely and added: 'It wasn't Daryl, he wouldn't do that.'

'But you understand that I need to speak to him?'

She shrugged, clopping in faded pink Crocs towards the back door. Opened it, looked at him: she expected him to follow.

Into the hot airless cave that was their little brick house.

'He's asleep,' she said. 'You know where.'

She left him there in the kitchen. A door slammed. Presently, he heard squeaky taps and shower water drumming against a plastic curtain. Taking a breath, Hirsch walked through to Daryl Cobb's battered door and knocked and waited. Knocked again, a hard, knuckling rap. Tough guy, he thought self-consciously, and decided simply to walk in.

The boy was asleep, wearing only boxer shorts, a big, soft, downy creature beached on a grimy sheet, his feet tangled in the top sheet. The room stank: sweat, dope, the rancid smell of unwashed flesh and clothing.

Hirsh regarded him glumly. Meanwhile Laura finished showering: he heard the water stop, the curtain rings clack. A quick towel rub later, her bare feet padded to her bedroom and a door slammed. Hirsch sighed again. Back to Daryl.

His footwear first: runners, black pointy-toed going-out shoes, thongs. No blood. The clothing on the floor, the chair, in drawers and the wardrobe. No blood.

Hirsch re-entered the hallway just as Laura emerged from her bedroom, her hair dampening the neck and shoulders of a yellow T-shirt, her legs thin and vulnerable in a baggy pair of shorts. 'Quickest shower in history,' he said.

She ignored him. Banged out of the back door and, a moment later, he heard her bicycle wheels.

The laundry next. The washing machine was bone dry. White knickers, a black bra and a Redruth High School summer uniform in the dirty-clothes basket.

But the absence of bloody clothing and footwear wasn't proof of Daryl's innocence. Hirsch took out his iPhone and replayed the video. He finally spotted Daryl near the end—with his sister, and his mother, cheering as Nan reached up to Santa for her Best Christmas Lights certificate and plum pudding. He was wearing blue boardshorts and a Kings of Leon T-shirt.

Hirsch returned to the bedroom. The T-shirt and the shorts lay where Daryl had stripped them off. Hirsch toed them open again: no blood.

It didn't mean anything. The kid could have changed his clothes, killed and slashed a few horses in the darker hours, buried his bloodied clothing in the backyard.

'All of them?' asked Daryl Cobb dazedly.

'Four dead,' Hirsch said. 'Couple more with stab wounds.'

He'd dragged two of the sticky kitchen chairs out into the sweeter air of the backyard, and now he watched Daryl stare at Laura's tomato plants as if answers lay among them. The boy's befuddlement might owe something to being hauled out of bed and plonked on a chair in the great outdoors hours before he usually awoke, Hirsch thought, but it owed a lot more to the enormity of the crime. The kid was staring vacantly, slack-jawed, unable to take it in.

He hadn't yet twigged that a policeman might view him as a suspect, and that counted for plenty in Hirsch's book. Not guilty, he decided. Daryl wasn't capable of concealing guilt. He hadn't butchered and mutilated any ponies, hadn't witnessed anyone else do it, hadn't heard talk of it.

Still, Hirsch had to be sure.

'Did you have a good time at last night's street party?'

'It was all right.'

Hirsch mentally reviewed Daryl's face in Katie Street's iPhone video clip: the uncomplicated enjoyment of a child. Uncool to admit that.

'What did you do afterwards?'

Daryl shrugged, struggling to make sense of where he was, who he was with, what it was about. 'Nothing much.'

'Mucked around with Adam?'

A ship at sea might change course faster than Daryl Cobb. He blinked, frowned. 'He wasn't...he didn't...I think he went home after. Or maybe down the hospital.'

'What did you do?' Hirsch repeated.

'Nothing much.'

Hirsch had the sense that Daryl barely recalled his evening. 'Watch TV?'

A cloud lifted. 'Yeah. *Game of Thrones*.'

'On DVD?'

The sun and the air defeated Daryl again. He frowned at the dirt. And said, slowly, 'Laura's.'

'It was her DVD?'

'Got it for her birthday.'

'You binge it? Late night?'

Daryl struggled again. 'Think so.'

'Did you go out afterwards? To look at the Christmas lights, that kind of thing? Meet up with friends?'

A dull intelligence stirred behind Daryl's blankness. He looked astonished, as if Hirsch was suggesting he'd piloted a private jet to Tahiti. 'Just went to bed.'

'Who was here last night?'

Another strange question. Overnight guests? Here? 'Me and Mum and Laura.'

'You all stayed in?'

Daryl woke a little more. 'I would never...We would never...'

'Never what?'

'Hurt Nan's horses.'

'What about Adam? Did he stay in town?'

Daryl shrank. He looked hunted. 'Dunno. Never saw where he went after.'

'He didn't pop in for a meal, watch TV for a while?'

Daryl folded his arms. It wasn't defensive, it was decisive. 'Nup.'

'I want to thank you again for apologising to Mrs Washburn, Daryl. It can't have been easy. Perhaps you boys felt we'd put you on the spot?'

Daryl blinked at the shift. And Hirsch realised that the boy had no sense of agency. It didn't occur to him to resent, or permit himself to resent, the burdens and expectations placed upon him by others. 'It was all right,' he muttered.

Another mantra of the bush: things were never terrible

or fantastic, merely okay. 'You didn't feel aggrieved at all?'

The boy didn't know the word. 'You didn't think Mrs Washburn and I were being unfair?'

Daryl's eyes swivelled wildly, as if he thought Hirsch were saying the apology was inadequate, more was expected of him. 'Better than going to court,' he said.

'What about Adam? Was he upset?'

Now Daryl could see where this was going. He shifted in his chair, his soft, pale thighs adhering to the vinyl. The rising sun had meanwhile begun to paint the yard, illuminating his bony feet.

'Daryl? Did Adam complain about yesterday?'

'Might of.'

'Was he just a bit pissed off? Or was he angry?'

A shrug.

'Any plans to see him today?'

Daryl went very still. He didn't know the correct answer.

'How's your mum been?'

Daryl struggled to find the words. 'She's, like, it's the start of a down time, you can tell the signs.'

'Things she says and does?'

'Yeah.'

'Did she enjoy last night?'

'She went to bed right after.'

'How long do the down times last?'

Daryl laughed, fully awake now. 'Weeks, months.'

'Laura's helping Mrs Washburn today.'

Daryl shrugged as if barely aware he shared a house with

his sister. Hirsch went on: 'Perhaps you could stay in and keep an eye on your mother.'

Daryl stared at nothing; at the layout of his life.

Hirsch walked back to the police station. It was probably his imagination, but already the town seemed stunned and cowed. The smell of slaughter hung in the air, which he knew must be a memory trace. He was several hundred metres from Nan Washburn's house now.

For distraction, he took the Santa suit down from his backyard clothesline, folded it as if Martin Gwynne were watching his every move, and tried to slip it back into the David Jones shopping bag. Gave up. The suit as folded by him proved unequal to the bag, full of fabric, clips, buttons and air, and Hirsch thought that pretty much summed up his day and his situation in this fucking town.

Five minutes later, he was parked outside the Gwynnes' house and knocking on their door. Joyce answered, and, as always, seemed to fall back as if he was carrying news of a death in the family. 'Paul,' she murmured, an acutely shy woman with short, wispy grey hair and thick-lensed glasses.

She rallied. 'I heard about Nan's ponies...'

Hirsch would have to deal with days of this. He was the law, he'd be able to fill in all the gaps. He gave her a non-committal nod.

'Nasty business,' Joyce Gwynne said harshly, as if he'd said it wasn't.

Hirsch nodded and proffered the Santa suit. 'I'm just returning this. Tell Martin it was very kind of—'

'Paul!'

The intrusion and eclipse were seamlessly choreographed; Martin Gwynne appeared in the hallway behind his wife and tucked her out of sight in the same movement. She seemed to evaporate, leaving a hint of floral perfume and muffled footsteps back in the dark reaches of the house.

Hirsch tried again. Thrusting the suit at Martin, he gabbled, 'Just returning this, many thanks, it's been washed.'

Gwynne took the costume automatically, his mind sharply on other matters. 'I hope you're looking at those two boys.'

'Excuse me?'

'Mark my words, there are times when a rap over the knuckles is worse than useless. An apology? Really, Paul. That was always going to rub them up the wrong way.'

'Early days, Martin...Look, I've got to dash. Thanks again for the suit.'

Martin looked down at it for the first time, bundled over both forearms. 'There was a shopping bag, I believe?'

'Oh? I'll look for it. Better go,' Hirsch said, gabbling again.

'It's a blight, you know that, don't you?'

Afraid that Gwynne was getting biblical on him, Hirsch waved and nodded madly as he made his way down the path and out to his police 4WD.

Sergeant Brandl called to tell him she'd arrived at the scene with the 'children'. 'Where are you?'

'Still in town, about to drive out to—'

'That can wait. I need you to show the forensics fellow

where you found the stolen copper. He's got another job on but he can give us five minutes.'

Hirsch said, 'Okay,' but she'd already shut him down.

He found the forensic van waiting for him at the corner of the Barrier Highway and Kitchener Street, one lazy arm waving him on when he appeared, and the two vehicles headed out of town. A few minutes later they'd parked at the farmhouse and Hirsch was standing at the edge of the hard pan of dirt in front of the barn.

He strove for an apologetic tone. 'I put up crime-scene tape and called it in, but when I checked the next day, the skip was gone.' *If you'd got off your lazy arses...*

The forensic technician picked up the implication. 'Mate, we've had a spate of thefts—Christmas presents, mostly.' He stared at the ground inside the barn. 'Not much to go on.'

Hirsch shrugged. The tech switched his attention to the tattered strands of tape. 'Might get prints off that, I suppose.'

My prints at least, thought Hirsch.

11

Before he could head out east, Hirsch was called back to help doorknock the town. Feeling pushed and pulled, the day no longer his, he returned to Tiverton, where he found his sergeant trying to soothe the CIB detective. Comyn was chafing.

'You're telling me there's a husband?'

'A bit of a hermit, apparently,' Hilary Brandl said calmly. She was a lean woman with a loping stride and dry, brown hair cut in a convenient bob.

'Wonderful,' Comyn said. He shot Hirsch a sour look. 'And yesterday a couple of town kids are forced to apologise for stealing her ute. Suspects crawling out of the woodwork, and I'm shorthanded.'

'So let Constable Hirschhausen do the follow-up,' Brandl said. 'My constables and I can help you here.'

She wore the lightweight summer uniform, a size too big, as if she'd lost weight, but had a habit of plucking at her shirt and pants as if she disliked the sensation of the fabric against her skin. 'He knows the district inside and out.'

I wish, thought Hirsch, standing back while they negotiated. One of Sergeant Brandl's young constables stood sentry at Nan Washburn's driveway, the other was guarding the crime-scene tape, which had been moved to the entrance to Kitchener Street. Not going to be enough, Hirsch thought, to keep the gawkers and ghouls away.

Then Comyn was looking at him. 'Constable Hirschhausen.'

Hirsch approached. He nodded, wary. Beads of perspiration stood out on Comyn's upper lip and temples. The heat of the day and the heat of arguing with Sergeant Brandl. It was tricky: she outranked Comyn, but she was uniformed police and it was CIB's case. 'Yes, senior constable?'

With some distaste, Comyn said, 'You were CIB before you got busted?'

I didn't get busted, Hirsch thought. I found myself in a corrupt suburban CIB squad that got busted. Some of the shit stuck to me, and I was sent to Hicksville as punishment. He said nothing. Screwed an expectant look onto his face.

Comyn went on: 'You've already questioned one kid?'

'Yes.'

'And?'

Hirsch summarised, concluding: 'I don't think he did it.'

Comyn waved that aside—he'd question Daryl Cobb himself. 'The other kid lives out in the sticks somewhere?'

'Just a few minutes away.'

'And Mrs Washburn's husband?'

'Out in the sticks somewhere,' Hirsch said.

Comyn gave him a look. 'Time is a factor. I need you to

take statements from both individuals.' He turned to Brandl. 'Sergeant, if you and one of your constables can help me with the doorknock?'

That's what I've been suggesting all along, her face seemed to say. 'Certainly.'

Hirsch got directions from Nan Washburn, promised not to harass or frighten her husband, and walked back down Kitchener Street to where he'd parked the police HiLux. A Channel 9 outside-broadcast van was arriving as he climbed behind the wheel. Not his headache.

Late morning now. He'd interview Adam Flann first, then Craig Washburn. Given that the latter was camped on the banks of Mischance Creek, in the general area of Hope Hill, he could look in on Denise Rennie and her daughter too.

After five kilometres of bumping along a narrow gravel road full of blind corners, corrugations and erosion channels, heading directly into a sun that flared on the lone windscreen of an oncoming farm ute, glass shards in the ditches, mica in the dirt and gravel, he breasted a rise and headed down into a dip in the hill folds. The Flanns lived in a pale green cube-shaped fibro structure, its iron roof standing up in steep surprise from a veranda closed in on all sides. Two small farm-implement sheds, an empty dog pen choked with weeds, ragged pine trees, a listing water tank. The property also consisted of a hundred hectares of stony hillside that might run a mob of sheep if you were ambitious, hard-working and able to keep up a supply of hay—which ruled out the Flanns.

Reaching the bottom of the slope, Hirsch coasted into the driveway. Here the neglect and helplessness were more pronounced. A wheelless Datsun Bluebird crouched in a patch of star thistles; an old latch-door refrigerator yawned at the weeds, a trap for small children; a trailer more rust than sheet metal sat piled with bald car tyres beside the front steps.

No sign of Wayne Flann's Holden ute.

Hirsch got out, locked up, approached the house. This was the time he hated most: alone in a land of suspicion, ignorance and untamed dogs. But the whole property was still and soundless and seemed to gather folds of apology, not belligerence, about itself.

He knocked, knocked again, and eventually walked around to the rear. The back veranda had been converted into a sleepout and someone was in there, moaning. Hirsch hesitated: it wasn't pain, it was exertion. With an unmistakeable erotic note.

What now? He stood back, observing proprieties, and waited. The sounds escalated, then stopped. He waited to be sure and then cleared his throat.

'Adam? It's Paul Hirschhausen. I need a minute.'

The whole world tensed, the whole world shot him an alarmed look, and then a voice that sounded like Gemma Pitcher's shouted, 'Don't come in!'

Right.

'Okay,' Hirsch said.

He waited. She'll be his alibi, then? Unless both of them spent the small hours hacking up tiny horses.

No, not Gemma. A few moments later she emerged from the house, scarcely able to meet his gaze. Embarrassed, he thought, but not ashamed. And as those first awkward seconds unfurled, she continued to shed her shy, pudgy shop-assistant persona. She took charge. Her hair was frazzled, her puffy face sleepy and slack with satisfaction, her fleshy legs mottled and bed-creased under the huge T-shirt. But it was with dignity and nerve that she reached a hand back through the door and gently tugged Adam Flann out onto the struggling couch grass. Adam had pulled on a pair of khaki boardshorts. He was also creased and dishevelled but, Hirsch had to concede, beautifully put together. Flicking Hirsch a sulky shy look, he stood hard against Gemma's side and their hands found each other. His thumb caressed her knuckles.

'Sorry to interrupt,' Hirsch said.

They waited.

'I'll explain why in a moment, but I need to speak to each of you separately.'

Adam went tight. 'Is it Mum?'

Gemma wrapped an arm around him, waiting.

'As far as I know, she's fine,' Hirsch said. 'Adam? Would you mind coming over here a minute?'

He took the boy to a pair of once-green plastic lawn chairs, which looked over nothing but a fraying clothesline and a dozen empty fuel drums. 'Sit.'

They sat, Adam shooting Gemma anxious looks. All of his smartarse confidence was gone—as if, having surrendered himself to vulnerability in his bed a short time earlier, he was yet to recover.

'May I ask your movements last night?'

The old Adam flickered into view. 'I never done nothing.'

'Just tell me what you did, and when, and I'll be on my way.'

Flann's expression was flat-out sceptical. 'I'm old enough,' he said.

Is he talking about having sex with Gemma? 'Yes,' Hirsch said.

Adam chewed his bottom lip. 'Me and Gemma went to the Christmas thing, you know, when you rode the horse.'

'Okay.' They hadn't been on Katie's video, but that was true of other people too.

'Then we come back here.'

'How?'

'Wayne.'

'What time was that?'

'Straight after.'

'Did you go out again?'

'Wayne did. Me and Gemma stayed here.'

'Okay,' Hirsch said, getting to his feet, 'stay put while I have a quick word with Gemma.'

Hirsch crossed the grass again. Gemma said, with some heat, 'He never did nothing wrong. He apologised and everything.'

'Take it easy. I just need to know your movements last night.'

'Me? I was with Adam at the Christmas street thing. You saw us, right?'

'Go on.'

'Then we came here.'

'How?'

'In Wayne's ute.'

'Did any of you go out again? The pub? A drive around? A party?'

She shook her head determinedly. 'Nup. Stayed here.'

'Wayne?'

'He might of gone out,' Gemma said, lifting and dropping her heavy shoulders. 'Wasn't here when I went to the toilet this morning. Why? What's he done? What do you think me and Adam've done?'

Hirsch turned, beckoned. Adam joined them.

'In the early hours of this morning, someone attacked Mrs Washburn's ponies.'

He waited. He watched. Gemma's hand crept into Adam's again and he saw both kids trying to get a handle on the news. Gemma said, 'What do you mean?'

'I mean some of the ponies are dead, and some are badly injured.'

'Shot?' said Adam.

'Hacked with an axe or a machete or some kind of large blade.'

Hirsch waited again. Tears welled in Gemma's eyes. Adam was slower to take it in, and when he did, he wrapped Gemma in his arms.

He looked at Hirsch. 'I would never do that. And me and Gemma were here all night.'

'Would Wayne do it?' Hirsch asked, even as he knew that brother would always protect brother in this family.

Adam's face was shut tight. 'Not him, neither.'

Gemma piped up. 'Wayne called Adam a fuckwit for stealing Nan's ute. Said it served him right he had to apologise.'

'Yeah. He couldn't care less about her horses,' Adam said.

'But he did go out at some stage?'

Adam toed the dirt and shrugged. 'Probably to the pub.'

Hirsch knew he'd just heard a lie, but where was the lie? Wayne had lied to Adam? Adam had lied to protect Wayne? And Adam had merely speculated, not made a statement. Everyone lied, every day—especially to the police. A one-off, outright lie, from someone unused to lying, could often be identified and disproved. Constant and habitual lying was harder to recognise, let alone challenge, because the liar no longer saw a distinction between a lie and the truth. They were all just words deployed in the interests of survival. In any case most people lied *some* of the time, generally layering it with the truth to deflect blame, to sugar-coat their cowardice or stupidity.

Separating the two could be a headache. And right now Hirsch was sure of Adam Flann's innocence in this matter, at least.

He nodded his thanks, wished them good day, and drove further into the back country.

Out where the bare red dirt was swept by the wind, the roads were rutted tracks. Eyeless stone ruins could be glimpsed through the stubby mulga trees or stood becalmed on a stony plain that would never nourish a grain crop, let alone a sheep. Stone everywhere: as white quartz reefs in the paddocks; as flat, erupted slabs around which Hirsch steered his police 4WD; as pebbles that pinged in the wheel arches when he picked up speed; and as rounded, water-tumbled rocks the size of footballs and tennis balls in the creek beds. Or as fieldstones harvested for long-ago farmhouses, barns, fences and stockyards.

He barely climbed out of third gear for the first half hour, the HiLux creaking and flexing like a stiff little ship in pitching seas, but eventually he reached a lonely intersection where a bunch of dead flowers rested on the grassy verge. Someone had died in a car wreck here, meaning that other poor souls continued to grieve. A short time later he passed a muddy dam where, according to Bob Muir and others in the town, a toddler had drowned. A landscape imprinted with death, thought Hirsch. Hopes died and people died. Mrs Keir's 'natives', children, motorists, gold fossickers, tourists. Some who wandered into the dry country intending never to return. A murder might pass unnoticed and undetected out here, he thought. Nowhere here is neutral. It's loaded, complicit.

He braked at a T-intersection. A sign pointed to *Mischance Creek (Ruins)* in one direction and *Mischance Creek* in the other. 'You want the creek itself,' Nan Washburn had told him. 'Drive until you see a wagon wheel, it marks the track to Craig's camp, if not Craig himself.'

Out of curiosity, Hirsch checked the ruins first. Nothing much to see. Mischance Creek had been a tiny settlement of houses a century ago but now was mostly stone walls sinking back into the red soil. He U-turned and headed in the opposite direction and turned off at the wagon wheel. A hundred metres down a rutted track he came to the creek and Craig Washburn's campsite. Hirsch was impressed. The main structure was a long caravan, squat and square, shaded under an extensive thatched roof supported by treated-pine poles. Palm tree fronds, he realised. In a clearing on one side of it, an array of solar panels and a battery. On the other side, an old rustbucket Kingswood parked under a slanted corrugated-iron roof fitted with a downpipe to an incongruous new poly tank the colour of the sky.

He got out, stretched the kinks in his spine, and wandered over to the car. It didn't look serviceable and there were no other vehicles that he could see. Two heavy-duty blue work shirts drying on a cord stretched between a couple of gum trees. A bucket with a hole-stippled base strapped to a tree—a showerhead? Tidy piles of used food tins and plastic and glass bottles. He crossed a dirt patch where bull ants teemed and examined the recyclables. Soup. Milk. Mineral water. No beer, wine or spirits.

The place felt deserted. Hirsch lifted his nose and sniffed cautiously, not wanting to detect decomposition on the wind. He sensed nothing. A man lived here but barely made an impact on the wider area, it seemed to him. He knocked on the door to the caravan. No answer. He tried the door— unlocked—and found himself stepping into a spartan world of folded bedding, textbooks and notepads, a metal detector on a rack above a sofa. No dust, odours, spills or clutter.

All that was left was to follow the creek. It was mostly dry. No running water, but reedy pools every hundred metres or so. In the distance, the pink-smudge Tiverton Hills. On either side, red soil flats with sparse mulga scrub and bleached dead grass. He came to a bend where a broad stretch of stagnant water showed between bulrushes. Small creatures had scribbled their tracks over a tight crescent of mud. Human footprints, too. Hirsch continued to follow the creek bank, and eventually the shape of a man coalesced beside a narrow cutting. It was probably fast in full flood; now it merely trapped a small pool.

He stopped to watch. Washburn—if that's who it was— wore a khaki shirt, trousers and a greasy Akubra hat. Kneeling with his back to Hirsch he was tearing at the dead grass that fringed a stone slab flat on the ground. That completed, he proceeded to swipe away dust and stalks with a new-looking banister brush.

Hirsch coughed. The man said, 'I knew you were there. Subtle as a mob of cattle.'

He stood and turned, revealing a seamed, whiskery face and heavy-rimmed glasses repaired with black electrical tape. Blue binder-twine in his belt loops. He removed the glasses and folded them into his shirt pocket, shrewd eyes watching Hirsch. Then he beckoned with a jerk of his head.

'Come and look.'

'Are you Mr Washburn?'

'I am. Come and look.'

He's more canny than crazy, thought Hirsch, approaching Washburn and his stone slab.

'Shepherd's son,' Washburn said. He'd been clearing a gravestone.

The slab, mossy and eroded, read, *James son of Geo. Taken by the Flood 5 April 1875 Aged Six Years and the Angel Sayeth Unto*, every carven S tilted forward as if straining at the torrent. The rest had been worn away and Hirsch felt an infinite sorrow, a rush of feeling, the place and the past fully there in him. He heard a scream—but it was only a bird, hunting. He straightened, stumbled a little, turned and, hands on his knees, found himself peering into a pool of water trapped below the bank. His face stared back with murky intent.

Washburn grabbed his elbow. 'Careful, it's not stable.'

Hirsch stepped back to safer ground. He was hot in the sun, his sweat salty.

He gathered himself and said, in a rush, 'Mr Washburn, I'm Paul Hirschhausen, based in Tiverton, where your wife lives.'

Anxiety crept over Washburn's grizzly old-codger face. 'Is she all right?'

'She's fine,' soothed Hirsch. 'But may I ask you where you were last night?'

Washburn couldn't believe his ears. 'Where would I be?'

'You were here?'

'If you mean my caravan, yes. No driveable car, Sonny Jim, no pushbike, no horse, no magic carpet, no broomstick, no—'

Okay, a bit crazy, thought Hirsch. 'Thank you. Now, the reason I'm here, some of Nan's ponies were slaughtered last night, and—'

'You said she was fine!' Washburn was horrified. 'She *can't* be fine. Let's go.'

He set out for the caravan, half-running. Hirsch trailed him. He didn't know what to do. Obviously, he could drive Washburn to town, but how might the guy react when he got there? What if Yvonne and Nan hadn't been fully forthcoming about his equilibrium?

'Mr Washburn, I—'

Washburn stopped and whirled around. 'I know what you're thinking. You've been told I'm nuts. But I'm not a threat to anyone. I just can't stand people for long. The way they're unable to leave things alone...'

He glanced about uneasily, as if the surfaces and boundaries of the creek and the nearby hills, roads and fences, were shifting. With effort, he gathered himself and said, 'For what it's worth, I still love Nan. She loves me. We understand each other. And right now she needs me. Just give me a minute to pack a bag.'

'All right,' Hirsch said. 'And I'll need to make a brief stop along the way.'

Hope Hill Road was seven kilometres from the Mischance Creek ruins, and when they got there, Craig Washburn said, 'Are you sure about the number? Sounds far too high to me.'

Hirsch checked his notebook again. 'Fifty-eight Hope Hill Road.'

'Who lives there?'

'People named Rennie.'

'Huh,' Washburn said, with an intonation that Hirsch couldn't interpret.

'Know them?'

'I keep to myself.'

Hirsch turned around where the road petered out and headed back along it. Thirty kilometres in length. No towns, only farms and station properties—seven in total.

'Why would she lie to me?' muttered Hirsch.

Washburn shot him a wry look. 'Maybe I'm not the only one wants to be left alone.'

They rode back to Tiverton in companionable silence, the weeds and the stones drifting past their windows until cultivated land appeared. It seemed anomalous to Hirsch. The road dipped and rose and turned in on itself, acknowledging the unruly contours of the land, while Douglas Keir and all who'd come after him had tried to stamp some symmetry onto it: straight fences, driveways and cypress hedgerows, ninety-degree angles, perfect rectangles of wheat stubble. And bright new galvanised rooftops here and there, as if the future mattered, even as the past was proximate and unsettling, stamped in stone: the grave of a shepherd's son, an abandoned hut, a Ngadjuri rock carving. Yet Craig Washburn lived contentedly out in that country. Now, as they descended from the hills onto the Tiverton flats, he seemed to shrink in his seat. Boundaries closing in on him, thought Hirsch. Or he's gearing up for the horror.

12

They rolled through the town. Hirsch's trip into the back country had taken hours, and now it was late Saturday afternoon. A second outside-broadcast van was parked near the entrance to Kitchener Street, and it looked as if a handful of locals were guarding the crime-scene tape alongside Constables Landy and Medlin, Sergeant Brandl's 'children'.

Craig's agitation increased. Close to panicking, Hirsch realised, seeing the heaving chest, the claw-like opening and closing of hands. 'Craig?'

'I can't...I can't...'

Hirsch did not stop but trundled to the northern end of the town and turned left onto the first farm road. All the while, he kept up a low, calming patter: 'Breathe deeply and slowly...I'll have you with Nan in just a minute...We'll go in the back way...Deep, slow breaths...'

It began to work, Washburn eventually sitting easier in the passenger seat. Hirsch drove for two hundred metres, glancing to his left until he judged they were adjacent to the rear of Nan's property, separated from her stable block by a stretch of just-harvested wheat.

'Okay?'

Washburn nodded.

They got out, climbed over a wire fence and crossed the paddock, the soil baked red and hard between rows of stiff, bleached stubble. 'Watch out for snakes,' Washburn said.

A good sign, Hirsch thought, if he's able to apprehend the world and the welfare of another man in it. So long as we can keep him sheltered.

Then they were in Nan's yard and already Hirsch could see that someone had been busy. The carcasses were gone; fresh soil had been raked over the blood pools. Expecting Washburn to notice, he turned to the man reassuringly, but Washburn was running to the railing fence with a little cry and Radish, trailed by the ponies, was trotting to greet him.

Hirsch had always believed you could read a dog's face. Now he was reading joy, or something like it, on Radish's.

Nan and Yvonne emerged from the back veranda, trailed by Detective Comyn, who immediately grabbed Hirsch by the arm. 'Over here.'

In the shade of a rainwater tank, his voice low, tense, he said, 'You took your sweet time.'

Hirsch explained.

Comyn wasn't interested. 'Did he do it?'

'No,' Hirsch said, outlining Craig's alibi.

Comyn gave another of his grunts, watching the tableau at the railing closely, as if hoping the surviving horses would finger Craig Washburn, rear up in terror at the sight of him and charge to the bottom corner of their paddock. But the scene was calm, Washburn stroking necks and snouts while the women patted his back.

Comyn sighed and shook his head. He spotted the roof of the HiLux in the distance. 'Used your brains, I see. Fucking media.'

'Did they film anything?'

'Nothing for them to film. Knowing they might send in a drone or a chopper or come in over the back fence like you did, I had a word with Mrs Washburn and the vet, and the upshot was a few of the locals carted the bodies off in a truck and delivered a load of topsoil.'

'Good thinking.'

'And Mrs Washburn—brave lady—walked down and fronted up to the cameras a couple of hours ago. No histrionics, no blame, just a few facts. Didn't take questions.'

But Hirsch knew that even with a victim statement, and without visuals, the evening news broadcasts would milk the story for all it was worth. 'Tomorrow could get messy.'

'A pleasant Sunday outing for some people,' Comyn said. 'Too bad there's nothing to look at.'

They were almost chatting like equals, Hirsch's lower rank and pariah status forgotten.

'About tomorrow...'

'Reinforcements,' Comyn said. '*Grudging* reinforcements, a *handful* of reinforcements, and not till about nine in the morning.'

Port Pirie and Clare would each send a car and two officers, he said. Meanwhile he was due back at Port Pirie and

Sergeant Brandl and her constables were about to go off-duty. A hard little grin: 'That leaves you, pal, on the front line, all night long.'

'Terrific,' Hirsch said.

What he didn't say, but wondered, had the area commander underestimated the incident? Thinking, who cares about a couple of mutilated horses?

Hirsch could answer that—about ninety-nine per cent of the population. Turn a blind eye to people hurting each other but weep buckets over an abandoned puppy.

'With any luck, tomorrow will be a fizzer,' Comyn was saying, 'but a bit of crime-scene tape's not going to stop anyone and nor is a wire fence, so: strategy.'

He laid it out for Hirsch. Beg, borrow and steal roadworks trestles and planks from the district council depot to block off the entrance to the street. Arrest anyone who came onto Mrs Washburn's land. A politely antagonistic approach to gawkers.

'Politely antagonistic?' said Hirsch, half-warming to the Port Pirie detective.

'Let them see you photographing faces and numberplates. If they want to know why, smile and say we fully expect the culprit to come back and gloat over his handiwork.' He shrugged. 'Could even be true.'

'The good old us-and-them approach to police work,' Hirsch said.

As darkness crept in, Hirsch—now the sole representative of law enforcement in the town—stood morosely at the entrance to Kitchener Street, contemplating his phone. He was supposed to celebrate Christmas with Wendy and Katie tonight: their place, a sleepover.

He dialled, Wendy answered, he explained. 'Another thwarted roll in the hay.'

A tiny but significant hesitation. 'They warned me not to get involved with a cop. *You* warned me.' Trying to make light, not quite succeeding.

She's disappointed, Hirsch thought. She almost never was, when his work intervened. But she might be forgiven for feeling something at Christmas time—for wanting to spend some time with him. And he might be forgiven for wanting that, too.

He found himself stumbling: 'I'll make it up to you after Christmas. I'll—'

'Doesn't matter,' she said, her voice warm again. 'If you can't come to us, we'll come to you.'

He liked that about her. She didn't dwell, she found positive alternatives. 'That'd be great.'

'But we won't man the barricades.'

'Fair enough.'

Mother and daughter reached the police station at seven-fifteen with the makings of a stir-fry. Katie asked where her Christmas present was as soon as she got out of the car.

'I can see I've trained you well,' Hirsch said, putting his arm around her while Wendy looked on, familiar with their routines by now. Giving Hirsch a complicated look. As if to say, don't take me for granted. As if to say, sorry about earlier.

Hirsch shot her a look of his own then turned to Katie. 'More to the point,' he said, 'where's *my* present?'

'It's so big we needed a truck.'

'And the truck broke down.'

'Got lost. No one knows where it is.'

The banter died away and was replaced by a strange shared anxiety, as if a malign force had rolled across the highway from Nan Washburn's street.

'Let's eat,' Hirsch said, ushering them into the police station.

They dined in his backyard, wearing paper hats and reading aloud their lame Christmas-cracker jokes. Then present-giving: from Wendy a history of the mid-north written by a retired headmaster of the high school where she taught maths, from Katie a CD she'd burnt for him titled *Old Fart Songs*. They exclaimed pretty convincingly over his gifts to them, and finally Wendy was saying, 'We'd better go, early start in the morning.'

Out on the footpath again, the highway silent, insects flickering in the street lights, Hirsch kissed them goodbye. 'Safe trip, speak to you Christmas Day.'

'If not before,' Wendy said, her warm shape briefly pressed to his.

Then she stepped back a little and gazed at him straight-forwardly. 'On Thursday Katie and I are going to my brother's for a post-Christmas lunch. We'd like you to come with us.'

Her brother and his family lived in Morgan, she said, on the River Murray, and wouldn't be attending the main Christmas gathering that year. 'They usually don't,' she said balefully, 'so we go to them. Otherwise I'd never see them.'

They never come to see you, Hirsch thought. 'I'd love to.'

She laughed. '...Because I've made it sound so inviting.'

Another round of hugs and then the two of them were in the car, Wendy sketching a goodbye wave, Katie waggling her iPhone in one of its new cases. Hirsch felt their absence at once, like a chilled space in the warm night air, and then they were nothing but receding tail-lights.

He crossed the highway, feeling bereft, tethered to nothing, a man of no account. Nan's street was quiet and empty beyond the barrier, and the town slumbered. He wandered back to his rooms behind the police station and his phone beeped for an incoming text. Martin Gwynne: *Re tomorrow, quick reminder, working bee at 9, dinner 6.30.*

Oh, for fuck's sake.

Sunday, 6 a.m., and Hirsch walked the town. He'd not been called overnight, and the highway was empty. Slipping aside a trestle, he walked up Kitchener Street and into Nan Washburn's driveway. The house and yard were silent, the horses standing at the rail, tossing their heads to see him—not in fear, he thought. He walked back to the highway and in and out of the side streets. The air was clean and mild, and nothing stirred but Hirsch and the morning birds.

The Clare police car arrived at 8.30, the Port Pirie car at 8.40, Sergeant Brandl's children—scowling at Hirsch as if this was all his fault—at 8.55. Coffee and a briefing on Ed Tennant's shop veranda. The only vehicles to pass through the town were a tour bus, a road train of hay and a handful of vehicles wearing inland dirt—headed for church services; making an early start on Christmas travel. Then Martin Gwynne's Camry rolled by and Hirsch remembered the tennis-club working bee.

His mood dropped instantly. One—Martin Gwynne. Two—surely he had the best excuse you could think of for getting out of it? Three—would anyone other than Martin be there, this close to Christmas? Four—he was due at Martin's for dinner at six-thirty; surely that would do? Five—Martin Gwynne.

Time passed. A couple of gawkers gathered at the barricade and a Channel 10 cameraman and reporter were turned away from Nan's back fence—which didn't stop them from filming the stable block, yard and surviving horses—but otherwise the town was quiet. Maybe the afternoon would be more hectic: it was a Sunday morning, after all.

Ten o'clock. No wind in the air now, just heat. The kind to set up a snap and a crackle in gum trees, timber beams and iron roofs. The briefing over, Hirsch left the newcomers to police the town and walked around to the tennis courts. Only six pairs of hands there—usually a working bee would attract twenty or more—Martin and Joyce, the former looking pointedly at his watch, Bob Muir, the primary school head—and the Bagshaw twins, who greeted Hirsch with sly humour.

'Hirsch, mate,' Ivan Bagshaw said. 'Pop by in the morning...'

Carl Bagshaw completed the thought. '...with the patching truck.'

'Fill your driveway potholes,' Ivan said. He was lubricating the net-tightening winder, Ivan stirring a tin of white marker paint.

Hirsch glanced uneasily at Martin, who was hovering nearby with the air of a foreman. 'That'd be great.'

'Crack of dawn,' Carl said.

'I'll be ready.'

The brothers were employed by the council to maintain roads, replace bullet-holed speed signs, repair broken swings and prune the war memorial roses. Unhurried, sleepy-eyed men who, with racquets in hand, were quick, precise doubles sharks. Off court, they viewed the world as mildly amusing: not much mattered, no point in trying to change things. They drove Martin Gwynne to distraction.

And now Martin was telling Hirsch he'd be helping repair the nets. 'Quickly now.'

The nets were beached at one end of the main court, ready to be unfurled for mending. 'There's needle and thread in the box.'

'Right.'

'You didn't think to bring leather gloves?'

No, Hirsch hadn't thought to bring leather gloves—or any kind of gloves. His life was full of things he hadn't thought to do, and things he knew he ought to have done.

'I've got a spare pair in the ute,' Carl Bagshaw said, ambling away with a lazy wink.

Hirsch gave them an hour of his time, then returned to Kitchener Street.

'Anything?'

'Nothing.'

*

Nothing all day, nothing they couldn't manage, and Hirsch, conferring by phone with Comyn and Brandl, sent everyone home at 4 p.m. He'd leave the barricade in place for a couple of days, but the weekend was over, and it was Christmas in a couple of days' time, so he wasn't expecting a last-minute influx of bored rubberneckers.

He spent the rest of the afternoon sluicing back-country dust from the wheels and panels of the HiLux, phoning his parents and contemplating the dingy walls of his office. Start painting the walls, or chill out with a beer?

That was easy. A short time later he was reading his present from Wendy under the ceiling fan, a beer at his elbow. The book proved to be more absorbing than he'd expected. The Keir family was there, Keir homestead, the Redruth copper mine, the Cornish miners, in text and photographs. The Razorback draped in snow; a field of wildflowers out east; the shepherd's son's grave; a Ngadjuri grinding stone; a bushfire in the Tiverton hills. He flicked through to the index: Muirs and Bagshaws had been in the district since records began.

Armed with Christmas chocolates and a bottle of Clare Valley riesling, Hirsch knocked on the Gwynnes' door at six-forty. He heard Martin on the other side: 'Can you get that, Mother?' Then Joyce Gwynne was opening the door with a curious bob—half shy curtsy, half sheer terror—and not meeting his gaze. Proffering the chocolates and wine, Hirsch said, 'Hope I'm not too late?'

Arriving ten minutes after the appointed time was his way

of showing passive resistance to Martin. Small-minded, but Hirsch didn't care; it was still satisfying.

'Come in,' Joyce said. She stood aside, eyes cast down, watching his shins cross the threshold before she lifted her head and shot him a brief, searching look. He couldn't read it. A warning?

The house was cool, hushed, dimly lit, everything in retreat from life. Down a long hallway to an open-plan arrangement of sitting and dining areas, with a kitchen on the other side of a long dividing bench. The table was set, with plain boiled potatoes in one bowl and pale iceberg lettuce and tomato wedges arranged depressingly in another. There was a pot on the stove. Some kind of stew? In this weather?

'Smells great,' Hirsch said.

'It's a work day for you tomorrow,' Martin said, 'so we thought we'd eat straight away. In any case...' He checked the time ostentatiously.

'Excellent,' Hirsch said.

'Sit here,' murmured Joyce.

'Thought we'd have a red with this,' Martin said, when they were seated. 'An interesting Barossa shiraz you might like.' He poured for Hirsch, for himself—significantly more for himself—and sparkling water for his wife.

Hirsch reached to take a swig, thought better of it because Martin was speaking. 'We like to say grace,' he intoned, and Hirsch felt the man's hot dry grip close around his right hand, Joyce's tiny damp fingers creep into his left.

'For what we are about to receive, may the Lord make us truly thankful, for ever and ever, amen.'

'Amen,' echoed his wife, barely audible.

Hirsch managed a strangled cough, and they ate.

'Delicious,' Hirsh said and, surprisingly, it was the truth.

The conversation didn't stray from the events of the town. What a good job Bob Muir had done, installing night lights around the tennis courts. Ed Tennant might want to think about getting Gemma some on-the-job training, the girl was a useless lump.

And poor Nan and her ponies...

Then, his face shining with expectation, Martin said, 'I know you can't comment on an ongoing investigation, Paul, but am I on the right track in assuming young masters Cobb and Flann had something to do with it?' He raised one hand and touched off the fingers one by one. 'They're friends. No other boys their age to spend time with. Crazy—for want of a better word—mothers. No father-figure to guide them. And they probably hated having to apologise to Nan.'

Hirsch mopped at his gravy with a potato. 'Actually, Martin, I'm pleased to report that neither boy was responsible. So it's still an open case.'

Martin raised his eyebrows. 'Really. I'm surprised to hear that.'

Wanting more, but Hirsch didn't oblige. The clack of cutlery in the silence, the soft whine of an overhead fan, a truck trundling through the town. Then Joyce said, 'How is Mrs Street? I was hoping she might have accompanied you this evening. She'd have been very welcome.'

It was the most she had ever said to Hirsch. And he appreciated the sentiment, even as he shuddered to picture

Wendy's take on a meal in this house. Gazing at Joyce Gwynne curiously, he saw that she was meeting his gaze. She seemed to be saying the evening might have been different if she'd had any say in it.

'Wendy's good, thanks,' he said warmly. 'She and Katie are away for a few days, extended family Christmas.'

'Too bad you have to work,' she went on.

'Well, it's the nature of the beast.'

Martin followed their exchange as if he couldn't believe its triteness. 'Let's repair to the sitting room, Paul. I have something to show you.'

It was a signal for Joyce to clear the table. She remained in the kitchen, from where Hirsch sensed a tentative scraping of plates and running of taps, while Martin ushered him to one end of a pneumatic tan leather sofa and seated himself at the other end. An iPad materialised in his lap.

'Are you on Facebook?'

Hirsch shook his head.

'I'd have thought it a useful crime-fighting tool. Never mind, Mother and I are on it, and there's also a Tiverton page you might be interested in.'

He scooted closer to Hirsch, angling the screen. Hirsch peered unwillingly.

'This is what Nan posted,' Martin said, scrolling, pausing at a photo. A dead pony in the dirt, outstretched neck, blood. 'She says: *Whoever did this has hit at my livelihood. I'll have to work on the surviving ponies for months now, they're so skittish. It's mindless, shameful brutality. No respect for harmless creatures who share the world with us. But what goes around, comes around, and the thugs who did this will get caught.'*

'She's right,' Hirsch said, feeling inadequate.

Martin ignored him. 'Look at the responses. *Whoever did this was most probably bored, selfish and stupid...I can't believe it could happen around here...Someone's going to start bragging and it will all come out.'*

'Certainly hope so,' Hirsch said.

'But that's not the main thing, Paul. I found this on YouTube.'

And there, after the ad-skip, was Hirsch. A wobbly video clip of him struggling with Denise Rennie outside Ed Tennant's shop. Denise looking down in astonishment at Hirsch's service pistol in her hand. Denise dropping the pistol.

'I won't make you look at the comments, Paul, I'm not a cruel man. But forewarned, as they say, is forearmed.'

13

Christmas Eve, 6a.m.

It is notorious that not a week passes without the Natives hereabouts displaying, in their greedy desires and untutored propensities, a characteristic cunning and base ingratitude.

Hirsch drained his coffee, closed Mrs Keir's journal and set out to walk the town.

The highway was empty; so was Kitchener Street. The barricade could come down today. The town was probably forgotten already. Too far from anywhere; nothing to see; the locals refusing to cooperate; some other atrocity awaiting.

He slipped past the barricade and walked up Nan's street, past her slumbering neighbours. Stood at her gateway awhile, deciding not to go in.

A voice said, 'The early bird…'

Craig Washburn was sitting on a veranda deckchair, difficult to see in the long, striping shadows of the rising sun. Hirsch took the greeting as an invitation and threaded through shrubs and over garden borders to join him. 'All right?'

'Me—or Nan?'

'Both.'

'She's knocked for a six, mate.'

'You?'

Washburn shrugged. 'I'll know I'm all right when I know it's time I went home to the creek.'

They chatted for a while, but Hirsch had things to do before driving to his pre-Christmas lunch and briefing at the Redruth police station. By seven-thirty he was showered, shaved, freshly ironed into his uniform and chomping on his second breakfast—a chalky muesli, the only kind stocked in the shop across the road.

'You do know there are other brands, Ed,' he'd told the shopkeeper one day.

'Uh huh. And this is the brand I stock,' Tennant said.

At seven-thirty-five, hearing air brakes and the beep-beep-beep of a vehicle reversing just outside the police station, Hirsch remembered the Bagshaw twins. He flung down his spoon and raced through the building to the front yard. He was grateful to have his potholes filled, but he was betting the brothers were asphalt dumpers, not artists.

The moment he appeared, Carl Bagshaw said, 'Some blokes sit around all morning.'

'While the rest of us slog our guts out,' his brother said.

They'd dropped a small, steaming pile of asphalt just inside the footpath gate and were walking shovelfuls to each pothole, filling, shaping, tamping down, melding the edges with the old, undamaged layer, their movements rhythmic, an effortless dance around each other on the narrow driveway. In five minutes, the potholes were patched over. No spillage, waste, lumps or rough edges. 'You guys are artists,' Hirsch said.

'Just don't drive that shitheap over it for a day or two,' Ivan said, indicating Hirsch's tired Nissan.

'What do I owe you?'

'It's council tar, mate, and you're a council employee—kind of. We're always dumping leftovers at the end of the day, so don't sweat it. A beer next time you're in the pub.'

'Your council rates at work,' Carl said.

There was a pause, both men eyeing Hirsch contemplatively, both propped on their shovels. Carl said, 'Don't let it get to you, what they're saying.'

'Arseholes with nothing better to do,' his brother said.

Unlikely as it seemed to Hirsch, the twins must have seen the YouTube clip. 'Thanks, I appreciate that.'

The men saluted him, climbed into their truck and left him alone beside his mottled driveway, wreathed in exhaust gases.

Half an hour later, Hirsch was across the road, stuffing potato chips, mince pies and soft drinks into a shopping basket: his contribution to Sergeant Brandl's Christmas lunch. She'd be providing sandwiches, the children were bringing napkins, paper plates and a plum pudding. No alcohol: 'We're all on duty, for the duration.'

As an afterthought, Hirsch added a packet of Christmas crackers. Then he looked over Ed Tennant's meagre range of Christmas cards. He didn't know how to word his greetings to his sergeant or her constables—he barely knew them. In matters of card-giving, humour was his default position, but the three Redruth officers were strangers to him. Did any of them have a sense of humour? Were they churchgoers? In the end he found three generic snowscapes with the single word *Peace* inside. That's all a cop wants at Christmas, he thought. Not heavenly peace, just a general absence of mayhem.

The shop was crowded by the usual standards—at least five locals doing last-minute shopping. They all said, 'Merry Christmas, Paul,' nodded and smiled, but none of them lingered. They were embarrassed for him. The YouTube clip.

What the fuck was Sergeant Brandl going to say? Or Internal Investigations, for that matter?

Gemma Pitcher was at the till. She blushed to see him—not, he thought, because she'd seen him on YouTube but because he'd sprung her in bed with Adam Flann.

He gave her a big, neutral smile. 'Season's greetings, Gemma. What's on tomorrow?'

She wouldn't look at him. 'Me and Mum are going to Auntie Trish's for lunch.'

'Where's that?'

Gemma gave him an astonished frown. 'Terowie.' Clearly everyone knew that.

'Right, right.' He'd encountered this quirk in many of the locals. It made him want to shout at them, 'Give me twenty years and I'll know all your fucking business.'

Gemma counted out his change, blushed again and said, 'Merry Christmas.'

By noon Hirsch was bowling down the highway, Chicago's '25 or 6 to 4'—one of the greatest songs ever written, and Hirsch didn't make these claims lightly—pounding from the police 4WD sound system. Some other hard, fast tracks came in after it. The music suited his mood: even if he didn't go viral on YouTube, he knew some other shit was coming his way.

Half an hour later, he was trundling through the outskirts of Redruth. Glancing up at the old mine buildings ranged across one of the town's little hills, he wondered if the museum—once an old pump shed—would be interested in Mrs Keir's journals. Who owned them, though?

At the town square he downshifted and crept around it, giving half-reproving headshakes to half-apologetic jaywalkers, and out along the Adelaide road for a short distance. He turned into a side street and pulled up behind a dusty SA Police patrol car. A further two police vehicles in the car park at the side of the police station. It was nothing like his little house in Tiverton: purpose-built, with red brick walls, tiled roof and aluminium window frames. Offices, interview rooms, a tearoom and a lockup.

Laden with his shopping, Hirsch went in, familiar with the place from weekly briefings. Nodding hello to the auxiliary support officer—a retired clerk of the council—he stepped through an inner door to the main part of the station. Voices and laughter drew Hirsch to the tearoom. A small Christmas tree in one corner, streamers looped around the windows, a huge felt stocking pinned to a noticeboard. A couple of rickety tables had been pushed together, laden with cups, plates, napkins and a bowl of rum balls.

And the children. 'You brought crackers—fantastic,' Jean Landy said.

She was short, pale, round-faced, pixie-like; black hair in a stubby ponytail. She'd worked for the ambulance service for five years, got tired of being attacked by strung-out ice addicts, and retrained as a police officer. Late twenties, but only recently out of the academy. Hirsch hadn't known her for long. She'd always eyed him coolly, as if she'd heard the rumours: Hirschhausen the dog.

But right now she was warm enough, her fingers resting on his forearm briefly before she helped him unpack the chips, drinks and crackers. Hirsch didn't quite trust it, until she said, 'Just so we're on the same page: me and Tim know about the YouTube thing and we think it's shit. So unfair.'

Hirsch assessed her briefly. 'Thanks.'

'Could've happened to any of us,' Tim Medlin said.

Younger than Landy, he was angular, awkward, balding prematurely. He shot Hirsch a shy smile, looked away again and said, 'Can you get it taken down?'

Could he? Hirsch doubted YouTube would listen if he complained, but maybe they'd listen to Police Command?

'It'll blow over,' he said, placing the last bottle in the tearoom fridge.

'Paul? A word,' said a voice behind him.

'I've been tasked to ask you certain questions.'

'Sergeant,' said Hirsch, seated on a stiff chair. Her office was generic, apart from the athletics ribbons hanging on one wall, and three desk photographs: Brandl with her parents, Brandl graduating, Brandl and a man with their arms around each other. Hirsch had never met the husband but knew he lived and worked in Adelaide, two and a half hours south. A modern arrangement, a kind of fly-in, fly-out marriage—a cop's timetable would wreak havoc on it, but it was none of Hirsch's business. He was waiting for a bollocking.

'Based on my recommendations, there may or may not be a formal follow-up—i.e., a trip down to the city, where you'll sit at one end of a long table to be grilled by a couple of faceless men.'

'No need to sugar-coat it, sarge.'

'Did you or did you not post the video on YouTube? Stupid question, but it's one they want answered.'

'Did not.'

'Do you know who did?'

'Could've been anybody. Quite a few people were there.'

'Was your sidearm properly secured in its holster?'

'Yes.'

'Loaded?'

'Yes.'

'Safety on?'

'Yes.'

'Did you give permission to the woman in the YouTube clip to remove your pistol from its holster?' *Another stupid question*, Brandl's expression made clear.

'I did not give her permission to do that.'

'In your own words, describe the incident for me, please.'

Hirsch complied. When he was done, Brandl said, 'So it's your belief she thought you were taking her daughter away and she overreacted?'

'Yes.'

'Had she been drinking? Was she on drugs?'

'No. She calmed down quickly when the doctor intervened.'

'You were in uniform. Clearly a policeman. Did she think you were going to sic Child Protection onto her or something?'

'I've been wondering about that. She was so over the top, maybe something else was going on. She said she lived with her husband, but what if she doesn't? Could he be violent? Trying to get custody? I ran her name, ran his; didn't find anything.'

'Have a quiet word with her.'

'Tried that. The address she gave me doesn't exist.'

'All the more reason to find out what's going on. Have another word with Doctor Pillai.'

'Will do.'

'Meanwhile, the powers that be have asked why you didn't advise Child Protection, or, at the very least, file some paperwork. I'm curious myself. She locked her kid in the car on a hot day. Could've died.'

Hirsch shifted in his seat. He'd been expecting the question—it had already cropped up a few times in the YouTube comments. 'One, her evident distress. Two, she apologised, she was mortified. Three, she struck me as a devoted mother in all other respects. Four, I don't think she's very well off. Five, it's close to Christmas. Six, I didn't think she deserved to be punished any further. Seven, I was surrounded by people I'm trying to forge good relations with. I didn't want to come across as bullying the poor woman.'

Brandl looked at him and said nothing. He said, 'Look, she ducked across the road to pick up a prescription, that's all.'

Better shut up now, he told himself. Brandl was stony-faced.

Then, a transfiguring smile. 'Ah, stuff HQ. We're at the front line, they're not.'

Police cultures, thought Hirsch, grateful. Police against the great unwashed. Front-line police against the pencil pushers.

A knock on the door, Landy calling out: 'Sangers just arrived, sergeant.'

Brandl looked at Hirsch. 'Hungry?'

They joined the others in the tearoom, pulled their crackers, put on their paper hats. Ate, drank their soft drinks, swapped police stories and Christmas stories. Like all good things, it didn't last.

'It's Christmas Eve,' the sergeant said as they went their separate ways. 'People are already getting into the grog.'

14

Dawn, Christmas Day.

> The Natives continue to effect depredations upon our flocks, determined to do as they please, and Douglas is very much of a mind to put a stop to it.

This sandwiched in with Mrs Keir's reports of a visit from a Shropshire cousin, the delivery by horse and wagon of a piano, afternoon tea on a neighbouring property and the despondency of a shepherd whose son had drowned.

Neither the shepherd nor his son was named. Hirsch wondered if Mrs Keir was as dreary and sour as her tone sometimes suggested. She'd written two thick volumes of a journal: she must have a curious, alert mind. But she did seem...easily irritated. Still, one thing Hirsch had come to rely on since his arrival in the mid-north: almost every week he'd meet someone who wanted to tell him about the pioneers, how tough they'd had it, and imply that they themselves were a chip off the same block.

Hirsch walked the streets of the town as the light that smeared the skyline threw his striding shadow ahead, alongside and behind him. His corner of the world at peace for now. Small children were awake here and there, filling the quiet town with giddy shrieks, filling Hirsch with memories. Presents in the sitting room, his parents beaming sleepily on the sofa as he tore open the wrapping paper.

No fun being a Christmas orphan, he thought suddenly. No fun being a small-town policeman on Christmas Day. He trudged back towards the police station, wondering when the shit would hit the fan. The expectation was unremitting. It was like a blanket in this godawful heat.

'Merry Christmas.'

He hadn't noticed Gemma Pitcher and her mother behind the grapevine draped along their veranda. He stopped, blinked. Creased faces, unruly hair, they were not long out of bed. Drinking tea and contemplating the soft morning light.

'Same to you,' he said.

Eileen Pitcher was tiny where her daughter was large, a dry, wizened woman with a flinty soul. She drew hungrily on a cigarette and extended a smidgin of Christmas cheer: 'Tea?'

The old Hirsch might have said, sorry, too much on, but today's Hirsch was consumed with his homesick blues. A cup of tea might be just the job.

'Don't mind if I do.' He perched on the veranda boards, his spine against a paint-peeling post. 'Plain black, please.'

Assigned, with the merest jerk of her mother's chin, the

task of making it, Gemma shuffled in pink slippers and huge T-shirt over satin pyjama shorts to the screen door and into the house, her thighs, branded with a criss-cross pattern from her chair, winking at Hirsch. He looked away. Presently tap water splashed, a kettle grumbled, a cup hit a saucer.

Meanwhile Eileen was staring out at the sun-lit world, ignoring Hirsch as if he was one of the veranda posts.

'Best time of the day,' he said.

She grunted and then he was saved. Gemma was there with his tea—and it was weak, milky, sweet. All at once the world was nothing worse than ridiculous. You had to laugh.

The conversation—Hirsch's conversation with Gemma— veered from Nan Washburn's horses to the TV vans and Hirsch in a Santa suit. Until Gemma said, 'Did that man find you?'

'What man?'

'He come in the shop yesterday.'

Hirsch waited. In his experience, no one ever just spat it out. They delayed and withheld as if they were on an hourly rate. 'Yesterday,' he prompted.

'That lady with the baby in the car.'

'Mrs Rennie?'

'He said her name was Reid.'

'A man came into the shop and...?'

'He wanted to know where she lived.'

'What did he look like?'

This seemed to be a difficult question. Finally Gemma shrugged, 'Average, I guess.'

'Age?'

She assessed Hirsch. 'A bit older than you?'

'Forties?'

'S'pose.'

'Did he say why he wanted to find Mrs Rennie? Or Reid or whatever?'

Gemma shrugged again.

'Do *you* know where she lives?'

Gemma shook her head. 'Told him to ask you.'

'Didn't see him,' Hirsch said.

With his small taste of Christmas spirit curdling in him, Hirsch carried on through the town, checking on the Cobbs, the Washburns and an elderly woman whose husband had dementia. These two were also on their front veranda, watching the sunlight advance across the quiet world. They were holding hands. Hirsch didn't go in, merely chatted briefly from the footpath. 'Going to be another scorcher,' he said, wishing them a happy day, lifting one hand in a wave goodbye. The woman smiled and nodded, but didn't wave, didn't break the spell of her husband's hand in hers. She's counting the Christmases left to them, Hirsch thought.

He showered, changed, brewed coffee, called his parents, then Wendy and Katie, then there was no one else to call. The walls of his cramped house drew in around him a little.

Relief came with a phone call via triple-zero: a crash reported on a bend of the Barrier Highway north of Mount Bryan. Hirsch raced down there on an empty road, through slumbering country, to find the witness had overreacted. A station wagon had gone straight ahead instead of around the bend and ploughed through a wire fence. No blood; minor damage. The car sat, barely scratched, a few metres inside a paddock. The greatest risk was a grass fire set off by the hot underside of the car, but there wasn't enough grass to burn. The paddock lay fallow, a dismal stretch of red dirt and sparse dead stalks.

A stocky, grey-haired man stood, bent at the waist, near the front of the car.

'Need a hand?'

The man straightened, brushing his hands. Dark trousers, dusty black shoes, a white short-sleeved shirt and a clerical collar. He winced to see a man in uniform.

'Checking the radiator and headlights.'

'Anything?' asked Hirsch.

The minister shook his head. 'Dents and scratches.'

Hirsch came closer to look for himself. 'Not the best day to run off the road.'

'You can say that again. I've got three services this morning and I'm already late for the first one.'

A country minister tending to dwindling flocks in dying country towns. 'What happened?'

'Act of God?' the cleric said, with cheerful vigour.

Hirsch grinned. 'You haven't, umm, been hitting the Christmas sherry?'

'That comes later. No, took my eyes off the road for a second.'

Hirsch glanced at the car's interior. Sheets of paper on the passenger seat, scrawled handwriting. 'Rereading your sermon?'

The man blushed. 'I was, as a matter of fact.'

'Don't you know them all off by heart?'

'Nothing is fixed or certain. My sermons evolve,' the minister said, with good-natured self-mockery.

Hirsch gave him a little salute. 'No harm done, except to the fence and your car.' He glanced around to the far corners of the paddock. No stock; the fence could stay as it was for the time being. 'If you give me your details, I'll pass them on to whoever farms this place.'

'To pay for the fence? Yes, of course,' the minister said.

Mid-morning, Liam Kennedy called. The family had returned from church in Redruth to find their house burgled. Most of the Christmas presents—yet to be opened—had been swiped from under the tree, together with a TV set and jewellery from the master bedroom, a phone and a laptop from the kids' room.

Their farm was ten kilometres west of Tiverton, a 1970s suburban-style brick veneer at the end of a winding track on a slope overlooking lucerne flats. As Hirsch turned off the approach road, he saw a sun-flash a short distance along a nearby side road. A car was parked there.

Check out the Kennedys first.

He parked behind a Subaru wagon on the gravel turning circle. That was the signal for the family to spill out of the house: Liam, Fiona, two girls of upper-primary-school age. They took him inside, the air close and warm, and showed him the back door. It had been forced open. Then the Christmas tree, an artificial one, with a couple of forlorn parcels under it. Then the kitchen.

'They raided the fridge!' Fiona said, her face tight with stress. 'I mean, you hear about people saying they feel violated when they're burgled...'

'It's a terrible feeling,' Hirsch agreed.

He glanced at Liam. A big man, scarred and scraped by a life on the land; combed and tidied now for church. Calmer and harder than his wife. A good thing he didn't walk in on the burglar, Hirsch thought.

That car he'd seen...

'Mind if I look around outside?'

'This way,' Kennedy said.

They were ten seconds into a sweep of the yard when Hirsch saw the dark gleam of a flat-screen TV under a rosebush beside the veranda steps. He said, very firmly, 'Liam, I want you to fetch Fiona and the girls and go sit with them in the car. Understand? Don't say anything to them, use hand signals.'

Kennedy twigged quickly. A rasp in his voice as he said, 'Let me—'

'Liam, you need to look to your family,' Hirsch said, putting some grit into his own voice.

'If it all gets away from you, I'm—'

'Understood, thank you,' Hirsch said.

He waited, watching the family troop out and into the Subaru before re-entering the house. He went through the place quickly, quietly: room by room; behind doors; under beds.

That left the wardrobes.

Master bedroom. Two teens, a boy and a girl, huddled

on the floor of the walk-in closet. Backpacks, a corner of Christmas wrapping showing at the top of one pack, the thin, silvery edge of a laptop in the other. They were frightened, scowling, the hems of jackets and dresses brushing their heads. As far as Hirsch knew, they weren't local kids.

'Stay where you are,' he said. 'You came by car?'

Silence.

'Heard the family come home and panicked? Dumped the TV outside when you heard their car and ran back inside with the rest of the stuff...'

Still nothing.

Hirsch wanted to say, 'Not very bright of you,' but they were kids; you didn't expect them to think.

'There's a car nearby, over on the other road. Is it yours?'

Nothing. And Liam Kennedy came lumbering in. 'Thought you were in strife. Thought—'

The girl shrieked. Burrowed deeper into her corner. '*Stay away from me.*'

The boy wrapped an arm around her, his face half-averted from the wrath of the adults, half ready to leap to the girl's defence. Kennedy stared in at them, stupefied, as if aliens had slipped into his house.

Hirsch said, 'You know them?'

'Never seen them before.'

Then why's the girl so scared of you?

Hirsch had his answer later, the kids in the car with him on the way back to town. Brother and sister, they were from Peterborough, an hour north of Tiverton. Their stepfather had lost his grain-handling job on Christmas Eve and gone on a bender. Wrecked the house and put their mother in hospital. When he flaked in the early hours of Christmas Day, they'd stolen his car and headed south. Low on fuel, hungry, no money, they'd turned off the highway and happened to see the Kennedys' Subaru head down onto the valley road. Took a chance that the house would be empty. Ate, fell asleep, woke up in time to start thieving just as the family returned from church.

Sorting that out, liaising with Peterborough police—who'd arrested the stepfather for assault and property damage in the meantime—and finding temporary accommodation for the kids, took Hirsch through to mid-afternoon. The Kennedys gave the kids fifty dollars each, said they wouldn't press charges—an expression they'd heard on TV. Hirsch knew it wasn't that simple. He could downplay the crimes, though.

Just another sad, Christmas Day fuckup. Could've been worse.

Then a third call came in.

15

It was Sergeant Brandl. 'I need you to do a welfare check.'

'Okay...'

'People named Redding. Family members are worried because they're not answering the phone.'

'Okay,' said Hirsch, writing down the address: 6 Hamel Road. Turn any corner and you'd find yourself on a road named for a Great War battlefield, he thought. He tried to place it mentally. Over near Mischance Creek.

'The call came to me,' Brandl said, 'but I'm dealing with a three-car pile-up near Farrell Flat and can't spare anyone.'

'I'm closer anyway,' Hirsch said.

Brandl continued, an odd tone to her voice: 'The thing is, the call came direct to my mobile, a man asking a series of questions to establish who I was before telling me he was from police headquarters in Sydney.'

A tone in her voice: suspicion. She hadn't been given the full story. Watch yourself.

'Right,' said Hirsch, reading between the lines. Why

would this man call her mobile and not the police station landline? And how would a policeman in Sydney even know her mobile number? And why had the call come from there? Sydney residents concerned because interstate relatives weren't answering the phone on Christmas Day would probably notify their local station first. They'd pass on the request to police in Adelaide, who'd ask the closest rural station to make the check.

'Perhaps headquarters gave them your number,' Hirsch said.

'Perhaps,' Brandl said, not buying it. 'Call me as soon as you learn anything and I'll get back to Sydney.' Pause. 'This bloke sounded a bit tense.' Another pause. 'Merry Christmas.'

Welfare checks were reasonably common in Hirsch's experience, often on behalf of someone who'd been unable to contact an elderly parent, an addict son or daughter, a friend in an abusive relationship, a neighbour whose newspapers were piling up. On one occasion he'd actually discovered a body—natural causes—but in most circumstances the explanation was mundane: the loved one or neighbour was deaf, off on an unannounced holiday or avoiding their relatives.

Late afternoon by the time he reached the Bitter Wash Road turnoff, heading east, the sun low behind him, flaring on the hills ahead. His sense of travelling back into the past was stronger than usual—roads that had barely evolved from bullock-wagon routes, old buildings, drooping telephone lines, ancient Austin trucks listing on perished tyres. But behind and beneath the things he could see was a more remote and comfortless past, at least if Mrs Keir's journals were anything to go by.

He slipped Katie's CD into the slot. Leonard Cohen, 'Closing Time'. Perfect for bringing order to his long line of jangled thoughts. Redding, 6 Hamel Road, Mischance Creek. You didn't ask for a welfare check on a whole family unless something was wrong. Even if they'd all spent Christmas Day at another location, or with other people, wouldn't at least one family member be contactable on a mobile? Or have posted their plans on Facebook, or texted someone?

The road wound through marginal country. Hirsch retraced the route he'd taken the day he located Craig Washburn until the crossroads sign. He turned right there, towards Mischance Creek (Ruins) and finally onto Hamel Road. A line of mallee scrub; tough merino sheep the colour of the soil; even a mob of emus. Hirsch stopped, blinked: he'd never seen emus in the wild. Leonard Cohen growling his dark urban poetry, a police vehicle on a mallee plain, emus raising outback dust...Where was the logic connecting those three facts?

He rolled on. The tyres shuddering on the corrugations, the tiny stones pinging against the chassis—the familiar music of his days. He'd seen a couple of distant farmhouses, rooftops above clumps of farmyard gum trees at the ends of long driveways. Number 6, when he reached it, was a stock ramp at the head of a dirt track lined with scraggly cypresses that led up a gentle incline and out of sight. He turned in.

The cypresses continued on the other side of the rise, down to a stone farmhouse with a sun-faded red roof. A house typical of the region—maybe smaller, squatter, than most—and a car-shed hard against the left-hand side wall. On the other side of the house were a corrugated-iron rainwater tank and a ten-metre-high tower topped with an old-style TV antenna.

Beyond the house, implement sheds, stockyards and a woolshed. Everything for a working farm, but this wasn't one: no sign of sheep, hay, tractors or any other machinery. A barren tree in the yard, its twigs and branches like forks of black lightning frozen against the sky.

He switched off, got out and stood for a moment, wary of dogs, wary of a homicidal/suicidal husband and father. Between the Toyota and the front door were a couch-grass lawn, some struggling rosebushes and a dedicated dry-country garden, only the second one Hirsch had seen. Shaped piles of stony dirt held together with tough little shrubs, succulents and ground cover, drab at first glance until you noted the subtle tones of pink, yellow, olive and khaki.

The shadows were long now, the sun beginning to smear the western hilltops. No wind. No sounds but for creatures claiming the evening. Surely someone had heard him arrive? He felt reluctant to cross the yard. The house wasn't repelling him, but nor was it just a pile of stone. It seemed to be gathering some shameful emotion to itself. It seemed not to want intruders.

Hirsch shook off the feeling. The car-shed's roller door was closed—not necessarily significant but, in his experience, the locals left their car-sheds open unless intending to be absent for some time. He pulled on crime-scene gloves and started with the shed.

The door was unlocked. It rolled upwards, revealing a dusty pink Hyundai Excel with a gaffer-taped sheet of black plastic sealing a broken rear window. Hirsch felt a jolt: Denise Rennie's car. Her fear and evasions; 'Redding' close in sound to 'Rennie'; the false address.

He peered in. The car was empty.

Not so the rest of the shed. He edged past the car to a workbench on the end wall—vice; scattered woodworking tools; hammers and saws on a pegboard. Set into the adjacent side wall was a door that presumably led into the house. It was locked.

He looked down. The car sat over an old-style service pit sealed with wooden slats. And, on the floor, evidence of hasty or interrupted gift wrapping: empty carton with an illustration of a pink tricycle, roll of Christmas wrapping paper, sticky tape, pink ribbon. No sign of the bike—and it hadn't been fully assembled. The saddle still lay on the stained concrete.

A tricycle for a little girl, thought Hirsch. Anna Rennie? It's Christmas Eve and she's asleep at last and now Mum or Dad can wrap her present from Santa. The shed door down, just in case she wakes up and gets curious.

Then an interruption. The wrapping didn't get finished.

Hirsch shuddered, then took himself in hand. He stepped out of the shed and advanced on the house. Onto the veranda. A knuckle rap on the front door.

Waited, tried the door: locked. Knocked again. No answer. Went around to the rear of the house.

The back door was open.

Hirsch nudged it with his forearm, stepped in when it was fully ajar, and saw that he was in a kind of mud room: work boots, rubber boots and old trainers against one wall, coats along a line of hooks, a small cupboard with a shoe brush on top, a broom rack. Two doorways: one to the kitchen, the other to the laundry. Both rooms empty.

But clean crockery gleamed in a rack beside the kitchen sink—several plates and bowls, from a main meal. Last night's dinner? Not Christmas Day lunch, not if the unfinished tricycle was any indication.

Hirsch stepped through to the dimly lit hallway leading to the front door, aware of three things: a beautifully patterned pressed-tin ceiling; wainscoting; a woman face-down on the floor at the end. There was enough light from a glass panel in the front door for him to see bare legs, pale blue shorts, a T-shirt once yellow but now mostly dark with blood.

Shot in the back before she could reach the door? Before she could warn somebody in one of the front rooms?

Hirsch scanned the floor automatically for spent cartridges before unholstering his service pistol. Stood for a while, listening. The house spoke like any old house, but he didn't have the sense of human hearts beating in it. He stepped quietly along the hallway and stopped at the first of the intermediate doors.

A teenage boy's bedroom: posters, scattered clothing, general mess. He went in. No bodies, no one hiding. The room opposite contained two single beds. Rumpled bed-clothes on one, with a scattering of soft toys and a Little Mermaid poster on the wall. The other bed, for an older child, hadn't been slept in. Novels in a fantasy series on a bedside table, boy-band posters on the wall, a little desk holding a lumpy pottery jar stocked with a range of colour-ful pens.

No blood, no bodies.

But Hirsch added another Denise Rennie falsehood to the list: she apparently had three children, not one.

He continued to the end of the hallway and knelt beside the dead woman. Flies had found her. She was cold, no pulse, and the blood had dried to a stiff scab on the T-shirt. Her head was turned to the left, her cheek against the floor, giving him a clear look at her face. Yes: Denise Rennie.

Hirsch gathered himself again. The doors on either side were partly open. The left led to the main bedroom: a queen-size bed, a massive old wardrobe and a modern desk with an ADSL modem, a printer and a computer on it. Two red lights among the green on the modem, indicating some kind of fault. The internet would be a problem this far from town.

He checked the wardrobe and the floor on the other side of the bed, then returned to the hallway. Stepped around Rennie to knuckle open the other door.

A sitting room with a Christmas tree in one corner, a mess of wrapping paper, boxes and presents strewn around it. Looted after they'd been wrapped and placed under the tree, thought Hirsch. All he wanted to do was make this mundane deduction and leave the room, but his gaze was drawn to the sofa and the overwhelming fact of a teenage boy slumped in death, facing Grand Theft Auto on a wide-screen TV, big headphones over his ears, a game controller in his lap. Wouldn't have heard his mother's screams or the shot that put her on the floor—but paused his game when the shooter entered. Shot in the chest before he could get up.

Hirsch stood there, thoughts in chaos. Mother dead, son dead. But where was the husband? Anna, the toddler? The older daughter? Had the husband run off with them? Butchered them in one of the sheds? Dead somewhere himself?

This was not the time for a churn of supposition. Checking again for ejected cartridges, he made a rapid, more thorough search of the house: under beds, in wardrobes, behind furniture. Drawers and cupboards had been rifled in some of the rooms. He went back to the main bedroom: no men's clothing or belongings anywhere. No sign that Denise Rennie was running an online business. He finished by photographing the bodies on his phone.

Then, as the light faded from the sky, he searched the outbuildings. No one in the boot of the little Hyundai or under the workbench. No one under the tank stand or in the implement shed. He entered the shearing shed. It hadn't been used for years but the odours lingered: lanolin, sheep shit; the wooden rails and floor slats still greasy. A place full of shadows. He stood a moment, listening for the susurrations of children in hiding, fearful of the next bullet. Only silence. He went through the shed quickly, found nothing and began a circuit of the house.

The phone line was cut.

Hirsch photographed it, returned to the Toyota and radioed Sergeant Brandl. She listened, said, 'I'll get back to you,' and ended the call.

Hirsch waited, darkness spreading around him, and ten minutes later Brandl was saying, 'I've informed the Homicide Squad and police in Sydney—who, incidentally, got very heavy with me. Don't touch anything, don't poke about, don't let anyone in. And have you found other bodies?'

'Negative—but how many other bodies might there be?'

'It was like dragging a state secret out of them. Last name Redding, mother Denise, son Nick, daughter Louise, daughter Anna. That's all they'd tell me. You're positive it's the woman whose kid was locked in the car?'

'Positive. She said her name was Rennie, no mention of other children, and she lived with her husband. Noel, Neil, one or the other. But there's no sign of a man living here.'

'Estranged? Tracked them down and snatched the girls?' Brandl said.

'Maybe. What happens next, sarge?'

'Short term? I'm supposed to join you and make sure you haven't, quote, fucked up the crime scene. We're to wait for CIB from Port Pirie, and eventually a Homicide team from Adelaide will take over.'

'Is anyone coming from Sydney? They wouldn't get here before tomorrow afternoon.'

'No idea,' Brandl said. 'See you soon.'

Hirsch continued his circuit of the house and outbuildings, thinking it would take Brandl an hour to reach him.

Finally, jittery, restless, he gazed out, away from the house. There was one thing he could do before the queer half-light disappeared.

16

Hirsch ranged on foot in all directions, across the patchy dry grass beyond the yard and the sheds, around and through a nearby huddle of gum trees, over the neighbouring paddocks, into the mallee scrub fringe and along a dry creek bed. Looking for bodies, breadcrumbs. For dirt powdery enough to hold shoe prints.

Fruitless. Too dark. He returned to the house and searched the weedy drainage channels on each side of the driveway. It ended at a stock ramp on Hamel Road, beside a fence gate. Here the soil was looser, part talc and grit, churned by vehicle tyres—his included. No shoe prints, not that Hirsch was expecting any. If the girls had been abducted, they'd be in a vehicle. If they'd run, they'd head across country, not along the driveway.

He wandered back to the house and the world had become a silent place, full of shadows cast by a slice of moon. With nothing else to do, he sat in the HiLux, listened to his CD. Dylan, 'Desolation Row'. Spot on.

Then his old training kicked in. Grabbing a roll of crime-scene tape and several garden stakes, he sealed off the tyre-churned dirt between the crown of the road and the stock ramp. Then he opened the paddock gate and marked out a path to the house parallel to the driveway, one stake every twenty metres, preserving his dwindling supply of tape by tying bows to each stake. Finally, he sealed off a parking area for the expected flood of official vehicles on patchy grass away from the yard, house and sheds. That was about all he could do to preserve the scene. He left the HiLux where it was and waited, seated on the ground this time, his back to the trunk of a pepper tree.

Sergeant Brandl arrived first, the headlights of her Commodore pitching and yawing over Hirsch's path of paddock stones, clods and grass tussocks parallel to the driveway. He stood so she'd spot him, pointed to the parking area he'd marked out, and watched her pull up and get out.

She said, 'I'd *like* to go in and look for myself, but it was made pretty clear I shouldn't go stomping over everything in my hobnail boots.' She glanced around at Hirsch's row of garden stakes. 'Good thinking with the tape.'

'Sarge.'

'Got any other photos?'

Hirsch handed her his phone, watched her flick through to the end. 'So where are the two girls?'

'I had a quick look around before the light failed. Didn't spot anything.'

'If they're not out there somewhere, dead or hiding'—she

indicated the endless plain—'then maybe they're with the killer.'

'Maybe. Let's suppose an estranged husband or boyfriend *does* find them. Why not kill all of them?'

'The girls are special to him?' Brandl said.

Hirsch looked away, wanting to anchor his gaze to something ordinary. But the pepper tree, the tank stand and the house were crouching shadows in the starlight. And like any member of a police force, he knew all about the chaotic thinking of a domestic tyrant.

They were silent until Hirsch broke it. '*Sydney*, sergeant?'

Brandl cocked her head at him. 'You're thinking they're a long way from home, if that's where they're originally from.' She shrugged. 'A good hiding place.'

'Or not,' Hirsch said. 'Someone found them.' Then a cold, clenching sensation. 'Oh, God...' he floundered, trying to squash the realisation. 'The YouTube clip.'

'Yeah.' Brandl turned to him and touched his forearm fleetingly. 'Not your fault, constable, okay? You might feel responsible, but you're not to blame.' She took a step back. 'Rather than twiddle our thumbs until the others get here, let's do a bit of brainstorming. What else can you tell me about the mother?'

'Nothing, really,' Hirsch said. 'Doctor Pillai might know more. But someone was looking for her yesterday.' He related his conversation with Gemma Pitcher. 'Except he didn't use the names Rennie or Redding—it was Reid.'

'We'll need a description from her. What did she tell him?'

Hirsch shook his head. 'She couldn't tell him anything. None of us knew anything about Mrs Rennie until last Friday. She only came in to Tiverton then because she needed a repeat prescription and Doctor Pillai has a clinic there on Fridays.'

Brandl brooded. 'The way she overreacted. Gave you a different name and a false address. Sydney police all cagey and officious. It's feeling more like witness protection than simply a family hiding from some unhinged bloke.'

The sounds of vehicles. Bumpy headlights. Port Pirie detectives and a crime-scene van, Hirsch guessed. He thought of his poor, damaged little town. 'Two atrocities in one week, sarge. I'll have reporters coming out of my ears.'

Brandl touched his arm again. '*I* will, you mean. The Homicide Squad's setting up a major incident room in the Redruth hall. Half the accommodation in town's booked out already.'

Hirsch doubted that would protect Tiverton from media attention. He watched an unmarked sedan park beside Brandl's Commodore. The crime-scene van parked beside the ribbon of tape closest to the house.

It was Detective Comyn driving the car, his passenger John Alwin, the new Port Pirie CIB inspector, in a wrinkled shirt, his tufts of carroty hair arranged around a vulnerable-looking white scalp. The man himself didn't seem vulnerable. He was a curt, take-charge type.

He scowled a hello to Brandl and turned to Hirsch. 'I know who you are.'

Hirsch was fed up all at once. 'Is that a fact. Sir.'

'Don't be a dick, constable. Now, you came out here because...?'

'Sir,' Brandl interrupted, 'I received a call from police headquarters in Sydney, requesting a welfare check. We were tied up with a traffic incident, so I asked Constable Hirschhausen to do it.'

'I'm asking Constable Hirschhausen. You arrived here when?'

'About three hours ago.'

'Found two dead.'

'Yes, sir,' Hirsch said. Beyond the inspector's shoulder he could see the crime-scene crew setting up external floodlights.

'Touch anything?'

Hirsch cast his mind back. 'I checked they were dead. Walked through each room. Knelt to look under beds. Opened doors, wardrobes and cupboards.' He added: 'I wore gloves.'

'Why did you go through the house? Weren't you told not to?'

'Not at that stage. I was looking for other victims.'

Either the inspector was obtuse or hadn't been told a thing—or he was being a prick. His words came at Hirsch in mocking, testing spurts. 'Looking for other victims. Then what?'

Hirsch used cop-speak. 'In what little light was available to me I undertook a search of the sheds and adjacent paddock areas.' He paused. 'Sir, we need a search party here first light tomorrow.'

'Oh, do we now? When you made this search, did you find anything?'

'No, sir.'

'It didn't occur to you that you might get shot?'

'I wanted to find the missing girls, sir.'

Alwin grunted. He turned away. 'Good thinking with the crime-scene tape. That was you?'

'Yes, sir.'

Alwin clapped his hands. 'Right. Detective Comyn will take your statement. Then when the crime scene officers have checked in and around your vehicle, you may go.'

'Sir.'

'Sergeant Brandl, I'll need that Sydney contact, and then you may also go.'

'Sir.'

'But I want you both working the phones tonight. Volunteers from all over, start searching at first light. If any of the local graziers have a spotter plane, well and good. I'll see if the air wing can give us a chopper.'

'Sir,' Brandl said.

'And Constable Hirschhausen, you'll need to make yourself available for interview sometime tomorrow.'

'Homicide Squad, sir?'

'Whoever they throw at you.'

17

Boxing Day. Hirsch, bleary in the dawn light, was walking along the creek bed, sandwiched between Martin Gwynne and a Redruth pharmacist named Delia Paley. Straggling lines of volunteers kept pace with them on each bank. The search helicopter chattered above the mallee scrub to the north-east. Separate line searches, fanning outwards from the house on Hamel Road, were covering the dry wheat flats.

And Gwynne was going on and on. 'It's just that I have had some experience.'

Miffed because he hadn't been put in charge of a search team.

'Out of my hands, Martin,' Hirsch said.

Thank God. He'd spent hours making calls and setting up a phone-tree last night, then, on four hours' sleep, had been one of the first to arrive at the kill house. He'd helped oversee the parking of the volunteers' vehicles, but after that he'd been told where to go and what to do, same as everyone else.

'For example, those tourists last Easter,' Gwynne insisted.

A Japanese couple who'd wandered into the bush after puncturing a tyre on a stone reef, to be found a couple of hours later by a scratch search party of Tiverton townspeople. Probably the quickest and least onerous search in mankind's history.

'We're all equal here, Mr Gwynne,' Delia Paley said—warm, polite, but with an edge.

A spasm of disparagement on Martin's face, what Hirsch could see of it under the sensible broad-brimmed hat. A blob of zinc cream on his nose, turning greasy.

Hirsch swung his attention back to the creek bed. It had been pointless trying to spot shoe prints in last night's half dark; he was hoping the sunlight would yield the clues they needed. The helicopter banked, swooped over them and disappeared towards the Mischance Creek ruins. It's going to be a morning of false sightings, Hirsch thought. A different note cut the air and he looked up: a crop-duster based at the Clare aerodrome.

Martin halted importantly, his palm pushing at the wall of hot, still air, and peered down at the pebbles and sand. Crouched. Straightened, took out his phone and photographed whatever was at his feet, then glanced left and right for markers. Photographed a bent tree on one side, a dimpled hollow in the red dirt bank on the other.

Delia Paley had stooped to look at Martin's find. 'Star Wars figure,' she said, reaching out a hand. 'Chewbacca.'

'What on earth do you think you're doing. That's evidence.'

Standing again, Paley flushed. 'It's old.'

'It could be significant.'

Hirsch said, 'I think Delia's right, Martin. It's been here for a very long time.'

Sun-bleached, cracked, missing an arm. He glanced up onto the bank, where Bob Muir waited patiently, looking in on them.

'Bob, do the locals use this as a picnic spot?'

Muir nodded.

Hirsch turned back to Gwynne and clapped him on the back. 'But thanks for spotting it, Martin. I would have missed it completely.'

Gwynne gave that some thought, then nodded. 'Can't be too careful.'

'Absolutely,' Delia Paley said, sharing a look with Hirsch.

He gave her a strangled grin. His life often consisted of standing between antagonistic parties. He took a swig of water from the bottle clipped to his belt. 'Better keep going.'

They walked for five kilometres, Hirsch relaying their progress to the other teams and to Sergeant Brandl, who was coordinating from the house. Hot, getting hotter, nothing to deflect the sun. Hirsch's bare arms were burning. Delia Paley turned an ankle when one round stone rolled against another, and switched places with Bob Muir.

After a while Bob said, 'Search and rescue dogs?'

'Two dogs and handlers expected late morning.'

'Police or SES?'

'Police.'

Trained in tracking and air scenting, probably. Hirsch

visualised it, the handlers offering a T-shirt to one German shepherd, a little singlet to the other, before setting them on their way.

'Have to do a damn sight better job than us,' Muir said, 'trampling over everything.'

'Yes, Bob, but as Paul said, they won't get here for some time,' Gwynne said. 'Meanwhile it's imperative that we conduct line searches.'

He's going to say *time is of the essence*, Hirsch thought.

'Time is the critical factor here,' Gwynne said. 'It could mean the difference between two dead girls and two live ones.'

'Mmm hmm,' Muir said.

Hirsch shot him a look. Neutral. Steadfastly sweeping the ground with his gaze. Irritation in the set of his head.

They came to a ford, the creek bisecting a dirt road. Hirsch glanced at his map: Hope Hill Road. Before they could cross, Martin Gwynne snapped, 'What are these idiots doing?'

The Flann brothers, approaching along the bed of the creek from the other direction. They stopped, Wayne offering a sleepy smile. 'Constable Hirschhausen, sir.'

Hirsch wanted to say, don't be a smartarse, but it would be wasted on Flann, who was lastingly derisive to everyone. He was slim, loose-limbed; on the surface a charmer, but no one was fooled. Women saw, beyond the good looks, a certain deadness and turned away. Men were wary.

Now, a little .22 rabbit rifle slung over one shoulder, he was wearing a tight khaki T-shirt with rolled sleeves, oil-stained jeans and elastic-sided boots. With the firearm, and his dark hair, lean face, olive-toned skin and lithe grace, he might have been playing a role. Not the hero, though.

Ignoring the rifle for now, Hirsch looked past Wayne to Adam. He seemed to be hiding behind his brother's shoulder. 'All right, Adam?'

'He's fine,' Wayne said.

Martin Gwynne cut in. 'Are you part of the official search? If not, how can we know that every area has been thoroughly checked?'

Flann smirked. 'I'm here, aren't I? I know what I'm doing.'

Hirsch touched Martin's forearm warningly. 'How far up did you boys start?'

'Three or four k's.'

'See anything?'

'Nope.'

'I suggest you register with Sergeant Brandl at once,' Gwynne said.

'That's what you suggest, is it?' Flann said. 'Good to know.'

Hirsch said, 'Why the rifle?'

Wayne Flann gave a smile and a slow roll of his shoulders. 'Don't know if you'd noticed, but we've got a murderer running loose. Plus, snakes.'

He glanced at his feet, and Hirsch's feet, then scanned the nearby dead grass. Hirsch scanned too, despite himself.

Which made Flann grin. 'Be prepared, mate, that's my motto.'

'A shotgun would be better against a snake,' Hirsch said, eyeing the rifle, a corner of his cop brain registering that it wasn't the murder weapon.

'Haven't got one, you know that.'

Hirsch nodded. One of his duties was checking firearm licences and storage. He needed to get Flann to stow the gun away without publicly embarrassing him. He was grateful when Bob Muir murmured, 'Wayne, it's not a good look, walking around with a gun. Not after what's happened.'

Not harsh. Not denigratory. Advising caution and good sense; sounding like a wise father. Hirsch saw a shift in Wayne, a nod of acceptance. 'Yeah, okay.'

'Anyway, good to see you both,' said Muir. 'How about you register with Sergeant Brandl and join one of the search parties so there's no doubling up?'

The Flann boys climbed out of the creek, Adam giving Hirsch and Muir a swift grimace of apology before following his brother across the paddock to the house on Hamel Road. 'What's the betting they don't register?' Martin said.

Hirsch shrugged. He didn't say that Wayne wasn't a team-player kind of guy.

'I don't trust those Flann boys.'

'Oh? Why's that, Martin?' Muir said.

'The older one especially. The way he looks at you.'

Hirsch understood. The lazy grace and flat-eyed insolence. He kept walking. And then Martin was grabbing at his sleeve. 'Have you looked at him for the horse mutilations, Paul?'

'Martin, can we keep our minds on the search?'

'It's just that they're very clannish, that family. I can well see the older boy getting back at Nan because she humiliated his little brother.'

Hirsch ignored him. Mid-morning now, the sun relentless. He'd almost drained his water bottle, and saw that the others had, too. He pointed. The Mischance Creek ruins were ahead, half-a-dozen lonely chimneys tethered to collapsed walls; a couple of corrugated-iron roofs held down by rusty nails and pointless doggedness.

'Let's find some shade and take a break. I'll call Sergeant Brandl and ask her to send us more water.'

They walked on. A short time later, Hirsch grew aware that Delia Paley had stopped pacing him along the bank of the creek. Thinking her ankle strain had worsened, he looked up. Her face shone with discovery and expectation. 'Shoe prints,' she said. There was a tremor in her voice.

'Secure the scene and wait,' Comyn told Hirsch when he called it in. 'The dogs are up and running. If they lead the handlers to you, then we'll know for sure.'

'We need water.'

'Just wait, all right?'

Hirsch joined the others in the stingy shade of a crumbling wall. They all stared at the creek bank, where a patch of powdery dirt held prints: shoes with patterned soles, and tiny bare feet. The girls had paused there, Hirsch thought. Maybe the older one had carried the younger one. She'd have been wearing sandals or runners if she was still awake, helping her mother wrap the tricycle. When the shooting stopped she ran inside, snatched the little one from her bed and made a run for it. Got to the road, set her down to rest and...

And apparently vanished. No other prints that Hirsch could see. If someone had stopped to pick them up was it the killer? No scuff marks in the dirt. Too exhausted to struggle?

Fifteen minutes later he saw the handlers and their dogs, shapes shimmering and coalescing on the flatland between Mischance Creek and the kill house. Their progress was inexorable, destination inevitable. Standing to greet them, he saw the dogs halt, run their noses along the ground, try to catch fugitive scents in the air. The end of the line. They panted, gulped, sat. One of the handlers called: 'This is as far as they went.'

Hirsch nodded glumly. He knew the road itself wouldn't reveal anything useful. He'd driven along it yesterday. This morning, Wayne Flann had driven along it; half the volunteers had driven along it. He looked up in the crazy hope that one of the airborne searchers might magically spot the vehicle that had saved—or snatched—the girls twelve hours earlier.

The volunteers straggled in. They were given tea, oranges, sandwiches that curled in the heat. And Hirsch was told he needed to get his arse down to Redruth.

'Sarge?'

'The incident room's up and running in the town hall, and a Homicide inspector wants a word.'

'Now?'

'Soon as you can get down there.'

Hirsch climbed back into the Toyota and drove away. Heading, he supposed, into the teeth of another bollocking.

18

It was mid-afternoon by the time Hirsch reached Redruth. The main street, which would have been deserted on any normal Boxing Day, was crammed with marked and unmarked police cars, vans and SUVs—all nose-up to the kerb outside the town hall–shire offices. He rolled on by and found a parking spot outside the Woolpack, the pub opposite the rotunda. Cutting across the square, touching the little rotunda for luck along the way, he headed uphill again.

Climbed the steps to the town hall entrance and into cooler, dimmer air. The creaky old ballroom had been transformed: phones, computers, desks; officers in shirtsleeves peering at screens, making calls, rippling their fingers over keyboards. It was like the floor of a stock exchange: an air of controlled panic. Hirsch glanced upwards. Dusty sunlight crept in from windows high on the walls. Lovely wainscoting, lovely pressed ceiling, and emotion surged through him as he recalled the walls and ceilings of the house on Hamel Road.

He swallowed and approached a plain-clothed officer wheeling in a whiteboard. 'Can you point me to whoever's in charge?'

She took in his dusty boots and trousers, the tidemarks of sweat on his shirt. Pointed to a long desk behind partition walls in a corner of the ballroom. 'Inspector Kellaher.'

Hirsch could see two men conversing on the far side of the desk, their chairs turned to each other. He crossed the room, the old polished floorboards creaking under his feet. It continued to be used as a ballroom—he'd attended the high school ball with Wendy a few months back—but his first experience of the room had been a public meeting, local people objecting to the thuggish enforcers then stationed at the Redruth cop shop. It had worked: the thugs were replaced by Brandl and her little team.

He knocked on one of the partitions and stepped in. 'Inspector Kellaher? Constable Hirschhausen, sir. I was told to report.'

The older man looked at his watch. White shirt, blue tie, sleeves rolled back on hard, veined forearms. A solid man with a bulky jaw and a shrubbery of brown hair salted with strands of grey. About fifty, his face stretching with tension as he leaned over the desk and tilted his chin up at Hirsch. 'I expected you some time ago.'

Hirsch wasn't going to let that go unanswered. 'I was taking part in a line search, sir. Quite some distance away.'

Kellaher grunted, then gestured at the man next to him. 'Sergeant Dock.'

Dock stood. About thirty, dressed in a pearl grey

open-necked shirt and tight charcoal trousers. A sleek man with carefully styled dark hair. Leaning across the table, he offered his hand, but with faint amusement, as if in anticipation of trouble coming Hirsch's way. The handshake brisk, dry. He settled back in his chair with little adjustments of his shirt and trousers. A man who can't abide creases, thought Hirsch. A man who walks around thinking about his next pair of sunglasses.

'Sit,' Kellaher said.

One chair faced the senior men—intended for me all along? Hirsch wondered. It was a straight-backed but bendy plastic thing. 'Sir.'

Kellaher stared at Hirsch awhile with fathomless eyes. It was an old interrogation trick, one that, from some people, was difficult to wait out. Remorseless, distant, exposing your faults. Hirsch faltered: he glanced at Dock, who gave him the ghost of a sharkish smile. Both men wanted to unsettle him, in their different ways. Hirsch began to feel that an air of suspicion hung over everything he'd said and done or would say and do.

When Kellaher finally spoke his voice was hushed and intense. 'I understand you had a history with the dead woman and her family?'

'Not as such, sir. I met her briefly, with her youngest child.'

'Explain.'

Hirsch began by describing the toddler-in-the-car incident, then readied his phone to replay the recording he'd made on the way to the hospital. 'You'll hear my voice, the voice of the woman known to me as Denise Rennie—and Doctor Pillai. And briefly the child singing.'

They listened. Hirsch paused the recording. 'Two things: she mentioned her husband, but none of the other children. And the address she gave me was false, as I found out a few days later, when I tried to find it.'

Dock said harshly, 'Any reason why you tried to find it?'

'My job,' Hirsch said mildly. 'I make two long-range patrols each week, checking up on people.'

With a look at Dock, the inspector said, 'And what did you make of that, Constable Hirschhausen?'

Hirsch was intrigued. Kellaher seemed to be inviting him to give his five cents' worth. As he thought about his answer, phones rang behind him, voices called, someone laughed.

He drew a breath. Said, 'Given what's happened, her earlier behaviour seems significant. Also, the request for a welfare check came directly to Sergeant Brandl's mobile from police headquarters in Sydney. As if they already knew who to contact if the family disappeared from the radar. It all seems to indicate the family was in hiding.'

'A tidy line of logic,' Dock said, still twinkling on Hirsch's flank.

Kellaher gave an almost undetectable grimace. Straight-bat player, Hirsch decided. But how far to trust him? 'Sir, is there a husband or boyfriend? Were they hiding from him?'

'Can't tell you—because I don't know. I'm hoping for answers when officers from Sydney get here later today.'

'Witness protection, maybe?' said Hirsch.

'Constable, I don't know. What else can you tell me?'

Hirsch suspected the two men did know at least a little more. They were probably receiving updates from their Homicide Squad colleagues at the kill house, too. He changed tack. 'It could be that Mrs Rennie was recognised from a YouTube clip I, ah, starred in.'

Kellaher wasn't amused. 'It's certainly possible.'

So, he's seen the clip, Hirsch thought. 'And someone recognised her and came looking.'

'Do you feel some responsibility, Constable Hirschhausen?' Dock said.

Hirsch ignored him, addressed Kellaher. 'A young woman who works in the Tiverton shop said a man came in asking if she knew where the woman from the video lived.'

'Description?'

'She was vague. Average, in his forties.'

'We'll need to speak to her,' Kellaher said.

'It might help if I sat in,' Hirsch said. 'She knows me.'

'Everyone knows you,' Dock said.

Now we come to it, Hirsch thought. He decided to face it head-on. 'Eighteen months ago I was unlucky enough to find myself in a corrupt outer-suburban CIB squad. It was disbanded. Some of the shit stuck to me and I was demoted to uniform and stationed up here in the bush. End of story.'

'Not end of story. You didn't keep your mouth shut.'

Hirsch leaned forward. 'Friends of yours wind up in jail, did they sergeant?'

'Enough,' Kellaher said. He breathed out. 'You were first on scene yesterday evening, Constable Hirschhausen, and you spent this morning there. Kindly describe what you saw. Feel free to speculate.'

Hirsch recounted his discovery of the bodies, his search of the sheds and nearby paddocks, the morning's line search with volunteers, the footprints. He concluded: 'It seems the girls escaped on foot and were later picked up by the side of the road. By the killer or a local weirdo or someone passing by—who knows. Where they are now, I have no idea. They could be lying dead somewhere, someone's sheltering them, or they're tied up in the boot of a car.'

Kellaher selected the contacts on his phone and passed it to Hirsch. 'Add your details.'

Hirsch complied. Kellaher said, 'Go home and take the rest of the day off. Get the shopgirl ready for interview tomorrow. Sharp at noon.'

'Bring her here?'

'That'll only intimidate her. Home turf, noon tomorrow.'

'Sir.'

Hirsch paused. 'Any ballistics results, sir?'

Kellaher cocked his head. 'Heavy calibre rifle, that's all I know at this stage. Why?'

Hirsch thought of Wayne Flann and his little .22 rabbit gun. 'What I thought, sir, judging from the size of the wounds.'

Hirsch walked downslope again, the sun blasting him between the shoulder blades. He was thinking only of a shower as soon as he got home. Aloe vera on his sunburn. Clean set of clothes, cold beer. Dinner with Wendy and

Katie—then he thought, damn, he'd promised to drive up to the river with them tomorrow. He agonised: the task force was in full swing and would manage without him—but it was important to be the go-between in the Gemma Pitcher interview.

Outside-broadcast vans had filled the town square. He climbed into the cab of the Toyota and drove slowly home along the Barrier Highway. Lengthening shadows striped the land; the glare was intense. Next up on his old fart's CD was Canned Heat, 'On the Road Again'. Hirsch listened through to the end, then tried the radio.

The five o'clock newsreaders were running with the story. He flicked from station to station: 'What evil links these sleepy communities?'...'The sisters are feared abducted'... 'Abducted, feared murdered'...'Believed to be originally from Sydney.' And sure enough, one newsreader had the YouTube connection.

Then a pundit: 'We can't rule out the possibility that one offender is responsible for both massacres—and yes, they are massacres.'

'Someone escalating? Horses, then people?'

'Can't be ruled out. The methods are dissimilar, but the... the rage, an excess of emotion of some kind—sexual frustration? That's evident at both sites.'

Hirsch switched off. All he wanted was his lover's arms around him, her familiar scent: banish the melancholy, bring back some peace, briefly, to his life. At least until he told her he had to work tomorrow.

19

Thursday.

Hirsch passed from death-like slumber to full alertness in an eyeblink, but could not work out why. He didn't know where he was. And, in the next instant, did know: he was in Wendy Street's bed, and deep habit had jerked him awake. His limbs and brain wanted to charge into the dawn light that slipped through her slatted window blind. He turned his head. She was sound asleep and her face, the scent of her, his memories of their lovemaking, let him downshift into slumber again.

Or was that a different memory, of an earlier time? His eyes popped open again. They had made love; they'd been loving with each other, but...Had Wendy been holding back? She knew how difficult it had been, finding the bodies. She understood that he had to stay behind today—and she'd known what she was getting into, dating a policeman. But it was clear she didn't always like it.

Hirsch closed his eyes and then it was 9 a.m. and he was swiping at his face.

Swiped again. What was happening to him? Opened his eyes and Katie Street was kneeling beside the bed, tickling him with a feather. She was expressionless, as if watching an experiment.

'Wakey, wakey.'

'Not amused, here,' Hirsch said.

'Mum says we're hitting the road in a few minutes.'

Hirsch turned his head. Wendy's pillow lay abandoned on the other side of the bed. 'Already?'

'Uh huh.' The feather tormented him again. 'So wakey, wakey.'

Hirsch glanced past Katie to what had become his chair when he stayed over, where he tossed or draped his clothing. Right now, he was naked under the sheet, his girlfriend's young daughter was between him and his pants, and he wondered, not for the first time, how that might look to anyone watching. He didn't know who might be, but they were always around somewhere.

'Er,' he said now.

She climbed to her feet. 'Mum says you can stay in bed as long as you like but I think you should come and say goodbye.'

'Is that so?'

A different Katie gazed at him. 'I know you have to work today, but work isn't everything.'

He said, 'Er,' again.

'There are *three* police at Redruth. One of them could've stood in for you today.'

'Katie,' Hirsch said, wondering how to follow up.

She got in first. 'Mum likes you. *I* like you.'

Hirsch struggled to sit upright and give a considered response, but Wendy had appeared in the doorway, her shower-damp hair darkening the neck and shoulders of a blue sundress. 'Give the poor man some peace.'

Hirsch just wanted her back in bed with him. He said, 'Give the poor man some *privacy*, more like.'

She smiled, distracted, and crossed the room to plant a brief kiss. 'You went back to sleep.'

He usually didn't. He usually slipped away from her bed before dawn. 'The brat says you're off soon?'

'Five minutes,' Wendy said.

Her hands on her daughter's shoulders now, she gazed at Hirsch sombrely, as if unpicking a tangle of feelings. She's wondering if I'm worth it, he thought. And probably hoping I don't stumble on any more scenes of slaughter. He tried a smile. She nodded briskly and bundled Katie out of the room.

Hirsch was showered and dressed inside four minutes and found the two of them stowing bags into the car. At the five-minute mark he was hugging them goodbye and then Wendy was adroitly looping her Mazda around the turning circle beside her veranda. They disappeared down the driveway.

Feeling faintly rebuked, Hirsch retreated to the house. It smelt of toast and coffee. The vase he'd given Wendy glowed on the sideboard. And he felt bereft suddenly. Anchored to nothing, unimportant. He made some toast and ate it on the veranda. It tasted of cardboard. Eyeing Wendy's roses, he fetched the secateurs for a spot of deadheading. Another hot day ahead.

Twenty minutes later, he headed back to town, Soundgarden cranked up to shake him loose. The road dipped and rose and turned in on itself as it followed the contours of a disorderly landscape. The music helped but he was still uneasy—loneliness creeping in, the Hamel Road house, the missing children. His thoughts took him to the shepherd's son's grave. The past was proximate and unsettling—stamped in stone, so if you lived here you'd never rid yourself of it. The graves and the abandoned lives out in the back country, the blood spilt and now unspoken about.

He reached the grain silos and rolled through the town. Baking under the mid-morning sun, its blinds were down, doors and windows shut, air-conditioners rattling. Everyone indoors. But, far from defending itself against the summer heat, the place seemed huddled tight this morning. Fear or shame, or something of both. Nan's horses; the Hamel Road killings.

He pulled up outside the police station, lowered the windows a crack, and got out. The shop across the road was shut, no cars at the kerb. The pub shut? That was a first.

He locked the Toyota, toe-tested his spotted driveway—the new tar was satisfyingly soft—and stepped onto the veranda. There was a note poking out from under the door.

Big, looping script: *Dear Paul Daryl never came home last night Laura.*

He turned around and headed along the street, the sun pounding on his shoulders again.

Hirsch wondered if Marie Cobb had moved from her chair at the sticky table since he'd last seen her. The same slumped posture, the same ashtray, the same long, amnesiac pauses between one desperate suck on her cigarette and the next.

But Laura was all business. Moving around the kitchen as if her mother was a permanent fixture, she fetched Hirsch a glass of water, plonked it on the table, sat opposite him.

'Gemma come and got him.'

'Last night some time?'

She nodded.

'Early? Late?'

'Late.'

'Did he say where he was going?'

'No,' she snorted. 'He'd never tell me.'

'Did Gemma say anything?'

'Never talked to her. She just tooted out in the street and off he went.'

'She hasn't got a car.'

'She had her mum's,' Laura said.

I bet they drove to Adam Flann's, Hirsch thought. 'Has Daryl got a mobile?'

'It just goes to voicemail.'

'I wouldn't worry too much. It's the holidays. They probably had a few beers at Adam's and decided to stay the night.'

'I rung the house six times this morning. No answer.'

Wayne would have been taking part in the search for the

missing Rennie girls. Was Brenda still in the hospital? If she'd gone home, was she too stiff and sore to come to the phone? Or too drunk. 'Do you have a number for Gemma?'

Laura shook her head—and then, exquisitely attuned to everything around her, she got up from her chair and stood behind her mother, wrapping the thin frame in her arms, resting her chin on the lank hair. Hirsch realised that Marie was crying silently, tears streaming down her cheeks. He glanced up at Laura. Laura gave him a look. *You know what you have to do.*

It seemed that Eileen Pitcher hadn't moved for days either, still perched like a twiggy bird in the speckled shade thrown by her grapevine.

Hirsch leaned against a veranda post and said, 'You're not worried she hasn't come home?'

'She's a big girl,' Eileen said, staring, in her dead-eyed way, past his torso. Nothing and no one to look at out there, only harsh sunlight on the empty street.

'Does she have a mobile?'

A ripple of astonishment crossed the woman's face: who didn't have a mobile?

Hirsch drew his phone from his pocket. 'Can I have her number?'

Eileen recited it, slowly, pauses between the digits. Hirsch called it. Voicemail.

He checked his watch: two hours before Kellaher and Dock were due in town. 'She didn't say anything to you about picking up Daryl Cobb? Where they were going?'

'Not her.'

'The man who came looking for Mrs Rennie the other day—has he been back?'

'I wouldn't know.'

'Gemma hasn't mentioned him again?'

The little shoulders shrugged.

'Did Gemma seem upset or anxious or scared to you yesterday?'

'Not her.'

Hirsch wondered if Eileen knew of her daughter's involvement with Adam Flann. He said carefully, 'Perhaps she and Daryl went to a particular friend's house? Adam Flann's, maybe?'

A pause, and, for the first time, Eileen Pitcher showed a flicker of feeling. It was like watching someone start to wake up. 'Is Gemma in trouble?'

'Not with the police, Eileen. I'm sure she just spent the night with her mates. But we do need to speak to her.'

The bony hands washed and rewashed themselves. The eyes looked inwards.

'I tell you what,' Hirsch said, 'I'll head out to Adam's house and if she's there, tell her to call you, how would that be?'

'Is he going to hurt her?'

Asking about the stranger, thought Hirsch, not Adam. 'No,' he lied. 'He was just a nosy reporter.'

Hirsch was running out of time for finding Gemma before the Homicide officers arrived. He climbed into the hot cab of the Toyota and called the Redruth hospital: Brenda Flann had palmed some painkilling meds and taken them all at once. Now she was sick as a dog.

'We're monitoring her condition. And she'll need a psych eval before we release her.'

'Are her sons with her?'

'Haven't seen them for a few days.'

Hirsch completed the call and headed out across the bumpy back country to the Flanns' rundown homestead. No sign of Wayne's ute but someone—presumably Wayne—had towed Brenda's old Falcon home from the Tiverton council yard. The crumpled front panels were gone and wrecking-yard replacements sat in the nearby dirt—a glimpse of a dutiful son.

He knocked: no answer, and the outer doors were locked. He peered in the windows, didn't see anyone, and wandered in and out of the sheds. No dead teenagers. Just dust, oil stains, beer bottles, split garbage bags and an old tractor. Rat droppings and hessian sacks. Only one gleam of new metal—a sizeable locked cabinet tucked in the corner of a hayshed. It was partly concealed behind some large sheets of splintery five-ply painted white and fitted with rolling mechanisms. Looked like the sliding doors of a built-in wardrobe. Hirsch had no means of searching the cabinet and no reason to obtain a warrant, but the itch was in him.

He walked back to the house, cocked his ear, phoned Gemma again. Then Daryl. Nothing. Silence inside the house.

It occurred to him that the trio might have gone up to Mischance Creek to join the search party. Heading across country to Hamel Road, he found Sergeant Brandl and asked her to check the log.

She scanned it, said, 'Nup, sorry, no Gemma Pitcher, Daryl Cobb or Adam Flann. Why the interest?'

'The Homicide Squad guys want to talk to Gemma about the man who came into the shop, and I can't find her anywhere.'

'Any reason to think this man's after her?'

'No idea. All I know is, late yesterday evening she picked up the Cobb boy in her mother's car and they didn't come back. Adam's her boyfriend, and Adam and Daryl are mates, but they're not at his place.'

'Daryl Cobb and Adam Flann—persons of interest in the horse mutilation, right? Perhaps it's a case of Ms Pitcher helping them disappear.'

Hirsch gave her an appreciative nod. 'It's a thought, but I'm pretty convinced they had nothing to do with it.'

'*They* might not think that. I bet Comyn gave them a hard time.'

'Yeah.'

'They might be thinking, okay, the police will stitch me up for something, some time or other, so they asked the girl to help them disappear. What're the dynamics between them?'

Hirsch considered the question. 'Gemma seems dull, but she's capable under stress. She's a year older than Adam, who is a year older than Daryl, who is easily led. I get the feeling Adam looks to her for some kind of stability. His dad's in jail, his brother's never around and his mother's reluctantly drying out in hospital.'

'You know what kids are like,' Brandl said. 'They huddle around half-baked theories, convince themselves the world's against them, and run off into the sunset to do something stupid.'

But what kind of stupid? He turned to go. Brandl touched his sleeve. 'Tell Homicide straight away.'

'Will do.'

Hirsch returned to the Toyota, leaned against a side panel and made the call. The sun tightened the bands around his skull.

Kellaher, predictably, was ropeable.

'Sorry, sir.'

'She at least agreed to talk to us?'

'I arranged it last night, sir.'

'No reluctance?'

'No.'

'Any ideas?'

'I think she's gone off somewhere with a couple of friends in her mother's car.'

Kellaher said, 'So she's being thoughtless? It's not a disappearance we should be worried about?'

'Disappearance' had an ugly meaning now, as in disappeared-believed-dead. Hirsch climbed into the Toyota, ran the air-conditioner and said carefully, 'I'm hoping the three of them went to a party last night and are still sleeping it off.'

Kellaher said, 'You've circulated the plate number?'

Hirsch swallowed. Should have done that an hour or more ago. 'Just about to, sir.'

'Get it done. Any other bright ideas where these kids might have gone—apart from some booze-up?'

'No, sir. I'll keep asking around.'

The phone went dead. Hirsch used the MRT to call up the registration details of Eileen Pitcher's car and issued an alert. Almost 1 p.m. and some search party volunteers were straggling in from the patch of mallee scrub behind the house, Nan Washburn among them. Probably a badly needed distraction for her, thought Hirsch.

Where was Craig?

He got out and joined Nan at a shaded table that was set with tea urns, water bottles on ice, and plates of sandwiches. 'Anything?'

'One snake, one sleepy lizard.'

Hirsch unscrewed the top from a water bottle and passed it to her.

'Thanks.'

He watched the motions in her throat as she drank. Dusty shoes, patches of perspiration on her shirt. 'Is Craig here?'

She shook her head. 'Too many people for his liking. Makes him jumpy.'

'He back at the caravan yet?'

Nan Washburn stretched her spine and ran her gaze around the dry land, the house and the vehicles on the stretch of dead grass allocated for parking and didn't meet his gaze. 'Still at my place.' She laughed grimly. 'I just want my life back. Everyone in town's been giving me space, but Craig's driving me nuts, frankly. He means well, and I liked having him with me for the first couple of days, but now

197

I just want him back where he belongs. Is that terrible of me?'

Hirsch shook his head. Some relationships withstood daily cohabitation. Others needed limits. He imagined the scene, Nan telling Craig he should return to the caravan, then the tense long drive to Mischance Creek with him beside her in the car...

'Look,' he said. 'In a day or two, when it suits you both, why don't I collect him and bring him back here? Save you the trouble.'

She put her hand to her chest. 'Oh. I wasn't...But that would be lovely.'

'Okay, give me a call,' Hirsch said.

He waved goodbye and bumped back along the temporary driveway to Hamel Road. He stopped the car. Had anyone searched Craig's place beside the creek? He turned right instead of left, away from Tiverton, past the ruins to the caravan. He knocked on the door. Waited, then tried the door. Locked. He walked into the clearing and waited a while, letting his senses register and sift. But it was a windless clear noon in the bush. The sounds of the caravan flexing in the heat, that's all. Perspiration salty on his lips.

He walked along the creek to the gravestone. It drew him—he supposed it always would—and he lingered for a while. Lichen crawled across the chiselled face, filling the grooves and channels that spelt out the boy's name and fate, and the father's appeal to God. Hirsch blinked. Realised he was holding his hand over his heart. Weird. He turned away to stare down into the creek, where murky water pooled around the bulrushes. A tiny ripple—a yabby or a water plant, shapeshifting as if woven into the water.

He walked on, curious about the creek beyond the gravestone and hoping to spot footprints in the moist soil at each of the stagnant pools, or creek-bed stones that had been rolled weather-side down by small feet. Mostly the creek was broad and straight, the bed barely two metres below the paddocks on either side, but where it curved, or cut between hillocks, the banks were significantly higher.

He was picking a noisy path through one such gulch—the tumble-smoothed stones, clustered pink, dry and weirdly testicular, tocking out a jerky tune under his feet—when a scree of dust and pebbles rattled downslope to spill over his shoes. He tilted his head, dwarfed by seven or eight metres of striated red soil embedded with rocks. A glimpse of dead grass at the top. Some creature up there, he thought. Or the dirt was unstable.

He turned back, passing the gravestone for a final silent tribute. Then the long drive home, thinking about Wendy, and when he finally reached the police station in Tiverton, a pair of Sydney cops were waiting for him with hard faces shut tight.

20

An Organised Crime Squad senior sergeant named Vita Roesch and a Homicide Squad senior constable named Robert Hansen.

Both shopsoiled, as if they'd spent the day sitting in a plane and then a car, which they had. Both still managing to crowd Hirsch's little sitting room, which was frayed and unloved to begin with, and put him on the back foot.

The ceiling fan chopped at the stale air. 'Pull up a pew,' Hirsch said.

Hansen glanced disparagingly at the sofa before perching as if fearing the fabric would soil him. 'Op-shop chic, mate?' he said.

Vita Roesch said, 'Now, now, Robert.' She turned to Hirsch. 'A quick word and we'll be on our way.'

She sat on the other end of the sofa; a woman of forty with the lean, searching look of a hunter, offset by a multi-coloured cotton sundress that showed sleek, tanned legs and shoulders. It all brightened up the sitting room, anyway.

Hirsch remained standing. 'Tea? Coffee? Cold drink?'

'Water, please,' Roesch said.

'Water, mate,' Hansen said. He sat back finally, surrendering to the sofa, a small man with pouchy cheeks and the tidy precision of a banker: a man who'd look brushed and combed whatever he did. Out on the street, your gaze would pass over him. But you'd look twice at Senior Sergeant Roesch and wonder when she'd come gunning for you.

Hirsch strolled through the archway leading to the kitchen nook and made a production out of opening and closing overhead cupboard doors and running the tap, and when the Sydney detectives were sufficiently disarmed by that bit of domestic flimflam, he sneaked a photograph of them on his phone. Then he filled three glasses, returned to the sitting room and sat opposite Roesch and Hansen. His fingers twitched: the print of Andrew Wyeth's *Christina's World*, on the wall behind the Sydney detectives, needed straightening.

'Quite a media storm you cooked up, mate, even in Sydney,' Hansen said. 'Big headline in this morning's *Daily Tele*: "Massacre central".'

Hirsch recognised the tactic: use disparagement to unbalance an interview subject, hoping they'll reveal a chink you can exploit. 'You don't think the media cooked it up by themselves?' he said lightly.

Hansen curled a grin at Hirsch, set for another swerve, when Roesch interrupted.

'Be fair, Robert. Constable Hirschhausen merely stumbled upon these, ah, crime scenes. I'm sure he doesn't welcome the attention. Isn't that right, constable?'

Hirsch nodded. 'Senior sergeant.' He didn't know if he could trust her smile.

'We flew in this morning and headed straight for Redruth,' Roesch said, all business now. 'Quick briefing from your Homicide Squad people then a quick look at the crime scene, and now here we are, gracing you with our presence.'

Kellaher would have told them about Gemma Pitcher, Hirsch thought, tensing up. 'How can I help?'

Hansen leaned forward, forearms on his knees, still intent on unsettling Hirsch. 'Where were you just now?'

Hirsch bit, wondering if he'd regret it. 'I'm the only copper in this district. I'm not going to be sitting in the station all day.'

Hansen smirked. 'One would hope you were out looking for a certain shop assistant we'd like a word with.' His features hardened. 'Someone you promised would be available for interview.'

'I was looking for her, in fact. And the two boys she's probably with.'

Hansen gave him an empty smile. 'But no luck.'

Roesch said, 'We really need to speak to this girl, Constable Hirschhausen.'

'Gemma Pitcher,' Hansen said, with the air of a man in possession of all the facts, 'who claims a man came into her shop and asked if she knew where a Mrs Reid lived. We'd like to know more about this man. Did she tell you anything—a description, for example? Did you ask?'

The guy was a prick, but Hirsch didn't want to bite again. 'She's young, vague, didn't take much notice. Average build, forties, that's about it. She only raised it with me because she wondered if he'd been to see me, which is what she'd suggested he do.'

'And now she's missing. Any idea why, or where she might go?'

Hirsch shook his head. 'All I know is, she's using her mother's car, and two boys, friends of hers, are probably with her. It's the holidays, maybe they've been partying and they're sleeping it off somewhere. It's just that they didn't tell anyone where they were going. On the other hand, we're not talking fully functional families. It wouldn't occur to them to tell anyone.'

Hansen looked all set for another snide comment when Roesch interrupted. Giving her colleague a glance that had a little slap in it, she said, 'Let's move along, shall we, Robert? Keep in mind that Constable Hirschhausen isn't this girl's keeper. At least he got her to agree to make herself available, right, constable?'

Hirsch nodded, grateful. There was an answering flash of warmth in Vita Roesch, something that glimmered and was gone. He cleared his throat.

Roesch went on, 'What matters is, two members of a family have been shot dead and two are missing.'

Hirsch waited.

Roesch said, 'We met your sergeant. She said the search is being wound back.'

Hirsch shrugged. 'I was out there yesterday morning. I'm not up with the latest strategic thinking. But...we haven't found anything, and if the girls were picked up by someone driving a vehicle, well, it makes sense to concentrate the search elsewhere.' He shrugged. 'Family, friends...'

Then he paused, waited. Another interrogation technique, aimed at eliciting information. Not that he expected it to work on them. It was more likely he'd be sidelined further.

But Roesch surprised him. 'Why don't you give us your take on the case?' she said. 'Not just the facts—theory and opinion as well.'

His mind raced, looking for traps. On the face of it he was merely the local plod, who'd happened to have a run-in with Mrs Rennie—and later happened to find her shot dead in her house. What else could he offer the Sydney detectives? Then he thought: they'd done their homework. Someone's said something and they'd dug around in his past and discovered he'd once been a detective and wasn't, in fact, merely the local plod.

Who were they, anyway? Roesch—Organised Crime. Hansen—Homicide. Some New South Wales task force? How well did they know each other? How well did they work together?

'It occurred to me that Mrs Rennie and her kids were in witness protection,' he said. He watched the pair of them carefully.

Hansen glanced at Roesch and said tightly, 'Why would you think that?'

There was an odd dynamic between them. Maybe they didn't work together, or hadn't for long. Was it Hansen who'd called Sergeant Brandl requesting the welfare check?

Hirsch shrugged. 'Mrs Rennie was very evasive. She lied

about her address, her husband and how many kids she had, so I wondered if she was in hiding.'

'There's a big difference between hiding and being in witness protection,' Hansen said. He put his head on one side, curled his lip. 'But that YouTube clip didn't do them any favours.'

Prick. Hirsch wanted to wipe the smirk off his face.

'Robert...' Roesch said.

Hansen shrugged.

With a last little frown, Roesch turned to Hirsch, her smile apologetic. 'You were saying...?'

He said, 'I'm wondering what Mrs Rennie's phone records might tell us, particularly calls to or from Sydney numbers.'

'Are you now,' Hansen said.

'We're looking into it,' Roesch said, cutting her colleague off. 'Now, presuming Mrs Rennie was hiding from someone—did you wonder who?'

'The usual: husband or boyfriend. And for her to end up out here, in the middle of nowhere, he must be pretty determined or well connected. But, you know, I'm guessing; *you* probably know exactly who she was hiding from. And why.'

Roesch gave him a tiny complicit grin. 'Let's keep guessing. Suppose this person found her—why didn't he shoot them all?'

'If he's got the girls,' Hirsch said, 'they're important to him in some way. Is he their father?'

Roesch smiled again. 'A good question. Would they willingly get into a car with him?'

'I have no idea. They might not have known he was the

shooter, so when he appeared in his car, they hopped in. Or they were exhausted and gave up. Or they knew he was the shooter but got into the car anyway, because they knew not to cross him.'

'Very Sherlock,' Hansen said, apparently amused.

Hirsch had had enough. 'I wouldn't have to guess if you people weren't so secretive and up yourselves. My sergeant gets a direct call to her mobile, from Sydney, asking for a welfare check—which suggests to me someone was a) keeping tabs on the Rennies and b) knew to contact the local police in an emergency.'

There was a silence, as if that information was new to them. Roesch shot Hansen a fraught glance. She smoothed her dress over one slender knee and said, 'I can confirm that a person of interest left Sydney a few hours after that video clip was posted. We have him in a silver Passat on the Princes Highway, before he dropped out of sight. Have you seen this car at all?'

'No. Who is he?'

Hansen said, 'This conveniently missing shopgirl. Did she see what kind of car this stranger was driving?'

'I don't know. We'll have to ask her when she shows up.'

'The thing is,' Vita Roesch said, 'if Ms Pitcher didn't know where the Rennies lived, how do you suppose the shooter found the right address?'

'I have no way of knowing,' Hirsch said.

'And I expect you're wondering if Ms Pitcher's going to turn up dead,' Hansen said, as if Hirsch might be to blame if that happened. He paused. 'Tell us about the YouTube clip.'

Hirsch complied, for the millionth time. 'And no, I didn't post it.'

Hansen smiled lazily. 'Some people like a bit of free publicity.'

Roesch interrupted. 'I think we should come clean with you, Constable Hirschhausen.'

Presumably, Hirsch thought, that meant mostly lies and a few half-truths. 'Okay.'

'I can concur that Mrs Rennie and her family were in witness protection.'

Expecting more, Hirsch waited. Nothing. He looked from one to the other. 'And?'

He continued to wait. Then: 'Am I allowed to know why?'

With a look at Roesch, Hansen said, a little more human now, 'I'm afraid not.'

Hirsch said airily, 'I'll just google them, will I?'

In a flash, an impregnable wall seemed to slam down between the Sydney detectives and Hirsch. He was being warned not to try scaling it. He raised his hands in surrender. 'Okay. What I think happened is, Mrs Rennie had been hiding from someone, only to be spotted in a YouTube clip, and this someone come looking for her—driving a silver Passat.'

'That's a working theory,' Roesch said, looking at her knees again.

Hirsch had to keep playing along. 'You know who he is, clearly. Why not wait till he goes back to Sydney and arrest him?'

'A little matter of evidence,' she said.

Hirsch looked at her. 'Can you at least tell me who he is?'

'Above your pay grade, mate,' Hansen chimed in.

Hirsch ignored him. 'Senior sergeant, shouldn't we have been told we had protected witnesses living in the district?'

'You know how it works, constable.'

That seemed to be that. Roesch and Hansen stood and shook hands with Hirsch; he showed them to their car. On the footpath outside the police station, Roesch stopped suddenly and turned to Hirsch. She placed her palm fleetingly on his chest, and withdrew it almost instantly, with a slightly apologetic grin. 'How's your grapevine?'

For a mad moment, Hirsch thought she meant the one he'd trained over the trellis in his backyard. But she meant contacts and informants. 'Not bad.'

'Tap into it. Maybe those children were picked up by a local person who hasn't listened to the news. Or someone's sheltering them.'

'Or a perv has them,' suggested Hansen. Cocked his head at Hirsch. 'You wouldn't happen to know any pervs?'

'There are various ways it could have gone,' Roesch said hastily. It looked as if she wanted to get Hansen out of there.

'I'll see what I can find out,' Hirsch said. As if it would never have occurred to him to do any actual investigating.

Late Thursday afternoon now, and Hirsch straightened the Wyeth print, dusted, vacuumed, wondered if he could bother the old woman next door for a bunch of her roses. It was all to tamp down his nerves: he'd been rattled by Hansen, and to a lesser degree, Roesch. Hansen's stance was simple: everyone's a suspect. Roesch was warmer and more agreeable—and she'd delivered him a little jolt of attraction that made him feel mildly guilty and noticeably more cheerful. And she didn't like Hansen: join the club. Her presence lingered in the shabby little room.

He called Wendy's mobile. Katie answered: they were in the car, heading back from the river, the twilight tricky, kangaroos on the road. Then Wendy's voice could be heard in the background; Katie passed it on: 'Speak later tonight, maybe tomorrow.'

'Safe trip,' Hirsch said.

Later tonight came and went. At ten o'clock Hirsch dragged on a T-shirt and surf shorts for bed and heard a knock on the street door. Vita Roesch stood there, still vivid in her summer dress but wearing a cotton jacket over it that gave her a stance of authority. Hirsch glanced past her at the hire car blocking his driveway. 'Senior sergeant.'

'It's just me,' she said, anticipating his question. 'I need a few more minutes of your time.'

Back to the sitting room, where she took off her jacket and the room brightened. Feeling clumsy, Hirsch said, 'Where are you staying?'

'Hotel in Redruth—forget the name.'

Taking charge, she perched on one end of the sofa and indicated the other. 'Sit, please, Constable Hirschhausen.'

He sat, and her long legs swivelled towards him. He could read everything or nothing into it, but she was all business as she took out her iPhone, poked and swiped, and proffered it.

'My bona fides. Recognise anyone?'

A photograph of Roesch with Denise Rennie. An office somewhere, shirt-sleeved men and women at desks in the background. Hirsch said, 'You worked together? She was in the police?'

'Yes and no. We were colleagues—friends, I'd say. Denise was a civilian—an intelligence analyst. The Covert Support Unit. We worked a big case together.'

'What happened?'

Roesch considered him for an uncomfortable moment. 'I'm about to fill you in a little more. Nothing I say can leave this room, understood?'

There's something about Hansen, Hirsch thought. He said, 'Okay,' wondering how much of the real story he'd get.

'Denise's actual surname wasn't Rennie or Redding, it was Reid.'

'Okay.'

'She was due to give evidence at a series of trials; her life was threatened, and we placed the family in witness protection. The location was compromised, her husband was killed, and she ran—disappeared with the children.'

'Who were they hiding from?'

'I'm not at liberty to say, Constable Hirschhausen.'

'She came here on her own? You didn't place her here?'

'No. We didn't know where Denise had taken the family until now.'

'Someone did. Someone called my sergeant and gave her the address.'

'That,' Roesch said, 'is a puzzle.'

'Has her landline history been checked yet?'

'Yes. She only called local numbers. The Redruth clinic, for example.'

Hirsch brooded. He said, 'May I ask who you are, exactly? Her original witness protection handler?'

A hardening of Roesch's face, her nose and cheekbones suddenly sharper. 'Do I detect a criticism, constable?'

Hirsch put up his hands in apology and, just as quickly, Roesch was subtly warm again. 'Senior Constable Hansen is Homicide—the murder of Denise's husband remains unsolved. I work major crimes including fraud and organised crime within the State Crime Command. That's how I got to know Denise. We became very close. This is personal for me.'

'It's a shame Mrs Rennie—*Reid*—didn't contact you again,' Hirsch said. The regret that creased Roesch's face making him feel clumsy and ashamed, he added quickly: 'Did you find out how their first location was leaked?'

'Constable, please. Don't you think I'd have kept her safe if I could?'

Careful where you tread in your size tens, Hirsch. 'Sorry.' He gnawed on his bottom lip. 'Would Senior Constable Hansen have known where the family was hiding?'

She seemed amused. 'The hackles certainly rose between you two—sorry about that.' She bent towards him minutely and grinned, a real smile. 'I barely know Hansen, but for the time being we're stuck with each other.'

Hirsch returned the grin, but he sensed she was trying to tell him something other than a version of the Rennie backstory. A warning about Hansen? 'Thanks for filling me in. I don't have much clout, but it's good to know a bit more about what's going on.'

'Don't hide your light under a bushel, Paul,' Roesch said. 'I know an intuitive copper when I see one.' She paused. 'You have told me everything?'

Hirsch glanced upwards, considered the question, and found an answer. 'Er, yep.'

Roesch said, 'The girls might need protection, wherever they are.' She touched his arm lightly.

'I don't know where they are,' Hirsch said, and wondered why he felt guilty.

21

On Friday morning Hirsch prowled the town, reliving the encounter with Vita Roesch as the dawn light dissolved into birdsong. Thinking he'd dodged a bullet. By much? What kind of man was he, anyway? Thank God she hadn't stayed long. The air was soft and clean around him, but he knew the dust- and heat-saturation would come soon enough. Meanwhile it was almost good to be alive—if you drew on your senses, not your memories.

It can be the little things that save you. His phone buzzed as he ambled past the grain-handlers on Hallett Street. Wendy: *Pancakes 9 am*. Hirsch walked home with a bounce, and it didn't matter that Sergeant Brandl texted him a few minutes later: *briefing 11 sharp*. Love and work, the twin poles of his existence. He returned to the police station, showered and changed for his pancake breakfast, and headed out of town.

Half an hour later he was seeing a side of Wendy he hadn't really encountered before, and finding he rather liked it.

She was venting about her brother and sister-in-law. 'Because Rose sees herself as vague and passive, she lets Matt make all the decisions.'

'Self-fulfilling,' Hirsch said.

'Exactly.'

They were in deckchairs on her side veranda, a little table between them, cluttered with the dregs of their breakfast. Katie was a few metres away, rocking in her hammock, reading, listening.

'Honestly, the family dynamics in that house,' Wendy said, looking down, shaking her head. 'Just as well you didn't come with us.' She lifted her head again. 'And they never eat the food I bring. I don't know why I bother.'

Hirsch reached out to lay a calming hand on her clenched fist. She turned to him, frustrated, and her eyes were damp. 'Sorry.'

He smiled. It was good just to sit on the veranda with her. And he liked a good rant if it was intelligent and amusing.

Wendy continued to deliver. 'Lunch was quite weird. Almost no conversation, they all just sat hunched over their plates, shovelling in the food. Peculiar. They never used to be as bad.'

'They sound like prisoners in a dining hall,' Hirsch said.

She gave him an intrigued look. 'And after lunch they all retired to a different part of the house and played with their fucking devices. Sorry, sweetheart.'

Katie's piping voice: 'That's okay, Mummy.' Pause. 'Tell him about Easter.'

'God, Easter,' Wendy said. 'We went to their place as usual

and there was an Easter egg hunt—the idea being everyone shared afterwards, right? But those kids—they just guarded their hoards like sticky-fingered little dragons and refused to share with my dear, sweet, wise, gracious daughter.'

'Tell him about the money,' Katie said.

Wendy closed and opened her eyes and shot Hirsch a rueful look. 'Do you want to know?'

'Give me all the dirt,' Hirsch said. The shoals and set-backs of ordinary life were mostly ridiculous, even funny. Definitely preferable to bloodshed.

'A year ago, I lent Matt seven hundred and fifty dollars—which was fine, he lent me money when Glen died, and I paid it all back. But yesterday he gives me *six* hundred and fifty dollars, as if the loan was settled. I didn't say anything. Now I don't think I can. It's only a hundred, but, you know, it's...'

'Symptomatic?'

Wendy grabbed Hirsch's hand, a tight, emotional squeeze. 'What about you? Any weird, screwed-up family I should know about?'

Hirsch cast his mind over them all. Generations of bland-ness. 'I could make something up.'

Wendy leaned across to kiss him. 'I'll settle for *your* weirdness.'

Pancakes heavy inside him, his mood better than it had been for days, Hirsch headed down the Barrier Highway to Redruth. Thirty minutes later, he was seated with Brandl and the children around the briefing table, playing catch-up.

Break-ins, traffic accidents, stock theft, a Christmas Day suicide.

'With New Year's Eve upon us,' the sergeant said, 'we need to prepare ourselves for more self-harm, not to mention pub brawls, domestics and drink-driving.'

Her face was drawn, her eyes pouchy with fatigue after her hours coordinating the Hamel Road line searches. 'I'm taking a rest-day tomorrow and need you to fill in for me, Constable Hirschhausen. The others will be out on patrol.'

'Sergeant.'

She clapped her hands. 'Right, anything else?'

Tim Medlin flipped through his notebook. 'A call came in from a Trevor Wesley, owns a property near Porters Lagoon, wondering why there's been no follow-up on a report he made back in May.'

Hirsch knew why. Back in May, the Redruth police district had been under executive management, a hiatus between the quiet removal of the old sergeant and his coterie of thugs and the appointment of the current team.

Brandl winced. 'The backlog. God, what a shemozzle. What did he report?'

Medlin frowned at his notes. 'He was getting ready for bed one night and heard a knock on the door. Wondering why he hadn't heard a vehicle, he answered holding a shotgun. Two men ran off and when he tried to call triple-O, he found his phone line had been cut.'

Hirsch tingled, stirred. 'The Rennies' line was cut. And I know of one other case.'

The sergeant looked at him tiredly, giving his words some

consideration. Finally she said, 'But is that enough for a pattern? It's only *two* instances if you factor in the likely how and why of the Rennie case.'

Hirsch felt stubborn. 'But can I do some digging?'

She was too weary to object. 'Knock yourself out. Just don't waste hours on it.'

The briefing over, they separated: Sergeant Brandl to her office, Landy and Medlin to their local duties, Hirsch to his Toyota. Armed with the Porters Lagoon address, he headed south along the Adelaide road for twenty minutes, until Google Maps directed him left along a side road leading into the hills. The lagoon was mostly a saltpan fringed with reeds now, but he'd seen 1920s photographs of it in full water, people rowing—yachting, even—and stilts, avocets and water fowl feeding along the edges. The road climbed in a shallow curve across a long, low hill, and then he was bumping up a driveway to an old farmhouse. Two storeys, which was rare, but the building was more an accumulation of rooms and extensions than a mansion. The arrangement was appealing, if a little random. It offered a big-sky view across the lagoon and valley farmland to hills and a broad horizon on the other side. Dusty pinks and tans over there, with khaki clusters that were distant farms and eucalypts.

Hirsch switched off, got out and was tackled by a slobbering kelpie. As he bent to pat it a piercing whistle sounded from a shadowy shed entrance and a voice growled, 'Get behind, you bloody red mongrel.'

The dog gave Hirsch a panting, apologetic grin and trotted

for the shed. A genial-looking man of about fifty emerged, wiping his hands with a filthy rag. He was solid-bellied, shirtless in a pair of overalls, with lace-trailing old boots on his feet.

'Won't shake,' he said. 'Trying to fix a carburettor.'

'Mr Wesley?'

'That's me.'

Hirsch introduced himself and explained the reason for his visit.

'Thought you lot had forgotten all about me,' Wesley said.

'As you know, there was a changeover of police staff,' Hirsch said. 'The new lot inherited a backlog.'

'Well, you're here now,' said Wesley. He looked at Hirsch shrewdly. 'But you're the Tiverton copper.'

Hirsch nodded. 'I can still make a formal report and give you the information you need for your insurance company, but the main reason I'm here is that I know of two other cases of cut phone lines.'

'True? I don't care about the insurance, I care about strangers lurking in the middle of the night. You want to know what happened, I take it?'

'Yes, please.'

Wesley launched straight in. 'It's only me and the missus here, the kids have flown the coop. Once in a blue moon we get someone come in off the highway to ask for directions or a can of petrol, that kind of thing, and usually in daylight. But when it's eleven on a still night and there's a knock on the door and no engine sounds or headlights, you err on the side of caution. I grabbed the twelve-gauge—don't worry, all legal, I've got the paperwork—and opened the door. Two blokes standing there. Took one look at the shotgun and ran off. I was in bare feet or I'd've gone after them. A minute or two later, I hear a vehicle take off halfway down the hill.'

'You tried to call it in?'

Wesley rubbed his chin, smearing it. 'I did. The line was dead. Went and had a look, cut clean through.'

'Anything stolen?'

'Chainsaw.'

'I'll give you a case number for the insurance—'

'Don't worry about it,' Wesley said. 'The saw was cactus. They're welcome to it.'

'Can you describe these men?'

'Not really. Youngish, wearing hoodies and jeans. Quick on their feet.'

'The vehicle?'

'No idea. There was a bit of moon to see by, and they didn't turn on their headlights till they hit the highway.'

'Which direction?'

'Redruth.'

Hirsch returned to Redruth, parked near the town hall and went looking for Kellaher or Roesch in the incident room.

Only Hansen was available, working on an iPad and not inclined to be available to Hirsch. In a nod to the heat, he was wearing shorts and a short-sleeved shirt. He looked less like a banker but not less like a prick. 'What do you want?' he said.

Hirsch told him. 'That's three cases of cut phone lines

now,' he added. 'There could be more, in other police districts.'

'Mate,' Hansen said, 'I'm New South Wales police. Nothing to do with me.'

'It could relate to the Rennie murders.'

Hating to be torn away from the screen of his iPad, Hansen said, 'Log it in, write it up, ask around, you know the drill.'

'You don't think it's important?'

'Everything's important. Log it in, et cetera.'

'Thanks for your help,' Hirsch said, but the irony passed over Hansen. He gave a shrug that said it was the least he could do and returned to his iPad.

Back in the Toyota, Hirsch checked his phone. Brandl: *Call me.* Not right now, he thought. Places to go, people to see.

He found Monica Fuller in her backyard, repairing an arrangement of stakes toppled by tomato vines heavy with fruit.

'Want some? More than we can eat.'

'A few would be good,' Hirsch said. Ed Tennant's tomatoes were generally soft and floury.

Monica took him to the kitchen, washed and dried half-a-dozen tomatoes and stowed them in a paper bag. 'Here you go. Tea, coffee, water?'

Hirsch settled for tea. He said, after a catch-up chat, 'That time your phone line was cut.'

'Yes?'

'You were both at home?'

'Yes.'

'Could someone have thought you were out?'

She considered. 'I don't see how. Both vehicles were in the carport.'

'Kip barked?'

'He was beside himself. Broke his chain.'

'And only the shovel stolen?'

'Even then Graham wasn't sure. It might've bounced off the back of the truck one day.' She swallowed. 'But if they'd got in the house...The TV isn't much, but it's not bad, and there was my laptop, that's pretty new.'

'Who fixed the line for you?' Hirsch asked, thinking a local telco technician might know of other, unreported cases.

'Bob Muir. No point calling Telstra; you get someone in Mumbai who doesn't have a clue what you're on about.'

Hirsch returned to Tiverton and called in at the Muirs'. Bob was rewiring a generator in his workshop. 'Constable.'

'Mr Muir.'

Hirsch watched for a while, mesmerised by his friend's deft fingers and the gleaming copper. 'I understand you fixed a damaged phone line for the Fullers?'

Bob's gaze didn't move from his fingers. 'I did.'

'Describe the damage?'

'It wasn't wear and tear, if that's what you're thinking. It was a cut, very neat, straight through, one snip.'

'Have you had any other cases?'

Now Muir lifted his gaze. 'No. But I'm betting you have.'

Hirsch explained, Muir listened.

'Not statistically significant.'

'No,' Hirsch admitted.

'But suggestive.'

'Yes,' Hirsch said, glad someone agreed.

He spent the rest of Friday afternoon searching for Gemma Pitcher, Daryl Cobb and Adam Flann. Eileen Pitcher was agitated because she needed her car for a hair appointment in Redruth, Laura Cobb was morose—her mother had been hoarding her meds again—and there was no one at home at the Flanns'.

Hirsch returned to the police station. Checked his phone when he got inside and remembered the sergeant's message. He called her, and she said, 'You're wanted in the city, Paul. Internal Investigations, first thing Monday morning.'

22

Saturday morning Hirsch phoned his parents.

'I was thinking of driving down tomorrow,' he said, 'and spending the night.'

His mother was pleased, and she was shrewd. 'Oh, good, a belated Christmas. Is everything all right?'

She was referring to his old troubles, the disbandment of his CIB squad, the Internal Investigations interrogations, the inquiry, the prosecutions. He came clean. 'I'm due at Angas Street at eight-thirty Monday morning.'

'Oh, Paul, what this time?'

'Mum, I have no idea.'

'Do you need a lawyer?'

'I'll ask for one if it gets tricky.'

His mother was brisk and practical. 'Will you be here for lunch?'

'Depends on traffic.'

'If we go out, I'll leave cold meat and salad in the fridge,' his mother said.

His parents were bound to go out. They were energetic in their early retirement, never home: golf, bridge, roadside clean-up campaigns, bushwalks, handing out how-to-vote cards. Hirsch's own busyness was more pragmatic: being neighbourly and civic-minded oiled the wheels of his police work.

Part of his police work was standing in for a Redruth officer now and then. Hirsch reached the town by 8 a.m., stationed himself behind the front desk and waited. The hours passed. He witnessed two statutory declarations, directed three German backpackers to the visitors' centre and had one of those conversations—fairly common, in his experience—that proved most crims were idiots.

A man came in and said, 'I was robbed.'

Hirsch tutted in sympathy, pen poised. 'Name and address, please, sir.'

Tony Alford, a street behind the old railway station.

'And what was stolen?'

'All of my weed.'

Alford was one of those men or women so tall they stand at a slant. About forty, greasy hair, three-day growth and bony arms and shoulders inside a Redruth High School polo shirt. His son's? Op shop? Grimy jeans barely clinging to his hipless middle.

'Your weed was stolen,' Hirsch said.

'All of it. In pots on the back veranda.'

'Your weed.'

'You know, grass,' Alford said. 'Dope.'

His eyes hadn't alighted on Hirsch or anything else in the police station. He was so twitchy, Hirsch couldn't stand it. 'You do know there are laws against growing it?'

Alford knew his rights. Folded his arms and stated that there were also laws against stealing.

Might as well roll up the whole drug empire while I'm about it, Hirsch thought. 'Do you happen to know who might have done it?'

But Alford shrugged. 'That's for you to find out.'

'How much weed are we talking about?'

'Three pot plants.' Alford sniggered. 'Three pots of pot.'

'Perhaps,' Hirsch said, 'we can send in our forensic team and go right over your property, inside and out, collecting fingerprints and other samples for the lab.'

A late-dawning gleam of awareness in Alford's glassy eyes now. 'No, she's right, I'll put it down to experience,' he said, hurrying out and down the street.

Hirsch entered it in the log.

Then nothing for a long stretch of time. At twelve-thirty he locked the station, texted Medlin and Landy that he was off to lunch and walked down to the Redruth town square. Even with the reduction in police numbers the bistro and deli were crowded, so he bought a salad sandwich in the milk bar and ate it sprawled in a patch of shade near the rotunda.

At 1 p.m. he crossed the road to wander back and, as he passed the bistro, a face in profile caught his eye. He stopped, looked in. No clear sightline to the back corner, so he shifted position. Vita Roesch and Inspector Kellaher.

Kellaher spotted Hirsch and nodded, prompting Roesch to turn her head. She rewarded Hirsch with a smile. Discomfited, he moved on, not wanting them to think he was spying.

He paused at the window of Redruth Real Estate, the only agency in the district. Houses, farms, businesses for sale. A couple for rent. And an idea tugged at him. He was about to push inside when Vita Roesch was nudging his arm and saying, 'Great minds think alike.'

The kind of cop who catches suspects, culprits, witnesses and victims unawares. Dressed in a plain, bold-patterned sleeveless dress, a hint of shampoo, warm and grinning, the air faintly electric around her. Hirsch said, 'Okay, what am I thinking?'

'You're thinking did Denise Rennie buy or rent the house on Hamel Road and if so, from whom, and what might the paperwork reveal?'

'I was, in fact.'

'Got there before you—we checked yesterday.'

'And?'

'Rented it, fully furnished. No takers for two years, the agency was glad she took it off their hands.'

Hirsch glanced past Roesch's shoulder, expecting to see Hansen lurking. 'Where's Mr Personality today?'

She gave him a crooked smile. 'Be nice.'

'Always,' Hirsch said. 'Did you find out who owns the place?'

'Some anonymous agri-company.'

'How did she pay?'

'Excellent question. Cash.'

'Cash,' Hirsch said. 'Did she have access to a bank account? You'd have monitored that, right?'

Vita Roesch gave him a sunny smile. 'We did. It seems the day before she and her husband went into witness protection, they withdrew fifty thousand dollars of their savings.'

Hirsch nodded. Forethought.

Roesch prodded him in the chest. 'You're wasted out here.'

'Not country-town cop material?'

'I'm from a country town,' Roesch said. 'Nothing against country towns. You just don't want to get trapped in one.'

The remainder of his workday was quiet; he was back in Tiverton by 6 p.m.

On Sunday morning he packed an overnight bag, pinned his mobile number to the police station door and headed south along the Barrier Highway again. On any other long drive, he might have slipped a CD into the slot, but his mind was racing today, his thoughts chaotic. He hated not knowing what the Internals had on him, or who'd be grilling him tomorrow. He tried to think it through: ran various scenarios in his head. Pictured himself clinically demolishing every accusation, holding his head high. Then the doubts. He imagined them dredging up old charges—supported, this time, by new and unanswerable proof.

Or was it something new? Had he fucked up in Tiverton without knowing how?

The YouTube clip? He'd thought that was old news.

His fingers were white on the steering wheel, his jaw tight.

He rolled through Tarlee and what took his mind from the turmoil a minute later was passing the old stone farmhouse where his father's grandparents had lived. His father remembered a gruff, remote, upright man haunted by his experiences of trench warfare on the Western Front. In the twenties he'd settled in Tarlee to manage the property for the cattle king Sidney Kidman, growing wheat and tending mobs of wild outback brumbies brought down by train and destined for the Indian Army. Hirsch told himself: *My concerns are not that important.* He felt the aggravations fall away.

By noon he was parking in his parents' driveway. Hugs, home cooking, uncomplicated evening company, his parents eyeing him with concern but always exquisitely tactful. His old room, his old bed...

23

At eight-thirty on Monday morning Hirsch was seated with two Internal Investigations officers at a bland table in a small, featureless room. He'd dealt with both officers and considered Rosie DeLisle a friend; Inspector Gaddis was a foe. Both had targeted him during the corruption inquiry; Rosie eventually believed that he was more or less clean, Gaddis was convinced Hirsch should have been charged.

It was Gaddis who began. 'Do you know why we've asked you here today, Constable Hirschhausen?'

The sun was behind the inspector, lighting up his thin hair in a wispy nimbus. Not holy, just distracting. 'No, sir.'

Gaddis was always colour-coordinated. For this warm summer day he wore a lightweight tan suit and sand-coloured shirt, the collar too big for his scrawny neck, with a beige tie. Gold-rimmed glasses; twig-like fingers adept at shepherding disordered paper into shape and stabbing the next bullet point.

He lifted a letter. 'I have here a communication from a

Damien Ablett of the district council of Redruth. Do you know this person?'

'I know of him,' Hirsch said, 'but haven't had the pleasure of meeting him.'

Prick though he no doubt was.

'Mr Ablett advises that rate-payer funded asphalt was used to fill potholes in the driveway of the Tiverton police station recently. What do you have to say in regard to this matter?'

Unnoticed by Gaddis, Rosie DeLisle rolled her eyes heavenwards then back at Hirsch. Apart from that, her face was flat, and Hirsch had to look away or he'd have started grinning.

He chose his words carefully. 'It was a donation, sir, from the crew of the council's patching truck. Apparently, they often have asphalt spoils left over at the end of the day, and rather than let it go to waste, they—'

Gaddis sharpened. 'Your driveway was patched first thing in the morning, Constable. Not the end of the day.'

Hirsch said nothing. If he waited, the blame might flow onto the Bagshaw brothers.

'The council employees will face internal disciplinary proceedings. Meanwhile you will appreciate that the South Australia police service cannot be seen to accept favours? Did you pay these men?'

I'll buy the Bagshaw twins a couple of beers one day, Hirsch thought, for laying asphalt worth about two bucks. 'No, sir.'

Gaddis turned jocular. 'So not a variation on the bitumen bandits who like to fleece the unwary, constable?'

Hirsch gave a hollow chuckle. 'No, sir.'

But he knew all about bitumen bandits. His parents had been scammed by a man who knocked on their door one day, saying he had a load of bitumen left over from a large road-repair contract and rather than take it to landfill, a terrible waste of good tar, would they like their driveway paved at a greatly reduced rate? They said yes, in their generous way, paid a deposit, and never saw the man again.

Gaddis tried for kindly uncle. 'Hardly a sackable offence, of course, Constable Hirschhausen, but perhaps you might be a little more careful next time. It comes down to image, and it comes down to perception.'

'Sir,' said Hirsch.

Rosie twinkled at him. 'Did they do a good job?'

'A great job,' Hirsch said. 'Every time I parked in the driveway, the potholes would put my spine out of whack.'

Gaddis said coolly, 'Moving along...'

While a part of Hirsch tensed for some fresh hell, another part raced through the asphalt back story. Someone in town had witnessed the pothole patching and informed the council office. The town and district councillor was Martin Gwynne. Martin saw and knew everything.

'The matter of your paperwork, Constable Hirschhausen.'

'Sir?'

'A number of important memos, in need of your immediate attention, remain unattended to. Would you care to speak to this matter?'

I would not, thought Hirsch. But his mind alighted on the 'information cascade' memo. Should have followed it up. He might have, if the damn thing had been written in plain English.

'What with long daily patrols and two major crimes in my district, I've had to let some things slide a little, sir. But I will clear my in-tray in the next few days.'

'Again, hardly a sackable offence, Constable Hirschhausen, but once a pattern of negligence is established, it can be difficult to shake.'

'Yes, sir.'

'Learn to make time in the day to attend to your paperwork. Now, failure to charge two teenage boys with the theft of a motor vehicle.'

Hirsch swallowed. 'A judgment call, sir. One boy's the carer, with his sister, of their mother, who has mental health issues. The other boy's mother is in hospital and his father's in jail. I felt a formal apology to the vehicle's owner was the best course of action.'

He paused, told a partial truth: 'Both boys were suitably chastened and apologetic.'

Gaddis stared at him without expression. 'Very well. Now, this brings us to the unauthorised use of your official police fleet vehicle.'

And instantly Hirsch saw Martin Gwynne: stationed at a window, hovering in his front yard, watching Hirsch sail by in the HiLux, Katie Street in the passenger seat.

He played dumb. 'Sir?'

It was his friend Rosie who took up the charge. She was all business now, no longer rolling her eyes, so Hirsch knew for sure he'd fucked up. 'You were seen, on numerous occasions, transporting a child in the passenger seat of your fleet vehicle, Constable Hirschhausen.'

'Her name is Katie Street and she's, er, the daughter of a friend who teaches at the Redruth high school and generally isn't able to pick her up after school,' Hirsch said. His face was burning. 'She's usually collected by a neighbour, but there were a few occasions when the neighbour couldn't do it so I gave her a lift home—in my own car, actually, except for twice when it wouldn't start and I used the fleet vehicle. I apologise. But it was only twice, not numerous occasions. And there won't be other occasions because she's going to high school next year—she'll be travelling with her mother.'

'That's hardly the point,' Rosie said. 'You may use your fleet vehicle to transport civilians in certain circumstances—giving a lift to a stranded motorist, for example, or taking someone to safety or to hospital—but not for private purposes.'

'Insurance obligations, for a start,' Gaddis said, his gold teeth flashing. 'Issues of propriety and image and good sense—the fact that you are a grown man and she a young girl...'

'What if you're accused of misconduct by mother or daughter, further down the track?' Rosie demanded. 'What if you fall out with them for some reason, and they decide to take it out on you? No matter how innocent those trips might have been, it's not going to look that way to the rest of the world.'

Hirsch felt mulish. 'There's not going to be any fallout from mother or daughter.'

'You can't know that, Paul—Constable Hirschhausen,' Rosie said.

She was right, of course. 'As I said, there won't be any further occasions.'

Gaddis said, 'Were you on duty, these times you took the child home?'

How to explain that a country copper is always on duty? That an eight-hour shift is meaningless in the bush? That often he was setting out on patrol at dawn and if he happened to be in town when school let out at three-thirty, he'd already worked a nine- or ten-hour shift?

'No, sir.'

'Did you consider the repercussions if, halfway through one of these trips, you were called to a road fatality or a suicide or a murder or to deal with an out-of-control ice addict? What that might do to the child?'

'Sorry, sir, didn't think,' Hirsch said.

'No. You didn't.'

'Just trying to help a friend.'

'Help that was detrimental to your police work and your professionalism, however, wouldn't you say?'

'Sir.'

'No disciplinary action at this stage,' Gaddis said, 'but it will be noted on your official record.'

'Thank you, sir.'

'Meanwhile the academy runs refresher courses throughout the year. Behaviour management and leadership, for example. You are strongly advised to enrol in a suitable course when classes begin again early next year.'

Hirsch knew that strong advice was in actuality an order. 'Sir.'

'And consider studying for the sergeants' exam,' Rosie said.

He flashed her a look, wondering if she was saying anything between the lines. Rosie, with her round figure, vivid eyes and glossy black hair, her air of looking for adventures, gazed back at him steadily, sombrely. Telling him to wake up to himself.

He nodded.

'We now come to the matter of the child locked inside a car on a hot day,' Gaddis said. 'Did you or did you not advise Child Protection?'

'Did not, sir.'

'Carry out a family check?'

'No sir.'

'Anything at all?'

'A firm chat, sir.'

'Chat. Why nothing stronger?'

'I weighed up the circumstances and didn't think a charge or a caution was warranted. As an officer on the ground, I made a judgment call. The offence didn't seem serious enough to warrant intervention from Child Protection or anyone else. There was no aggravated behaviour, no violence, it was just a bit of carelessness.'

'That might have cost a child its life.'

Hirsch swallowed. He didn't answer.

'What about the assault on your person, Constable Hirschhausen. You didn't think to pursue charges for that?'

'No, sir. Again, a judgment call. The poor woman was

distressed. You may not know, sir, that she's subsequently been murdered? She and her family were in hiding and she clearly thought her daughter was in danger. She wasn't thinking clearly.'

'She got hold of your gun.'

'Yes, sir, but not deliberately. She seemed shocked when she realised—she dropped it straight away.'

Gaddis was running with this line of questioning. Rosie DeLisle looked on, leading Hirsch to think she supported his case.

Gaddis paused a while to gaze at Hirsch. 'We've all been there, Constable Hirschhausen.'

Not you, Hirsch thought. You were born with a pen in your hand. 'Sir.'

'Heat of the moment decisions. Judgment calls.'

'Sir.'

Gaddis lifted another sheet of paper. 'Your sergeant gives you a good report. "A sound officer," she says.'

'Good to know, sir.'

'Quit the bloody shortcuts, all right?' Gaddis said, his headmaster veneer slipping. 'People are noticing. You risk bringing the force into disrepute, not to mention your own career and reputation.'

'Sir.'

'By the book,' Gaddis said, gathering his paperwork. 'Dismissed.'

They left Hirsch there. Rosie gave him a rueful smile goodbye, and soon after he left the building, he received a text:

Count yourself lucky, mate. I've got your back, but... xx.

24

As he returned to the long-term carpark there was another text. *Any chance of an update? Rex.*

Rex Dunner. Owner, with his wife Eleanor, of a grazing property named Pandowie Downs, whose heritage-listed woolshed had twice been spray-painted with swastikas and ejaculating penises. Hirsch reacted as he always did when reminded that he'd neglected, avoided or evaded his police duties—screwed his face into a mad grimace and stifled a groan. His fault for making promises, then putting the matter on the backburner.

He checked the time. He'd reach the mid-north by mid-afternoon, too late to do anything more than make reassuring noises to Rex and his wife. Spend all day in a hot vehicle again, in other words. He climbed behind the wheel and took South Road to Port Wakefield Road and the Northern Expressway. Here the traffic was fast, sparse, giving him breathing space.

*

Martin Gwynne.

The man's physical appearance dominated Hirsch's thoughts before he could shake it off. Martin's looks were hardly noteworthy—but maybe that was the most significant fact of all: Martin Gwynne was a monster disguised as a man you wouldn't look at twice. His little pot belly, skinny legs, innocent round cheeks, neat scrape of greying sandy hair. Avid eyes behind prissy rimless glasses. An earnestness to make an ordinary person run for the hills. A small man at home in corners, scurrying away from searching eyes.

But look behind that and you'd find a man with an infantile need to be wanted, noticed and appreciated. Hirsch doubted the need was ever fully satisfied. Martin often alluded to people and circumstances that had let him down. Until coming to live in Tiverton, he'd been a senior manager in an insurance company. Then, aged fifty-five, he'd been retrenched—fallout from murky office politics, was how he'd put it. Or, Hirsch thought now, Martin had been an underperformer or a pain to work with. Anyhow, he'd not been able to find other work. Hirsch had commiserated at the time, only to see Martin's morose face flip 180 degrees. 'It was the best thing that could have happened, Paul. A new lease of life. Mother and I downsized and came north to enjoy honest country living.'

Not entirely true. The attraction for the Gwynnes was that their daughter Annette was living in Tiverton with her husband and son. Moving to be close to the little family gave Martin a heaven-sent opportunity to meddle in their lives. Martin babysitting, issuing gratuitous advice, dropping in at all hours of the night and day. Martin teaching his grandson to play tennis. Martin sitting on the primary school council, taking the lone teacher aside for a quiet word; directing traffic and ushering children across the road at school drop-off and pick-up. Wendy Street referred to fierce primary school mothers as mumzillas. Martin was a grandpazilla.

Then daughter and family moved back to Adelaide, ostensibly because their rural handicrafts business had failed; probably to escape the smothering, and their departure left a hole in Martin's life. Unfulfilled by his roses and wife-bossing, he threw himself into town and district affairs: he had expertise, he explained, and wanted to give back to his new community. Soon he was representing Tiverton on the district council, chairing the tennis club committee, organising fetes and working bees for the Anglican church and writing letters to the *Stock Journal* and the *Redruth Argus*, dispensing wisdom.

Interfering in Hirsch's work life.

Mindful of law and order issues, having a keen interest in police procedures, and being Tiverton's elected district council representative, he was concerned to keep abreast of local policing activities. He had theories to offer. Advice to give. And wasn't it a lucky thing he'd been on hand to save Hirsch's life from Brenda Flann's out-of-control Falcon?

A man who'd sulk if he wasn't fully appreciated, Hirsch thought. A man who'd hoard his grievances.

He realised he had no idea how to deal with Martin. And what if it wasn't Martin who'd snitched to the Internals?

*

Hirsch's shortest route to Pandowie Downs from a southerly approach was to cut across country at Mount Bryan and wind around to the dark side of a stony spine known as the Razorback. The land out there was parched, the roads powdery and chopped about. Hirsch headed up and down the folds of the earth, dust boiling thickly in his wake. His wrists juddered on the steering wheel.

He came to the intersection of two flat, empty roads and took the Pandowie Downs turnoff, a sunken road between stony erosions and weedy paddocks dotted with dun-coloured merino sheep. Ten minutes later, reaching the stone pillars that marked the driveway entrance, he almost turned around and headed for town. Did he really want to face Rex and Eleanor Dunner just now, after the day he'd had? He took a breath. *Build bridges. Forge healthy community relations.* He was sure he'd read exactly those words in a memo. But had he replied to it? Joke, Paul. He checked the time. Almost five o'clock. If he was lucky, he'd be home by seven.

He turned in. A sign on one pillar read: *Pandowie Downs Unique Outback Experience Accommodation Horse Riding Mustering Seasonal Shearing Demonstrations All Welcome.*

A theme-park take on old rural Australia, thought Hirsch, taking in the solar panels on the shearers' quarters, a stone building that had been converted into a block of four pricey self-catering units. Two faced the woolshed, sharing a back wall with the two that faced the stony ridge overlooking the little settlement. Antenna arrays, fresh paint, parking bays marked by red-gum sleepers. Irrigated lawns dotted with old ploughs, wagons and tractors. Curtains drawn on one of the units, a dusty white Audi SUV parked outside it. Impossible to tell from this angle if there were guest cars parked at either of the rear-facing units.

But the Dunners were about. Spotting their glossy-dusty black Range Rover parked at the rear of the woolshed, Hirsch steered down the flank of the long building and pulled in alongside it. Got out, took a moment to admire. The woolshed was a vast, beautifully proportioned structure of local stone. One of the side doors was open. He stepped in.

High ceiling; massive posts and beams; holding pens with slatted floors; an odour of lanolin. Silent and empty now, but suggestive of a time when a grazier might shear sheep by the thousands.

He stepped outside again and headed for the office, a partitioned space at the rear. Paused: a patch of the side wall was cleaner, sharper than the rest. It had been sandblasted. He peered: traces of white swastika and penis clung to the porous stone and friable mortar.

'Expected you last week, young fella.'

Hirsch turned. Rex Dunner had emerged from the office. He wore cream moleskins and elastic-sided R. M. Williams boots, all part of the unique pastoral-Australia mystique. Until five years ago Dunner and his wife had run a real estate agency in North Adelaide.

Hirsch shook Dunner's freckled, wrinkled old hand. He was a desiccated seventy, but wiry and brisk. 'Mr Dunner.'

'Constable. You bearing good news? A gang of graffiti artists locked up, keys thrown away?'

'Afraid not.'

'I see.'

He thinks I'm a sloppy policeman, thought Hirsch, or he knows it was a lost cause. Or both.

'I'm afraid there's only one of me,' Hirsch said. 'In a perfect world I'd station someone here overnight for a few weeks, or drive past every hour, but that's out of the question. Have you thought of installing CCTV?'

Dunner jerked his head, inviting Hirsch to walk with him to the office. 'What good would that do? A ghostly image of some idiot with a spray can? It would only illustrate what I already know.'

'We might get an ID.'

Dunner shook his head. 'Costing me a fortune in cleaning.'

Everything would boil down to cost with this man. Installing cameras, for example. They reached the door to the office. 'It seems significant that the attacks have been recent.'

Dunner paused in the act of turning the doorhandle. 'How so?'

'It's not tourist season, is it? Too hot. Were there any guests staying the nights the place was graffitied?'

'Well...' Dunner gave a slow nod. 'Now that you mention it, no.'

Was it that helpful, knowing the place had been empty? Any fuckwit could drive past, see there was no activity and think: hey, let's spoil some rich bastard's day.

Someone local, thought Hirsch. He followed Dunner indoors. The reception area comprised a desk, armchairs and a drinks machine, with a spacious office behind it.

Eleanor Dunner was in there, listening on a landline phone. Dressed similarly to her husband, and just as skinny and vigorous. She twinkled her fingers at Hirsch.

Rex Dunner crossed to the drinks machine, yanked on the door. 'Coke? Lemonade?'

'I'm fine. Who belongs to the Audi?'

'Film producer. Scouting locations,' said Dunner, with a little inflation of his chest, as if touched by Hollywood glamour.

'One big location.' Hirsch gestured towards the endless landscape beyond the thick, cool walls. 'Is he travelling alone?'

'Yes.'

Hirsch cocked his head. 'You heard what happened at Mischance Creek?'

Dunner turned his face north-east unconsciously, as if the creek ran just outside the building. 'Nasty business.' He paused. 'Hang on, are you saying he's involved?'

'Nothing like that,' said Hirsch easily. 'But I do need to ask if you've seen any odd activity in the past few days. People, vehicles, anything at all.'

'Mate, any passing car is strange. People drive past just to see the woolshed, they don't necessarily call in. Quick selfie at the side of the road and off they go to the next tree or hill or ruin. I've stopped noticing.'

'Any other guests?'

'A nature photographer in four,' Eleanor Dunner said, emerging from the office, her hand out.

Hirsch shook. Her fingers were strong, her palm dry. 'Man? Woman?'

'Man.'

'What's he drive?'

She shared an amused glance with her husband. 'His car's there now, Paul, if you'd like a look.'

'Bear with me, Mrs Dunner. What's he drive?'

'A car's a car to me,' she said. 'A silver car, will that do?'

Just happy to look down on other motorists from the cockpit of her Range Rover, thought Hirsch. 'Would you mind showing me the reservation book? It's important.'

She was amused. 'We are computerised, Constable Hirschhausen.'

She stepped behind the counter, tapped on a keyboard, swivelled a monitor so that Hirsch could read the screen. Philip Whiteman, an address in Ultimo, Sydney, a New South Wales registration number. Hirsch was uneasy. Parked where it was, his police Toyota was not presently in view of the shearers' quarters, but had he been seen driving in? Making a note of the Whiteman number plate, he asked for the film producer's reservation details.

'Paul, what's going on? I don't feel comfortable about any of this.'

'I'll be out of your hair in just a moment. I just need to run both plate numbers and if there's no cause for alarm, I'll leave you and your guests in peace.'

'Now there's a statement to put our minds at rest,' Eleanor Dunner said. She tapped the keys. The film producer was named David McAuliffe; an address in Crows Nest, Sydney; South Australian car registration. The Audi was probably a rental.

Hirsch didn't have the capacity to check interstate plates using the Toyota's onboard computer, so he called to ask Sergeant Brandl to run both sets.

'I'm with Inspector Kellaher and the others in the incident room,' she replied. 'Soon as I can commandeer a computer I'll call you back.'

Marooned with the Dunners, Hirsch made awkward conversation for five minutes, and then his phone buzzed.

'Sarge.'

'I'm putting you on speaker phone. The New South Wales plates belong to a silver Camry owned by Whiteman Photography, an address in Ultimo.'

'Thanks.'

'The other plates belong to a blue 2007 Holden with lapsed registration, last owner a used-car dealership in Hahndorf, since closed down.'

The Adelaide Hills, thought Hirsch. One of the main routes into the city from the eastern states.

He wandered over to the door for privacy, murmuring, 'Those plates are currently fitted to a white Audi SUV, Sarge.'

Another voice cut in: Inspector Kellaher. 'What name did the driver book under?'

'David McAuliffe, said he's here to scout locations for a film company.'

'Is he alone?'

'Yes.'

'Sit tight. He could be the Passat driver our New South Wales colleagues were tracking. We'll run a check for stolen Audis and abandoned Passats.'

'I could have a word with him in the meantime, sir.'

'Don't be a hero, Sonny Jim. You could get yourself shot. Wait until I can get you some backup.'

'That could take a while, sir.'

'Not necessarily. I still have people finalising things at the Rennie house. I'll call you in five.'

Hirsch wandered back to the desk, where the Dunners were vibrating.

'Is anything wrong?'

'Is it to do with the shootings?'

Hirsch made a noncommittal noise. 'Could you google "Whiteman Photography" or "Philip Whiteman"?'

Disappointed, Eleanor Dunner complied. Hirsch peered at the screen with her: a logo, a selection of birds, kangaroos, skyscapes and wildflowers, a beaming, bearded man festooned with cameras in one corner. 'Is that the man staying in number four?'

'That's him. Should we be worried?'

'No. He's not involved in anything.'

Rex Dunner said, 'But the film fellow is?'

Hirsch was thinking of a reply when his phone buzzed. He said, 'Excuse me a moment,' and wandered back to the door. 'Sir?'

'A white Audi SUV was stolen in Balhannah a few days ago.'

Another Adelaide Hills town. Hirsch chewed on the information. 'He's in his cabin. I've got enough to—'

'No, Constable Hirschhausen, sit tight, and that's an order. Senior Constable Hansen is running a check on

McAuliffe as we speak; I'll contact the Hamel Road team as soon as I get off the phone. They should be with you in less than half an hour.'

'And if McAuliffe makes a run for it in the meantime?'

'Follow discreetly, if you can. Just don't get shot.'

'Sir.'

Hirsch rejoined the Dunners. 'I don't mean to alarm you, but I'd like you both to drive home now. Go inside, lock the doors, don't open to anyone. I'll let you know when it's safe to come out.'

They exchanged numbers. Eleanor, jittery, said, 'Hadn't you better tell us what's going on?'

'There are stolen numberplates on the film producer's car. It might mean nothing, but with the shooting at Mischance Creek, we're not taking any chances.'

'What about Mr Whiteman?' Rex said.

'Good thinking. Can you call his room for me, please?'

When Whiteman answered, Hirsch said, 'This is Constable Hirschhausen, South Australia police, Mr Whiteman.'

A shocked pause. 'My wife? My—'

'Nothing like that,' soothed Hirsch, 'but I do need you to pack a bag quickly and get in your car and drive somewhere safe. Turn right at the gate and follow the signs to Mount Bryan.'

The photographer, alert to the tension in Hirsch's voice, simply said, 'Will do,' and they exchanged phone numbers. 'Now your turn,' Hirsch said, turning to the Dunners.

They shook his hand. Eleanor gave him a brisk hug and said, 'Take care.'

He watched from the office door. Doors slammed, and the Range Rover crunched away on a bed of expensive white gravel. A short time later he glimpsed Whiteman's silver Camry head slowly out along the driveway.

Time passed. He wandered outside, retreated to the office again, beaten back by the heat. Fifteen minutes, twenty minutes. He idled by the door, looking down the driveway to the road. Four cars passed the property, slowing, one stopping for a stickybeak, perhaps curious to see a police vehicle parked at the rear of the woolshed. Thirty minutes.

He left his station at the door, fetched a can of lemonade, returned. Thirty-five minutes.

Then, as he stood looking out, waiting for his backup to arrive, Hirsch saw movement. A shape flicking away from the rear of his police Toyota.

25

He raced out, cut between the woolshed and the Toyota, stopped short. Hissing air. Slashed tyre. A precious moment lost, he ran to the corner of the woolshed and pounded upslope to the accommodation block. Too late: the Audi was fishtailing down the slip road, onto the driveway, and speeding towards the entry pillars. Hirsch saw brake lights flare, a wing mirror spin away in a sideswipe, and then the Audi swung right and powered out along the Razorback road.

Hirsch ran back to his Toyota and reached for the radio: the handset cord dangled, cut cleanly. He ran in circles for a mobile signal, called Sergeant Brandl, then hauled out the jack and spare tyre. The jack slipped; the nuts felt glued on; situating the spare was like wrestling a fridge onto a trailer. Knuckles barked, blood and grease on his hands, he lost thirty minutes. Then he was opening the driver's door again, heat pouring out, the seat burning hot. He fumbled the key into the ignition, cranked the aircon to high and planted his foot. Everything about his take-off seemed clumsy: weak aircon, sluggish acceleration.

Then he was out on the road, trying to coax speed out of a vehicle designed for endurance. He called Redruth again: two cars had been dispatched to his location; a roadblock had been set up in the town.

'But he could be headed for Broken Hill, sarge.'

'I'll notify Peterborough.'

A few minutes later he topped a rise overlooking a broad, shallow basin, like a giant claypan. Was it his imagination or was there a lingering dust haze from the long-departed Audi? He'll be on the Barrier Highway by now, Hirsch thought. Not mad enough to head south, surely. He steered along the road's slow curve through the depression and out the other side.

The minutes passed. The sun, dropping behind the Razorback, cast him in shadow for a couple of minutes. And then he was on the final stretch to the Barrier Highway with no sign of the Audi.

He turned north, figuring if the man calling himself McAuliffe had turned south, he'd run into the Redruth cars or the roadblock. Two kilometres, three, four, the highway empty, nothing along the farm tracks or minor roads. And then, as he passed the Booborowie turnoff, he saw the Audi a hundred metres in, parked at an odd angle. He braked, reversed, sped down to it.

McAuliffe had overshot a slight bend. The car was nose-down, cocked over, in a culvert. The trouble with you city boys, Hirsch thought—don't know how to drive on dirt.

Never throw a vehicle into a corner, you'll lost traction. He pulled over, switched off, reported to Redruth and stepped onto the road. About to unholster his pistol, he thought, *petrol*, and ran for the SUV.

He could see that the driver's side window was down, but the vehicle was tipped too far onto the passenger side for a clear view of the interior. He slid to the bottom of the culvert and peered through the windscreen. The driver had toppled sideways over the console and head-first onto the dash, his lower limbs partly secured behind the wheel by his seat-belt. Blood: on the dash, the passenger-side window. Why? Nothing about the Audi's front-end damage indicated a high-speed collision or major road trauma. He half-expected to see the man lift his head and reach for a gun, but he didn't move. Gave, in fact, every appearance of being dead.

Even so, Hirsch thumped on the bonnet. 'You need to get out,' he shouted. 'I can smell petrol.'

It was a lie: there were only the usual odours of hot metal, oil and grease. No reaction from the driver.

The Audi was tipped at such an angle that Hirsch couldn't open the driver's door. He scrambled out of the culvert and around to the other side. The front passenger-side door was jammed against the culvert, so he pulled out his service pistol and tugged open the rear passenger-side door. Still no movement from inside.

Hirsch climbed in and edged along the tilted rear seat until the gap between the two front seats gave him a clearer view of the driver. About forty, dressed in chinos and a short-sleeved cotton shirt, a tanned, thin-faced man with dark hair, recently cut. You'd think: surgeon on his day off; film producer scouting locations.

You'd also think he'd been shot. A large exit wound behind his left ear was seeping blood.

26

Hirsch called Redruth again. Having been ordered to keep car and driver intact, he took a series of photographs in case the Audi caught fire, then settled in to wait.

Time passed. He was restless, itching to search the SUV. Eventually he got out a pair of crime-scene gloves, returned to the precariously tilted car and began to rummage awkwardly beneath the seats. Searched the glove box, under the mats, tyre-changing kit and spare tyre. No rifle. No mobile phone. No personal possessions apart from a wallet.

Stepping clear of the car, he flipped through the wallet. Credit cards, $560 in cash and three driver's licences— same face—in the names David McAuliffe, Shayne Elliott and Christopher Baldwin. He took close-up photos of each licence and returned the wallet to the car.

Still waiting, he ran through some possible narratives. Why had McAuliffe run? Had he seen the police Toyota arrive; suspected something was wrong when first the photographer then the Dunners drove away? A cool character, since he'd had the forethought to walk downhill with a knife and slash the tyre and the radio handset cord before he bolted...

But none of that explained what he was doing on this side road, shot in the head. Puncturing Hirsch's tyre had bought him time to run—but it had also bought time for someone to set up an ambush. A partner, thought Hirsch. He thought about the vehicles that had slowed or stopped to look at the woolshed. A partner who'd spotted the police car and told McAuliffe to run. A partner who'd decided he was a liability and eliminated him on an obscure back road. His side window was down, Hirsch recalled—as if he'd opened it to talk to someone, maybe an oncoming driver. He's shot in the head, his foot slips off the brake, the Audi rolls into the ditch. The killer lingers long enough to grab his phone—presumably the call log would have been incriminating—then clears out.

Detectives and crime-scene officers arrived, Comyn among them, and Hirsch was told to get his arse down to Redruth and report to Kellaher.

'In a moment,' Hirsch said, heading for his Toyota. The killer had taken a great risk, knowing Hirsch would call for back up, change his tyre and come looking. Would he be stupid enough to hang onto the murder weapon and risk a search?

'Now, constable,' Comyn said.

'In a moment,' Hirsch said.

He climbed behind the wheel and drove at a walking pace

further along the Booborowie road, eyes sweeping left and right, taking in stones, dirt and stunted bushes. The sun at a shallow angle across the land. *May it flash on metal...*

A kilometre later, a dull glint.

He stopped, got out, stepped through the grass, crouched. A 9mm automatic pistol.

He photographed it in situ. Debated fishing it off the ground with a twig through the trigger guard but marked the spot with his cap and drove back and reported his find.

Comyn grunted, the most thanks Hirsch might expect, and followed him in a police car to the marker. Hirsch watched him retrieve the pistol with a gloved hand and slip it into a paper bag.

'You still here?'

'On my way,' Hirsch said, gathering his cap. Then he was bouncing and jarring his way back to the Barrier Highway as the day dimmed all around him.

The Redruth town hall sat like an ocean liner on a dark sea, lights blazing where the rest of the town had retreated for the evening.

Now that extensive searches had failed to find the Rennie girls, the main police presence was winding down, but figures still flickered past windows, gathered on the front steps or huddled, smoking, in the shadows at the side of the building.

Hirsch rolled by and turned into the alley leading to a carpark at the rear of the hall. Switched off, got out and found his way through to the incident room. Little of the original fit-out remained: a scatter of computer stations, phones, chairs, desks and wall partitions, like islands on a vast sea of hardwood floorboards.

Kellaher and Dock were conferring at a whiteboard beside the stage. They broke off when Hirsch appeared.

'Start at the beginning, keep it brief,' Kellaher said. 'I need to start bringing police members back in again.'

Hirsch laid it out for them: stolen plates on a stolen car; the proximity to Mischance Creek; McAuliffe making a run for it; dead behind the wheel; the tossed pistol.

'A pistol, not a rifle?'

'Correct.'

'Is he the Passat driver?'

'Don't know, sir.'

'Do you have anything tying him to the shootings?'

'No, sir.'

'So for all we know, he could've been planning to hold up the Tiverton bank.'

There hadn't been a bank in Tiverton for twenty years, but Hirsch saw the inspector's point. 'The fact remains, sir, it's possible he was warned, and it's possible he was shot by whoever warned him.' He took out his phone, isolated the McAuliffe licence photograph. 'This is him.'

Kellaher peered at it. 'His prints are being run as we speak, so let's hope he's in the system. Meanwhile, Sergeant Dock will take your statement.'

Dock took Hirsch to a card table beneath a wall photo: the Pandowie Downs shearing shed, appropriately, in its heyday, with 1950s Austin trucks, loaded with plump wool bales, lined up for the camera.

'That's where it kicked off,' Hirsch said, pointing at the photograph as he eased onto a foldup chair.

Dock shrugged. The photo was old, and he was not a man with any use for history. He sat down opposite Hirsch and said, 'Been busy, mate.'

Hirsch said nothing. He reached an exploratory finger to the green, mock-leather surface of the card table. A small brass label along the edge facing him read: *Property of the Redruth and District Bridge Club.*

Dock removed a digital recorder from his pocket and set it on the table between them. 'No objections?'

'Go your hardest.'

Dock also took out a notebook. He thumbed through it. Trying to intimidate, Hirsch thought. Second nature.

'Okay, let's get started.'

But before the Homicide sergeant could form the first question, a voice called, 'Mind if I sit in?'

Vita Roesch was striding towards them. Hirsch expected irritation from Dock, but he clattered to his feet, pulled in his stomach and worked his eyebrows at a fair demonstration of wry charm for the attractive police officer from Sydney. Hirsch, less flustered, also stood.

'Do you mind?' said Roesch again, with a small, disarming smile. 'I need to hear this.'

'I'll get you a chair,' Dock said.

He fetched it from a stack beneath a window, placed it at the card table and watched Roesch settle herself. She tucked a strand of hair behind her ear. Almost 8 p.m., Hirsch thought: hair immaculate, dress barely wrinkled. She shot him a look, a smile.

Hansen joined them, carrying a fold-up chair that he placed at the card table. Now they were a small, over-populated island.

'Go on, Sergeant Dock.'

Dock cleared his throat. 'In your own words, Constable Hirschhausen, starting with why you went to the location in question.'

Again Hirsch outlined the day's events, concluding: 'Whether or not McAuliffe—or whoever he is—shot Mrs Rennie and her son? I don't know. That's for others to decide.'

'He registered under the name McAuliffe?'

'Yes.'

'Then let's call him that. Did you search his room?'

'No. There's a team doing that now.'

Roesch interrupted: 'I've had their preliminary findings. A change of clothes in a weekender bag, that's all.'

'No rifle?'

'No rifle.'

Dock turned to Hirsch. 'Did you search the Audi?'

'Well, yes...' Hirsch shifted on the flimsy little chair. 'I thought if there was a petrol leak...'

Dock waved that aside. 'What did you find?'

'Wallet with false ID. No firearm.'

Roesch leaned in. 'You replaced the wallet?'

'Yes.'

She shook her head as if frustrated. 'Did you at least take note of the names?'

Hirsch nodded and took out his phone again. He scrolled through the three licence photographs. 'I'm betting you know him, senior sergeant.'

A quick glance and Roesch frowned. 'Vaguely familiar. Rob?'

Hansen leaned in. Shook his head. 'Don't know him. Let's hope his prints are on file.'

That was enough of that. 'Next question, sergeant?' said Roesch.

Dock complied. 'The pistol you found. Could McAuliffe have ditched it?'

Hirsch shook his head. 'I found it past where he was killed.'

'The shooter ditched it?'

'I'd say so.'

Roesch inclined her head towards Dock. 'Perhaps your people could have a thorough look tomorrow, in case the driver himself ditched anything.'

Dock blushed very slightly. 'Will do,' he said.

Hirsch thought of all the kilometres of road between the woolshed and the Audi. With any luck he wouldn't be part of that particular search.

Dock shifted his attention to Hirsch again. 'Was there any indication McAuliffe had company with him? An accomplice?'

'Nothing in his car to suggest it. I haven't seen his room.'

Roesch cut in again. 'As I said before: just a weekender bag packed with clothing.'

Dock nodded, accepting that. He said to Hirsch, 'What about the kids? Any sign they'd been in his car?'

Hirsch shook his head. 'If he'd snatched and disposed of them, he'd hardly stick around.'

'Mmm,' Dock said. 'So he was sticking around to finish the job, or he was there for some other purpose entirely.'

'Yes,' Hirsch said.

Roesch cocked her head at Hirsch. 'Why don't you tell us what you think this fellow was up to, Constable Hirschhausen? You've been on the ground from the start, after all.'

Hirsch was weary. 'One scenario, he shot Mrs Rennie and her son—in which case he'd been staying somewhere else at the time, because he didn't check in at the woolshed until after the shooting—and got rid of the rifle. When he heard on the news there were survivors, he stuck around to finish the job.'

'The survivors were children. Why risk hanging around to kill them?'

Hirsch shrugged. 'Maybe, for whatever reason, his brief was to wipe out the entire family. Or he thought they could identify him.'

'Okay. Any other scenarios come to mind?'

'Honestly, senior sergeant, this is above my pay grade.'

'Humour me.' The little smile again.

Hirsch took a breath and wished he hadn't. The room was warm from the heat of many days, stale from the respiration of many people. 'Okay. Someone else was the killer. Job done, he clears out. Then news breaks about the girls, and

McAuliffe is sent in to clean up. Or there are two different outfits, after the same thing.'

Roesch was expressionless, but for the first time he felt a wave of coolness from her, a warning: he was alluding to the witness protection betrayal: bent police. Only Dock reacted. 'A lot of trouble to go to if Mrs Rennie's already dead. And is it such a big deal if the kids see something? They're traumatised. Not likely to be viable witnesses.'

Roesch said, 'Or he was there for some other reason.'

Hirsch was busy trying to decipher mood and body language. '*Do* you know who McAuliffe is, Senior Sergeant Roesch?'

Hansen's phone pinged before she could reply. She glanced at it with a brief frown, then addressed Hirsch, speaking in sharp volleys, as if time was wasting: 'We're going around in circles. Why wasn't this woolshed place checked days ago? How far is it from the Rennie house?'

'Excuse me,' Hansen said. He was staring at his phone, one hand raised.

'What?'

'We have an ID. Ian Lavau, an address in Sydney.'

'Yes, thank you, Senior Constable Hansen,' Roesch said, clipped.

Hansen, ignoring her, continued to recite from the screen of his phone. 'He was police for many years. Regional— mainly in the Riverina. Not covered in glory but no red flags; more recently a compliance officer with Border Force.'

Hirsch gave a laugh without much humour in it. 'Maybe there's an international drug ring operating from Tiverton.'

This was Roesch's show; she leaned forwards. 'Don't be a smartarse, constable.'

I'm not flavour of the month anymore then, Hirsch thought. He wondered how much information she'd given her SA Police colleagues. He said nothing. Watch, listen and learn.

Dock was interested. 'Anything else you can give us, Rob?'

Hansen was still looking at his phone. 'That's about it.'

'Nothing to explain why he's here? Links to Mrs Rennie?'

'Nothing so far. He worked in the Compliance Audits Unit. They check that tax invoices don't understate the value of imported goods, so...no obvious reason why he was here carrying a false ID.'

'We're going to need anything and everything you can give us on Lavau,' Dock said, addressing Roesch and Hansen. 'We've got bodies piling up and two kids missing, presumed dead. He's the only one in the frame, so who was he working for? Or with? Who knows him? Et cetera.'

Good on you, thought Hirsch.

Roesch said, 'I'm afraid I can't—'

Dock cut her off. 'The Passat you were tracking—it was driven by Lavau, right?'

'I can't really say.'

Hirsch pitied Dock. He could keep pushing but Roesch would just keep stonewalling.

Just then his phone buzzed. A text from Nan Washburn: *Can I please take you up on your kind offer, take Craig back to his camp tomorrow?*

Hirsch felt flattened with weariness, and the day wasn't

done. He'd have to drop his tyre off at Redruth Motors, reassure the Dunners, reassure Whiteman the wildlife photographer, drive home...

'If no one minds, I'm knocking off. I've been at it all day and I'll be on all day tomorrow.'

New Year's Eve: drunks on the road, tempers unleashed in kitchens and bedrooms.

Roesch gave him a look. He could feel it digging around in his head and soul.

'You may go,' she said. Imperious—as if she wasn't a mere visitor but in charge of the investigation.

27

Early morning, New Year's Eve. A cool, cloudy start to the day.

Old-timers had assured Hirsch they could recall temperatures below twenty degrees in the Christmas and New Year period, thunder clouds bunching, teeming rain: 'We even had to light the fire!' So it wasn't unheard of, a cool change this time of the year. Hirsch walked the streets as he always did, and the town slumbered, except that Martin Gwynne was standing on the other side of his neat hedge, sprinkling his roses with a craft-shop watering can—a pastel blue thing with yellow flowers that Hirsch wanted to boot into oblivion.

'Martin, I—'

'Paul!' cried Gwynne, as if Hirsch had never been known to walk the town at dawn.

'Look, Martin, I—'

'I expect you're on duty all day, not to mention tonight, what with drunken idiots on the roads, but Mother and

I were wondering if you'd care to have a bite to eat this evening? Earlyish, around six?'

'That—'

'Strictly no wine, of course, wouldn't want to get you into trouble.'

Hirsch gave that last statement some consideration. Amazing how the guy's mind worked. One gleeful part of Martin Gwynne was saying, 'I hope you do have a drink, so I can report you,' and another was saying, 'Bet you don't know I've already reported you.' The remaining parts of Martin Gwynne were pure trash.

Hirsch stepped through the fussy wrought-iron gate and into Gwynne's personal space. 'I was raked over the coals by Internal Investigations yesterday. Do you know anything about that, Martin?'

'I beg your pardon?' The watering can dropped like a rock, splashing their shoes.

'You reported me. Not once, several times. Why did you do that, Martin?'

Gwynne stepped back, eyes darting.

'Paul. What on earth are you on about?'

'Why, Martin? What is your problem with me?'

'I have no idea what you're talking about,' Gwynne said, with the weak bluster of a man caught out in lies.

'No more meddling, Martin, let me do my job. And for god's sake find yourself a hobby.'

Gwynne straightened his back, inflated himself. 'I'm sorry you feel that way, Paul, Constable Hirschhausen. Now if you don't mind, I'd like to finish watering.'

There was a shape in the front window, hazy behind a lace curtain. Poor old Joyce; imagine being married to him. Hirsch turned away and stalked back along the street towards the police station, feeling better—but not much better.

He was halfway there when a memory surfaced. It was the day he'd freed Anna Rennie from the backseat of her mother's Hyundai. Martin waving his phone around. It was Martin who'd filmed the tussle and uploaded it to YouTube. Martin who had brought killers to the district.

Whether or not that was the case, Hirsch would deal with it later. He showered, dressed, ate a second breakfast, checked in with Sergeant Brandl by phone, locked the police station and pinned his mobile number to the door. Contemplating his patched driveway gloomily, he backed the Toyota out onto the highway and trundled around to the pub.

Kev the publican, a thin man with bulky, unrealised dreams for his establishment, was hosing down the veranda. He told Hirsch he wasn't expecting trouble, there hadn't been a New Year's Eve punch-up in the main bar for as long as he could remember—but every year he hired the Bagshaw brothers as bar staff and bouncers, just in case.

Hirsch eyed the metal struts supporting the roof section damaged by Brenda Flann and said, 'Have a good one.'

Two minutes later he was parked in Nan Washburn's driveway. Craig's voice floated to him from the veranda again, disembodied behind the screen of ferns in hanging pots. 'All packed and ready.'

Hirsch mounted the steps. How long had Craig been

waiting? At his feet were an old kitbag and supermarket bags distorted by cans, bottles and packets. 'Nan still asleep?'

'The sleep of the dead.'

Hirsch hoped not. 'Let's go. I need to make a few house calls on the way, if that's all right.'

'Fine by me,' Washburn said, hitching up his binder-twine belt, adjusting his duct-taped glasses.

They left the town behind them, Hirsch curious about the altered light. He'd grown accustomed to weeks of cloudless days, a vast blue dome above, sharply-etched objects all around. Today he was traversing a piebald landscape, the sun pouring intermittently through ruptures in the clouds. Sun, shadow. Pouring, retreating.

Meanwhile his passenger was silent, as if contemplating a return to solitude. What did Craig do or think about all day? Hirsch didn't mind companionable silences, but this one seemed fraught. Had Craig squabbled with Nan? Was he rethinking his self-imposed exile? Hirsch wanted to dispel the mood—he was tempted to play the CD Katie had burnt for him. But if Craig was allergic to the twenty-first century, a burst of Leonard Cohen might tip him over the edge.

Hirsch's first stop, the woman with the rehab daughter. He knocked—no answer—and the car was gone. He checked doors and windows: the house felt unoccupied rather than touched by junkie-offspring violence, so he left it at that. It was a sense that all cops developed, knowing when a situation behind closed doors was right or wrong.

He climbed behind the wheel. Craig said, 'Lovely woman. Sad about the daughter.'

Hirsch said nothing, surprised he was keeping tabs on events in the district.

Then along a looping side road to a small 1970s brick-veneer house on a struggling carob-tree plantation, the home of a seventy-year-old widow and her son Trevor, who had Down syndrome. 'Mrs Watts always serves a cuppa; I could be a while.'

Washburn waved that off. 'I'll stay here, don't worry about me.'

The widow, answering Hirsch's knock, spotted Craig in the Toyota. 'That idiot,' she muttered, gesturing at Washburn with a frail hand, veins like pulsing cords over the fragile bones. Then she smiled and stood aside for Hirsch to enter.

Half an hour later, fuelled with leftover mince pies and rumballs, Hirsch stuck his card under an Eiffel Tower magnet on Mrs Watts' fat old fridge and said goodbye. Unspoken between them, as always, the question: What happens to Trevor when I die?

Feeling like a change of scenery, Hirsch decided to keep going rather than retrace his route back to the main Mischance Creek road. Craig Washburn remained subdued. The powdery dirt and corrugations marked their passage; the minutes passed. So much for a change of scenery, though: this was a road like all of the others and Hirsch realised he could be anywhere out east. Then the detour rewarded him: a kilometre of new pine fence posts and taut strings of shiny wire and a gleaming galvanised gate bearing a sign: *Great Wall Pastoral*.

'Fucking Chinese,' Craig muttered, 'buying up family farms left, right and centre.'

It was an old refrain. Hirsch drove on, merging with the Mischance Creek road again. At one point a few kilometres short of Washburn's caravan he saw the flash of a windscreen down at the creek. A farmer? There was an old hayshed on the opposite side of the road, but no sheep that Hirsch could see between the fence and the creek.

Then they were crossing at the Hamel Road T-intersection. 'Almost here,' he said.

Washburn said nothing. Instead, he glanced in the direction of the kill house and crossed himself. Hirsch was astounded. Washburn might be a little bonkers but he was a scientist—surely a man of reason. Not someone who'd fall back on superstition to ward off evil.

The cloud cover was almost fully gone when Hirsch turned at the wagon wheel marking the track that led to the camp. Washburn sighed and smiled. 'Still the same.'

Had he been worried someone would tow his caravan away? Hirsch pulled into the speckled shade of the gum tree. They got out and stretched their spines, then retrieved the kitbag and shopping from the back seat and carted them across the red dirt to the caravan.

Hirsch stopped suddenly at the door, a bag in each hand. Something...

He glanced around the immediate area, trying to spot the source of his disquiet. The day was like all the others: hot, still, peaceful. Then a water droplet, seeping from the base of the shower bucket, was struck by the sun. It hung, blazing like a diamond for a moment, before it fell to earth.

Hirsch placed the supermarket bags at his feet and said, 'Craig.'

Washburn had unlocked the caravan. 'What?'

'Come here.'

Intrigued, a little spooked, Hirsch stood beneath the bucket, looking up, then down. He heard the kitbag thump onto the floor of the caravan, heard Craig's boots. Then they were both peering at damp soil; a child's heelprint.

'Something to tell me, Craig?'

Washburn's stare was unfocused, but his face was mobile, one memory or emotion touching off another.

'Craig?'

Washburn blinked, turned, hurried to the caravan. Hirsch, hard on his heels, found him halted beside the sink, opening cupboards and drawers.

Empty spaces. Hirsch said, 'You're missing containers of food and water, right?'

'Yes.' A murmur.

Running his gaze around the interior, Hirsch pointed and said, 'And a mattress.' From the spare bed. Thin foam, easily carried.

'Yes.'

Hirsch gripped Washburn's bony elbow and squeezed hard to wake some sense in the man. 'Come and sit at the table.'

Washburn, dazed, let himself be guided to one of the bench seats, Hirsch taking the other. The table top was dusty, untouched. Old nicks, stains and burns.

'Did you hide the Rennie girls here?'

Washburn struggled towards comprehension. 'No.'

'You didn't come back here at any stage?'

'I've been at Nan's since you took me there.'

'Has Nan been out here?'

'No. She doesn't know anything.'

'But you do. You've met the girls?'

A long pause. A nod.

'So, just now, when you saw the footprint and the empty cupboards, you thought at once it was the girls, not some stranger. Correct?'

New expressions flickered over Washburn's face. Calculation. Equivocation. 'I don't know what I thought.'

'Craig...' Hirsch said harshly.

'All right, all right, I met the kids exploring the creek one day.'

'When?'

Washburn shrugged. 'Last year some time. Winter. The creek was running.'

'A long walk from their place to here.'

'Not here, closer to the ruins. I was walking in one direction, the kids in the other.'

'They didn't run away, try to hide?'

'No.'

Hirsch saw another new expression on Washburn's whiskery face: he'd grown close to the family and possibly knew their secrets.

'You met Mrs Rennie, too? She told you why they were living out here?'

Washburn considered that. 'Eventually. A long time later, once we got to know each other. I don't know if I should—'

'She was shot dead, Craig. Her son was shot dead. Your friends were murdered, and it's possible her daughters could be next. Why the hell didn't you tell me you'd met the family?'

'Why should I?' Washburn said with heat. 'It wasn't like I had anything do with anything. I wasn't even here when Denise was shot, and the news said it looked like the girls were picked up by the side of the road. Didn't occur to me they'd come here.'

'But it was a possibility, surely?'

Washburn shrugged. 'I wanted to protect them.'

'By keeping quiet.'

'Yes.'

'Well, they're clearly not sleeping here, but it seems they sneak in and pinch your stuff and help themselves to a shower now and then, so they can't be far away. There's a spare key they know about?'

'Yes.'

'Where are they, Craig?'

'No idea.'

'You're not protecting them by keeping your trap shut. Did you hear on the news about the man who was shot yesterday?'

'Don't know.' Washburn's eyes wouldn't settle on anything. 'Might have.'

'I'll take that as a yes. It's possible he was looking for the girls. An accomplice shot him before he could be arrested. What does that suggest to you, Craig?'

Washburn pouted. He wanted to be left in peace.

'Craig?'

Washburn sat up straight. 'Okay, okay. It means the girls could still be in danger.'

'Exactly.'

Now Washburn cocked his head and gazed curiously at Hirsch. 'Was he police?'

Hirsch went very still. 'What exactly did Mrs Rennie tell you?'

Washburn's eyes slid away. 'Things.'

'I've had enough of this. Where are the girls?'

Washburn agonised, twitching the seams and whiskers that made up his face. 'I think they're hiding in the dugout.'

An old miner's dugout in the bank of the creek, Washburn explained: probably been there for a hundred and fifty years.

They set out, passing the gravestone, passing through two or three stretches where the left-hand bank loomed above them, Hirsch glancing up, hoping to spot the dugout entrance. 'Much further?'

'No.'

'I'm assuming you showed it to the kids one day?'

'Yes.'

They walked the length of another shallow reach, which led into another deep gully, and finally Washburn stopped. He pointed. The hint of an aperture fringed with grass halfway up the bank. You'd never know it was there. Rocks and stones protruded. Useful foot- and handholds, thought Hirsch. And, as he watched, a hint of movement. Not a trick of the cloudy light but a sliver of face—forehead, blonde hair and eyebrow—appearing and gone again in a flash.

Washburn formed a megaphone with his hand. 'Louise! It's okay!'

Silence.

'He's a policeman, the good kind.'

A long wait and the face looked down, young, full of doubt. 'Did anyone see you?'

'There's no one else here. We're coming up.'

'Be quick.'

'Quick as we can, love,' Washburn said.

28

Hirsch found himself in a space that was part natural hollow, part pick-axed cavern. About two metres high, at least in parts, and ten or so metres deep. Two small pairs of knickers were drying on a rudimentary clotheshorse fashioned from twigs in one corner, a styrofoam cooler packed with food and water bottles stood in another. The spare caravan mattress rested beside one wall, a candle stuck into a puddle of wax next to it. Face-down on a folded blanket, an illustrated guide to Australian birds. Craig's book, he thought. The kids wouldn't have picked up their favourite books as they fled. A cool, dim, oddly comforting space—except for the odour from a far corner, which the girls had been using as a toilet, kicking a thin layer of dirt over it.

The girls. Hollow-eyed and wan. Cabin fever, Hirsch thought. Grief. Uncertainty. And fear of everything outside this hole in the ground. Sitting cross-legged on the mattress, they made room for Washburn and snuggled against him. Beaming up at Hirsch, he said, 'This is Anna, and this is Louise.'

Hirsch nodded hello, looked about for somewhere to sit, and paused. On the wall opposite Washburn and the girls there was an ochre hand. Beside it, three stick figures armed with spears chased a stick-figure kangaroo. He stared at the images, complicated feelings settling in him. He felt like an interloper, somehow; a despoiler. He found himself looking at his heavy footwear. Finally selecting a spot in the dirt, his spine uncomfortable against knobs in the lower part of the wall, he realised Washburn was looking at him with some sort of emotion he couldn't place.

'Apart from the girls,' Washburn said, 'I'm about the only one knows about this place.'

Hirsch nodded. 'Pretty amazing.'

'Certainly is,' Washburn said. He looked at the top of one head, then the other. 'Clever of you girls to come here.'

The little one, sucking her thumb, burrowed deeper into Washburn's chest when Hirsch glanced at her. The older girl, Louise, glittered with hostility, waiting for Hirsch to show his true colours. He guessed she was thirteen or fourteen, with the temporary plumpness of early adolescence. Hirsch could picture her carrying Anna over the stony ground, all the way to the dust beside the road at Mischance Creek. He thought of Katie Street. She looked nothing like Katie, but she was similarly self-contained, a kid who played out the available options in her head before she acted. Right now, she was waiting and watching and keeping her trap well shut.

'Craig, are you sure no one else knows about the dugout?'

Washburn shook his head. 'I've never seen a soul out

here, not once, and the entrance is hard to spot from the creek. The girls are safe.'

'They can't stay here forever.'

A bird came to the mouth of the dugout, seemed startled to see them and flapped off again in a disturbance of feathers and beaten air. Anna jumped, briefly removed her thumb, sucked it again. Her shortie pyjamas needed a wash. Dust and scratches on her legs and feet.

Hirsch said, 'Louise, before we work out who does what, would you mind if I ask you a few questions?'

She continued to scowl at him. She wore pale blue shorts, a white boy-band T-shirt, socks and runners. Her legs were badly scratched. But he thought she gave a faint upwards tilt of her chin. He said, 'Anna was asleep in bed when it happened, but you were still up?'

This time, the ghost of a nod.

'When it was safe, you ran inside and grabbed her and carried her across the paddocks? That took a lot of strength and courage.'

Another tiny movement of her chin: pleased for the acknowledgment but not about to be taken for a sucker.

'What I *think* happened,' Hirsch said, 'it was Christmas Eve and you were in the car-shed with your mum, wrapping the'—he glanced at Anna—'wrapping a present to go under the tree, when someone arrived. Your mother went out to see who the visitor was, and...'

He trailed away. Louise Rennie finished for him: 'Mum screamed and there was shooting so I hid under the car.'

Craig Washburn pulled her tighter against him.

'A pair of sniffer dogs tracked you across the paddocks to the road where someone picked you up,' Hirsch said, with a glance at Washburn. 'How did you know to wait just there? How did you know it would be safe?'

'We didn't know. We just had to get away. Then a truck came along.'

'A truck.'

'A hay truck.'

Hirsch had been seeing them since October, drought-relief hay trucked in from Victoria and New South Wales. 'The driver picked you up?'

'Yes.'

'Had you seen him before?'

'He wasn't the man who came to our house,' Louise Rennie said, eyes narrowed, anticipating his thinking.

'Where did he take you?'

'Craig's.'

Hirsch thought about it. An interstate truck driver on a tight schedule, wanting to get home by Christmas morning, bemused to find a pair of kids at the side of the road asking to be taken to a caravan in the middle of nowhere. But Craig's campsite was tidy, and the solar panels and the old car would have shown the place to be inhabited. The man hadn't shown much duty of care—but nor had he harmed the girls. And, what with Christmas, maybe he'd missed the news or didn't connect picking up the girls with the shootings.

'You asked to be taken there?'

'Yes.' Louise Rennie stared at Hirsch, unflinching, straightforward, wary. She went on, 'We've known Craig for ages.'

'How?' said Hirsch, expecting Craig to interrupt.

'We were exploring the creek and ran into him.'

'And you've all been friends since then?'

She nodded.

'I showed you the dugout, didn't I girls?' Washburn said.

Louise touched his wrist.

Hirsch said, 'Okay. Let's go back to what happened at the house, Louise, is that okay? I don't want you to go into detail, I don't want...' He cleared his throat. 'But we need to catch whoever...hurt your mum and brother.'

Her voice hoarse and hollow, she said, 'Okay.' The wariness was still there but the hostility had gone.

'You were wrapping presents and you heard a vehicle arrive?'

'Yes.'

'Did you see what kind? A car or a ute or a four-wheel drive? A motorbike?'

'It was a ute.'

'So, a cabin for the driver and passenger at the front, and a tray for carrying stuff at the back?'

She frowned. 'I know what a ute is.'

Hirsch scooted a couple of centimetres sideways, seeking a smoother patch of wall for his spine. 'Your mum stepped out of the car-shed to see who it was?'

'We're always super-careful about visitors. Mum said, "Stay here," and when she pushed up the main door to go outside a man by the house ran back to the ute and brought out a gun.'

Cutting the phone line, Hirsch thought. 'The door was shut when I got there.'

'I shut it.'

'Why?'

She looked baffled. She shut it out of habit, he thought—but not until the killer had gone. 'Doesn't matter. Did you see what happened?'

'Mum ran around to the back door and the man chased her.'

The words tumbled out; her face collapsed, and, like her little sister, she burrowed hard against Craig Washburn.

Hirsch waited, feeling like a bully.

'You did the right thing, staying in the shed, love,' Washburn said.

She tilted her face to him. 'But I could've...' She didn't know what she could have done. She broke into tears again.

Hirsch said gently, 'And after a while you heard him drive away?'

'Yes.'

'Was he in the house for very long?'

'I don't know. Ten minutes? He came in the shed.'

'Looking for you?'

'I stayed under the car.'

'Thank goodness,' Hirsch said inadequately.

'He took stuff.'

'Took stuff?'

She nodded, trembling. 'Stole stuff. Nick's toolbox and... other things.'

She's reluctant to mention the bike, thought Hirsch. 'He left after that?'

Another nod. 'I went inside and saw Mum on the floor...'

She looked at him, a painful entreaty: she was saying that she hadn't checked on her brother.

Hirsch shifted uncomfortably, unable to conceal his distress, and she read it in him. Checking that her sister wasn't watching, she mouthed the words: '*He's dead?*'

Hirsch gave an abbreviated nod. She closed her eyes tightly.

To distract her, he said, 'Did you see the man's face clearly?'

'Fairly clearly.'

'Do you think you'd recognise him again?'

'Yes.'

Get her together with a forensic imaging specialist. Let her look at mouth, nose, chin, hairstyle and profile templates in the hope of creating a composite. 'There was only one man?'

'Two.'

'Two? Where was the other one?'

'He didn't get out. I could see him sitting in the ute.'

'The man who got out. Was he young? Old? Fat? Thin?'

'Do we have to do this now?' Craig Washburn said.

Hirsch felt chastened. 'Sorry, Louise. Too much, too soon. Let's—'

'It's okay.'

'Pet,' Washburn said, craning to look down at her as she craned to look up at him.

'It's okay,' she reassured him.

The other child said nothing but was curious, listening. Hirsch would have to be careful. If Anna had been woken by the shots, she might also have seen the shooter, who surely had checked the bedroom—and spared her life, through some skerrick of humanity. But would she be able to describe him?

He returned to Louise. 'Perhaps just give me a general impression?'

'He wasn't old, or fat or anything. Just normal.'

'Short or long hair? Beard?'

'No beard. Kind of short hair.'

'What was he wearing?'

'Jeans and a shirt.'

'How about the other man? Would you recognise him if you saw him again?'

'No.'

'How long were they at your place altogether?'

She shrugged. 'Not long.'

'Can you describe the gun?'

'It was long.'

'A rifle?'

'Yes.'

Hirsch took out his phone and showed her the David McAuliffe licence photo. 'Is this the man?'

She peered. 'No. Who is he?'

How much to tell her? 'His name's Ian Lavau. He was staying in tourist accommodation not all that far from here.'

She craned her head towards the mouth of the cave, as if Lavau might appear there. 'He's dead, someone shot him,' Hirsch said.

She began to crumple. 'What's happening? They're every-where. How did they find us again?'

'We need to get you kids somewhere safer than this,' Hirsch said.

'No!'

She was breathless, close to panic. Hoping it would reassure her, Hirsch walked in a crouch to the lip of the dugout and peered both ways along the creek. No one. He returned to the mattress. 'There's no one out there. It's safe. I'm parked at Craig's caravan, we can walk there in a few minutes.'

'No! We need to stay hidden.'

Then, as Hirsch watched, she grew calm. Gave herself a shake, swallowed, and said, firmly, 'No.'

'Well. Let's return to the other night: you okay with that?'

A curt nod.

'Did you stay in the car-shed for very long after the men had left?'

She shook her head. 'I could hear Anna screaming.'

Hirsch felt his eyes moisten. 'You raced in, grabbed Anna and ran off over the paddocks, where a truck picked you up.'

Washburn broke in. 'You did the right thing, going to the caravan.'

Louise Rennie tucked herself against him. 'You're my safe place.'

Hirsch blinked. Washburn's eyes watered, too.

'And you've been here ever since?'

'We sneak down to Craig's when we need stuff and have a shower.'

'Clever girls,' Washburn said. 'The dugout's perfect: safe, sheltered, and no one knows about it.'

'They can't stay here forever, Craig.'

'We'll work something out.'

'You don't understand. The search has been wound back, but people are still looking. The girls need to be checked over and then we can put them with a relative or a family friend, someone they know and trust. And I'm afraid they'll have to answer a few more questions from people more senior and experienced than me.'

He turned to Louise. 'We need to get you somewhere comfortable, with a bathroom, proper beds, people to look after you.'

'This is safe! Out there's not!'

Hirsch turned to Washburn for support but Craig shook his head. 'The wrong people know that the girls are unaccounted for.'

Hirsch shrugged.

Washburn persisted. 'And these same people know that Louise is old enough to be a reliable witness.'

He's not stupid, Hirsch thought. He gave the girls an uneasy look. 'We don't know that anyone's after them in particular.'

Washburn seemed disappointed in him. 'Don't we?'

'Craig, let's get the girls in the hands of the police as soon as possible.'

'We can't trust the police!' Louise Rennie shouted. She was ragged, snotty, furious and frustrated.

'But what about your mother's friend? Vita? They worked

together.' Hirsch took out his phone, found the image of Roesch and Hansen in his sitting room. 'This is her. She arrived here from Sydney a few days ago. She's worried about you.'

Louise Rennie glanced at his phone with her face half-averted as if fearing an attack. She shook her head, uttered a mad, choked laugh and shrank away. 'You're not listening to me.'

'The man sitting next to Ms Roesch. Know him?'

'No.'

'On Christmas Day my sergeant received a call from a policeman in Sydney asking us to check on you. Could it have been him? Was your mother in contact with anyone there?'

She was rocking in distress. 'Yes, but I don't know who. She bought a satellite phone.'

That explained the lack of Sydney calls from the Hamel Road house. No satellite phone had been found. Stolen, presumably, along with the toolbox and the bike.

Louise Rennie was pointing heatedly at Hirsch's phone. 'Are they outside? Did you bring them here? Did they follow you?'

'No,' Hirsch said, harsh and definite. 'They're in Redruth. There's no reason for them to be interested in anything I'm doing, and I didn't even know about you and Craig or this place till half an hour ago.'

She shoved her jaw at him. 'I don't trust any police.'

'Louise,' Hirsch said, shaking his head in frustration. He looked at her. 'Did you think the man who came to your house on Christmas Eve was a policeman?'

'Maybe. Probably.'

'You can trust most of us, Louise.'

Washburn interrupted. 'Better hear her out, Paul.'

Hirsch shrugged. 'Go ahead. Start at the beginning. Why was your family placed in witness protection?'

Louise Rennie took a breath, released it again, a way of ordering her thoughts. Then she started, rattling it off: 'Our real name is Reid. We used to live in Sydney. Mum and Dad were in the police. Dad was just in the Dog Squad, but Mum was an analyst. She worked on big cases. One night we all had to pack a bag and some people took us to this town up near Moree. They said it was only for a while, till Mum gave evidence in court. We couldn't text or call or Facebook. We had to be home-schooled, never went out, never went any-where.' She looked away. 'Then one day someone shot Dad.'

Washburn interrupted. 'He was home when normally Denise would have been. She'd have been the target. Someone leaked their location. Someone in the police. So you can see why Louise doesn't know who to trust.'

'I can see that,' Hirsch said, even as he was thinking: What if the husband was the intended target? What if it had been a local crime—he'd had an affair in Moree, for example? 'But I hope you can trust me,' he added.

All three looked at him as if he were the last person they'd trust. He shrugged and said, 'Why wasn't your mother there that day?'

'Usually she would've been, and Dad would've been at work—he did some gardening for the shire—but he was home sick.'

'And your mother left the house...'

'To do some shopping. Normally she didn't go out.'

'Where were you kids?'

Louise was scraping shapes in the dirt with her big toe. 'We went with her in the car.'

'How did you know what happened to your dad?'

More patterns in the dirt. 'We came back from shopping and there was a police car there, so we just drove past and then a bit later heard it on the news. Didn't dare go back.'

Hirsch tried to see the world through Denise Rennie's eyes. Even as a civilian analyst, she'd have known all about the lies, whispers, nods and handshakes that glued a police force together. So, she disappeared with her children into her own version of witness protection.

'How did you end up here, in particular?'

'Mum grew up in Broken Hill,' Louise said, as if that explained it. Perhaps it did, Hirsch thought. Broken Hill was dry country not so many hours north of Tiverton, and many Broken Hill families holidayed in Adelaide, which meant driving through the mid-north.

'Did your mother contact anyone after you came here? Your witness-protection handlers, for example?'

'Not for ages.'

'But she was speaking to someone more recently?'

Louise nodded. 'She started saying, "We need to come in, we can't live out here forever." But I don't know who she was talking to or what they said. All she said to us was, until she could work something out, we were on our own. We couldn't trust anyone.' She glanced up at Washburn. 'Except Craig.'

Hirsch tried to imagine their lives. Cut off from everything and everyone they knew. Home-schooled. Quick in-and-out trips to town. The kids walking along the creek to visit a crazy old man.

'You had enough money to live on?'

'Mum says it's starting to run out,' Louise said. Tears spilled. '*Said* it was running out.'

And before they could come in out of the cold, Denise Rennie was spotted, by the wrong people, on YouTube. 'Louise, we need to think of something more secure than this. I should tell my boss. She's a good person.'

'No! If you do, we'll just run away again.'

'I'm sure I could find somewhere safe for the meantime, while we work out who to trust.'

As he said it, Hirsch had doubts. It wouldn't matter where he took the girls, they'd be spotted eventually; someone would say something. And he didn't want to ask a favour of anyone close to him, risk the lives of Wendy and Katie, the Muirs', his parents or Nan Washburn. Child Protection? Any government agency would leak like a sieve.

'Let me put my thinking cap on. I'll get back in touch later today.'

'Don't trust *anyone*,' Louise Rennie said, the conviction hard in her.

Hirsch made one last try. 'I have a police friend named Rosie whose job is investigating corrupt police. I trust her. She'll find somewhere safe for you and keep it under the radar until we find a more permanent solution.'

'No.' Louise went rigid. 'No police.'

'We're not all villains, Louise.'

'Even if that's true,' she retorted, 'Mum said the police have to follow procedures. Things get written down and put in files. You can't keep a lid on it.'

Hirsch pictured Denise Rennie talking to her kids deep into the night. Her paranoia catching: *Don't trust anyone.* Except the family had put some trust in Craig Washburn. And right now, Hirsch thought, I've also been granted a smidgin of trust.

'Louise, are you going to grow old in this cave?'

A cheap shot, and she was disgusted. 'There's only one way we'll show ourselves.'

'What's that?'

'When you lock up everyone responsible. All of them.'

Hirsch thought about it. Did he keep their location a secret for now? He visualised the killer more as a force than a person—malign but diffuse, floating out in the back country somewhere, poised at any second to take on a clear shape and pounce. And a checklist had been drilled into him at the academy. Before acting, a good cop will ask: will it pass scrutiny? Is it lawful? Is it ethical? Is it fair?

He didn't get far with his thinking because just then the creek started to sing. The rounded stones below the dugout entrance were tocking, scraping, grinding. Louise scuttled to the lip of the dugout, came back at once, hyperventilating. 'It's him. The one who...the one on Christmas Eve.'

Hirsch scrambled half-bent to the entrance and dropped to his belly. He peered out.

Wayne Flann.

29

The windscreen flash Hirsch had seen from the road: Flann's ute. Reminding himself to study a topographical map should the creek ever feature in some future crime, search party or picnic, he watched Flann cast about, alert, as he receded in the direction of Craig Washburn's camp. Flann was dressed as before, the rifle strapped to one shoulder. His T-shirt was dark with sweat and dotted with flies. Dust on his jeans. Without the rifle, you might overlook him, a bush drongo like any other. To Hirsch he was as sharp and poised as a dart.

Flann disappeared around a bend. He'll see the police Toyota before long, Hirsch thought, and wonder what it was doing there. Or he'll spot the dugout entrance on his way back.

Hirsch shuffled back to the others, murmured, 'Stay here, don't show yourselves to anyone, don't make a sound. If anyone other than me calls out your names, ignore them.'

Then he was dropping into the bed of the creek. But the

stones were noisy under his boots, so he climbed onto the bank, passing through dead grass that whispered against his trousers. Even so, he was posed against the sky. And there were snakes. Hirsch shuddered. He was trained for street shadowing and surveillance and couldn't relate any of it to tracking someone in the bush.

He checked his phone: no signal. The terrain grew rougher, more difficult. Where the creek was shallow, Flann's head and shoulders would appear above the bank and Hirsch would duck. He passed through the stabbing spines of star thistles, over a limestone reef, around a stretch of rabbit burrows and a handful of deeper, more treacherous holes that he guessed were collapsing mine shafts. A snake flicked into movement and reared. Hirsch bolted.

Slid over the bank to the noisy safety of the creek bed. Began to pick his way carefully, keeping off the stones as much as possible, looking for stretches of sand. Two reedy waterholes put him temporarily on the bank again. Looking down, he saw a yabby disappear, disturbing his soulless reflection in the water. His pistol was in his hand, he realised, safety off. He'd trip and shoot himself if he wasn't careful. He reholstered the gun and carried on.

He couldn't hear his quarry. He judged that Craig's caravan was about a hundred metres ahead. He tried to get inside Flann's skin, his thoughts jumping madly. Wayne was here to mop up. The killings had had nothing to do with Sydney or witness protection. It was a nasty, brainless local crime.

It felt to Hirsch that he was picking his way over

booby-trapped eggshells. He reached the final bend. Heard the music of the stones ahead and—too late—found himself only a few metres from Wayne Flann, who was turning towards him.

Startled, Flann shrugged the rifle strap from his shoulder, swung the barrel tip towards Hirsch and stepped back onto a stone that turned under his heel.

His ankle buckled. He grunted, winced with pain, and placed all his weight on the other foot as he tried to work a cartridge into the breech and, in the same movement, nestle the rifle butt into his shoulder. He tipped to one side, his footing unstable as he fired, and the shot went wide.

Hirsch was moving, already on him, deflecting the barrel, powering his shoulder into Flann's mid-section. They bounced apart again, slipping and slithering and windmilling for balance, almost comic. Toppling slowly onto his back, Hirsch propped himself on his elbows and hooked his right foot behind Flann's injured ankle. Flann flipped onto his spine, the fall driving the breath from his lungs, and Hirsch was on him again.

Grinding the barrel of his pistol under the man's jaw, Hirsch said, 'Wayne Flann, I am arresting you for assaulting a police officer and for the murders of Denise and Nick Rennie.'

A twist of savagery on Flann's face. Then it cleared, replaced by his usual sleepy-eyed charm. Almost as if he might seduce Hirsch into some harmless shared wickedness. 'Jeez, Paul, didn't mean to shoot at you. We're mates, right? I'm out here looking for those kids. No one's thought to search this part of the creek. Suddenly I hear someone coming and I think, shit, who's that, the killer? Bit quick on the draw; sorry buddy.'

Hirsch ignored him. Took the handcuffs from his belt and manacled Flann, right wrist to left ankle.

'Jesus, how am I supposed to walk?'

'You're not. You're staying put for a few minutes.'

Hirsch patted him down briskly. Found keys, a wallet and an old Samsung phone in the front pockets of his jeans.

Flann smirked. 'That how you get your kicks?'

Hirsch turned him over; nothing in the tight back pockets. Rolled Flann onto his back again, stepped clear of him and checked the Samsung. It was locked.

He tilted the screen towards Flann. 'Password?

'Fuck you.'

'Something you don't want me to see?'

'Fuck you. Get a warrant.'

'Wayne, I found the girls. You were recognised.' He wondered, too late, if he should have kept his mouth shut.

As if unable to stop himself, Flann said, 'The dugout, right? My old man said—'

Then his face shut down. 'Time for me to go no comment. No comment from here till fucking eternity.'

'Who was in the ute with you the other night? Was it Adam? Is that why he's disappeared? Couldn't stomach what you'd done?'

'No comment.'

'Wait here.'

'No fucking comment.'

Hirsch set out to fetch the HiLux. First secure his prisoner, then deal with the Rennie girls.

Five minutes later, parked beside the creek, he shoved Flann up the bank and into the boxy prisoner-transport compartment in the back of the Toyota. Snug, white inside and out, no windows, no sharp surfaces. Stifling just now, but the car aircon was ducted through. Flann would survive.

Before locking him away, Hirsch twisted the cap off a bottle of water and handed it over. 'It's not a bribe, it's not poisoned, no added truth serum.'

Flann showed a flash of bewilderment and curiosity. Then his empty, no-comment face reappeared and he merely stared at Hirsch, received the bottle with an abbreviated nod, and drank deeply—an unguarded action, and when he'd taken it from his lips, face regaining its composure, Hirsch snapped his photograph.

'You cunt.'

Hirsch smiled, handed him a second bottle. 'Make yourself comfortable.'

'I get claustrophobic.'

Hirsch got behind the wheel, aircon on high, and checked the CCTV feed: Flann looked resigned but was muttering fuck and cunt and copper a lot.

'That's the spirit,' Hirsch murmured, and bumped the Toyota across the dirt and grass until he reached the dugout. Leaving the aircon and engine running, handbrake on, he slapped his palm against the box and shouted, 'Back in a few minutes.'

Flann began to shout, kick the walls. 'I'm dying in here. I'm claustrophobic, you fucking arsehole.'

The Toyota protested meekly, rocking on its springs. 'Few minutes,' Hirsch shouted.

He climbed down to the bed of the creek, stood beneath the dugout and called, 'It's Paul, you're safe now, he's locked up.'

He scaled the bank. At the dugout entrance he said it again: 'I arrested him. He can't get at you. He's locked away.'

Craig Washburn gave one of his vacant grins, Anna sucked her thumb, eyes wide, and Louise was suspicious. 'How do we know?'

'Here.' Hirsch swiped at his phone, showed her the screen.

She peered briefly and nestled back in against Washburn. 'Who is he? Police?'

'He's called Wayne Flann. He lives near Tiverton. Did you ever have anything to do with him? Was he ever at your house? Did your mum, I don't know, cut him off in a carpark? Anything like that?'

She shook her head. 'No.'

Then her face creased; grief and bewilderment saturated her voice. 'Why would he want to kill us?'

Hirsch touched the back of her hand. 'I honestly don't know. I think he and possibly his brother liked to go around breaking into houses on quiet back roads and this time it was your bad luck. Maybe this time he was high on drugs, I don't know. The thing is, there's no need for you girls to stay here now. Hop in the car, I'll take you somewhere safe.'

She shook her head wildly. 'No way.'

'We won't go anywhere near any police, okay? We'll figure out somewhere safe you can go, then I'll get your statement and we'll start an investigation.'

She shrieked it. 'Start an *investigation*? While people can see us sitting in your car? And you said that man you arrested has a brother? Where is he? Is he coming after us, too? We're staying here. Craig'll look after us.'

Hirsch was patient. 'You'll be safe travelling with me. There's plenty of room and—'

Her voice rose an impossible notch. '*You honestly think we're riding in the same car as him?*'

Anna took her thumb from her mouth, her face wretched, and began to wail. 'Shhh,' her sister said. 'Sorry, bub.'

Hirsch, looking to Washburn for help, saw only a benign, philosophical beam on the old creased face, and a tiny shrug that said: *What can you do, eh?*

Hirsch sighed. 'Will you at least let me contact my friend in the police in Adelaide? The one who polices the police. She's straight, she's honest, she has no contacts with anyone in New South Wales...'

Louise gave it some reluctant thought, rolling her shoulders. 'Maybe.'

'How about this?' Hirsch said. 'I take Mr Flann to jail and come straight back and collect you and drive you to Adelaide. I won't say anything to anybody about finding you. We'll put you somewhere safe until everyone involved has been arrested.'

Another 'maybe' shrug.

'You can't stay here, Louise. You just can't. Another week?

296

Out of the question. Think of Anna. Think of yourself. Food, clean clothes, a proper bathroom, proper bed...'

'Sounds like a plan to me, girls,' Washburn said. An arm around each sister, he rocked them gently, looking down at the tops of their heads. 'What do you think?'

Louise Rennie looked directly at Hirsch as she answered him. 'I think if Paul comes back, we might be okay. And if he doesn't it means they've got him.'

30

As Hirsch headed away from the creek, past Craig's camp and out along the track, it occurred to him how unwise it would be to hand Wayne Flann over to the Homicide Squad in Redruth right now. Or even to Sergeant Brandl. As soon as the arrest was made public, everyone would get wind of the Rennie girls. Flann himself would probably broadcast the story that he'd merely been looking for them and how come Hirsch wasn't telling anyone he'd found them? Meanwhile if a killer was still lurking, time was an issue. Taking Flann down to Redruth, booking him in and answering inconvenient questions would eat too much of it. The sooner the girls were secure, the better.

Reaching the wagon wheel at the turnoff and seeing that he had two signal bars, Hirsch pulled over and called Bob Muir. Flann immediately began shouting and kicking the wall panels.

Hirsch muted the CCTV. Now he could hear Bob's voice in his ear: 'Well if it isn't the local law.'

'Are you at home?'

'Working in the shed.'

'Are you free for a couple of hours? I need you to babysit Wayne Flann.'

Muir didn't waste time on incredulous questions. 'Where?'

'What used to be the lockup.' A room at the rear of the Tiverton police station, now used for storage but still fitted with good locks and a barred window.

'When?'

'I'll be there in half an hour,' Hirsch said.

'Okay.'

'He knows you,' Hirsch said. 'Sit in a chair, read a book, talk to him, give him water and food. I don't want him hanging himself with a shoelace.'

'What's he done?'

'Shot Mrs Rennie and her son.'

A pause. 'Okay.'

'See you soon,' Hirsch said, but he'd lost his signal.

Clear in his mind now, Hirsch turned onto the Tiverton road and cranked up the speed. Using the old hayshed as a marker, he glanced out of the other side window and caught a brief glimpse of Flann's ute down beside the creek. He'd secure it when he got back. Have a forensic team test it for blood traces, fibres; stolen goods from the night of the shootings.

He drove on, his mind turning to Rosie DeLisle. Would she help him hide the girls? What if she played it by the book? Or went into full-scale major-operation mode, informing everyone—including a work colleague who might happen to let it slip to a Sydney colleague involved in the original witness protection betrayal? Better to turn up in Adelaide unannounced, he thought.

He checked his phone: still no signal, and it stayed that way until he was ten minutes from Tiverton. On three bars, he pulled over again. Flann kicked the side panels. Finding Gemma Pitcher in his contacts list, Hirsch texted the photo of his prisoner in cuffs, saying: *Wayne locked up. Safe 2 come home.*

Soon after he pulled back onto the road, his phone rang. Gemma's number on the screen.

He tucked the Toyota into a farm gateway and accepted the call. 'Gemma.'

'You've really got him?'

'Yes.'

'You know what he done, right?'

'Yes.'

'Adam says if you can get into Wayne's phone there are some photos.'

'Ah. Excellent.'

'He can't get away?'

'No.'

'They won't let him out? You know, on a technical whatever?'

'No.'

A long pause. In the lockbox, Flann yelled and kicked the walls.

Gemma said, 'Adam was with him, but he never shot no one and he didn't know Wayne would do it and now he's scared he'll go to jail.'

'I'll look after Adam, that's a promise,' Hirsch said. 'But the three of you need to come in. Everyone's worried.'

Another pause and Gemma said, 'Maybe tomorrow.' Then she was gone.

With Flann's phone stowed in the office safe and Flann secure in the old lockup, supplied with Pepsi, a microwaved supermarket pizza and the company of Bob Muir, perched on an Ikea garden chair, Hirsch got behind the wheel again and headed out of town. His phone rang: a number he didn't recognise.

'Paul?'

Sergeant Brandl. Should he tell her about the Rennie girls and Wayne Flann? Not yet. 'Yes, sergeant?'

'I'm on an incident-room phone. Apparently we had a call from a truck driver an hour ago.'

'Truck driver...' Hirsch said, and he knew at once. The air grew chill around him.

'A hay carter from Tamworth. Seems he wandered into his local cop shop to say he'd only just heard about the Rennie kids. Said he was on his way back to New South Wales on Christmas Eve after delivering a load of hay to a station out east of Tiverton and gave a lift to a couple of kids who might have been them.'

'An hour ago? Sarge, I—'

'He gave the coordinates.' She recited them to him. 'Can you check it out? I can't spare anyone. Inspector Kellaher's gone back to the city, Sergeant Dock's at lunch, I have no idea where our Sydney friends are, and the children and I are flat chat.'

Hirsch accelerated, driving with one hand on the wheel, the Toyota juddering on a narrow road shouldered with talc-like dust and loose gravel. 'Who talked to the truckie, sarge?'

'One of the support staff. I'll put her on. Let me know how you go.'

There were phone-fumbling sounds. Hirsch pictured one of the civilians at a desk in the town hall, logging information into a computer. He said, 'Hello?'

'What can I do you for?'

'Sergeant Brandl said you took the call from the truck driver?'

'From someone at the Tamworth police station originally, then the truck driver, and when I realised what he was talking about, I passed the phone to one of the Sydney detectives.'

'Which one?'

'I think his name's Hansen.'

'What did he do?'

'Took off straight away.'

An hour ago. 'Did he say where he was going?'

Hirsch could hear a shrug in her voice. 'To check it out, presumably.'

'Alone, or with Senior Sergeant Roesch?'

'That one?' scoffed the woman. 'She came barrelling up a few minutes later, wanting to know where he was off to.'

'And she also left?'

'Just grabbed the coordinates and took off. Rude cow.'

To head off Hansen before he hurt the girls.

Hirsch tried calling Roesch. No answer and his signal kept

cutting out. He reached for the radio handset—no, the cord was still cactus.

The minutes passed. He increased speed; the temperature gauge rose—the radiator, he thought. Cleaning off dust and chaff was on his to-do list, which was long. Cleaning the radiator had been on it for at least two months now.

The sun beat down. Mirages shimmered, vanished, renewed themselves further along the road. The distant hills were grey-blue, the closer hills mottled: dead grass, a dirt underlay and stone reef striations. The Toyota shuddered on the corrugations. Dust boiled in his wake. Then he was braking, swerving, straddling a lizard. He sped on, checking the rear-view mirror. No roadkill, thank god. He'd been responsible for a few squashed creatures in his time and wasn't yet blasé about it, unlike the locals.

Finally he was slowing at the wagon wheel and bumping down the track to Craig Washburn's caravan—where a car was parked. One of the patrol cars on loan to the investigation; driven, presumably, by Hansen. No sign of Roesch's rental car. Hirsch got out, locked up and headed for the creek.

Then stopped. One hand went to the butt of his service pistol.

A gunshot. Curiously flat, as if contained by the creek, but with an echo that snapped around the sky.

31

But the shot had come from the direction of the old ruins, not the dugout. Hirsch thought about that; decided it made sense. Downstream was all untamed nature, and city-boy Hansen would have been drawn by instinct to signs of civilisation—the old ruins—after searching Craig's camp.

Had he stumbled on Craig and the girls? Had something persuaded them to leave the dugout? Or was Hansen shooting it out with Roesch? Had Roesch parked at the ruins and walked downstream?

Hirsch thought all of these things in an instant but, before he could take another step there was a shriek—a man's voice—followed by a flurry of shots, so rapid they spelt panic or anger. Or sheer enjoyment.

Another shriek—unearthly, despairing. Hansen? Craig Washburn? He ran, and as he ran the shrieking faded, dissolving into something more like keening: a sound of loss, or of grief. No other voices.

Arms spread for balance, Hirsch picked his way over the

stones. Faster when he reached a stretch of sand, slowing at pools of brackish water collared by bulrushes. At each bend he'd pause to dart a quick glance at the stretch ahead. No sense in tearing blindly around a corner and getting a bullet in his belly. But there was no sign of Hansen. Surely he could hear Hirsch coming?

He powered on, dreading the next bend, and the next, his shoes clicking and rattling on the impenitent stones. There was silence for some time, then a low, distressed moan, close by now. Reaching the next bend, Hirsch stuck his head around. A shot whanged past his cheek, spitting dust and grit into his eyes.

'Jesus.' He jerked back, reeled, sat.

Touched himself gingerly. A trace of blood on his finger-tips; a coarse paste of dust and tears in the corner of one eye. He blinked, trying to make sense of what he'd just seen: Hansen, wearing shorts, sandals and a short-sleeved shirt, on the ground, propped on his elbows. No one else.

Unholstering his gun, he called, 'Rob?'

A pause, and Hansen croaked, 'I thought you were Vita coming for me.'

Hirsch thought about that. He said, 'Where are the girls?'

'No idea.'

'What was all the shooting?'

Hansen moaned. 'A snake bit me. More than once.'

Hirsch's insides curdled. He found himself listening—for what, he didn't know.

'You shot it?'

'Killed it.'

'Rob, could you put the gun down? I'm coming to help you.'

'What if there's another one?' fretted Hansen, sounding loosely wrapped. 'What if there's a mate?'

Keeping his tone mild and even, Hirsch said, 'Look around. Do you see another one?'

A pause. 'No.'

'Okay, I'm coming. Don't shoot.'

Hirsch chanced a quick look first. Hansen was still on his back, the pistol loose in one hand, looking down along his body to his sandalled feet, where the snake was draped sinuously over the bloodied creek stones. A potent-looking force even in death.

Hansen turned to Hirsch. Startled by the grimness etched in the man's face, Hirsch ducked.

'I'm not going to shoot you,' Hansen said, looking down at the snake again.

Hirsch reholstered his gun. 'Okay.'

He crossed the ground, crouched, removed a little Glock from Hansen's slack fingers, all the time with one eye on the snake. The head looked hacked about—pistol bullets at close range—but he recognised it as a brown, one of the most poisonous on the continent, a metre and a half long and almost as thick as his forearm. More deaths from a brown than any other snake. And to be bitten several times...

Hansen had shot himself in the foot, too.

Hirsch stood up, stepped over to the snake. Steeled himself, and flipped it away with his shoe.

'I must've trod on it,' Hansen said, trembling, dusty tear

tracks on his cheeks. 'It just kept biting me, so I shot it. I don't feel very good.'

Hirsch crouched again, put a hand to Hansen's forehead. Clammy. He examined the pale legs: a mix of scratches and puncture wounds.

Hansen said dazedly, 'Help me stand. I'll drive myself to hospital.'

Hirsch pressed gently down on his shoulder. 'You need to keep still. Movement increases the blood flow.'

Hansen screwed up his face. He seemed to be breaking down. 'Have you got a knife? Cut open the bites?'

'They don't do that anymore.'

'Ambulance.'

Hirsch felt his jitters vanish, a cool pragmatism settling in him. Hansen would probably die: too much venom, too late, too far from medical help. 'Rob, I need to know: you shot Lavau, and you're here to shoot the kids for some reason?'

'What? No!' In all of his wretchedness, Hansen was shocked. 'Not me. *Roesch*. I need to get to them before she does.'

32

Hirsch crouched, wondering if he and Hansen were about to become the fulcrum of each other's worlds. He shaded Hansen's face with his hat, and asked the question.

'Why?'

Hansen's voice weakened. 'The older girl can ID her as the one who shot her father.'

And I showed her a photo of Roesch sitting on my sofa, Hirsch thought. No wonder she was on edge.

Hansen, staring dazedly at the snake, now looked up at Hirsch. 'Do you know where the girls are? Have you always known?'

'Found them this morning,' Hirsch said. He explained about Craig and the dugout.

Hansen coughed. 'They've been there the whole time?'

'Yes.' Hirsch paused. 'Rob, I need to see they're all right.'

Hansen was agitated. 'I know she's coming,' he said, the words tangling on lips and tongue. 'You need to watch out.'

Hirsch glanced back along the creek, undecided.

Hansen—or Craig and the girls? 'I've got pressure bandages in the car. I'll run you to hospital. But I need to check the dugout.'

'Go,' Hansen said, rallying, then he leaned to one side and vomited neatly, unfussily, a thin gruel that darkened the dirt. The acrid smell rose. He lifted his head to Hirsch and croaked, 'Go.'

Hirsch stood. 'I'll be right back.'

Hansen gasped, 'Feel pretty bad, mate. My head. I'm going to chuck again.'

Hirsch had no knowledge of the mechanics of snakebite death. Given the amount of venom in Hansen, a cardiac arrest of some kind? Very soon? He squeezed Hansen's shoulder. 'I'll call an ambulance, we'll meet it halfway.'

Call triple-zero as soon as he had mobile reception, is what he meant. He couldn't radio it in, with the HiLux's radio still fucked. A repair job for Bob Muir...Christ, why was he thinking that at a time like this? 'Sit tight,' he said. He placed his hat gently over the flushed face.

Then he ran, checking the grass and the dirt the whole way: snake-watching ingrained in him now. And as he ran, he recast Roesch's second visit to his little suite of rooms behind the police station. She'd been trying to get him on-side and Hansen offside. He was supposed to distrust Hansen, and warm to her because she'd confided in him. And she'd have wanted him close, because he was closest to everything that had happened. He'd met Denise and her youngest kid, he'd found the bodies. For all she knew, he was hiding something or unwittingly holding some key information. A person steeped in secrecy and manipulation would expect secrecy and manipulation in others, he thought.

Stumbling past the caravan—still no sign of Roesch's car—he continued downstream to the dugout. Waiting a moment, hoping they'd heard him, he called softly, 'Craig? Louise?'

Nothing. Gone already. Or lying there dead. Sick, jittery, Hirsch clambered up the hand- and footholds. Reached the lip of the dugout, chanced a quick look in. Empty. Climbed down again.

They must have left as soon as he'd driven off with Wayne Flann. Louise and her poker face. Despite his fine words, she knew why Vita Roesch had come. She knew it wasn't finished.

Hirsch had to trust them to be safe, to be wise. He ran back to the HiLux and bumped along the creek bank to where he'd left Hansen. Fished around for the pressure bandages and bottled water and slid down into the creek where Hansen lay unmoving.

Dead.

Hirsch checked for a pulse, but it was unmistakeable. Hansen lay in the loose, collapsed attitude of death, flat on his back, eyes open, head angled to one side. He'd vomited again: a crusty mess of it around his mouth, down his shirt front and on the ground. And he'd evidently tried to call for help: one hand, slack in death, nursed his mobile phone.

Hirsch retrieved it, the movement animating the screen, revealing Hansen's final action. Not calling. Recording.

Hirsch took out his own phone, checking automatically for reception, and began to photograph the dead man and the site of his death. The legs, the riddled snake, the blood-splashed stones. Then he hauled Hansen up the bank and draped him along the back seat of the HiLux and strapped him in. He glanced uneasily along the creek. There was no need to rush now—not for Hansen. But Roesch...

He'd call for backup when he had a signal. Right now he needed to find Craig and the girls.

They would have run downstream, not back to Craig's camp—the first place someone like Roesch might look—so he drove along the creek as far as he could go. Wayne Flann's ute was parked in a patch of dead grass—both doors open, windows down, curiously. Hirsch got out, approached cautiously: no one inside it, no loose ignition wires. The ground was baked too hard for shoe prints, but that didn't mean the girls and Craig hadn't been here. Meanwhile, any evidence it might contain could be contaminated or degraded by the sun, the wind and the dust that forever lifted from the plains. He wound up the windows, shut the doors.

The terrain beyond the ute was impassable, the creek petering out. Hirsch felt the perversity of the day: a sense of control removed from him; of waiting for something worse to happen. All he could think to do was drive, and he found himself bumping along in Flann's wheel tracks across the dirt and grass to a gate on the Tiverton road, the smell of vomit hanging in the air.

The hayshed. He parked between the gate posts and ran across to the listing walls. The hay was rotting but he found a hidden nest among the bales; an empty spring-water bottle, not a speck of dust on it.

Where now? Prowl up and down the roads? Their instinct would be to head for Tiverton. Back in the Toyota, he placed Hansen's phone in the bracket on his dashboard, and set it to play the man's dying declaration.

At first, only ambient sounds crackled from the little speaker: a breeze in the grass stalks; a tree heat-flexing; a crow cawing. Then Hansen's voice emerged: slow, reedy, a man becoming weak.

Denise Rennie, he said, was a New South Wales police civilian analyst working with Federal Police and Vita Roesch and other Major Crimes detectives on a large-scale arms and drugs smuggling ring comprising immigration agents, bikie gangs, Border Force officers and bent police. Along with the smuggling there were ancillary crimes including extortion, bribery and money laundering.

At the midpoint of the investigation, an attempt was made on Rennie's life—she was shot at by a motorbike pillion passenger—and the family was placed in witness protection near the town of Moree, in northern New South Wales, until the trials.

Six weeks later her husband, Neil, was shot dead at home.

Normally he'd not have been there—he worked part-time for the shire—but he and the older girl, Louise, were home sick. Louise witnessed the shooting and recognised the shooter as her mother's work colleague, Vita Roesch. She escaped from the house with a mobile phone and called her mother, who was out shopping with the other children.

The family fled. They made no contact with anyone for eighteen months. 'Except,' Hansen said, slurring his words, 'Denise made a classic angry-idiotic move—she called Roesch and told her she was going down. You could say Vita was highly motivated after that.'

Roesch, a major player in the very crime ring she was investigating, was in a position to manage the flow and storage of information. She'd have known when Denise Rennie was getting too close.

'Then back in October,' Hansen said, 'Denise made contact with us.'

She was cagey and she was patient: started with untraceable thirty-second calls from public phones to her dead husband's Dog Squad friends. Quick, in-and-out questions, random times of the day and night, until she reached Hansen's boss and decided she trusted him. Hirsch imagined those calls: she must have driven all over the state looking for phone boxes.

'The money was running out and she was lonely I guess, and sick of living out in the sticks and worried about her kids' futures,' Hansen said, 'but mainly she was pissed off about something she'd read online.'

Her old case, adjourned when she disappeared, had been reopened in a watered-down form: minor charges only, against a handful of baggage handlers and couriers. What about the main players? What had happened to all that evidence she'd gathered?

'Vita Roesch happened to it,' Hansen said. He coughed, spat, groaned.

Then Denise had dropped her bombshells. Not only had she saved some of that evidence to cloud storage but her daughter could ID Roesch as the shooter of her husband.

'The boss set up a team to investigate Roesch. Small, hush-hush.'

Hansen became Denise Rennie's point of contact. He talked her through ways to bring the family in. How their ongoing safety would be secured. How Roesch and anyone involved with her would be kept in the dark.

'This went on for about three weeks. She was paranoid about wiretaps, call monitoring, email hacking, so I talked her into getting a satellite phone.' A pause while Hansen coughed wetly. 'I don't know where it is now. It wasn't at the house, and Lavau didn't have it.'

Here Hirsch experienced an odd sense of time and place dislocation. Hansen hadn't known about Wayne Flann.

Finally, Denise Rennie revealed her address and Hansen obtained a number for Sergeant Brandl, just in case. Then, less than a week later, the Hamel Road murders. Hansen was sent to South Australia to monitor Roesch and safeguard the girls, if they could be found.

Hirsch imagined Roesch's eighteen months of gnawing anxiety—and then, the YouTube post, like a gift from god. She sends Lavau, but by the time he reaches the mid-north, Wayne Flann's been and gone. Lavau would have reported back to Roesch, saying that whoever had shot Denise and Nick Rennie had either snatched the daughters or let them escape. What would Roesch have made of that? Someone in the organisation acting on their own initiative—one of her bikie mates going rogue? She would have told Lavau to stay put, keep his eyes and ears open, until her arrival. Her reason for being there? Ostensibly to safeguard the smuggling-ring investigation; actually to contain and mop up. And work out what the hell was going on.

'She tried to seize Denise's computers et cetera, but your people wouldn't have it.'

Hansen's voice grew weaker. 'There never was a man in a silver Passat. Classic Roesch misdirection. But Lavau was part of it and I think she shot him. He'd have been a liability if you'd caught him that day. I remember she made herself scarce for a few hours.'

A long silence. Then: 'Christ, I feel like shit. Head hurts. And I...ah...coupla things you need to know. I looked into Lavau yesterday. He was at the academy with Roesch. Twenty years ago, no contact since. But his file says he went to Barrenjoey High School. That's a name you don't forget... anyway, back when Neil Rennie was shot, when we were looking closely at everyone on the team, I remember one of the support staff...same school.'

Hirsch was making mental notes as he drove. Tell Hansen's boss.

He waited for more from Hansen, but all he heard were the birds and the wind again, and, some time later, the sounds of his own feet scrabbling down the bank to find a dead man.

Just as he reached to switch off Hansen's phone, it rang. Hansen's boss? Roesch? Hirsch slowed down and glanced at the screen. The caller ID simply said *Denise*.

33

Hirsch pulled over, spooked. He answered cautiously. 'Hello?'

'Is this...Is your name Hansen? Are you the police?'

Craig Washburn, sounding typically befuddled. Hirsch said, 'Craig, this is Paul Hirschhausen on Senior Constable Hansen's phone.'

Couldn't get much clearer than that, but there was a silence, Hirsch reading bewilderment into it. *He* was bewildered. What phone was Washburn using? 'Craig, where are you? Are the girls with you?'

He heard the scrape of fabric in his ear like a clamorous seashell: Washburn holding the phone against his chest? Then muffled voices laced with agitation, broken when a woman said, 'Give me that, you idiot. Paul? This is Nan.'

Her voice cheery and bright, as if she'd just stepped in from watering the garden. Hirsch, wondering if he was in some kind of parallel universe, said, 'What's going on? Are you at home?'

More precise than her husband could ever be, she still gave an account that unfolded in disconnected stages with prompts from Hirsch. He was on the move again, one hand on the wheel, the other holding the phone to his left ear. Moving again because Vita Roesch had appeared.

As he'd supposed, Craig and the girls had walked south along the creek, eventually spotting Wayne Flann's ute. They'd had no luck finding an ignition key, but Denise Rennie's satellite phone, with only Hansen's number in the contacts list, was in the glove box: another nail in Wayne's coffin, Hirsch thought.

Reluctant to stay with the ute or return to the creek, they crossed the road, concealed themselves in the hayshed and called Nan to come for them. When she got there, they made a run for the car—just as Roesch drove past. She swerved in front of them. Got out of her car with a big fake grin on her face. Nan had the others on board by now—she shot through the fence and across the paddocks to Hamel Road.

'Where are you?'

'The girls' house. We couldn't think where else to go. That woman was right behind us. She *shot* at us, Paul.'

The house? Hirsch couldn't see them defending a place with so many entry points. 'Can you lock yourselves in a room?'

'We're in the car-shed. We managed to lock the roller door and the inside door, but she's right outside. First she tried bashing the doors, now she's trying to sweet-talk us. Louise says not to trust her. Is that right?'

'I'll say,' Hirsch said. 'Stay where you are, I'm a few

minutes away.' He paused. 'Look, can you get into the service pit under Mrs Rennie's car?'

'Yes. Why? Oh...'

Right. In case Roesch starts firing shots through the shed walls.

Hirsch said, 'I want you to call Sergeant Brandl. She'll know what to do.'

He gave her the number, U-turned—hearing Hansen's body shift in its restraints—and shot back towards the ruins, then onto Hamel Road. Gave himself a moment to think. Roesch would have gone via Tiverton. A longer route on better roads. If she'd cut through behind the Razorback, the GPS coordinates would have stopped her at Craig's camp, well before the hayshed. Or she'd got lost. Or...Whatever. Her present location was what mattered.

Hirsch pulled up at the driveway entrance for 6 Hamel Road, unsure of his next move. With the house over a small rise, he was invisible to Roesch. But he'd lose that advantage if he drove in. She'd hear him coming and have time to ambush him.

He'd have to walk in.

Blocking the driveway with the Toyota—it might slow her down if she bolted—he got out, locked up, unholstered his pistol and ran upslope towards the house. Halfway there his phone rang. *Jesus.* He switched it to silent as he fumbled it from his pocket and checked the screen. Sergeant Brandl.

She's spoken to Nan, he thought. He'd better answer. If he moved even a step he might lose his signal.

'Sergeant,' he said, his voice low.

Her voice crackled. 'Is what Mrs Washburn told me true? The sisters are alive? And Sergeant Roesch of all people is trying to shoot them?'

'Yes.'

'You sound short of breath. What's going on?'

'I'm on foot, just approaching the house now, and—'

'Wait for backup,' she said briskly. 'That's an—'

And he'd lost the signal.

He lay on his stomach at the top of the rise. Nan Washburn's Volvo was parked at a crazy angle in front of the car-shed, all of its doors open, Roesch's car behind it. Roesch stood in the open, apparently addressing the shed, looking, from the way she moved her arms as if she was laying down the law.

No sound from the shed.

Hirsch ran at a crouch down the slope, keeping to the edge of the track, ready to duck into the meagre shelter of the cypresses that lined it. He heard Roesch shouting, then cajoling, as he neared the bottom. Was she unravelling? When he was within twenty metres of her, she swung around and he froze in the lee of a tree trunk.

She hadn't seen him. She ran to the Volvo, ducked her head in for a quick look, then climbed behind the wheel. The keys must have been in the ignition: a puff of exhaust and the car shot towards the shed and slammed into the roller door. She reversed: the door was badly buckled, lifting at one corner. She rammed it a second time, reversed again with a tearing-metal sound, and now the gap was large enough to crawl through. The driver's door swung open. One foot hit the ground.

Hirsch sprinted. Coming in behind Roesch, he tucked the tip of his pistol behind her ear. 'Stay right there. Throw your—'

She yanked on the door. It cracked his forearm; his nerveless fingers opened; the pistol dropped to the dirt. Then she was tumbling out, shoving him in the chest, kicking the gun under the car, kicking him, and running for her rental car.

She got in and looked at him, an odd, opaque expression, then sped away, up and over the rise. A few seconds later, he heard a shot. Then another. His tyres? He glanced at the Volvo. It was barely driveable.

He approached the shed. 'You can come out. She's gone.'

They were nearly silent. Some kind of muttered debate. His body was too drained—not a supportive bone in it—to crawl in and show them a reassuring face.

'It's okay,' he said.

It was a long time before they straggled out. All four of them seemingly intact.

34

When he left them five minutes later, they were arranged along the edge of the veranda, backs to the house, feet in the dirt, the girls in a fresh set of clothes fetched by Nan from their bedroom.

They didn't want him to leave them for even a minute. 'Be careful. She could come back.'

'She won't,' he said. 'She's blown her cover—nothing to gain by coming for you now.'

He was itching to check the damage to the Toyota. Clearly, with Hansen's body stretched out along the back seat, he couldn't take the whole gang with him. 'A couple of minutes,' he said.

Finally Nan Washburn made a shooing gesture and he ran up the incline and down the other side. The HiLux was listing. Roesch had put a bullet through each passenger-side tyre.

He ran back to the house, watching the relief flow through all of them. He'd been gone for less than five minutes.

'Did you see her?'

'No sign of anyone,' Hirsch said.

'She shot your tyres?' Craig said.

'She certainly did,' Hirsch said.

They were still lined up along the veranda. He swung a garden chair around to face them. 'I'll need to borrow the phone again.'

He'd made several calls already: reporting Roesch, with a description of her car; arranging for the collection of Hansen's body and the transportation of Wayne Flann from Tiverton to the Redruth lockup; reassuring Bob Muir; requesting search warrants; and asking the sergeant to update the Homicide Squad and track down Hansen's boss in Sydney.

Now he made two more calls using the satellite phone: to Redruth Motors, requesting a truck to collect the Toyota, and to Brandl again, saying he'd need a replacement vehicle if he was to fight crime in the dark hours of New Year's Eve.

'Very droll,' she said. 'I'll see what I can rustle up.'

They settled in to wait. Louise was jittery—and no wonder, thought Hirsch: Roesch was still at large and the deaths of her mother and brother lingered inside the house behind her.

He tried his warmest smile. 'You'll be in good hands. No need to hide now—too many people know about Sergeant Roesch. She has no motive to hurt you. She's running for her life.'

A grubby leg jittered. Teeth nibbled at fingernails.

*

Jean Landy arrived first, driving a Redruth patrol car, followed by a mix of uniformed and plainclothes police to escort the sisters to Adelaide. 'The boss is on the way,' Landy said. 'She stopped off in Tiverton to have a squiz at your prisoner.' She paused. 'You know for sure he's the one?'

Hirsch nodded. 'Any news on the ambulance?'

'On way.'

Hirsch walked back to the road just as the ambulance appeared. He raised a hand to stop it, pointed to the rear of the HiLux and watched the ambulance pull up by the back door.

The driver, a morose man with day-old black stubble, wound down his window. 'You sure he's dead?'

'Pretty sure,' Hirsch said, opening the door. The other paramedic, a small woman with brisk, expert hands, got to the body first. 'Dead all right. *Several* bites. What kind of snake?'

'A brown.'

'Nasty.'

Hirsch watched them load Hansen onto the stretcher and into the ambulance, then he walked back to the house. He was crossing the yard to the veranda when another vehicle arrived: Sergeant Brandl, driving a HiLux exactly like his wounded one. 'Yours for the next couple of days.'

'Thanks, sergeant.'

'Walk with me,' she said, striding off towards the shade of the first cypress tree as if she was controlled by wires. She stopped, turned, tucked a sweaty tendril of hair behind her ear. 'How sure are you that Mr Flann shot Mrs Rennie and her son?'

Arse-covering, thought Hirsch. He nodded towards the house. 'The older girl can ID him.'

'So, nothing to do with witness protection?'

'Correct.'

'Why? What was his motive?'

'He's been robbing remote farms. Might have been on ice that night.'

'We'll need better than that. He's swearing black and blue he didn't shoot them. Is the girl credible? It was night, she was scared, a lot happening...'

'She's credible.'

They both glanced at Louise, who still sat on the veranda looking up at the detective questioning her, Craig Washburn's arm around her shoulders. Brandl swung back to Hirsch. 'It'll be good when we get her statement,' she said crisply. 'Without that, what do we have? Mr Muir showed me the rifle you took off Mr Flann. It clearly isn't the murder weapon. And Flann was adamant he'd never met Mrs Rennie or her family, never been to her house before, he was simply carrying out his own little search of the area, yada yada. And he's accusing you of prejudice against his family.'

Hirsch heard the sharpness. He'd disappointed her; he should have confided in her about Flann. 'Boss, his own brother can put him at the house.'

'Correct me if I'm wrong, but isn't he still missing? And how credible is he likely to be—assuming he's found soon? Some actual evidence would be good.'

'There is some,' Hirsch said. He explained about the photographs on Flann's phone.

'Have you seen them?'

'No, but—'

'Perhaps they don't exist. Perhaps he deleted them afterwards.'

'Okay, what about the phone Mrs Washburn called you on? It was Denise Rennie's. It was in Wayne's ute.'

'So? He can say he found it in the creek.'

Frustrated with her now, Hirsch said, an edge to his voice: 'Boss, he took a shot at me.'

'He says it was accidental,' Brandl said.

Then her manner changed in its mercurial way. She grinned at him. 'But taking a pot-shot at a policeman is enough to keep him locked up for the time being. Meanwhile, Jean's got the search warrants. How confident are you that you'll find something?'

Less confident than he sounded: 'There'll be something.'

The big metal cabinet on the back wall of the Flanns' main shed. He was pretty keen to get a look inside that.

Half an hour later, only Hirsch and Jean Landy remained. Landy had a quiver on. 'My first official search.'

'Don't get too excited. It's generally dirty, dusty and thankless,' Hirsch said. 'You see things you can't *unsee*. You—'

'Like what?'

'Things.'

Like violent porn, mouldy food, shit-smeared walls...Once he'd been searching a drug-couriering great-grandmother's bedroom and tripped over a brimming chamber pot.

Mid-afternoon now. The New Year's Eve drunks would be well on their way. Hirsch had been working all day; he'd be working through to the early hours. 'You on duty tonight?'

Landy nodded. 'Patrolling the mean streets of Redruth.'

Hirsch decided he liked her. He eyed her patrol car. 'Convoy, or come with me?'

She was practical. 'Convoy, in case I have to head back in a hurry.'

The replacement HiLux drove exactly like Hirsch's shot-up one. He headed down Hamel Road to the Tiverton road, Landy behind him, and half an hour later they were at the Flanns' miserable cluster of house and sheds. Watching Hirsch select the house key from the bunch he'd confiscated after the arrest, Landy said, 'Looks like no one's lived here for years.'

Hirsch grunted. Brenda Flann was a nightmare, but at least she'd had a smattering of pride in the place; perhaps even some vague maternal streak. With her in hospital, Adam on the run and Wayne out scouting the countryside, the house, yard and sheds had grown forlorn surprisingly quickly.

Once inside, they made a rapid search of the obvious areas—under beds, in drawers and wardrobes—then the usual hiding places for people's miserable secrets—in freezer packets and flour tins, taped to the undersides of drawers, under floorboards.

Such meagre lives, Hirsch thought. No books, barely any magazines. Clothes worn too long between washes. Greasy water in the kitchen sink, tide marks in the bath and the toilet bowl. There was a small stash of pot in an old tobacco tin, but nothing else to suggest inner lives apart from a vast new TV, a couple of Xbox consoles and an eBay receipt for a military-tactical rifle sling from a Kentucky gun shop.

That left the sheds.

In one, remnants of hay, a set of rusty harrows and an old Massey Ferguson on perished tyres. In the other, nothing of note but that shiny steel cabinet behind the sheets of plywood. 'Tucked away,' observed Landy, 'but not in an obvious way. At a second glance you'd think it was a locker for expensive tools.'

'There probably *are* expensive tools in it,' Hirsch said.

Landy completed the thought: 'But not his.'

They drew on crime-scene gloves. Hirsch found the correct key, turned it in the lock and tugged gingerly on the handle.

'Expecting a booby trap?'

'It's been known,' he said.

They weren't blown to kingdom come and the first thing they saw was a child's tricycle missing its saddle. Scraps of Christmas wrapping clinging to the frame.

'Got him,' said Hirsch.

He told Landy the story and watched fear, pity and sadness flicker on her face as she pictured Christmas Eve at the Rennie house.

Stacked upright in an open space behind the bike were three fishing rods, a whipper-snipper, an archery bow and a couple of cricket bats. Next to it, a set of shelves: toolboxes, an electric sander, a bowsaw, chainsaws and a leaf blower.

Landy reached in, tilted one of the chainsaws. 'There's a name texta'd on this: T. Wesley.'

'The Porters Lagoon guy,' Hirsch said.

Landy grunted in satisfaction. 'We've got Mr Flann up, down and sideways.'

For thieving, Hirsch thought. We need to put that murder weapon in his hands. We need Adam's testimony. Just then Landy's mobile chirped. She checked it, muttered, 'Didn't think I'd get reception out here.'

Hirsch guessed. 'The boss wants you.'

'Brawl in the main bar of the Wheatsheaf.'

'You go, I'll finish up here.'

When he was alone, Hirsch photographed the contents of the cabinet and locked it again. He took the long way back to Tiverton; called in at the little house on Bitter Wash Road.

'Thought I'd wish you happy new year for tomorrow.'

'On account of you'll be busy,' Wendy said. She took his arm and steered him down the corridor. 'You need a shower.'

'On the nose?'

'Scrambled eggs and bacon when you're done.'

Their relationship was oftentimes brisk, Hirsch barely getting a word in. 'Breakfast food?'

'It'll get you through the night.'

When he stepped out of the ensuite bathroom, a towel around his waist, the spare uniform he kept hanging in her wardrobe had been draped over the bed. No sign of that day's sweat-stained mess: no doubt soaking in the laundry sink.

The eggs and bacon washed down by strong black tea, the imprint of Wendy's lips on his, Hirsch headed for town. Checking Kitchener Street automatically as he passed the shop, he saw a silver station wagon and a journalist in a short-sleeved white shirt interviewing Mr Cromer. Good luck with that, Hirsch thought. He'd been hoping the vultures were gone for good, but maybe pony mutilation had unexpected shelf-life.

As he parked outside the police station, the reporter came running up. 'Constable Hirschhausen? If I might have a word?'

'Sorry,' Hirsch said, 'I have things to do.'

'Any nearer to catching whoever mutilated Mrs Washburn's horses?'

I am, actually, Hirsch thought.

'It's been said that the same person was responsible for the killings out on Hamel Road.'

Hirsch turned around in the act of unlocking the front door. A car shot into town, saw the HiLux in the driveway of the police station, lurched to an anxious crawl and trundled through as if butter wouldn't melt in its mouth.

'Your views on that, Constable Hirschhausen?'

'A busy night coming up, you understand,' Hirsch said, staring at the reporter, who faltered, seeing something daunting in him. Hirsch nodded. 'Have a good night, you'll be busy yourself,' he said, and disappeared inside the police station.

Airing his office and the rooms he lived in, Hirsch was catching up on emails and phone calls when a text came in from Gemma Pitcher: *C u tomorrow afternoon.*

He replied: *C u then* and went out to keep the peace.

*

By 8 p.m. he was patrolling, south to Mount Bryan, north to Terowie, calling in at the pub in each town, taking a swing in and out of their side streets. Then a fast trip back to Tiverton: apparently a guy was swinging a machete around in the pub.

Machete, pub, New Year's Eve—a recipe for disaster. But when Hirsch had parked nose-up to the wonky veranda post and hurried into the main bar, he found only cheery noise and heightened amusement.

'All over, mate,' Carl Bagshaw said.

'Dealt with it,' his brother said.

Hirsch glanced at the patrons: a couple of station jillaroos, a handful of farmers and farmhands, a driver for the lucerne seed business, the primary school headmaster, the town's beautician. The publican was pouring beer. Behind him, on the other side of the U-shaped bar, was the lounge, the tables taken by a faintly more genteel crowd: mums, dads, kids and grandparents. Like a Saturday night, except with the electric charge that lingers after a bit of drama.

Kevin Henry was the least amused. No one had been hurt; hiring the Bagshaw twins for crowd control had paid off. But there had been an incident, hard on the heels of Brenda Flann's parking trick. 'Could've been nasty.'

He gestured at the sodden towel running the length of the bar. 'Machete' was stretching it: Hirsch recognised the weapon as a World War II bayonet, rust-pitted and blunt-looking. His grandfather had brought one back from Borneo in 1945.

'What happened?'

One Bagshaw twin glanced at the other. 'This bloke came in.'

'Pissed as a fart.'

'Trolleyed.'

'Waving that around.'

'Said, "Where is she?" We said, "Who?"'

'He didn't say. Wife? Girlfriend?'

'Never seen him before.'

Hirsch cut in, lifting his voice above the noise: 'Anyone recognise him?'

A lull, then a murmur of denials and headshakes.

'Okay, did anyone see where he went?'

More headshaking, but one scrap of information: the maniac had driven away in an old Subaru wagon.

'When I took the blade off him,' Ivan said, 'he just burst into tears and scarpered.'

'Anyone other than you touch the bayonet?'

'No, only me.'

Hirsch lifted it off the bar with a handkerchief around his fingers, placed it in the Toyota and returned to make the rounds of the patrons. Did you see what happened? Did you know him? Had you ever seen him before? Film him, by any chance?

One blurry photograph: a short, barrelly guy, about forty, shorts and a wifebeater singlet. None of the women knew him.

No damage, no bloodshed, but a lethal weapon had been brandished. Hirsch would have it tested for fingerprints, see if the guy was in the system.

The rest of his night was uneventful. Hirsch patrolled his domain, and, as far as he could tell, no crimes were committed, or regulations infringed. May that be a harbinger for the new year, he thought.

35

The first of January. Hirsch slept in. So did everyone else.

Then, early afternoon, he offered his second happy new year of the season.

'Yeah, happy new year.' Gemma Pitcher's response was clear and confident, a sense almost of grace in her heavy round face. The boys, seated on either side of her, barely muttered. All three kids looked bleary. Wherever they'd been hiding, they'd given the new year a thorough welcome.

Hirsch had decided to use his sitting room for this: private, not too formal—but also not too much like home, with the police station just through the door behind them. 'I'll need to speak to each of you alone at some stage,' he said, knowing that in a perfectly managed police operation he'd have split them up immediately and gone in hard against each one.

Gemma shrugged; Adam scowled; Daryl looked as gormless as ever.

'But let's just establish the main facts. First, where have you been the last few days?'

'We don't want to get them in trouble,' Gemma said.

'That won't happen. It's just to satisfy my curiosity.'

'My cousin's.'

'Did your mum know?'

'No.'

'Where?'

Gemma shrugged, the stretched neck of her black T-shirt halfway down one fleshy shoulder. 'Does it matter?'

Probably not. Hirsch took out his phone, found the snap of Lavau. 'Do you recognise this man?'

Gemma peered. 'He's the one come in the shop.'

Hirsch nodded. 'Thought he might be.'

'Who is he? He going to come after me?'

Hirsch his head. 'Nope. Dead.'

'Okay,' Gemma said, unconcerned. The boys looked cowed and sullen. Young.

The next stage would need a light touch. Go in too hard and the kids would clam up. 'Just to deal with a couple of other matters first,' he said, fixing on Daryl, 'did you guys spray-paint Mr and Mrs Dunner's woolshed, by any chance?'

The Cobb boy merely looked more vacant. Adam Flann gave a delayed blink, a little frown. 'Who?'

'Doesn't matter. How about copper wiring, copper pipes, can you tell me anything about that?'

Adam hardened. 'We never did no copper.'

'What about Wayne? Was he into stealing copper?'

'Nup.'

Hirsch made a mental note: check Wayne's prints against the ones found on the crime-scene tape at the barn.

'What about Kip?'

'Who?'

'Mr and Mrs Fuller's dog, over on Munduney Hill. It went missing a few weeks ago. Know anything about that?'

Gemma knew about Kip being found on the road. Affronted, she looked at the boy seated on her left, the boy on her right. 'They wouldn't hurt a dog.'

But Daryl stirred, a light coming on. 'Him? He went mental at us.'

'Tell me about it,' Hirsch asked. The mild tone that meant business.

Daryl realised he'd said too much and subsided.

'Daryl? When was this?'

A shrug. 'Ages ago.'

'You were there with Adam and Wayne?'

Another shrug. Hirsch checked Adam, expecting him to shut his friend up.

Interesting. The boy was all tight wilfulness behind his veneer of boredom.

Gemma intervened. She clasped Daryl's gingery hand. 'It's okay, Daz. We talked about this. You have to tell him.'

Daryl was silent. Gemma sighed and said, 'They told me they done the Fullers, but Kip freaked them out.'

'Is this true, Daryl?'

Daryl lifted his head. 'He went mental. His chain broke.'

'You almost had an arse full of teeth,' Hirsch said, expecting a grin, but the kid remained blank. 'Did you guys steal anything?'

'Wayne took a shovel.'

'Did you always go out with Wayne and Adam on these expeditions?'

A head shake.

Hirsch turned to the other boy. 'Adam? Did you go with Wayne each time?'

Adam lifted his chin. He stared at Hirsch with a thin, hard smile: 'Not worth the hassle *not* going with him.'

Hirsch imagined the boy's home life. Bullied by the older brother, father in jail, some scant stability and home comforts from Brenda—when she wasn't on the grog. 'Okay, what about Mrs Washburn's horses?'

'We never done that! Never would.'

'Okay,' Hirsch said. 'But what about Wayne?'

'Nah,' Adam said, as if a spot of horse mutilation would have been more trouble to Wayne than it was worth.

'How about Mr Wesley, over near Porters Lagoon?'

Adam had to think about it. 'Chainsaw?'

Hirsch nodded. 'Did Wayne have a particular grudge against the Fullers or Mr Wesley or—' he slipped in the name '—Mrs Rennie?'

Adam shrugged. 'Not that I know of. They were just, you know, like, in the middle of nowhere.'

'Isolated properties.'

'Yeah. Before Dad went to jail, we used to go spotlighting.'

Driving around at night, picking out a fox in a beam of light and shooting it. 'Is that how you found places to rob?'

Adam nodded. 'Wayne would go, "What about this place? What about that place?" and Dad would say yeah or nah.'

Hirsch grunted. 'Okay, let's now talk about what happened on Christmas Eve.'

Adam shrank. Daryl looked half-asleep. Gemma straightened, a square-shouldered heft that said Hirsch should watch himself, she'd be looking out for her boyfriend.

Easy does it, Hirsch thought. 'Daryl, did you go out with Wayne on Christmas Eve?'

Daryl had to think about it. 'No.'

'He didn't,' affirmed Gemma. There was the merest hint of emphasis.

'But you did, Adam?'

Adam seemed to look for a way to shade his answer. In the end, he nodded.

'Did you get out of the ute at any stage? Go inside the house?'

'Nup.'

'Wayne did?'

'Yep.'

'What happened?'

'The lady come out the shed when Wayne was cutting the phone line and he got a shock and got the gun out,' Adam said flatly. 'He told me to stay where I was and chased her inside and just, you know, started shooting.'

'Why did he do that?'

'Ask him.'

'I will. Why do *you* think he did that?'

'He was flying, man.'

'Drugs?'

The answer seemed obvious to Adam. 'Ice.'

'Does he use often?'

'When he can get it.'

'Every time you've gone out?'

'Not really.'

'So he went in shooting. Then what happened?'

'Freaked me out.'

Hirsch found himself offering the boy a defence. 'You were scared of your brother.'

Gemma caught it. She glanced at Adam and nudged him. He said, 'He's fucking scary, man. Always having a crack at me.' He lifted his T-shirt. A mottled bruise under the ribs.

'Did he steal anything?'

'Yep. A toolbox, a phone and a kid's bike. I never touched nothing.'

'He took photos?'

Adam winced. 'He showed me.'

'Did you both go home after that?'

'Yep.'

'And the next day? Boxing Day—I saw you with Wayne in the creek, remember.'

'He freaked out when he heard on the news there were two kids missing. He thought they might of seen him and said we had to find them before anyone else did.'

'Adam had no choice, he was that scared,' Gemma said, hugging Adam hard against her cushiony torso. 'But soon as he got a chance, he rang me, and I come and got him.' She shrugged. 'I wasn't going to let him get blamed for everything.'

36

Two solicitors practised in Redruth. By mid-afternoon on that first day of the new year, Hirsch had arranged representation for each of the boys in their interviews with Homicide Squad detectives at the Redruth police station.

After dropping them there, he continued through town and out to the Wesley farm above Porters Lagoon. He showed Trevor Wesley two arrays of photographs. The sun, dropping on the other side of the valley, flared on a stretch of water not yet evaporated in all the days of heat.

Wesley was clear. 'That one.'

Wayne Flann. 'How about this lot?' said Hirsch.

Adam Flann and boys of Adam's age and appearance. Wesley shook his head. 'It was dark, mate. The second one hung back, hoodie on. He was younger, though. I think.'

On Thursday afternoon, Hirsch headed across country to Munduney Hill. Kip wandered out to greet him; Graham Fuller, seated on the veranda picking grass seeds out of his work socks, offered Hirsch a beer.

'Won't say no,' Hirsch said. He could go hours without any kind of refreshment on this job.

'Inside. Too hot out here.'

Monica joined them in the sitting room. Hirsch realised how alike they were: calm, solid and attentive, seated opposite him on a fraying sofa.

'Been busy,' Graham said.

'I'm here about Wayne Flann, in fact,' Hirsch said. 'Did you ever have a run-in with him?'

'Barely know the bloke.'

'He never did any tractor driving for you, shed-hand work?'

'Mate,' Graham said, 'I could barely afford to pay myself, let alone Wayne Flann.'

Monica interrupted, in her quiet, careful way, her tough blue eyes fixed on Hirsch. 'Is there a reason you're asking about him?'

'There's a fairly good chance he's the one who cut your phone line and stole your shovel,' Hirsch said, 'before Kip scared him off.'

She swallowed, crushed the neck of her blouse in one hand. 'Are you saying he might've shot us, too?'

Hirsch rolled his shoulders uncomfortably. 'I can't speculate about that. The main thing is, he didn't, and now he's locked up.' He paused. 'Which brings me to Kip.'

'You think Wayne took him? Whatever for?'

'No, not Wayne,' Hirsch said. 'Is there anyone else you've had a run-in with? Last two or three years?'

Monica was amused, but sad with it. 'Us?' She gestured

at their slightly-better-than-threadbare existence: outdated furniture, low ceilings, small rooms in need of a new coat of paint.

Hirsch steepled his fingers. He'd have to prod them. 'Specifically regarding Kip.'

They reached the answer together. 'Redruth Show,' Monica said.

'Two years ago,' Graham said.

'Kip won best sheepdog a couple of times prior. That year he won best in show as well.'

'And the runner-up?' said Hirsch, anticipation pulsing through him, a little burst of adrenaline.

'Annette Thorburn.'

Martin Gwynne's daughter.

Then out to Pandowie Downs, where he found Eleanor Dunner in the office; Rex had gone to the dentist in Clare.

'About the graffiti.'

'Yes?' she said brightly.

He wondered what it was like for her, stuck out here. Any visitor must brighten her days. 'I'm thinking it wasn't random.'

'I don't think so, either. We had a bit of resentment from the neighbours who didn't want the extra tourist traffic.'

Hirsch let that go: the nearest house was five kilometres away. 'Cast your mind back a year or two. Any tiff or argument or full-blown confrontation you can remember?'

She had to think. An argument with the accommodation-block plumber, but that was soon sorted. Some argy-bargy with a council inspector over the position of their road-side noticeboard. She paused: 'Speaking of which, Martin Gwynne came by one day and said there shouldn't be an apostrophe in "Demonstrations". We corrected it but I'm rather afraid I told him to mind his own business.'

Hirsch cocked his head. 'Told him a little forcefully?'

She smiled lazily. 'A little.'

Hirsch returned to Tiverton in the dwindling hours of daylight, shadows lengthening over the dusty paddocks, some clarity now to his tangle of thoughts regarding Martin Gwynne. A man who never let go of his grudges. A man you didn't cross. A man you mightn't even know you'd offended. Patient. Patiently stewing. Never at peace.

Finally that day he logged on to his SA Police email account. Two messages: the lab had found the selfies on Flann's mobile, Wayne posed with his victims; and the YouTube clip would be taken down—the IP address of the offending computer having been traced to a library in the Adelaide suburb of Rostrevor. Hirsch was bleakly satisfied: that was where Martin's daughter lived now.

37

On Friday Hirsch decided to take the day off—for what that was worth in his line of work. Three things on the agenda: stock up on groceries, swap the loan Toyota for his old one, dinner at the little house on Bitter Wash Road.

He breakfasted in his backyard, flicking through Mrs Keir's journals again:

> A great many of the shearers and hut-keepers are the off-scourings of English prisons, and a more insolent set of scoundrels you could not find. They are much given to spending their money on drink and bad women, but there are a few good men of the labouring classes hereabouts, and, from their long servitude on the Sydney side, they know a good deal about sheep-work.

Thinking that not much ever changed, he walked across to the general store at eight-thirty, nodded hello to Gemma Pitcher and filled a basket with bread, milk, wrinkled apples, wrinkled vegetables, painkillers and frozen meals. He heard glass smash behind him and turned around.

Joyce Gwynne stood gaping at her left hand, a shopping basket in the crook of her right arm, a spill of shards and gherkins and brine at her feet.

A stroke? Swiftly setting his basket on the floor, Hirsch crossed the space separating them and held her upper arms. 'Joyce? You okay?'

She winced. Pain, but he'd barely touched her. Releasing her, he stepped back. 'Let's find you somewhere to sit.'

'It just slipped out of my hands,' she said, blinking behind her glasses.

No slurring. He eased the basket from her arm and led her to the front of the shop and around to the seating area at the 'library'—a plain wooden chair beside a case of books.

Then Gemma was hovering. 'I'll get her a drink of water.'

'Thanks. And a jar broke.'

'On it,' she said.

She returned with water in a glass and disappeared again. Presently Hirsch heard sweeping and mopping.

Joyce was trembling. 'He wanted gherkins for lunch, with his cheese.'

She looked tiny in the creaky old chair. Flushed, wispy grey hair awry. She sipped the water, then took a long swallow. The movements of her little stick-like arms and thin neck shifted the lines of her collar and sleeves so that Hirsch saw bruises on the pale skin.

'Joyce,' he said carefully, 'how did you hurt yourself?'

She shrank as if she wanted to disappear inside her clothing. 'Oh, I'm such a clumsy thing.'

She closed her eyes, swayed and toppled. Hirsch caught her, set her upright. 'Let's get you to the doctor.'

He expected resistance but Joyce Gwynne shuffled out of the shop with him and across the road to Dr Pillai's Friday clinic. The waiting room was unoccupied; the surgery door open, Dr Pillai at her desk, tapping notes into a laptop.

She rose to her feet. 'My first customer,' she said, helping Hirsch settle Joyce onto a narrow bed under a mothercraft poster. The only other furnishings were a sink, a cabinet and a set of steel shelves containing bandages and surgery gloves.

'What seems to be the problem?' Pillai said, her hand on Joyce's forehead.

'I had a dizzy spell in the shop,' Joyce said. She looked comfortable on the little bed: eyes closed, limbs loose.

The doctor looked to Hirsch for confirmation. Jerking his head towards the door, he mouthed, 'Quick word?'

She nodded, said, 'I'll be right back, Mrs Gwynne,' and joined Hirsch in the waiting room.

Keeping his voice to a murmur he said, 'She dropped a jar on the floor, and I saw her looking at her hand as if she had no control over it. Which may or may not be related to the fact she's got bruises on her upper arms and under her collar.'

Pillai cocked her head. 'She falls down a lot? Or she falls down a lot.'

'Exactly.'

'I'll see if she'll open up to me.'

'Thank you.'

'You'd like to know, either way?'

'Yes.'

Hirsch finished his shopping, stowed it away and returned to the clinic. Three people in the waiting room now, a teenage girl with her mother and a windfarm worker holding a bandaged hand upright, face tight with pain.

Hirsch waited. When Joyce emerged, she hurried past him with a shy, frightened, 'Thank you.' Then Dr Pillai appeared, spotted Hirsch and beckoned him into her room.

Shutting the door, she said, 'Mrs Gwynne wasn't forthcoming. She said some cans fell on top of her when she was cleaning the pantry. I didn't press it, and when I raised the issue of the DV support options available to her, she shut me down.'

Hirsch nodded. 'Thanks for trying.'

'But for what it's worth, I think someone hit her.'

Hirsch returned to the police station and a short time later Laura Cobb came in. 'Please, Mrs Flann's upsetting Mum.'

They trotted along the footpath. 'What's she doing at your place?'

'Apologising.'

'For what?'

'Wayne and Adam.'

They reached the house, Hirsch recognising the station wagon at the kerb. It had been repaired with wrecking-yard panels and hammered-out dents.

'Is she drunk?'

'I don't think so. She keeps going on about how it was all her fault her boys turned out bad and got Daryl into trouble.'

They raced down the side yard and in through the back door. The kitchen looked clean and orderly except for the disorder of the women seated at the table. Brenda Flann was pouring her words out, one arm stretched out across the table towards Marie, who was rocking in her chair, hands over her eyes.

Laura went immediately to her mother and embraced her thin shoulders from behind as Brenda said, 'It's my fault, it was the drinking, I wasn't there for them. No surprise they went wild, now they've got your boy in trouble, and I'm so, so sorry.'

Brenda looked and smelt clean. Not drunk, just over-wrought. And quite oblivious to Hirsch and Laura, and to the distress she was causing. Hirsch said sharply, '*Brenda*.'

She blinked. Dragged her hand back across the table. The words dried up. Then, still blinking, she lifted her still-bruised face to Hirsch. 'I need to say sorry to you, too.'

'Let's do that back at the station—what do you think?'

He eased her out of the chair. Tried to turn her away and through the door but she wriggled free and stood over Marie Cobb and said, 'I mean it, I'll make it up to you and—'

Then Marie said the only words Hirsch had ever heard her utter: 'It's okay, Brenda. I forgive you.'

A low voice, creaky from disuse. Brenda Flann nodded and let herself be ushered towards the door. Hirsch cast a look over his shoulder: *You okay?*

Laura shrugged. It didn't say *No*. It said: *Business as usual*.

*

Outside, the hot sun beating down, Hirsch said, 'Are you okay to drive, Brenda? It might be best if you went home.'

She looked around dazedly, long nose sniffing, moist sad lips tasting the dusty air. 'Sorry, what?'

Was she on some kind of medication? 'Would you like to see the doctor?'

In the next instant she was almost her harsh old self. 'I've had it up to here with doctors and hospitals. I need to make amends, then I can go home.' She poked his chest. 'I tried to run you over. I'm sorry about that.'

'Apology accepted.'

'I'm not touching another drop.'

'Good for you.'

'You don't believe me I can tell, but it's the simple truth.'

She wheeled around and crossed the road to the pub. Amusement bubbled up, bringing back some of the old you-have-to-laugh attitude Hirsch thought he'd lost. He watched her disappear through the door to the main bar. Time went by. When she didn't reappear, he investigated, finding her at the bar, deep in conversation with Kevin Henry, nursing a clear fizzy drink.

'Lemonade,' she said, spotting Hirsch. Then: 'It's okay, we went to school together.'

Hirsch nodded, returned to the police station, pinned his mobile number to the door and drove the loan HiLux down to Redruth.

Sergeant Brandl was at her desk. She gave him a look. 'Aren't you off-duty today?'

'Swapping vehicles, sarge.'

She grunted. 'While I've got you—Vita Roesch was arrested this morning.'

Hirsch felt the easing of tension he hadn't been aware of. 'Where?'

'Lightning Ridge.'

An outback opal-mining town, a place where people went to hide. Hirsch nodded. 'See you at the Monday briefing, sergeant.'

'Wait: where are we on Mrs Washburn's horses?'

Hirsch knew exactly where he was on Nan Washburn's horses, but he couldn't prove anything yet. 'Still sniffing around, sarge.'

He was approaching Tiverton, the Doors' version of 'Light My Fire' blasting his eardrums, when his phone vibrated in his pocket. He pulled over to take the call.

Joyce Gwynne, sounding frantic. 'It's Martin and Mrs Flann.'

Shit, bugger, damn. Brenda's saying sorry to everyone she can think of, Hirsch thought, pulling onto the road again. 'Two minutes away.'

He found Martin and Brenda scuffling, dragging each other in circles on the footpath. Joyce was trying to intervene, tugging ineffectually on her husband's arms whenever he came within reach.

Hirsch piled out shouting, '*Break it up, break it up.*' He barrelled in and strongarmed them apart.

Brenda was weepy, dishevelled. 'I only wanted to say sorry. He didn't have to hit me.'

'Oh, I did no such thing,' Martin said.

One of his few saving graces was neatness. If he'd been brawling with Brenda, you wouldn't know it. Shirt tucked in, hair in place, face barely flushed.

Hirsch dropped his arms but stayed where he was, standing between them. 'You both going to behave?'

'Behave? I am behaving, more than could be said of this silly cow,' Gwynne said.

'Martin.' Hirsch put some grit in his tone.

'All I wanted was to say sorry,' Brenda said. 'I know I must've been rude sometimes, Martin. I'm very sorry.'

'Rude? Try drunk and disorderly.'

This time Joyce said it, as harshly as Hirsch: 'Martin.'

He swung around on her. 'Stay out of it, Joyce.'

'Not if you're going to be like this.'

'I came here...I came here...' Brenda tailed off as if unable to get the words straight in her head.

Feeling a swift, protective tenderness, imagining her life just past and soon to come, Hirsch wrapped an arm around her shoulders and led her to the Toyota. 'Sit here for a while. I'll sort things out with Mr Gwynne, all right?'

'I never...' she said.

'I know.'

Hirsch rejoined Gwynne and looked at him. Gwynne blanched. He said, 'What, you're taking her side? The woman's a menace.'

Hirsch felt toxic in his soul and in his bones. 'She came to apologise, that's all. She's genuine about it, can't you see that?'

Apparently not. 'Drunken cow.'

His wife said, 'That's unfair, Martin. She's not drunk. She's upset, and you didn't have to hit her.'

A flare in Gwynne's eyes but he controlled it. With ghastly calm he said, 'Let me talk to Constable Hirschhausen, Joyce. If you don't mind?'

'I'm staying right here.'

'Is it true, Martin?' Hirsch said. 'You hit Brenda?'

'You do know who she is, don't you? The mother of a murderer. *Two* murderers, if truth be known.'

A transformative surge of feeling flowed through Hirsch. All the misery Martin had wreaked, on all of his days on earth. His voice a low rumble, Hirsch said, 'I know who you are, Martin. I know everything.'

Gwynne tried for bewilderment, but there was a fugitive glint behind it. 'Know what?'

Your imagined grievances, nourished by hate, thought Hirsch. Your vicious little dreams and vendettas. Your nasty churchgoing spitefulness.

He reached out. He patted Martin's cheek. 'I know. And I'm patient.'

Brenda was weeping. She was afraid to go home, she said. Home contained memories. Things had gone wrong there that couldn't be put right.

Hirsch said gently, 'Adam's there?'

'He's that ashamed,' she said.

'He needs you just now,' Hirsch said, knowing it was a cliché; knowing it was true.

Brenda sniffed. 'He's angry with me.'

'It'll pass,' Hirsch said. He paused. 'Gemma's his girl-friend, did you know that?'

Brenda went still and Hirsch could see her mind working. There was an unexpected dimension to her son if he had a girl.

Hirsch decided to press the matter. 'Invite her for dinner.'

A few minutes later he watched her drive off in her old wreck and went inside to check his email.

There was one that mattered: the fingerprint branch had found two sets of prints on the pub bayonet. One set matched a Clifford Edward Palmer of Peterborough, two convictions for assault. The other set were not in the database but did match prints found on the copper-skip crime-scene tape.

Hirsch rocked in dismay.

Ivan Bagshaw had handled the bayonet. Ivan and his brother, likeable ratbags whose job took them all over the countryside in their council vehicles. Seeing and knowing everything. You wouldn't question their right to be any-where in the district.

Fuck, fuck, fuck.

Perhaps he groaned it aloud; a voice said, 'Sorry?'

Joyce Gwynne, standing in the main doorway, sunlight spilling in around her.

She entered, clutching a big Myer shopping bag to her chest, shut the door and stood at the counter. It wasn't steel in her spine, exactly, but she held herself with some resolve, without the shy ducking away.

'I would like,' she said, 'to make a statement.'

*

Hirsch took her to the other side of the counter and settled her in a chair across from his desk. Set out a digital recorder, notepad and pen.

'Go ahead.'

She went back to the beginning. She'd been a lecturer at the teachers' college, and some of her old fluency and authority returned as she told her story. In her fifth year of lecturing, aged twenty-eight, she'd met Martin. She didn't use his name, talking to Hirsch: 'That little man,' she said.

The first years of marriage were okay. She worked, the little man worked, they made a home together. They had a daughter, and Joyce enjoyed staying home to raise her. But when she felt ready to go back to work, the little man thought it unwise. Her duty was to look after the home they'd made together. 'I was a cliché,' she said.

Depression crept up on her over the long years, chronic and incapacitating. She felt useless. Her friends drifted away, and Martin seemed to have none of his own.

'That little man and his disappointments,' she said. The missed opportunities he suffered, the forces that acted against him—anything from losing a job promotion to losing a parking spot. It was never just bad luck, and never involved a deficiency on his part.

Hirsch eyed the Myer shopping bag. Stuffed with something soft. Running-away clothes? She was holding on to it for dear life, anyway.

'And he'd hit you sometimes?'

'Not at first. Not for years. But recently, yes. You know what decided me? Or what decided me on top of everything else? When he hit poor Brenda. The exact same look on his face, the hatred.'

Coming to be near their daughter and her family in Tiverton had not been the cure for their miserable life. Annette had moved back to the city to get away from Martin and his obsessions. 'So he immersed himself in this godforsaken place,' Joyce said. 'No offence.'

'None taken. I was sent here. It's growing on me, but I take your point.'

'And when I say immersed, I mean he was into *everything*.'

'I've worked out some of it,' Hirsch said. 'The Pandowie Downs apostrophe. Kip winning a dog prize he thought should have gone to your daughter's dog.'

'Kip was just the better dog,' Joyce said. She shook her head as if you wouldn't credit what made her husband tick. 'Poor thing. We had him shut in the laundry for a week. I let him out one day when the little man was at the tennis club. I told him Kip shot out between my legs when I opened the door to feed him. I got a fist in the stomach for that little bit of defiance.'

'He reported me to police headquarters in the city, you know. I had to go down and get hauled over the coals.'

Joyce closed her eyes briefly as if distressed on his behalf. 'He was furious with you because you kept fobbing him off with the dinner invitations.' She gave Hirsch a crooked grin. 'Those evenings you did come must have been fun.'

Hirsch shrugged and smiled. 'Good tucker, though.'

She nodded, as if appreciating his kindness. 'He was

hoping to be Santa again, even though it meant he couldn't enter the Best Christmas Lights competition. Then the council chose you to be Santa, so he went all-out with the Christmas lights. Expected to win, of course.'

'A compensatory thank-you from the town?'

'Very good. You're getting the hang of how he thinks.'

'His light display was pretty good. Nan's was better.'

'Much better. But let's not ignore the elephant in the room: she won when she shouldn't have.' She paused. 'He hit me just now.'

'That's what brought you here?'

'You have to understand. My mind...for years it was a tiny, inward-looking thing,' Joyce said. 'I could only see what was right in front of me: was the mantelpiece dusty? Had I set the table properly? Had I ironed his handkerchiefs perfectly? *I couldn't see the world*, Paul. I couldn't see the ripple effects of everything he did and said and thought.' She cocked her head. 'Like that film he put on the internet. He was having a go at you, he wanted to hurt you—and look what happened. It brought bad people here, evil people.'

Hirsch was uneasy now. He kept his voice mild, unhurried: 'Where is Martin, Joyce?'

He eyed her clothing, her arms and her hands. She was as neat as a pin. If she'd stabbed or clubbed the little man, there was no evidence of it.

'Oh, he's messing about on his iPad. There's always some chat room where he can post a message, always some site that will feed his misery and resentment.'

'You didn't have to explain where you were going?'

'I told him I was taking some old dresses to the charity bin outside the church.'

She placed the Myer bag on the desk. She nudged it. Nudged it again with more confidence, as if taking the biggest of all her big steps. 'I expect,' she said, 'they can test for equine DNA?' Another nudge. 'With any luck, where he's going someone else will do his laundry for him.'

Hirsch pulled the bag closer. He plucked at the opening, revealing a neatly folded pair of overalls, neck uppermost, *M. Gwynne* on the nametag sewn inside the collar. Slowly he slid the stiff fabric into view, and saw where jets and smears of blood two weeks old had darkened the folds, and even though he'd long figured it out, he still felt the need to brush his palms against his chest, and he jerked back as something dank and rotten drifted past his nose and spread, and settled—and then Joyce, in her wisdom, was coaxing him outside, into the peaceful street. Saving him, when it should have been the other way around.

ACKNOWLEDGMENTS

Peace was written in partial fulfilment of a doctorate at LaTrobe University. The author thanks his supervisor, Professor Sue Martin, and Text Publishing editor Mandy Brett for helping to make it a better book.

ABOUT THE AUTHOR

Garry Disher has published fifty titles across multiple genres, and is best known as Australia's King of Crime. He has won the Deutsche Krimi Preis three times, the Ned Kelly Award twice, and his novel *The Sunken Road* was nominated for the Booker Prize. In 2018 he received the Ned Kelly Lifetime Achievement Award.

garrydisher.com